TOOTH AND NAIL

Also by Craig DiLouie
Paranoia
The Great Planet Robbery

TOOTH AND NAIL

CRAIG DILOUIE

Schmidt Haus Books
Portland, Oregon

TOOTH AND NAIL
Copyright © 2010 by Craig DiLouie

Schmidt Haus Books
A Salvo Press Imprint
Portland, Oregon
www.salvopress.com

Main cover istockphoto image by Ninjaprints, London
Cover istockphoto image of gas mask by Andreas Gradin

Library of Congress Control Number: 2009941202

ISBN: 9781930486980
1-930486-98-7

Printed in U.S.A.
First Edition

For Christine and Mieka

Acknowledgments
A lot of people helped make this book possible, but I owe special
thanks to two: Anthony McCurdy, friend and veteran of the 101st
Airborne Division (Air Assault), and Chris DiLouie, my brother, writing comrade and always ready editor.

ABBREVIATIONS

AG: Assistant gunner
AO: Area of operations
AWOL: Absent without leave
BDU: Battle dress uniform
BGE: Brigade
CDC: Centers for Disease Control
CO: Commanding officer
FEMA: Federal Emergency Management Agency
FPF: Final protective fire
HE: Heavy explosives
HEAT: Heavy explosive anti-tank
HK: Hong Kong (as in Hong Kong Lyssa)
HQ: Headquarters
H&S: Headquarters & Supply
HVAC: Heating, ventilation and air conditioning
ID: Infantry division
IED: Improvised explosive device
KP: Kitchen police
LAV: Light armored vehicle
LAV-R: Light armored vehicle (recovery model)
LT: Lieutenant
1LT: First Lieutenant
2LT: Second Lieutenant
MIA: Missing in action
MG: Machine gun
MGR: Machine-gunner
MP: Military police
MRE: Meal ready to eat
NCO: Non-commissioned officer
PFC: Private First Class
POGs: People other than grunts
ROE: Rules of engagement
ROTC: Reserve Officers' Training Corps
RPG: Rocket-propelled grenade
RTO: Radio/Telephone operator
SAW: Squad automatic weapon

SINCGAR: Single-channel ground and airborne radio system
SPC: Specialist
TOW: Tube-launched, optically tracked, wire-guided missile
USAF: United States Air Force
USAMRIID: United States Army Medical Research Institute for Infectious Diseases
VCIED: Vehicle-concealed improvised explosive device
WP: White phosphorous
XO: Executive officer

"Never will I fail my country's trust.
Always I fight on—
Through the foe,
To the objective,
To triumph over all.
If necessary, I fight to my death."

—From "The Infantryman's Creed"

"Battle not with monsters, lest ye become a monster."
—Friedrich Nietzsche

Chapter 1

The end of the world will not come without a war

Standing at the checkpoint behind concertina wire and sandbags, sweating in his body armor and holding an M4 carbine, PFC Jon Mooney closes his eyes and instantly falls asleep on his feet, nodding under the weight of his Kevlar helmet. Then his eyes flutter open and he believes, just for an instant, that he's still in Iraq manning a roadblock in Baghdad's Adamiyah District, with Apaches throbbing overhead and Iraqi kids hawking cold sodas and sniper rifles popping in the windows.

His heart racing, his eyes flicker, assessing threats, and settle on the giant billboard across the intersection for what seems like the hundredth time. The big ad, packed with models frolicking in a frothy pink bubble bath, is mounted over a Burger King nestled between a nameless electronics store and a discount clothing shop. He doesn't understand the ad, doesn't even know what it is supposed to be selling. It calls to him, promises some sort of escape he desperately wants right now, but cannot name.

This is not Iraq. This is New York City.

The Burger King and all of the stores are closed on this part of First Avenue due to the epidemic, their fronts screened by black metal grates as if the street were a giant prison. Abandoned cars and litter choke the streets and sidewalks radiating out from the checkpoint up to the concrete roadblocks placed a block away.

This is supposed to be home.

Midtown Manhattan looms over this grimy street scene, skyscraper windows winking in the sun. Mooney squints into the light until he finds the gleaming crown of the Chrysler Building. Everything looks quiet, almost serene up there. A man could stop and rest for a while in the breeze.

Forty-six hours ago, he was sitting on a runway halfway around the world with the rest of Charlie Company's Second Platoon, waiting for his ride home. Of course, they weren't calling it a retreat. The Brass called it the Emergency Redeployment, the officers on the ground called it the Extraction, and the enlisted called it Suckfest and the Mother of all Clusterfucks and "a great way to get killed." Whatever you wanted to call it, the military began pulling out tens of thousands of soldiers all at once while the Iraqi government folded up into the Green Zone and the tribesmen returned to settling old scores when they had time between fanatical attacks on the retreating Americans.

The soldiers, returning home on anything that could fly or float, were redeployed throughout the United States. The logistics of the withdrawal of forces from bases around the world back to the homeland boggled the mind. Mooney's light infantry rifle platoon, still burned by the Middle Eastern sun and digging sand out of their pockets, got assigned this stretch of First Avenue in Manhattan.

The mission: Provide security for Trinity Hospital.

Not exactly the homecoming that Mooney had been looking forward to for the past year, but at least nobody was shooting at him anymore.

Near the checkpoint, the old man has returned and is again hounding people trying to get through the soldiers and into the hospital. "I wouldn't go in there if I was you," he warns. He's clean shaven, with long, scraggly gray hair. He wears a T-shirt that announces: THE SMARTEST DUDE IN THE ROOM.

"But I'm hungry," a man says. "The stores are low on food and I've got nothing."

Corporal Eckhardt, Mooney's team leader, waves through a young woman obviously infected with Hong Kong Lyssa, supported by a man who could have been her husband or boyfriend. The woman is lit up with fever and twitching.

"Sorry," Eckhardt is saying to those next in line. "We are not doing food distribution at this post. Here's a list of sites you can try. The list is from the City Government."

"People go in there," the old man says, nodding at everybody within eyeshot. "But they don't come out."

The old bastard is practically gloating over this news.

Mooney sighs as he watches people streaming through the abandoned cars, seeking care among Trinity's rapidly dwindling beds. The infected never seem to stop coming. He's tired of military service. But soon it will all be over for Jon Mooney. Twenty-seven days and a wakeup, his discharge comes through and he's out of the Army, and Alpha Mike Foxtrot—*adios,* motherfucker—to Iraq, New York and the rest of it.

The days are crawling by. He and most of the other guys in the platoon are kids, nineteen or twenty years old, but they wear patches on both shoulders, indicating that they have combat experience, that they are veterans. They are infantry: lean and fit and hungry. Mooney is tired and he has already seen too much that he'd like to forget. He just wants to go home and return to collecting vintage records and staying up until two in the morning watching bad TV. He'd like to see if he can get things going with Laura again. Maybe get his own place, some secret refuge where he can be alone for a while.

"Next!" barks Eckhardt. "Come on, let's go, people."

"Everybody goes in there, but nobody ever comes out!" the old man crows.

"Mister, I believe it's time for you to shut your dicktrap," says Specialist Martin from Weapons Squad, leaning over his tripod-mounted .30-caliber M240 perched on a pile of sandbags and aimed up First Avenue. Sitting on the ground next to him, the assistant gunner, the guy everybody calls Boomer, laughs.

"So is this how you treat—?" the old man starts, then begins jogging away as Martin swivels his machine gun just enough to communicate threat. "You boys are in the right business, all right," he calls over his shoulder as he weaves through the abandoned cars. "Because the end of the world will not come without a war!"

"Alpha Mike Foxtrot!" Martin calls after him with a grin and a friendly wave, making the assistant gunner cackle again.

"A war of fratricide!" the man calls back.

Mooney is only vaguely aware of what that word means, but it makes him shudder for some reason.

"Only in New York," says Boomer, shaking his head.

This place is starting to sound like Baghdad

At the south checkpoint, a small crowd is arguing with Second

Platoon's CO about whether the Army is hoarding a secret government vaccine in the hospital.

Second Lieutenant Todd Bowman of Fredericksburg, Texas has pale blue eyes and the blond, all-American good looks of a choir boy. Bowman studied history in college before joining the Army to see first-hand how it is made. Tall and lanky, he has been a competent leader but has not yet shaken his habit of glancing at Sergeant First Class Mike Kemper, a thirty-year-old veteran from Louisiana, for confirmation of his boldest orders and deepest fears. Kemper, small but with large hands and a wiry, lethal build, usually winks back. With his short-cropped hair and intense stare, his normal expression is menacing until he smiles, which dramatically changes his appearance. To the boys, the platoon sergeant is a rock. They call him Pops.

On the other side of the double line of coiled concertina wire pulled across First Avenue and weighted down by sandbags, a large woman is pleading with the LT to share whatever vaccine his troops are guarding inside the hospital.

"Ma'am," says the LT, "if we had a vaccine, why would we be wearing these masks? Do you know how uncomfortable it is to wear these masks all day and night?"

The woman stares at him uncertainly. "Well, it could be just for show."

"That makes no sense to me whatsoever, Ma'am."

"I told myself I was going to come down here and I'm not budging an inch until I get some vaccine for my babies. Do you understand me?"

Another man says: "Look here, officer."

"How old are you, anyway?" the woman says. "Twelve?"

The man continues: "Look at me, officer. Thank you. The President of the United States said you have a vaccine. Why would the President say that if it weren't true?"

Bowman answers matter-of-factly, "Sir, the Commander-in-Chief passed along no such information to his chain of command, who surely would have told me about it."

"Hey, I asked you if you understand me," the woman says.

Another man jumps in: "My wife's got it and I asked her sister to come over and help but now she's got it and I can't control both of them. They're back in my apartment doing God knows what, ripping the place apart. I need help. What should I do?"

"The best you can," Bowman answers. "You can bring them here for care or try to get a neighbor to help or maybe call the police, if they have the resources. But I can't spare a single man to leave this post to help you. I'm sorry. I really am."

A long series of single gunshots erupts to the north, popping against the steady background roar of New York, the sound of eight million people trying to stay alive. Bowman stiffens for a moment and turns towards the gunfire's distant echo, his instincts aroused by a vague sense of threat. Moments later, the sound is drowned out as a Blackhawk helicopter zooms overhead, skimming the rooftops.

Corporal Alvarez has meanwhile hustled up, and reports to the LT that the Trinity people want to talk to him. It's urgent, he adds.

The man is still talking: "You're not listening to me—"

Bowman nods vaguely, unable to shake his feeling of unease, and tells the crowd: "We're done here."

Dr. Linton, the hospital chief, and Winslow, one of several heavily armed city cops providing security inside the building, stand outside the city transit bus parked in front of the hospital emergency room doors, wearing N95 masks and looking worried. Behind them, the line of victims of the Hong Kong Lyssavirus and their families wait their turn to go into the bus, coughing and blowing their noses. Inside, nurses perform military-style triage to separate those infected with HK Lyssavirus from those with other infections or nothing wrong with them at all other than panic and imagination.

Those who have Lyssa are separated into priority groups using colored tags. If you get green, the nurses send you back home for home care. If you get red, you are considered a high priority for the ICU if one is available. If you get yellow, you might do well in the ICU and you might not, so you are hospitalized but have to wait.

If you get black, they make you as comfortable as possible until you die.

The HK Lyssavirus' mortality rate is high, somewhere between three and five percent of clinically ill cases, as much as twice as during the Spanish Flu of 1918-19. Hundreds of thousands of Americans are already dead and another two to three million are expected to die later. So many are dying, in fact, that corpses are being stacked in refrigerated trucks continually idling on the other side of the hospital, which, when full, drive their loads out to mass graves being dug in New Jersey.

The problem is not the number of dead, however, even though the number is horrifying.

HK Lyssa is a new airborne flulike virus—likely to have originated in Indian fruit bats, according to the CDC—that evolved to become easily transmissible between humans. It knocks you off your feet like severe flu, with additional symptoms such as twitching, rapid blinking and a powerful sour-milk body odor. Most people recover in about two weeks, but if infection is severe and the virus enters the brain, it causes dementia: The victim foams at the mouth, refuses water, becomes paranoid and prone to sudden violent movements, and eventually cannot speak except to make an unnerving growling sound like an idling motorcycle. Somebody on cable news called them Mad Dogs, and the label caught on. It fits. They are dangerous, and the soldiers know to be careful of them. Mad Dogs have hurt and killed people, even their own family members. They always get the black tag. They always die, usually within three to five days.

But the small numbers of Mad Dogs complicating an already horrifying epidemic is not even the real problem.

The biggest challenge facing the United States is simply the staggering number of people who are sick, unable to do anything except lie there and require constant help.

Because the human immune system has never encountered this virus before, it has no natural defense and almost everybody is susceptible to catching it. As a result, tens of millions of people are sick around the country, including many of the people who treat them, maintain public order, produce and distribute food and pharmaceuticals, make the water flow, and keep the lights and air conditioning and refrigerators and elevators and gas stoves working. America is already starting to come apart at the seams.

There is a proverb that says the USA is always just three days from a revolution. Stop delivering food to the supermarkets and see what a country of three hundred million citizens, with a strong sense of entitlement and more than two hundred fifty million guns, has to say about it. This is why the government declared a national emergency and recalled its military forces from overseas—to protect America from itself.

"Stay close, Mike," Bowman tells the Platoon Sergeant. "I have a feeling I know what they're going to want this time."

Kemper takes off his patrol cap and runs his hand over his closely cropped skull. "It was inevitable, sir," he says. "We knew this would happen."

"But we couldn't really plan for it. We're not equipped."

"We trained with non-lethals, but now that we have to actually use them, there's none to be had," says Kemper, refitting his cap. "All that training, down the drain."

Linton foregoes the usual token effort to make some sort of friendly contact with the military men protecting his hospital, and gets right to the point.

"Lieutenant, we have no more room for new patients. No beds, no staff, nothing. We're running out of gloves and gowns and masks. We're shutting down and will be focusing on our current caseload for the near future."

"I understand," Bowman says.

The hospital chief extends a clipboard with one gloved hand. "I've had the addresses of several local alternative care sites written down. Last I heard, they are still in business. Hospices, too, for the Mad Dogs." The doctor clears his throat politely at his use of the common but politically incorrect term. "I'm asking if you can tell people who come here wanting care that they should go to one of these other sites."

Kemper takes the clipboard while Bowman says, "We'll take care of it."

Linton opens his mouth, closes it, then says simply, "Thank you, Lieutenant."

Watching the men return to the hospital, Bowman shakes his head and Kemper nods in agreement.

"It's a bag of dicks, sir, that's for sure," he says dryly.

Bowman sighs loudly. "I've got to report this up to Captain West. Mike, find me my RTO."

A sudden crash of automatic weapons fire to the west, deep inside the city. The soldiers turn towards the sound, their faces wearing expressions of puzzlement. They exchange a quick glance. Every day, it seems, there is a little more gunfire. They're thinking: This place is starting to sound like Baghdad.

And the epidemic is only a few weeks old.

If you shot a dog, you couldn't eat it

Eight days earlier, Charlie Company sat around for thirty hours surrounded by their gear on the runway in Logistical Support Area King

Cobra in Iraq, alternately sweltering by day and freezing by night while waiting for a ride home. King Cobra was a virtual city of sandbagged tents and concrete bunkers sprawling for miles in all directions and surrounded by concertina wire and guard towers. The Army's ongoing exodus from the country was a marvel in its overall speed and orderliness, but LSA King Cobra nonetheless steadily unraveled in the confusion, constant attacks by insurgents, and the massive ongoing labor of trying to provide shelter and medical care for the infected. An estimated twenty percent of the forces in Iraq caught Lyssa and were suffering in quarantine tents.

At the time, the boys thought they were being redeployed to Florida, which started a debate about the relative merits of Miami girls versus girls from every other state represented in the Company. They shouted to make themselves heard, as some POGs—people other than grunts, support troops—in a nearby motor pool company had started a musical duel, one side picking gangster rap, the other heavy metal anthems.

The second night, the boys began to worry. Nobody in charge seemed to know they were there, and they were out of food and hungry. Some snuck out to beg or steal some MREs and barely made it back alive. One couldn't walk to the latrine without being attacked by wild dogs or shot at by nervous replacements. Dogs caught Lyssa too and you needed to bring a shotgun to the can so you didn't get bit, and for the same reason, if you shot a dog, as a sniper from Third Platoon did, you couldn't eat it.

A Humvee parked near the edge of the runway took a hit from an RPG and was burning, its ammo cooking off and popping. Marine Cobras roared overhead in the darkness, setting up strafing runs. In the middle of a densely populated camp with fires all around, thermal and night vision optics were useless, so the boys sent up flares and took potshots at the shadows. The swacked Humvee exploded, shooting flaming shards of metal fifty feet into the air, making the boys whoop. A SAW gunner in Second Platoon showed up laughing with a bottle of cheap Iraqi gin he'd bought from some kids at the perimeter, and the boys passed it around, savoring the slow burn on their parched throats.

A firefight broke out in the distance, then another, red tracer flashes bursting along the wire. A single mortar round whistled and burst in the center of the camp, sending pieces of tent flying. A squad of heavily armed MPs jogged by, telling everybody to keep their heads down. Buses packed with soldiers drove onto the runway as if nothing was happening, their headlights playing on the tents and Stryker vehicles lined up in neat rows while a C130 cargo plane touched down dangerously close. The headlights briefly illuminated two soldiers locked in a fist fight, then swerved away, returning them to darkness. Somebody in the quarantine tents was screaming. Shots rang out.

The boys lay on the ground shivering in their armor, using their helmets to rest their heads, dreaming of forbidden pleasures—hot showers, plates piled high with French fries and, of course, sex. Some were so exhausted they dreamed of sleep, or not at all. In the middle of the night they woke up, Iraqi dust caked in their ears and mouths and nostrils, to the sound of gunfire close by. The air stank of oily smoke and hot diesel fumes.

At least it's not like this at home, they thought, and sighed. Soon, it will all be over.

Green tracer rounds from Russian guns streamed into the cold night sky over Baghdad. The city appeared to be tearing itself apart. Word went around that the militias were shooting Lyssa victims down in the street. People went Mad Dog and roamed the city along with animals who'd also caught it, spreading infection.

It was a disaster beyond the soldiers' comprehension.

"We tried," PFC Richard Boyd said, watching the distant fireworks, his voice quivering with rage. "We really did. Now they can die for all I care."

At dawn, Lieutenant Colonel George Custer Armstrong, silver-haired and looking fierce with his arm in a bloody sling, mustered the battalion and gave everybody a rousing speech just before they boarded chartered United and Air France planes and started the long journey home.

Operation Iraqi Freedom has been scrubbed, he told them.

We're going back to the World.

The mission has changed. Our new mission is more important. In fact, it is possibly the most important thing the Army has done since the founding of the Republic.

We've got to see America through the Pandemic, he said.

The boys glanced at each other in formation, exchanging quick, discrete grins. It was actually happening. They were finally going home.

As Charlie Company boarded the planes, First Platoon found that Private Tyrone Botus, the kid everybody called Rook, had gone Elvis. He had ventured out near the quarantine tents to refill his squad's canteens the night before. They couldn't find him anywhere.

We have bayonets. That should make an impression

Jake Sherman, the platoon's radio/telephone operator, hands Lieutenant Bowman the handset attached to the SINCGAR radio pack on his back. "War Dogs Six on the net, LT," he says, his mouth full of gum.

War Dogs is Charlie Company's call sign and War Dogs Six is the commander of Charlie Company, Captain West.

"This is War Dogs Two actual," Bowman says into the phone. "I send 'Metallica,' over."

This is War Dogs actual. I copy "Metallica." Wait one, over. Um, roger that, over.

"Request riot control gear, over."

Wait one, over. That's a, uh, no go, over.

"Request to be relieved by riot control units. How copy? Over."

That's another no go, War Dogs Two. I've got nothing to send you. You'll have to make do, over.

The LT grinds his teeth and says, "Roger that, sir."

Hearts and minds, son. Good luck. Out.

Bowman turns to face his squad leaders. His rifle platoon is divided into three rifle squads of nine men plus what's left of Weapons Squad, decimated by Lyssa infection back in Iraq, leaving a single gun team. Each of the rifle squads, in turn, is led by a staff sergeant easy to pick out because, like Bowman, they are the only ones wearing patrol caps instead of Kevlar helmets. The men lean into the conference.

To the east, across the river somewhere in Brooklyn, a splash of small arms fire.

"Gentlemen, our position here is changing," says the LT.

The platoon occupied the block in front of the hospital, where the City parked a bus in front of the emergency room doors. Double strands of concertina wire were laid across both ends of the block, weighted down by sandbags, with nests for the platoon's thirty-caliber machine gun. In the intersections beyond, concrete barriers blocked off the adjoining streets, but people simply drove around them using the sidewalks and abandoned their cars in the intersections. Beyond the roadblocks, the streets are jammed with cars in slowly moving traffic, drivers yelling at each other and leaning on their horns. Looking at the bumper-to-bumper traffic only a block away, you could almost believe things are still normal here. At least normal for New York.

"Until now, our mission has been to protect the hospital and ensure the orderly flow of cases through the triage process," Bowman adds. "Now the hospital is full up, as I've just informed Captain West using the mission code. This means the orderly flow of cases is about to hit a dam. We're shutting off both entrances in thirty minutes."

"The good citizens of New York are not going to like that one bit," Sergeant Ruiz points out. "Could get ugly fast."

"Any word on the non-lethals, sir?" asks Sergeant McGraw in his heavy South Carolina drawl.

"The Captain says that's a November Golf, Pete."

In other words, a "no go."

McGraw rubs his nose. With his barrel chest, handlebar mustache bristling on his upper lip, and heavily tattooed forearms, he has an intimidating appearance. When not soldiering, he is usually riding a Harley across the Bible Belt with his young biker girlfriend, hammering down on the big slab. "Kind of hard to do crowd control with what we got, LT," he says. "We're armed to the teeth and can't use any of it. You know that."

"We have bayonets. That should make an impression. Hopefully, it will be enough."

"And if it ain't, sir?"

Bowman looks into his non-coms' eyes. He knows what they are thinking. Back in Iraq, they're thinking, the streets are still littered with American good intentions, blood and bodies and undetonated munitions. Hundreds of thousands of civilians died there, many as a result of stray American ordinance. You simply can't use the kind of firepower that American infantry carries around and not expect civilians to get killed, especially in built-up areas. Accidents happen and they cannot afford accidents now that the civilians are their fellow citizens. To do this mission properly, the soldiers need batons, shields, riot control dispensers, snipers on the roof and birds in the air. But they have none of these. There are Army units all over the country needing the same equipment and there is simply not enough to go around. Due to the usual logistical foul-up, they do not even have CS gas grenades commonly issued to infantry in urban deployments.

Instead, they are packing heavy firepower and plenty of bullets.

"We stick with the ROE," Bowman answers. "Remember that we're in somebody's house here." The rules of engagement for this mission in urban terrain: Return fire only if you are fired upon directly by a hostile force that is clearly visible. Which should be almost never.

He adds: "And we keep our force concentrated. Between Lyssa and everything else, we're down to seventy-five percent strength. I don't want to see any part of this platoon peeled off and overrun by a mob of pissed-off civilians looking for medicine."

They know they are basically in a no-win situation, a "bag of dicks" in Army lingo. Ruiz whistles through his nose. Lewis mutters, "Man, this is jacked up." Kemper smiles and says: "Embrace the suck, gentlemen."

Bowman raises his eyebrows. "OK. If the crowd gets out of hand, we'll put on respirators, fire some smoke grenades and maybe the civs will think it's tear gas and run for it. It's a long shot, I know—"

McGraw is grinning. "Satisfactory, sir. It's worth a try, sir."

"All right, then. Get your men ready to muster in thirty minutes."

The best way to take down a police helicopter with an RPG while playing *Grand Theft Auto*

The boys of Third Squad are the night shift, and this being day, they are enjoying some rack time, sprawled on their bunks in a large room in the cool basement of the hospital, where Second Platoon has been billeted. Three of the boys are sleeping soundly after a debate on the best way to take down a police helicopter with an RPG while playing *Grand Theft Auto*. Corporal Hicks, sweating bullets, does push-ups on the floor. Grunting, he switches to sit-ups. Boyd smokes quietly and reads a letter from home, idly running one hand over his bristling skull and mouthing the words *oh, man* repeatedly, while McLeod, the platoon ne'er-do-well, leafs through a copy of *Playboy*, calling out, for anybody caring to listen, names, hobbies, measurements and, assuming unlimited funds, how much he would pay to have sex with them. The Newb sews a rip in his uniform, cursing steadily at having to perform yet another goddamn mind-numbing Army chore when he could be dreaming, while Williams cleans and oils his M203A1 carbine and grenade launcher and at that moment is pretty sure he'd shoot somebody in the face for a hot fajita burrito with sour cream and extra corn salsa. A good soldier can break down a rifle in fewer than thirty seconds and reassemble it in less, and Williams knows his business. He grew up in Oakland hustling and gang banging, and he is a long way from that world, even though he feels right at home with the big, dumb, earnest kids of his platoon, this melting pot Army. He shakes his head, smiling and remembering. He has some stories to tell when he gets back. He is still alive to tell them. A boom box stolen from an upstairs nurse's station plays a loud, steady stream of music. Today it is hip hop, yesterday it was rock and roll, tomorrow who knows. As long as it's loud.

"Man oh man, at least a million dollars," says McLeod, checking out the centerfold. "At least. I mean, Jeezus. Hey guys, what'll you give me for a quick look at these hooters? Do I hear a buck? I swear they're real. Any takers?"

Williams shakes his head. It's all they ever talk about—that special Suzie Rottencrotch back home, their mythical sexual prowess, the hot nurses upstairs and what they are going to do to the world's women when they get out of the Army. He looks up as Sergeant Ruiz enters the room and says, "Hey, Sergeant. What's the word?"

"The word is you morons aren't sleeping when you're supposed to be getting your Zs," Ruiz barks back at him, glaring with his intense eyes. "And not wearing your masks when you're supposed to, either."

"We didn't wear the masks in Iraq, Sarge," McLeod says. "How come we have to wear them here?"

"Because in Iraq, we weren't living in a hospital filled with people dying from the Black Death, shit-for-brains."

McLeod grins, racking his wit for a good retort, but Ruiz has already moved on. "Get out of your fartsacks and get your shit on, ladies. LT has some work for us and we're on the move in ten minutes."

Boyd looks up, his eyes gleaming. "My sister's got Lyssa. I got this letter from home."

The boys stop and stare at him.

"My mom says they're burning bodies outside town. She even told me how they do it. They dig a trench to make an air vent, right, and then they build the pyre with wood. They put the bodies on top and burn them up. The town council got totally freaked and started doing this. This is all the way on the other side of the country. The letter took over a week to get to me."

"Sorry about your sister, Boyd," Ruiz offers.

"This was over a week ago," Boyd says, staring at the letter in disbelief. "She could be dead by now."

"Did somebody say they were burning up bodies?" says Ross, whom everybody calls Hawkeye because of his uncanny accuracy with an M4 carbine. He has just woken up and is still bleary from sleep. "Man, that is extreme."

"It's got to be bullshit," says McLeod. "Some cities are digging mass graves to store the bodies temporarily, but they're not burning them up, for Chrissakes."

"If they were paranoid enough, they might," Williams says.

"What I'm saying is: What am I doing here in New York?" Boyd wonders. "Why aren't we guarding a hospital in Idaho, like in Boise? I should be there. I should be home with them. I could at least be in the same lousy state. I have to call my mom."

"I'll bet we got guys in Boise and the towns around it just like we're here in New York," Ruiz tells him. "Some of them are probably New Yorkers and wishing they were here. And they're watching over your family just like we're watching over theirs. The same way that everybody in this platoon has each other's backs. All right?"

"Hooah, Sergeant," says Boyd, without enthusiasm.

The boys quietly begin to pull their gear on: battle dress uniform, boots, kneepads, body armor, harness, watch, ammo, knife, gloves, primary weapons and Kevlar.

"Okay, so we've reached the point where we're setting people on fire, but if you look at this whole global plague of death in a glass-half-full kind of way, there are some things we could actually be pretty happy about," McLeod says to break the ice after a few moments. "For example, we're getting three squares a day, eight hours of rack time a night, and we even got running water. Plus we don't have to go out on patrol in neighborhoods that all look like Tijuana after it's been cluster-bombed, getting our balls blown off by elevated IEDs and crazy Hajjis."

"Shut up, McLeod," growls Ruiz.

"I'm just trying to cheer everybody up by pointing out it may be true that two hundred million people are going to die and the world is probably ending, but at least we got out of that Arab Hell with our butts and balls intact and we don't have to shit in an oven covered in flies, so mission accomplished, am I right or am I right?"

Most of the boys are laughing, but Ruiz is now standing in front of McLeod, who snaps to attention, staring straight ahead into the void, his mouth carefully zipped and primly holding back a smile. Ruiz takes a step forward until their eyes are inches away, Ruiz's probing, searching for an excuse, McLeod's respectfully vacant. Finally, the sergeant shakes his head in exaggerated disgust and walks away. "*Vamos*, ladies!"

Williams slaps McLeod on the back after Ruiz leaves the room. Their friendship goes back to basic training, where they were battle buddies and McLeod often got them both smoked with pushups and barracks maintenance—usually scrubbing toilets—by falling asleep in class and otherwise pissing off the drill instructors.

"You go on being a buster and Magilla is gonna chunk your ass good, dawg," Williams warns. He means it: Ruiz is an articulate and thoughtful NCO but has a short temper and, thanks to constant exercise, a thickly muscled body, making him resemble a bulldog. The boys call him Magilla behind his back, short for Magilla Gorilla.

McLeod replies with a cartoonish shrug.

Corporal Hicks, watching Boyd slowly pull on his gear while muttering to himself, says, "Get yourself squared away, Rick. Almost everybody in this platoon has somebody on the outside who's got the bug."

"I should be there with them," Boyd says. "They're all I've got in this world."

"If we stay focused, we'll all get through this and I mean everybody. If we start falling apart, with everybody going off his own way, well, then God help us all because we are surely jacked. Because this thing is going to get a hell of a lot worse before it gets better. Until then, make the pain your friend and it will make you stronger."

McLeod grins and says, "Wouldn't it be cool if the Sergeant got Lyssa in his brain and turned into a Mad Dog? 'Get out of your fartsacks and get your shit on, ladies!' Snarl, snarl!"

The boys burst into laughter.

I'm going to kill you dead

Sergeant McGraw roars, "Squad as skirmishers, move!" and watches his squad deploy in a line, weapons held at safe port so the friendly citizens of New York can clearly observe their bayonets. Beyond the concertina wire and the sandbags, people keep on streaming through the cars. They break into a run after seeing the soldiers begin to close the checkpoint, and when they finally reach the wire and confirm their dashed hopes, they try to shout or beg their way in.

Help me, they say. I think my kids have it and I don't know what to do.

Their faces are turning blue.

Corporal Eckhardt hands them the yellow sheets, but the people do not want to leave. Many of them brought a sick loved one with them, and the prospect of walking ten blocks to a Lyssa clinic set up in some school or bowling alley does not seem promising. They scream, they shout, they beg. They fall to the ground and sit, numbly clutching their yellow pieces of paper. The air fills with that sickly sour smell people give off when they've got Lyssa—the stench that keeps on giving.

A woman is crying, I can't do it by myself, I can't, I just can't.

"Couldn't we let in just a few more people?" Mooney hisses.

"Shut up," says Finnegan, standing next to him. "You know the answer to that."

"This is horrible."

Sergeant McGraw says into his handheld, "We're good at this end, sir."

Gunfire rattles just a few blocks away to the west, loud and echoing among the buildings. The seemingly constant wail of police and ambulance sirens appears to multiply in volume.

McGraw pauses, looking west, and says, "I've got—"

A deafening boom sends a brief tremor through the ground and shatters windows in nearby buildings. The soldiers break formation to look as a fireball mushrooms into the air on a plume of black smoke, rising up over the buildings across the avenue to the west. A shrill wail goes up from the civilians.

"Holy crap!" says Wyatt. "I felt the concussion."

"Back in formation!" McGraw roars, his face red. "Right now!"

"Whoa, what was that?" says Rollins. "It practically blew out my eardrums."

"Dude, this is seriously jacked," Mooney whispers.

"We got to trust the Sergeant," Finnegan hisses at them. "He'll get us through this. If he don't, Pops will. Now just shut up and do what you're told. It's all going to be okay."

"No talking in the ranks, you hear?" McGraw says, then finishes his report to the LT on his handheld.

Mooney is not listening. He is watching two men jogging towards the crowd at the wire. There is something not right about them. The way they move as they weave purposefully through the cars. A strange, loping gait with their hands splayed into claws pressed against their chests. Like they aren't people, but some kind of animal. The thought chills him.

"Sergeant?" he says.

"Next man who talks is going to get my boot," McGraw growls, fed up.

Mooney has lost sight of the two men. One of them had no shirt on and what looked like blue pajama bottoms. The other wore a baseball cap, denim shirt and blue jeans and had a black stain on his face, around his mouth.

The civilians are screaming. Mooney cranes his neck, trying to see past McGraw's broad shoulders.

Then the sergeant moves, running fast, and Mooney can see the checkpoint. The two men are there, one of them pulling the long dark hair out of a woman's head by the handful while the other systematically bites her stomach, drawing blood and leaving a smear of drool. The other civilians are screaming and trying to get out of the area fast. The men wrestle the woman to the ground. She lets out a horrible high-pitched whine and suddenly seems to give up, her body starting to go slack, her eyes glassy and pleading.

McGraw is shouting, stop, stop or I will shoot.

Corporal Eckhardt takes a step forward. "Sergeant—"

The sergeant sees what they've done and screams, "I'm going to kill you dead—"

But remembers his training, fires his Beretta into the air. Warning shots. The men's heads jerk up with a spray of blood and spittle, looking like birds startled while feasting on carrion. The one wearing pajama bottoms leaps to his feet and takes a run straight at McGraw but immediately becomes entangled in the concertina wire, thrashing and making sounds like a dog being strangled.

Concertina wire is lined with two-inch-long razors set four inches apart. The man shreds himself until he falls to the ground, his legs soaked with blood and bleeding out from a severed femoral artery in his thigh.

The other man jumps to his feet, runs, leaps over the wire—

Several carbines *crack* and *pop* at once and the man twitches in mid air, lands on the ground in a heap. Instantly, a widening pool of blood begins to form under him.

"Cease fire! Cease fire!"

Mooney lowers his carbine. The sharp tang of cordite hangs in the air.

"Did you see that?" McGraw says to nobody in particular. "What was that?"

Bowman is shouting, running towards them from the other checkpoint, demanding to know why weapons are being fired.

The woman is still alive, lying on the ground and in the throes of some sort of convulsions. The two assailants lie still in their own blood, obviously dead.

"Ma'am, it's all right now," McGraw says, holding the Beretta behind his back and extending his other hand across the wire. "Come to me. We'll take care of you."

The woman stares at him in terror, panting as she pulls herself unsteadily onto her feet.

He lowers his mask. "Look at me. Miss. You're going to be okay."

She begins twitching and blinking rapidly.

"No, don't—"

But she has already turned and started running. By the time the squad can make an opening in the wire enough for McGraw to give chase, she is gone.

Chapter 2

Beginning to wonder if we actually did leave Iraq

The night is alive with police sirens and car horns and shouting and gunfire. The warm, muggy air smells like smoke. The streetlights dim and occasionally flare up as the city juggles its power problems. Down First Avenue, past the roadblock, the traffic lights are all blinking red and the traffic is snarled and honking with fury as thousands continue their flight from Manhattan in anything that can get a little gasoline in it.

Everybody thinks things are better somewhere else.

The boys of Second Platoon's Third Squad pace the wire nervously, wired on black coffee. A police helicopter roars overhead, its powerful spotlight exploring the area briefly and ruining their night vision before moving on.

"I can't believe this," Corporal Hicks mutters to himself, squinting down First Avenue and listening to the deep thuds of heavy machine-gun fire. "Are those tracers?"

"No, I'm just happy to see you," McLeod says, strolling up with his SAW. "Sounds like a fiddy-cal. So what?"

"Because this is New York, not Baghdad, shit-for-brains. What is somebody down there doing firing an MG in the middle of New York?" Then, as an afterthought: "Beat your face, McLeod. Give me twenty."

"Are you serious? We're in the middle of a war zone here."

"You want thirty?"

While McLeod counts off his pushups, Hicks raises his carbine's telescopic close combat optic to his eye. A red dot is centered in the optic for easy targeting. The tracers form a stream of light over the hoods of cars crawling in bumper-to-bumper traffic and the heads of people running through the cars.

Hicks can't see through buildings, though, so he can't tell who is laying down this steel rain and who is getting rained on. Just a few hundred meters away, and yet even this close he feels isolated and can barely tell what is going on. He wonders where all those big bullets are ending up. A fifty-cal round can travel four miles. It can blow through vehicles and, at close range, concrete walls.

Now imagine what it can do to a human being.

"Six. . . . Seven. . . ."

The firing stops. It lasted only a few seconds. Somebody screwed up big time, probably some green recruit in a Humvee who got spooked. Hopefully, nobody got killed.

Rather you than me, he thinks.

Hicks is about to lower his weapon when he notices two people at the periphery of his scope image and focuses on them. One is a middle-aged man wearing boxers. The other is a teenaged girl dressed in a long T-shirt that comes down to her knees. They're staring vacantly and doing that strange, jittery neck roll that people with the Mad Dog strain of Lyssa often do and that always gives Hicks the creeps. Their hands are clenched into fists in front of their chests. They look in his direction, open their mouths, and bolt away in the direction of where the MG fire had come from.

He mutters, "And what are all these Mad Dogs doing running around without a leash?"

The last thing we need, he tells himself, is another bunch throwing themselves at our perimeter and getting themselves shot. Getting caught in that kind of fire incident will follow you around for life.

The MG starts thudding again.

"I'm beginning to wonder if we actually did leave Iraq," McLeod says, then resumes counting.

Things will be just fine, sir, if we keep right on moving

The armored Humvees, butterbar Todd Bowman commanding, race up Haifa Street through dense smells of burning trash and gasoline fumes. The boys in the lead vehicle bob their heads in time to Dope's "Die Motherfucker Die" played loud enough to be heard in the mosques. A year ago, the government of Iraq tottered on the edge of collapse and the U.S. Army reentered the cities in force to prop it up, unleashing a new generation of martyrs, foot soldiers and mad bombers in a war that has no end.

The street karma is constantly shifting, but Bowman, brand new to the country and command, is not prepared for how much hate he has to eat here on a daily basis. The walls of the high-rise apartment buildings, pockmarked with bullet holes from years of strife, radiate it. The very streets cry infidel. The very bricks want him dead.

"Contact, right!"

The RPG zips across the front of his Humvee and strikes a parked minivan, which explodes and rockets a spinning blur of metal against his windshield, where it bounces with a heart-stopping smash and leaves a spider web of cracks. Kemper, driving the rig, whistles through his teeth but otherwise barely even flinches at the impact.

They did not prepare Bowman for this in ROTC.

The air hums and snaps with small arms fire while the fifty-cals on the Humvees chew up the walls of nearby buildings. Tracers flicker and zip through the air. The top of a palm tree explodes, scattering burning leaves and blistering their windshield with pieces of shrapnel.

Bowman, wide-eyed and shouting himself hoarse, forces himself to calm down. His men are counting on him to lead them, and he doesn't want to let them down on his first mission. They need to stop and start directing aimed fire at the insurgent positions. In an ambush, if you can't withdraw, you assault.

He starts to key his handset, but Kemper turns, winking, and tells him that things will be just fine, sir, if we keep right on moving.

The cops aren't answering the phone

Bowman's eyes flutter open and he looks around the facility manager's office with a flash of panic. Had he been dreaming? For a moment, he'd thought. . . . Then he'd heard a noise. A knock? He listens to the hum of machinery in the hospital basement.

Somebody is muttering outside his door.

"Come in," he says.

Kemper enters the room, dimly lighted by a single desk lamp, followed by the squad leaders. Bowman is expecting them. He requested a squad leader meeting. The room's smells of sweat, stale coffee and lived-in gear grows stronger.

"Pull up a chair, gentlemen," says the LT, rubbing his eyes. "Yeah, Pete, just push that aside. Ah, coffee's not fresh but it is hot if you want some."

Ruiz stands, grinning, and heads for the pot. "Don't mind if I do, sir." His squad will be manning the wire for the rest of the night until relieved at oh-six hundred.

Bowman clears his throat and says, "Gentlemen, the situation has changed. Again. In fact, it's become fluid."

Puzzled expressions behind their masks. "Sir?"

"About thirty minutes ago, the RTO came to see me," Bowman tells them. "He shared with me some interesting information about messages he's been intercepting on the net. Gentlemen, there are units in our area of operations that are under attack by civilians."

The sergeants are squinting in disbelief.

"Confirmed, sir?"

"Captain West confirmed it."

"Coordinated?"

"No," Bowman answers. "The attacks are entirely random."

"Just what do they hope to gain from doing that?" says Sergeant McGraw. "Are they looking for food, vaccine or are they, you know, lashing out at the government?"

Bowman looks him square in the eye. "We were one of the units that was attacked."

The men gasp. These are men not easily surprised. But they have just learned the attacks are being made by Lyssa victims suffering from Mad Dog syndrome, and it floors them.

"We were attacked," McGraw says slowly.

"Yes, Sergeant. We were attacked."

"By unarmed Americans. American civilians. Sick people."

Bowman turns to the other sergeants. "As I said, the situation is changing."

McGraw shakes his head. "Sir. . . ."

"Pete, you may feel that your men have something to atone for after what happened on the wire today. I don't. Captain West agrees with my view on this. Whatever your feelings are, you're going to have to get yourself squared away on this."

McGraw chews on his mustache and mutters, "Yes, sir."

"Well, this makes sense," Ruiz says. "We've been turning away a lot of people who caught the bug, but also a lot of people asking for help controlling a Mad Dog, or saying a neighbor's gone Mad Dog and attacking people. More than we should be hearing about."

"What do you say to them?" Sergeant Lewis asks. He is a giant of a man, nearly six feet and four inches tall, and was once considered the unit's finest athlete. Back then, the soldiers called him Achilles behind his back, with admiration, but not anymore, not for some time. After his son was born and he quit smoking, he got a little soft and put on some weight. It did not dampen his natural aggression, though. If anything, he has only grown more aggressive over time. He adds, "What do you tell them to do?"

Ruiz shrugs. "To go back home and call the cops."

"And is that all right for them?"

"They, um, say the cops aren't answering the phone."

Lewis gestures with his large hands and says, "We got to get out there and start helping these people."

"Negative," says the LT, shaking his head for emphasis.

"It's why we're here, ain't it, sir?"

"It's a no go. It's not our mission. The Army is a weapon of last resort in civil disturbance situations. We're not cops. We trained with the non-lethals but we don't have any. We go out there, and we'll end up in situations like today where civilians get killed."

"Sounds like people are getting killed all over, and we're sitting with our asses in the wind," Lewis says bitterly. "What's the Army for if not protecting the people here?"

"I don't have the answers you'd like me to have," Bowman tells him. "What matters is our position here. Our orders are the same. Keep this facility safe. Out there, we'd only do more harm than good."

Kemper nods. It makes sense. You can't kill a fly with a hammer.

Bowman clears his throat and adds carefully: "I should add, however, that in light of recent events, the rules of engagement have changed."

The NCOs begin swearing.

If you're AWOL for more than thirty days, you are technically a deserter

PFC Richard Boyd follows the girl down the street, both of them sticking to the shadows to avoid being seen. He had no idea things have gotten this bad out here. The streets are alive with packs of healthy and infected hunting each other in the dark.

The girl's name is Susan. He guesses her to be about nineteen, his own age. Pretty face. Nice body, slim and athletic. A girl next door type who seems out of place in New York. Being in a Muslim country for the past ten months made Boyd forget how much skin comes out in the West when the air is warm and muggy like tonight. She is wearing a tank top and cut-off jeans and the humidity is making her sweat. He pictures droplets of sweat trickling between her breasts and feels the pull of arousal. Maybe she will kiss him for helping her out. Maybe she'll do more than that.

Susan disappears into the doorway of a jewelry store and he follows.

"What is it?" he whispers near her ear.

They are standing close and he wonders if he should try to kiss her.

After a few moments, she says, "Nothing. They're gone."

She showed up at the post just after midnight, while Sergeant Ruiz was in the hospital with the LT, and asked for help. Williams said she had a junkie look and suggested some sort of quid pro quo if he could get her something tasty out of the hospital pharmacy, which got the guys excited and joking. They stopped laughing when she told them her story: Her father was sick and went Mad Dog and starting beating the crap out of her mother. Mom hid in a closet in their apartment and Dad was tearing the place apart. She called the cops but kept getting a recorded message saying all circuits are busy. That's when Corporal Hicks showed up and told her that there was nothing they could do for her in any case. If the cops could not help her, she was on her own. The boys suddenly ached to help, although Williams hooted and said it was all BS, you white boys almost got taken.

Some of them wanted to get taken. She really is pretty, they thought.

That's when Boyd decided to go "over the hill." AWOL. He waited a few minutes, then slipped out through the wire and joined up with her. They have been making painfully slow progress to her apartment building in the Lower East Side ever since.

His plan: Save the girl's mom, be the hero, split for Idaho. He should be there, with his family, right now. Donna had Lyssa and Mom needed him. She said so in her letter. She said she was afraid his sister would go Mad Dog and then the Sheriff would come and shoot her and throw her body on one of the big fires outside town. The fact that everything in the letter happened a week ago does not matter to Boyd.

The only problem with this plan is he is not even sure where he is right now, much less how he is going to get to the suburbs of Boise during a plague, when all the planes are grounded and the streets, apparently, are alive with homicidal maniacs.

If you're AWOL for more than thirty days, you are technically a deserter. If he becomes a deserter, they might even shoot him if they find him. After what he has seen tonight, he is certain they will. These are hard times and getting harder.

Maybe he will go back after he helps this girl out. The idea of being executed is starting to loom large in his imagination, and he does not like it. He did not really think things through before slipping out of the post. His plan is already falling apart.

Susan darts into another doorway, and he follows.

"What is it?"

She shushes him, their bodies pressed together.

Then he hears it. Mad Dogs howling in the dark.

Two teenaged girls enter the glow of the sputtering street lamps, crossing the street. One stops and stares directly at where Boyd and the girl are hiding in the shadows, and emits a low guttural growl, shoulders slouched and trembling, her hands balled into fists at her sides. Drool drips from her clenched teeth, staining her T-shirt.

The other girl, her long hair falling in tangles over her face, continues limping along, dragging a leg that appears to be bleeding and broken. Then she too stops and begins growling at where Boyd and Susan are hiding.

Boyd raises his M4. The first girl growls louder. Susan is shaking, breathing in short, panicked gasps.

"Shoot her, shoot her. . . ."

He licks his lips as a sickening wave of horror blanks out his mind. His heart begins hammering against his ribs and he can feel his bowels turn to water. He blinks, tries to shift his mind back on his training, but he never trained for this. The fact is he has no idea what he will do if the girl charges him. In Iraq, things were never clear cut but fighting American civilians who have turned into some kind of psycho zombie is something new and beyond training. Instead, his mind begins obsessing on the theory he heard that Mad Dogs are not really growling when they make that noise, they are actually talking, but their throats have become partially paralyzed so it comes out as a creepy gurgle. Once he thinks of this, he cannot get it out of his mind.

He wonders what they are trying to tell him.

A mob of young, muscular Asian boys, wearing wife-beaters and jeans, emerges from the darkness and falls upon the girls with metal pipes and baseball bats. The girls' bodies topple to the ground under the blows. Except for the scuffing of their sneakers against the street as they lay convulsing and flailing and dying, they don't make a sound. Boyd hears the pipes and bats connecting with flesh and cracking bones when they hit, clanging off the asphalt when they miss.

"Jesus," he says, sick to his stomach.

One of the boys straightens and stares in their direction.

"Shut up," Susan hisses beside him.

"Why? They aren't infected."

"I've seen those guys before," she says. "You do not want to fuck with them."

Their work done, the mob moves on without a word, stretching and swinging their homemade weapons.

"Come on, Rick," Susan says, sighing. "We're almost home."

War has rules

In Bowman's headquarters in the hospital facility manager's office, the rules of engagement are changing and the non-coms are swearing.

Bowman presses on, "You are now authorized to use deadly force against any civilian who makes a threatening gesture towards a member of this unit. Even if that civilian is unarmed."

Now everybody is shouting.

"This comes straight from Battalion and presumably from Quarantine and the Old Man himself."

War has rules. Rules of engagement are spelled out by command authorities to describe the circumstances under which military units can use force, and to what degree.

They are also supposed to follow the basic precepts of law.

The LT runs his hand across his buzz cut. "Gentlemen, I'm honestly not sure what to make of it. I'm open to suggestions."

Kemper glances at him sharply.

"It's illegal," says McGraw. "We don't have to obey an unlawful order."

"Suppose we don't pass on the new ROE to the men," says Lewis. "What happens if we are attacked? How do we defend ourselves, and with what force?"

"I'm not shooting American citizens," McGraw says, his face burning. "I took an oath to defend them, not slaughter them, for Chrissakes. Even the goddamn dirty hippies."

"So we're going to let the Mad Dogs here attack us and kill us or infect us," Lewis says. "That's your ROE?"

McGraw snorts. "How many people are we talking about here? We can handle a few at a time without killing anybody. Not that many people go Mad Dog. It's pretty rare."

"If that's true," says Ruiz, "then why are we getting these reports of Mad Dogs attacking Army units?"

Nobody has an answer to that.

"I mean, did you ever wonder why America had to pull its forces out of almost every one of its military bases around the world? We've got what, more than seven hundred bases? More than two hundred fifty thousand people overseas just in the Army? Think about it. Almost every one of them is home now."

"They're not telling us something," Lewis says. "That's for damn sure. You can take that straight to the bank."

"Our situational awareness is very limited," Bowman says.

"What happens later, sir?" Ruiz is asking. "Suppose we do shoot some people who are honest to God trying to kill us. What happens after, when the Pandemic is over? Do we end up in court charged with murder or what? Could we get sued?"

"They're going to die anyway," says Lewis.

"I want some assurances," says Ruiz. "About the legalities."

"So I say if they're trying to kill us, we should be able to kill them first. They can't give the whole Army a court martial, can they?"

"I'm not shooting anybody," McGraw says. "The question is not whether we refuse the order, but whether we tell the Captain that we're refusing the order to make a point up the chain of command."

"We can't be the only unit refusing to fire on sick people," Ruiz says.

"These are dangerous times," says Lewis. "I wouldn't go around announcing to the chain of command that you're refusing to follow orders, know what I mean?"

"Are we even supposed to be here?" says Ruiz. "Isn't it against the law for the Army to be pointing guns at people at all in our own cities? You know, Posse Comitatus?"

"We trained for this type of domestic emergency before we shipped out for Iraq," Lewis tells him. "Why would they do that if they didn't mean for us to use that training now?"

"Yeah? Then where's the non-lethal equipment?"

Lewis glances at Kemper. "Back me up on this, Pops."

Kemper wants to shout them down, remind them that they are professionals and that they should shut up and listen to the LT, but Bowman is not doing anything, only sitting there with his mouth open and grumbling to himself that the whole thing does not make sense: If only three to five percent of the sick develop Mad Dog symptoms and die within a week, how can they be that big of a threat? At any given time there cannot be more than ten, maybe fifteen thousand of them in all of Manhattan. That's a lot if you put them all together, but they are scattered far and wide.

How can there be this many Mad Dogs?

Kemper looks away, suddenly wondering if the Lieutenant is going to be able to get them through this in one piece. After serving together a year in Iraq, it is a disloyal feeling, and he does not like it.

He also finds himself agreeing with Lewis: The Army is not telling them something vital. Like the LT said, their situational awareness is very, very limited, and Kemper wonders what it is going to cost them when the bill comes.

The worst thing I ever smelled

PFC Jon Mooney lies awake on his bunk in the dark, restless and staring and dry-mouthed from wearing an N95 mask all day and night. He plays the shooting over and over in his mind: Did they do the right thing? He can't get the image of the Mad Dog squealing and flopping in a puddle of blood, tangled up in the wire, out of his head.

Around him, the boys of First Squad snore gently in the dark. Collins is speaking in tongues while he slumbers, gibberish for the most part but ending with, "Fried chicken?" and a throaty chuckle. Somebody else farts and turns over. Mooney likes these guys, they are like brothers to him, he and them have gone to hell and back together, but he can't stand them anymore and he would really, really like to be alone for a while.

He turns onto his side and sees PFC Joel Wyatt staring back at him, his

27:03

eyes gleaming in the dark. Wyatt takes off his headphones and says, "You still awake, Mooney?"

"Can't sleep. You?"

"Chillin' like a villain, partner."

"All right. Well, good night, Joel."

"'Night."

Mooney closes his eyes, forces the shooting out of his mind, and tries to remember what Laura looks like. They are technically not together but he is trying to forget that. Before he left for Iraq, he told her that maybe they should break up. He still thinks that was a sound decision at the time. Plus he'd been feeling spiteful because sometimes he wondered if she is really all that good looking and that maybe he deserved better. He hadn't anticipated, however, how hard things would be overseas, how lonely he would get, and he clings to the idea that he still loves her—a lifeline in his violent world.

Plus she had agreed a little too readily to his suggestion of seeing other people, and it has been eating at him ever since he deployed.

"Hey, Mooney."

"Yeah, Joel?"

"I feel like some TV. They got TV upstairs in the patient rooms, right? You in or not?"

Something like electric current floods Mooney's system, jolting him out of bed. Within seconds, the boys are quietly pulling on T-shirts and pants and tip-toeing into the hallway on bare feet, trying not to laugh as they dart past the facility manager's office where the LT, platoon sergeant and squad leaders are huddled together in a tense pow wow.

They pause to listen.

"My wife and kid are out there and I am going to protect them," they hear somebody saying.

Lewis? Mooney mouths to Wyatt, who shrugs.

"That's right," says somebody else. "She's out there. So what happens if she becomes one of them? Do you want us to shoot her too?"

"I'll tell you what," says Lewis. "If I become one of those things, I want you to shoot me in the grape."

"What the hell, over?" whispers Mooney.

"What the hell, out," Wyatt whispers back, shrugging.

As enjoyable as the spying is, the lure of mindless entertainment is stronger, calling them back to their original mission. The hallway is dark and shrouds their movements. The hum of machinery conceals their footsteps. The whole basement stinks of ammonia and disinfectant. We are ninja, Mooney thinks, totally hidden. The thought makes him smile.

"What's on this time of night?" Wyatt wonders as they reach the stairwell and begin climbing the stairs.

"Who cares? I just want to turn my brain off and forget who I am for an hour."

"Better than sleep!"

"Who can sleep?" Mooney wonders.

"So where are we going, anyhow?"

"Let's go up to the sixth floor and then walk back down, checking out each floor until we find a room that has a working TV in it. Hooah?"

"Whoop," says Wyatt.

By the time they reach the sixth floor, the boys are panting and stop for a rest. They are in good shape but exhausted from months of hard work and lack of sleep and barely enough calories. They sit on the top step and share a cigarette. Mooney is starting to warm up to Wyatt, the tall, skinny red-haired replacement from Michigan with Army glasses who always seems to be looking over your shoulder while he's talking to you. Most of the boys think he is a little off.

"Ready for some infomercials, cuzin?" Wyatt says. "Some *Girls Gone Wild*?"

Mooney flicks the cigarette down the stairs, where it bursts in a shower of sparks, and puts his mask back on. "OK. Let's do this."

Wyatt hands him some latex gloves, which Mooney pulls on.

"Remember, Mooney, if a nurse or somebody sees us, we just say we were sent to find that cop. Winslow. That'll be our cover story."

They open the door and immediately gag as the stink assails them, the horrible sour body sweat of Lyssa victims lurking under a sickeningly sweet combination of air fresheners and perfume that the Trinity people apparently sprayed everywhere.

Mooney hears people moaning, and realizes that the walls of the darkened corridor are lined with gurneys, a Lyssa patient in each connected by a tube to an IV bag to keep them hydrated. Some snarl and struggle against restraining belts, while most simply lie moaning, their breath rattling in their chests.

Other than the Lyssa victims, there's not a soul in sight.

Wyatt whistles at the ambiance. "Spooky."

Mooney nods.

"I mean," Wyatt adds, "wouldn't it be cool if they all jumped up and attacked us?"

They turn a corner. There are no patients in this part of the corridor and the lights are on for the night. Mooney and Wyatt blink at the fluorescent light.

"We shouldn't be here," says Mooney. "This whole place is crawling with virus."

"Dude, how about that smell? Every time I think I'm used to it, I get the urge to puke. And I even got a scratch-and-sniff perfume sample in my mask from an ad I tore out of a magazine."

"Abort mission?"

"Hell, no! These are patient rooms up here, yo. There's gotta be a TV in one of them. Wouldn't it be awesome if they had PlayStation?"

"I'd love to play *Guitar Hero*," Mooney admits.

Pinching their noses, they creep up to a doorway. Inside, Lyssa victims lie in the dark in their own sweat and stink. Mooney can hear their ragged breath. One of them, a young woman lying on a cot on the floor, is alternately weeping and apologizing to somebody named Ron in fevered delirium.

"Bingo," says Wyatt. "The sound's turned off, though. Gotta find the remote, unless you like the close captioning they've got on. Me, I can't read that fast."

"What's on?"

"CNN, I think. Some kind of riot going on in Chicago. No, wait. Now they're talking about Atlanta."

"Hello?"

The raspy voice electrifies them, making them jump.

"You scared the shit out of me, whoever you are," Wyatt hisses, and starts laughing.

"Same here," the voice says. "Are you the cops?"

"No, sir," Mooney answers. As his vision slowly adapts to the dark, he can now make out the figure of a man sitting up in bed. "We're U.S. Army."

"Somebody was screaming down the hall earlier tonight. Probably just somebody out of their head with fever, right? But it sounded awful. Like an animal being slaughtered. You might want to check it out. I'd tell a nurse but I haven't seen one in hours."

"How are you feeling, sir? It is bad?"

"A little better today, thanks. My fever's broke, but I could use some water—"

They jump again as they hear the crackle of small arms fire coming from outside the building. Stepping carefully, the soldiers approach the window and peer through the closed blinds to see who is shooting at whom. Far below, they see muzzle flashes and hear the reports.

Third Squad is lighting somebody up.

"What the hell, over?" says Wyatt.

Mooney is starting to feel naked without his rifle.

"Oh, God," he says, and runs from the room.

Wyatt chases after him, finds him retching over a wastepaper basket.

"I breathed it in," Mooney says, spitting and trying to catch his breath. "I forgot to hold my nose for a second. It was the worst thing I ever smelled in there. Holy shit. It smelled like a rotting grave."

"Dude, put your mask back on before you get sick," Wyatt says nervously.

"Are you guys all right?" the Lyssa patient calls from the dark room. "Don't leave me alone, okay? Bring me some water, please?"

"Hey, look at that," says Wyatt, pointing at the floor.

The bloodstain begins five feet from them and ends at a pair of doors twenty feet distant. The blood is smeared, as if somebody dragged a mop soaked with blood through the doors.

"You gotta be kidding," Mooney says as Wyatt approaches the doors.

They should be getting back. If Third Squad's engaged outside, McGraw's probably mustering the squad. Right about now, he is working himself into a blind rage looking for his AWOL riflemen, chewing his massive handlebar mustache and grinding the molars in that big square jaw of his.

Mooney also has no interest in seeing what's on the other side of those doors. What did that guy say?

Awful, he said. It sounded awful. Like an animal being slaughtered.

"We'd better go back," Mooney says. "McGraw's gonna kill us."

Wyatt grins. "I'll just take a quick look. Dude, this place is like a haunted house. Wouldn't it be cool if there were zombies on the other side of these doors?"

He presses a button on the wall with the palm of his hand. The doors swing open automatically.

Clear the fucking net

Jake Sherman, the platoon radio/telephone operator, sits in a janitor's closet with his feet up on a box containing cheap toilet paper, eating a packet of instant coffee mixed with hot chocolate powder and washing it down with Red Bull while listening to the traffic on the military nets. He started mainlining caffeine after too many sleepless nights in Iraq, and hasn't yet kicked the habit of getting completely wired while on duty.

Blackhawk flight, this is War Pig Three directly below you, what's your call sign?

War Pig Three, this is Red Baron Two.

Red Baron Two, request flyover east of us, about three blocks. We hear a high noise level in that direction, possibly a firefight in progress. What is happening at that location? Confirm, over.

Wait, over. . . . War Pig Three, we see multiple, uh, estimate fifty, civilians at an intersection three blocks north and two blocks east of you. Break. Riot in progress. Break. Some are armed. Break. They appear to be fighting each other. Over.

Roger that and thanks for the eyes, Red Baron Two. Out.

Then the excitement is over and the company's voice traffic quickly returns to the ongoing rhythm of units talking to each other in the night about location, condition, supply and all the other mundane communications required to keep two infantry brigades functioning on the ground in New York. Sherman switches from the company to the battalion net and listens in on the chatter. War Pig (Delta Company) continues to collect and pass around intelligence about the riot. War Hammer (Alpha Company) is requesting a medevac for a grenadier who got his ear bitten off by a Lyssa victim. Warmonger (Bravo Company) is asking the last calling station to authenticate its identity.

He switches to civilian traffic, looking for more information about the riot. The authorities provided more frequencies than normally needed based on the extreme nature of the epidemic, and he has access to everything. The police are aware of the riot but cannot scrape together enough manpower to do anything about it. A fire is also raging in a warehouse in Queens but there are not enough firefighters to respond to the call. Police units are overwhelmed with domestic disturbance calls and looting. Violence is reported inside Lyssa clinics and one of them has apparently been firebombed with Molotov cocktails. Despite several major arteries in the City being blocked off for official vehicles only, traffic has virtually ground to a standstill almost everywhere.

Sherman laughs to himself: The voices on the SINCGAR, while edgy and tense, could still make the Apocalypse sound like just another logistical foul-up. Glancing at his watch, he switches back to the company frequency for a commo check. He hears:

War Dogs Two, War Dogs Two, this is War Dogs, how copy, over?

Sherman recognizes the man's voice at the other end. It's Doug Price, Captain West's RTO. He fires back, chewing on hot chocolate powder: "War Dogs, this is War Dogs Two, I copy, over."

War Dogs Two, message follows, over.

He takes out a small notepad and pencil.

"Roger that. Send message, over."

War Dogs Two, I send "Nirv—"

Sherman can't hear for a moment; men are shouting in the background and it sounds like somebody is shooting a rifle.

"Negative contact, War Dogs. Say again, over."

I send "Nirvana." How copy? Over.

"That's a good copy, War Dogs; I copy 'Nirvana.' Wait one, over."

He looks up "Nirvana" on his code card, his cheat sheet for routine communications requiring encoding, but it's not there. He digs out his mission code book and looks up the term.

It means: "Unit is under attack."

Sherman coughs on hot chocolate powder. He takes another swig of Red Bull to clear his throat and lights a cigarette, thinking for a moment. Who would be stupid enough to attack a platoon of heavily armed U.S. infantry in Manhattan in the middle of the night? But there it is: an authentic message from the company commander, announcing that the company HQ and First Platoon is under attack.

He says, "Roger, War Dogs."

War Dogs Two, this is War Dogs, second message follows, over.

"Standing by to copy, over."

I send "Motorhead Slayer November Sierra Oscar November," over.

"War Dogs, I copy 'Motorhead Slayer November Sierra Oscar November,'" Sherman says, scribbling the message in his notepad. "Wait one, over."

He looks up the code, translating: "Rendezvous at our location at oh-seven-thirty."

LT needs to hear this message right away.

"Roger that, War Dogs. Stand by. Wait, out."

Jake? Jake, are you there?

Sherman tenses for a moment, unsure how to answer this breach of protocol. Finally, he says, "Yeah, I'm here, Doug."

Be careful coming over here, okay? There are thousands of them.

"Thousands of who?"

Somebody lied to us, Jake.

The radio screeches, making him flinch.

War Dogs, this is Quarantine. Clear the fucking net.

A place we can hold up while the world ends

"That's it," says Susan, pointing at one of several rundown-looking pre-war apartment buildings across the street. "Home."

"Don't worry," says Boyd, trying to put on a brave face.

He cannot understand why he is so scared. He's a soldier. He has seen men die. He's even killed some himself. Well, at least the one that he is sure about. He has a locked and loaded carbine and should not be afraid of one homicidal but weaponless guy tearing apart some crummy New York apartment.

And yet he's so scared he can barely think straight.

They enter the building, and Susan points up.

"Fourth floor."

They walk up the stairs slowly, quietly, Boyd first, holding his carbine, Susan hugging the wall behind him, clearly terrified.

On the second floor, Boyd flinches as he hears screams behind one of the doors. A woman's voice pleads with somebody named John not to hurt her. The screams become high-pitched until they dissolve into sounds of furniture being tossed aside and an ensuing struggle on the floor and a long, shrill peal of terror.

Then silence.

Boyd swallows hard and turns to Susan, sees tears running down her face.

"I know that woman," she says. "I know her and her husband."

"Can you go on?"

"They have a baby."

"I don't know what to do. I don't think there's anything we can do."

"I'm so sorry, Rick."

"You're a brave girl."

He feels very close to her now.

I could fall in love with this girl, he thinks.

"Don't give up yet," he adds.

She nods, visibly trembling, and they continue their climb. On the third floor, he hears an ominous gurgling growl behind one of the doors, the sound of pacing feet, reminding Boyd of an animal in a cage.

The wall vibrates from an impact.

"Let me call home first," she says. "See if anybody answers. Okay?"

"All right," he tells her, thankful for the break in the tension.

Susan takes out her cell phone and calls the number, but hangs up after a few seconds.

"Nothing," she says, paling.

He wants to comfort her, but can only nod and glance up at the ceiling.

They climb the next set of stairs. She points to a door and says, "This is it right here."

Boyd wipes sweat from his eyes, blinks, nods, steadies his carbine against his shoulder. "Let's do this," he says.

He hears a door open behind him. Before he can turn, something heavy cracks against his right leg, which gives out beneath him, forcing him onto his knee. Hands tug at his carbine. The barrel of a pistol is pushed roughly against the side of his head.

"Let go of it, man," he hears.

"Susan!" he cries, reaching out, but the girl flings herself into the arms of a tall, muscular boy. "I did it, baby," she says, kissing him passionately. "I did it." Her boasting quickly turns into hysterical sobbing, her face buried against his chest. "I did it, you goddamn bastard."

The boy says to another holding a length of pipe, "She should never have had to go out there to do this."

"And yet she did, and she got back alive, and mission accomplished."

"She's a wreck, look at her. She could have died out there."

The whole thing was a setup, Boyd realizes. The cell phone call was the signal.

"Williams said your story was shit and that you were a junkie," he cuts in, blinking tears of shame and rage. "I should have listened to him."

"Junkie?" says the grinning boy holding the gun. "We're NYU students. I'm pre-med. Susan's a freaking philosophy major."

The boy with the pipe crouches and looks Boyd in the eye. "It's nothing personal, guy. I'm really sorry I had to hurt your leg. We just need your rifle and any ammo you got, then you can go home."

The boy with the pistol chimes in, "We need to cross over to Jersey tonight, and we got to have some weapons in case we have to fight our way through any drooling wackos. We grabbed this pistol off a dead cop. Then Bob and Susan cooked up this lunatic idea to get a couple of you guys out here and do a snatch-grab on your guns." He laughs crazily. "Seeing you actually here in the flesh, I can't believe it worked. It was a stupid plan."

Glaring, Boyd asks, "What's in New Jersey?"

"A place we can hold up while the world ends."

"The world's not ending."

"Are you blind? Did you not see what's going on out there, friend?"

"I'm not your friend," Boyd seethes.

The jock holding Susan says, "You know, you could always come with us." His friends try to shout him down, but he presses on: "We got your rifle but we don't even know how to use it right. We need a guy like you with us. I almost had a heart attack when we mugged you. But you have experience with this sort of thing. What do you say?"

The others look at him expectantly.

Fifteen minutes later, Boyd limps briskly down the street, wincing at the jolt of pain lancing through his leg with each step.

He is alone.

Those crazy dumb kids won't make it to New Jersey, he thinks. They're not going anywhere. Weapon or no weapon, if it's going to get as bad as they say it will, they're going to die.

He sees a body lying face down in the middle of the street, twitching, and gives it a wide berth.

After everything he has seen and heard tonight, the safest place to be is smack in the middle of Charlie Company's Second Platoon, with natural born killers like Hicks and Ruiz watching his back. He would rather be with them, with Ruiz kicking his ass black and blue for going over the hill and losing his M4, than take his chances with a bunch of gun-slinging, middle-class, smart-ass college kids.

Another three blocks and he'll be home.

He tries again to think up some good excuse for abandoning his post and losing his weapon and ammo, but his tired brain still isn't giving him anything. An infantryman losing his rifle is like a *Samurai* losing his sword. He is never going to live this down.

He hears gurgling in the dark. He turns, seeking refuge, a place to hide, but nothing is in easy reach. Down the street, two dark figures are moving towards him at a loping gait. He quickens his pace, but the pain in his leg flares until he sees stars. The figures have already drawn closer, their faces in shadow.

Nothing to do but fight, then. So be it.

For the first time all night, Boyd is perfectly calm. This he understands.

The college kids took his carbine and bayonet but they did not take his personal knife, a bad-ass pigsticker he keeps in his boot.

He draws the knife and waits.

Run, run, goddamn run

The hospital corridor beyond the doors is packed with people standing or shuffling along in pajamas and paper gowns and hospital scrubs. They twitch and roll their necks in the bright fluorescent light, their eyes wide and staring at nothing, snarling and scratching as they bump into each other in their aimless wandering.

Their faces are scarlet and shiny with sweat. Their eyes gleam with fever. Their bare feet track blood and excrement along the floor.

The stench is incredible.

"Holy shit," Wyatt says aloud.

Heads turn. Eyes flicker and focus. The snarling grows louder.

"Joel, come away from there," says Mooney, taking a step backward.

One of the Mad Dogs, a woman with long graying hair, takes three rapid strides forward and screeches at Wyatt, spraying spittle.

"Help," Wyatt says quietly.

An enormous balding man with a nose shaped like a potato and a tattooed arm gurgles, leaking drool, and begins shoving his way through the others to get at Wyatt. A small boy, no more than six years old, dashes up to him and begins jumping up and down, wild-eyed and whimpering and pawing at his running nose.

"Run, Joel," Mooney says, his voice shaking.

"Help. . . ."

The corridor suddenly comes alive with bodies pushing and shoving at each other until a boiling point is reached and they all come rushing forward in a flood.

"Run," Mooney screams. "Run, run, goddamn run!"

He turns and sprints on bare feet, sparing a single glance over his shoulder to see Wyatt gaining on him, his eyes big and watery, a horde of maniacs snapping at his heels. They reach the stairwell and plunge down the stairs two, three steps at a time, wincing at the jolts of pain in their feet and screaming their lungs out.

"Mooney, wait for me!"

A skinny, bearded man in a hospital gown hurtles from above, kicking and clawing at the air in his descent, and strikes the floor below with a sickening smack.

"Mooney! Don't leave me here!"

"Keep moving, Joel!"

Mooney reaches the door at the bottom of the stairwell and holds it open, sweeping Wyatt inside with his arm and then slamming it shut.

"Get the Sergeant! Go, go, go!"

Wyatt bolts down the corridor, limping on a hurt ankle, yelling bloody murder while Mooney pushes against the door with all his might. Instantly, he is almost thrown to the far wall as the first Mad Dogs press against it. Regaining his balance, he leans against the door again, digging in his heels, but the crush of bodies is too strong.

He can't hold them, slowly loses ground.

Finally, he lets go and rushes after Wyatt, shouting the alarm.

The boys are already spilling into the corridor, some still in their underwear and rubbing their eyes, all of them armed and swearing and asking for orders.

"What's going on?"

"Who's that chasing Joel?"

"Are we shooting or what? What's going on?"

"God, what's that smell?"

"What the hell is that?"

"Out of the way!"

The LT pushes through them, unholstering his nine-millimeter handgun and flicking off the safety.

"Halt!" Bowman calls out.

The Mad Dogs ignore him.

"Halt or we will fire on you!"

He is almost pleading now.

"Please. . . ."

His panic evaporates as he realizes he has no choice.

"Get down!" he shouts, waving at Mooney and Wyatt. "Now!"

Mooney, his lungs and legs burning, makes a last dash at Wyatt and tackles him to the floor.

"LT—" Kemper says behind him.

Bowman takes careful aim and shoots the lead Mad Dog in the face.

The other Mad Dogs do not even notice. They keep running at the soldiers, howling.

"Fire!" he says, squeezing off another shot. "Fire!"

The soldiers form a firing line and start shooting with their carbines at almost point-blank range. The effect is devastating. The rain of hot metal rips through flesh and muscle, cracks bone. A fine mist of blood and smoke fills the hall. Some of the boys close their eyes while they shoot, unable to watch the slaughter.

In less than a minute, it's over and Kemper is calling, cease fire, cease fire.

"What the hell just happened?" one of the boys is shouting. "What's happening?"

Bowman blinks and sees the corridor carpeted with broken, bloody bodies, some moaning and thrashing in puddles of blood. The battle was a blur to him. Despite the incredible firepower delivered into the narrow kill zone, the Mad Dogs almost made it to the firing line. His ears ring and his teeth are still vibrating from the deafening rifle reports. He feels oddly exultant, then fights off an urge to vomit.

He turns and sees a few of the boys crouched against the wall, puking and retching and bawling. A flash goes off as one of the soldiers takes a picture with a digital camera, then resumes staring at the carnage in disbelief.

Third Squad is probably crapping itself in front of the hospital as well, Bowman tells himself. They had their own firing incident, reported moments before this crazy horde showed up, and they've got a man AWOL.

We will all be like that within a few minutes, puking and paralyzed with guilt and shame, unless we can stop thinking and keep moving.

The LT still has doubts that he made the right call to order his men to fire, but he has a job to do and he must keep his unit combat effective.

What he wants to know is: Where are all these Mad Dogs coming from?

"Sergeant McGraw!" he barks. "Pull your men out of there and get them cleaned up and disinfected. I expect a full report on how exactly they brought these civilians down here. Sergeant Ruiz!"

"Sir?"

"Check on your squad," the LT orders. "Not with your handheld. Go in person. I expect a full report on their firing incident. And go easy on them. Sergeant Lewis!"

"Sir!"

"Stay close to me, Grant."

The discord of their meeting in the basement office is gone. Bowman is pleased to see the NCOs pulling together as a team. These men are professionals.

Wyatt and Mooney are already trying to stand, pushing bodies off of them, moaning at the mauling they received as the Mad Dogs trampled over them.

Wyatt gets to his feet unsteadily and starts laughing. "That was so freaking cool!"

Mooney, covered in blood and swaying drunkenly, takes a wild swing at him and by sheer luck manages to connect with the side of his head, knocking Wyatt against the far wall and sending his glasses flying. Then the boys pull them apart.

"Sergeant Kemper!" Bowman calls.

"Sir," says the platoon sergeant.

"Get these people sorted," he says. "Separate the dead and wounded and find a place to put each."

"Morgue's full, sir."

"Find something, Mike. I want them out of here."

"I'll see to it, sir."

"Sergeant Lewis will lead a squad to round up any stray Mad Dogs and then re-establish contact with Winslow and the hospital staff. If you're not helping here, I want you helping him. I want everybody doing something." Bowman notices two soldiers waiting for a chance to speak to him. "Well, what is it? What do you men need?"

"Just what the hell is this plague, Lieutenant?" asks Finnegan.

"We just shot all these people," Martin chimes in. "What are we going to do, sir?"

"Sergeant Lewis, see to these men."

"All right, morons! You heard the Lieutenant! Get your dicks out of your ears and un-ass this hallway!"

The effect is electrifying on the boys, who snap out of their funk and spring into action.

"Hey!" a voice calls from the stairwell. "You all right?"

"Come forward slowly and show yourself," Lewis orders, raising his rifle.

Winslow steps into the corridor holding his pistol at his side, breathing heavily, looking at the dead and dying with wide-eyed horror. Stepping carefully through the bodies, he approaches Bowman.

"Are you infected?" Winslow asks him.

"We were attacked," Bowman explains. "We fired in self defense."

"Are you infected?"

"We're trying to see to the wounded, but we could use some of the hospital people down here. Some of these people are still dangerous. They have to be sedated before they can be treated."

"Hospital people?" Winslow says, looking confused.

Bowman steps forward. "Sir, are you all right?"

The cop's voice cracks. "These monsters killed half the night shift. They tore my men to shreds. Like tissue paper."

A wounded middle-aged woman moans at their feet, wide-eyed and panting, holding a bleeding hole in her ribs.

He adds, "Stand back, Lieutenant."

And shoots her through the forehead.

Chapter 3

I'm Security, not Facilities

After the mob swarmed into the lobby, the Bradley Institute of Graduate Microbiology and Virology Studies went into lockdown. The scientists couldn't get out, and the mob couldn't get upstairs and into the laboratories.

Most of the staff went home last night, leaving only a few diehards in the labs working on a vaccine for Hong Kong Lyssa. They are now trapped for the duration of the siege.

Bleary from lack of sleep and his large belly growling with hunger, Dr. Joe Hardy, director of research, watches the tall, beautiful blonde on the security screens and wonders where he has seen her before.

"There she goes again," Stringer Jackson, the security guard, says next to him. "Check it out. She's writing another message."

The mob easily overwhelmed the two National Guardsmen posted in the lobby and took them hostage. The blonde, apparently the leader of the group, has been communicating their demands by holding up signs to the security cameras and miming shooting the soldiers in the head.

"She a tough bitch, that one," Hardy says with respect, his hands buried in the pockets of his labcoat. "Like my ex-wife."

Jackson grins appreciatively.

The blonde triumphantly holds up a sign. It says: GIVE US VACCINE OR FREEZE.

Hardy snorts derisively, then blinks. "Uh, can they do that?"

Jackson says, "I'm Security, not Facilities."

But air conditioning is blasting through the air vents and the temperature in the Security Command Center, already maintained at a chilly sixty-five degrees to keep the guards awake, is already dropping.

"Lovely. Is there anything we can do to shut it off, chief?"

"Not that I can think of, Dr. Hardy," Jackson shrugs.

The Center is about twice the size of the scientists' private offices, with a desk in the center of the room where Jackson is now sitting in an ergonomic chair, reeking of nervous sweat and stale cigarette smoke. The operator's workstation contains a control console and PC with a graphical user interface, telephone, randomly scattered office supplies, and storage. A digital projector mounted on the ceiling displays the security camera images on large screens on the wall facing the workstation.

Hardy has only been in this room once before. It is strange to think that behind a random door in one of the Institute's utilitarian, blindingly white corridors is a highly sophisticated security apparatus enabling a single operator to monitor all of the public spaces in the building on giant wall screens.

Unfortunately, while the Security Center's equipment allows them to watch the mob downstairs, it offers nothing in the way of help to get rid of them.

This is too important, Hardy thinks. The nation is counting on us. We have grown pure samples of the virus. We are working on genetic characterization. And after that is wrapped up, we can start in earnest on a vaccine. If only you will let us.

There are so many lives at stake right now.

"Actually, there is maybe one thing we can do," Jackson says quietly.

"What's that?" Hardy says with interest.

"We could always, you know, give them what they want."

"But we don't have a vaccine yet!" Hardy explodes.

Jackson shrugs, unconvinced.

"Maybe I should go down there with some syringes and pump them full of saline," Hardy sneers. "Then they'd leave and we could get back to, you know, trying to save millions of lives by developing a real vaccine."

"I don't know," Jackson says. "I don't think that would be very ethical."

"Say it with me, Stringer: 'There is no vaccine!'"

"I heard you. You don't have to shout at me."

"And we're not going to get one with this mob of assholes down there, either. We've got maybe ten people at most working in the labs right now."

"I mean, they really don't pay me enough to put up with this. I used to be a cop, you know. People in my neighborhood used to show respect when I walked down the street."

"CDC said they were coming to secure the facility, but so far they haven't come. We have almost no food, no place to sleep, and no way to keep up the current level of our research effort with this skeleton crew. And that means no vaccine, okay? All these people are doing is taking a big risk of getting themselves killed when the Army shows up."

And even if they could work without interruption, it would still take months before a vaccine is produced in any real quantity, Hardy reminds himself. After they create the formula, factories have to manufacture enough of the stuff to inoculate the health workers and then the government and then the Army and then the rest of America's population of more than three hundred million. By the time they start inoculating the general population, it will be months after the vaccine is created.

By then, the Pandemic will be over—in North America, anyway.

But that's not the point. The point is they have to make a vaccine to stop the virus from flaring up again months after that and starting this whole nightmare over again. Pandemics occur in two to three waves. A vaccine will stop the second wave in its tracks. It could even purge the world of Lyssa entirely.

On the five-foot-tall security screens, the blonde's gloating smile gradually fades and she eventually tires of holding the sign. She passes it on to somebody else. The mob has become listless after a long night of doing nothing. When the facility went into lockdown, not only were they locked out of the labs, they were also locked inside the building.

It's called Code Orange. Nobody goes in or out.

The two National Guardsmen sit on the floor looking glum, their hands tied behind their backs. Behind them, a teenaged boy turns away from his friends, takes a sandwich out of a brown paper bag, and begins wolfing it down.

Hardy watches him, his belly snarling, practically drooling with hunger. He tries to guess what kind of sandwich the kid has. Ham and cheese with mustard? Turkey with tomato and bacon? One of those Cuban sandwiches they make around the corner with ham, roasted pork, salami, Swiss cheese, pickles and mustard on Cuban bread?

His belly roars.

"Well," Jackson says, "that's fine, but all I'm saying is there's only about thirty people down there. If you had a vaccine, surely you could give them a little."

Hardy feels himself start to burst, but his large shoulders deflate and he shakes his head sadly. "There's no magic cure, Stringer," he says. "I wish there were."

Then he sighs loudly and begins walking towards the door.

"Where're you going, Dr. Hardy?"

Hardy pauses at the door. "To the labs, Stringer," he answers in as heroic tone as he can muster, like something out of a movie. "I have a lot of work to do yet if I'm going to defeat this scourge."

Then he snorts and leaves the Security Command Center in search of something resembling breakfast.

Chapter 4

New York has always seemed like a foreign country to me

Sergeant First Class Mike Kemper nods to Mooney and Wyatt, who are busy mopping up blood from the floor in the hallway, and enters Bowman's makeshift office, all the while wondering if the LT is still cut out to command the platoon.

Kemper knows Bowman better than anybody in the unit, even better than Captain West does. It is his job to do so. The NCOs take care of the enlisted men in their unit. As platoon sergeant, however, part of his job is also to take care of and advise the LT.

Earlier tonight, the Lieutenant waffled over new orders and opened those orders up for debate by his NCOs. Then he ordered the platoon to fire on civilians.

Kemper showed Bowman the ropes for nearly a year in Iraq, and watched him mature into an intelligent officer who respects his men and leads from the front, not the rear. But this is an entirely new situation. In a horrifying situation like this, a commander can become indecisive, rash or both. Rash or indecisive commanders can get their men killed.

It was the right call to open fire on the civilians, given the size of the crowd attacking them. If Bowman hadn't ordered the platoon to shoot, it would have been overrun and destroyed. But it turned out to be the right call only in hindsight. It could just have easily turned out to be a small group coming at them. In that case, the LT would now be considered an officer overeager to implement a new ROE allowing him to shoot civilians.

The point is the LT could have been wrong. Horribly wrong. And this has Kemper wondering whether Bowman made an intelligent, calculated risk or whether he panicked. He wants to believe it was a thoughtful decision, because he actually likes the man, but he isn't sure.

He finds Bowman sitting in a pool of light from his task lamp, glaring at the radio on his desk. The LT looks up and gestures wearily. He's not wearing a mask.

"If you've come to arrest me, I've already tried," he says.

The Platoon Sergeant blinks. "Arrest you?"

"For violating Article 118 of the Uniform Code of Military Justice, Mike."

"Murder?"

The LT nods and says, "For turning my men into a bunch of baby killers."

"Hell, I was just coming to see if you wanted to do an After Action Review."

Bowman says, "In a way. . . ."

Kemper sits, takes off his own mask, lights the stub of a foul-smelling cigar and sighs, exhaling a long stream of smoke.

"You want to know what I think?"

"Yeah, Mike. I do."

It is a hard thing to explain, but Kemper is not concerned right now about the morality of shooting those people. Morality is a luxury in a situation like this. What worries him instead is the open question of the Lieutenant's judgment.

A question to which he may never learn the answer.

"LT, what happened here tonight was a terrible thing, but you were acting within the ROE and had only a few seconds to make a decision to protect the platoon," he says truthfully. "While a man's conscience is one thing, the Army will say you made the right call."

"That's what Captain West said."

"You told him what happened? What'd he say?"

"He said his own hands are full and that I should follow my fucking orders. End quote."

Kemper leans back in his chair, absorbing this information.

"All this. . . . It doesn't make much sense, does it?"

"It makes no sense at all."

"Have you talked to any of the other platoon leaders?"

"That's just the thing, Mike. Quarantine is restricting the net to emergency traffic only. Something big is happening, and we're isolated. I've got no intel. No big picture."

Kemper is beginning to understand what is going on inside the LT's brain. The situation has changed and with it, the ROE, and Bowman is trying to figure out why. If he understands why, he can make good decisions and, perhaps, justify to himself why he ordered his men to shoot down more than forty civilians in cold blood.

"Everybody's feeling like crap right now and unfit to wear the uniform. Morale is shit. But we're the professionals. We can't appear indecisive in front of the boys. They need us to lead them."

Bowman stiffens, then smiles shyly. "So this isn't all about me then, is it."

"No, sir, it ain't," Kemper says quietly.

"What's so weird about this whole mess is it's like this is a foreign country and we're the enemy. I feel like we're in this *Twilight Zone* episode where we did something terrible in Iraq so God warps reality and turns America into Iraq. And we have to figure out what we did wrong or repeat the same mistakes against our own people."

"Sir, with all due respect, you think way too goddamn much."

Bowman smiles grimly. "Mike, I just saw a cop shoot a wounded American citizen in the head. A cop who watched his best friends get ripped apart by a crazed mob in a rare terminal stage of a new disease. I'd say anything is on the table at this point."

"We're all tired." The NCO exhales another cloud of smoke and grinds his cigar against his boot heel. "We're wiped out. In any case, New York has always seemed like a foreign country to me."

The LT regards him for a moment, then laughs out loud.

"It gives me an idea," he says. "The situation demands that we treat the city as hostile. So we do just that. If your force is isolated in hostile country and you need to move from a place of security to a new AO, what's the first thing you do?"

Kemper suddenly smiles.

"You reconnoiter," he says.

"Right. We have just enough time to do a recon mission before we have to be on the move. It might give us the answers we need so we know what we're facing here."

"Satisfactory," says Kemper. This is the Todd Bowman that the platoon sergeant trained to be a commander in Iraq, and it is good to have him back. "I know just the men for this mission."

We could use a gun, though

Morning brings a cool, dewy feel to the air. The windows on the taller buildings gleam in the first light. Several buildings near the site of yesterday's explosion are still smoldering, and a sudden change in wind rains ash and the acrid stench of burning furniture. The boys check their rucksacks and top up their ammo, coughing into their fists. They're getting ready to move.

Second Platoon is exhausted. They spent hours clearing out the hospital and cleaning up the mess. Small groups of infected attacked the wire through the night and had to be shot down, their bodies left out in the open until dawn among the ruins of the cars.

The scuttlebutt about the platoon moving to rejoin the company is they might be lined up and shot for what they've done, the LT included. The boys fought in Iraq and they know their duty but they signed up to shoot bad guys, not Americans, and what they are doing doesn't feel like real service anymore. Instead, they feel like war criminals, regardless of what the new ROE lets them do. Some have had it and are ready to quit and go home. Others want somebody to blame. This is a dangerous mood. The NCOs sense it, and kick ass to keep the boys hopping while keeping an eye peeled for symptoms of post-traumatic stress.

In the lobby, the LT says his goodbyes to the hospital chief and the cop.

"Sorry we can't stay and continue to support you," Bowman tells Dr. Linton, who appears to have aged another ten years overnight. "What are you going to do?"

"We're staying right here, Lieutenant," Winslow cuts in, answering for Linton. "The doc and I are going to try to keep the place running and convert it into a recovery clinic."

"We've got plenty of food and water, gas and a generator," Linton adds. He clears his throat politely. "We could use a gun, though."

"Are you sure, sir?"

"I'm certain."

Bowman hands Winslow back his Glock 19 handgun.

"I'll arrange for the sidearms and ammunition to be returned to you that we recovered, um, from your men, sir," he says.

"Thank you, Lieutenant," the cop says, grimacing.

"Well. Good luck to you both, then. You're very brave."

Brave and doomed, he thinks.

One psycho cop with a couple of handguns won't be able to protect an entire hospital against people who will certainly use force to break in and demand medical care for their families. That, or junkies looking for drugs, will finish them.

If only his platoon could stay in place, they could remain secure and finish what they started here. But orders are orders.

"Somebody has to survive, Lieutenant," Winslow tells him.

Bowman frowns in response to this odd statement. He puts on his patrol cap and salutes, then leaves Trinity Hospital without looking back.

Outside, the boys are sitting on the ground with their gear, cleaning their weapons and chowing down on MREs. They look at the LT expectantly, with scared eyes, but say nothing. The silence, in fact, is the first thing Bowman notices upon walking out of the hospital. The boys are all business. None of the usual sparring and grab-ass this morning. They are still trying to wrap their heads around what they have done.

Today, Bowman will lead them northwest to a middle school that has been turned into a Lyssa clinic and is the current area of operations for First Platoon and Charlie Company HQ. The distance is over a mile. They have no transport, so they will hoof it.

Bowman nods to Sergeant McGraw and says quietly, "All right?"

"Managing, sir," replies the leader of First Squad.

"Find Private Mooney and Private Wyatt and bring them to me, Sergeant."

"Right away, sir."

Kemper approaches and salutes. Bowman returns it.

"Good morning, sir."

"All right, Mike?"

"All present except for Private Boyd. He's still MIA."

"Well, we combed the hospital good last night. We'll have to assume he slipped out past the wire and went AWOL. Let's take a walk and see what we can see."

They move out past the wire and climb onto the roof of an abandoned car to get a good view down First Avenue. Bowman uses the close combat optic on his rifle, Kemper a pair of Vortex Viper binoculars. The road is choked with abandoned vehicles as far north as they can see. Smoke hangs like a pall over the scene, drastically reducing visibility. Some of the cars are on fire, billowing thick, oily smoke.

They see no people.

Gunfire snarls in the distance, intense and violent.

A chill trickles down Bowman's spine.

"Other than that shooting, things seem pretty calm this morning," the Platoon Sergeant says.

"Right. No sirens. No traffic. For that matter, I don't see any new patients trying to get into the hospital. It's eerie."

"I sure would like to know where all the people went who were driving those cars. Looks like some kind of battle took place out there last night, just outside those roadblocks. Maybe you are right about one thing, sir."

"What's that, Mike?"

"Maybe we are in a *Twilight Zone* episode."

Behind them, Mooney and Wyatt hustle up in full kit, followed by McGraw.

"Sir, Private Mooney reports!" says Mooney, standing at attention.

Wyatt repeats the ritual.

Bowman turns and regards them. "So you're the guys who like recon missions."

Mooney and Wyatt exchange a glance, fidgeting.

Wouldn't it be cool if you could kill everybody you hate?

The endless lines of abandoned vehicles stretch into the gloom, surrounded by piles of luggage, clothing, junk and dead bodies. The soldiers weave slowly through the wreckage, carbines at the ready, heading north. Mooney fights the urge to vomit as he notices that the driver of one car has been mostly decapitated with the exception of his jaw, which sprouts a red beard. Wyatt excitedly points out another car that plowed into a McDonald's restaurant and now stands riddled with bullet holes, blood splattered across the windshield, the driver nowhere to be seen.

Shock and awe, Mooney thinks.

"Some kind of war happened here, cuzin!" Wyatt says. "Hey, lookit!" He rushes forward, leans his carbine against a car, and starts stuffing his pockets with something he found on the ground. "I'm rich! Too bad all the stores are closed."

Mooney coughs on the toxic haze. The unending horror of this patrol is sucking the life out of him. Every step feels sluggish, like swimming through air, like running from his worst fears in a dream.

"This lady is naked!" Wyatt crows. "Oh, gross, I can see her brains! Hey Mooney, you want some of this money? It's everywhere."

"Joel, put that back. We're already in enough trouble without you looting. And you're going to get sick if you keep picking stuff up off the ground."

The stress is causing an incredible headache to bloom in the front of his skull. He can feel the veins in his forehead begin to throb. He squats, leans forward and retches over a pile of clothing soaked in black oil. Baby shoes, a bra, a couple of pairs of gym pants.

Wyatt appears in front of him and says, "You don't look so good, dude. Maybe you're the one who's got the bug."

"I don't have it."

"Oh, you got vertigo. Just pretend we're back in Iraq. Then it's all good." His eyes widen and he does a double take. "Wow, that cop car is upside down!"

"Shut up, Joel," Mooney says, spitting. "Please shut the hell up."

"Don't tell me to shut up when I'm just trying to help!"

"Just keep your voice down. You're going to bring those things down on us again."

"Oh my God, wouldn't it be cool if we woke them all up and they came at us again in a human wave, like a million of them?" Wyatt laughs his shrill laugh. "No sweat, boss. I've got a gun this time. There are many like it, but this one is mine! If the crazy people show up, I will terminate them with extreme prejudice. It's like Christmas came early this year. It's legal to kill people!"

Mooney stands, ready to resume their expedition, but immediately sees a dead young girl with vacant eyes seemingly staring back at him from the rear window of a Volkswagen Jetta. He closes his eyes.

Shock. And. Awe.

Wyatt says, "I mean, wouldn't it be cool if you could kill everybody you hate?"

"No, Joel, I don't want to kill anybody."

"More for me." Wyatt swaggers away, puffing his chest out. Exhaustion has only made him more manic. "Back to work then, dude. The Lieutenant said to haul ass."

"In fact, I swear to God I'm not going to kill anybody if I can help it."

Wyatt checks his watch. "It's almost time to report in on these cool

Icom radios they gave us. You coming or what?"

Mooney sets his jaw and hurries to catch up, his boots crunching on broken glass. He dulls his sense of vision until he has "fly eyes," not focused on anything in particular but able to take in subtle movements everywhere across his entire field of view. He used this technique during patrols in Baghdad.

As he passes a truck in the next block, he hears a rustling.

And beneath that sound, a bestial growl from deep in the throat.

He whistles at Wyatt to halt.

Wyatt immediately crouches, looks around, then turns back and signs, *What?*

Mooney shakes his head. He's not sure what the sound was or where it was coming from. It could have been a plastic bag caught in the wind. Except there is no wind.

Wyatt motions for Mooney to join him.

Mooney stands and out of the corner of this eye sees the leering face in the truck.

The creature lunges, snapping its foaming jaws and slapping its hands against the window, leaving bloody smears on the glass.

Yelling, Mooney staggers backward and fires a burst point blank into the face, which disappears in an explosion of smoke, glass and blood.

"Holy sheepshit, killah!" says Wyatt, appearing at his side. "You smoked that chick. Give her a chance to surrender next time, why don't you?"

Mooney turns away from the wreckage, holding his hand over his face, and groans.

Romeo Five Tango, this is War Dogs Two actual, over.

"Uh oh, War Dogs Two-Six wants to know who you murdered for scaring you," Wyatt says, then keys his handset. "Standing by to copy, over."

We heard shots fired in your vicinity. Give me a sit-rep. Over.

"Private Mooney got surprised by a cat and accidentally discharged his weapon. Break." Wyatt grins at Mooney and pumps his fist to produce the universal sign language for masturbation. "Be advised that we are within a block of our designated turnoff and about to head west. Over."

Your mission is to observe. Do not attract any unwanted attention. How copy, over?

"Roger that loud and clear, sir. Solid copy, out."

Out.

"LT's cranky." Wyatt winks at Mooney. "Let's move out, killah."

They've gone about half a mile. The soldiers step over scattered open luggage strewn across First Avenue, then turn onto Forty-Second Street.

Halfway up the block west of their position, they see a soldier standing guard outside an office building. Beyond, far down the street, they can see cop cars parked at roadblocks set up to keep sections of Forty-Second clear for official traffic. Figures are moving around the cars, barely visible through the smoky haze hanging in the air.

"Hey!" Wyatt says, giving a big wave.

The soldier turns but does not react to them.

"Does he see us?"

From the east, across the river, they hear intermittent bursts from a heavy machine gun, the sound distant and booming and angry, like a primitive war drum.

"Hang on," Mooney says. He raises a pair of binoculars to his eyes.

The soldier is PFC Richard Boyd.

"It's Rick Boyd," he says, his eyes stinging.

Wyatt grabs the binoculars, takes a look, and gasps.

"Jesus Christ," he says.

"I'd better report this to the LT."

"Jesus Christ," Wyatt repeats. "They bit his nose off."

"War Dogs Two-Six, this is Romeo Five Tango, over," Mooney says into his handheld, sounding calmer than he feels.

"There are goddamn flies in the wound," Wyatt says, gritting his teeth.

This is War Dogs Two actual. Standing by to copy, over.

"We found Richard Boyd, over."

Good work. What's his status? Over.

"He's, ah, wounded, over."

Can you provide medical attention and get him moving, or should we send you the doc? Over.

"Negative. There's more to it than that."

Wyatt snorts and whispers, "You could say that again."

Mooney waves at him to zip it.

Speak clearly, over.

"He's one of them, sir. He's been bitten and he is . . . one of them now. Over."

Explain "one of them," over.

"He's showing symptoms of being a. . . ." He suddenly can't remember the politically correct term the soldiers have been told to use. Finally, he sighs and finishes, "A Mad Dog, sir. He's a Mad Dog, over."

A long pause.

"Negative contact. How copy, over?" says Mooney.

Are you absolutely sure of these facts, over?

"Affirmative. One hundred percent, sir. Over."

Roger that. Wait, out.

The soldiers crouch and keep an eye on Boyd, who wanders aimlessly around, then stops and stands still, his jaws moving.

"There are flies in the hole, laying babies," Wyatt says, lowering the binoculars and glaring at Mooney, "where his nose used to be."

"We can't do anything about that right now," Mooney says. "Keep an eye out behind us, will you? We don't want anybody sneaking up."

"Okay," Wyatt says, sounding strangely tamed.

They wait like this for several minutes. Mooney sighs loudly. "Come on, already. Let's get on with it."

As if on command, his handheld comes to life.

Romeo Five Tango, this is War Dogs Two actual. Message follows, over.

Mooney keys his handset and says, "Send message, over."

You will mark Private Boyd's position but take no further action related to him. Break. Abort mission and return to base immediately. Avoid detection by civilians. Break. Follow the new ROE strictly if you are threatened. How copy, over?

Mooney and Wyatt exchange a glance.

"Um, roger that, sir. You want us to avoid detection and abort mission. Wilco, out."

Out.

Mooney stands. "You heard the man. Time to go home, Joel. Joel?"

"We can't leave him out here like this, Mooney."

The skinny soldier raises his M4 and takes careful aim down its barrel using its iron sights.

Mooney says, "He's one of us, man."

Tears are streaming down Wyatt's face. His eyes are wild.

"I'm just going to put him out of his misery. I knew him, too."

"Stand down and secure your weapon, Joel."

"I just want to help him."

"Put the goddamn gun down."

Wyatt says, "But he's already dead."

He pulls the trigger.

Nothing happens.

His M4 jammed on a double feed. He has two rounds stuck in the firing chamber.

"It's not fair," Wyatt says, racking the bolt back.

Down the street, a car alarm blares. Boyd's head jerks towards the sound. He runs off.

"I guess it's Rick's lucky day," Wyatt adds bitterly.

"Let's just get back to base," Mooney tells him, utterly exhausted. "Before you give me a heart attack."

He starts thinking about what the Lieutenant said. It was strange: The LT explicitly ordered them to leave behind a member of their unit who is sick and wounded. This offends him but he knows better than to refuse orders or even question their wisdom. Besides, as a grunt, he's used to receiving orders he thinks don't make a lick of sense. Something to do with his limited situational awareness, or the incompetence of his superiors, take your pick. This is not what is bothering him. What's bothering him is the way the LT's tone got under his skin. The LT sounded worried.

No, scratch that.

The LT actually sounded terrified.

There is some major shit going down here and we are walking into the middle of it and that's wacked

At oh-six-forty-five hours, with the return of daylight, the invisible war slowly resumes, filling the air with scattered booms and popping of gunfire from all directions. In another time, one might mistake the sounds for fireworks. The boys of War Dogs Two-Three huddle around Sergeant Ruiz. Toting an M4 Super 90 shotgun and wearing rows of red shotgun shells across the front of his outer tactical vest, the Sergeant tells Third Squad that they will be leading the platoon to rejoin Charlie Company, and that they are authorized to shoot civilian targets, even those who do not have a weapon.

PFC McLeod considers Ruiz a gung ho mo fo when it comes to God, guns and the Army. It's not just the man's freaky black eyes, his intense stare. The man is something of a legend in the Army as a natural born killer. Without his shirt on, the Sergeant's thickly muscled torso is emblazoned with a large, ornate black cross tattooed on his chest and abdomen.

Once, in Iraq, he surprised an RPG team and when his weapon jammed, he killed the men, by himself, in a struggle lasting fifteen minutes, with his knife.

McLeod often tells people that it is because of psychos like Ruiz that pussies like him can sleep at night no matter how bad things get in the field.

But now the world is turning upside down. In the middle of America's biggest city, Sergeant Ruiz's voice shakes with something like fear as he tells them they are authorized to shoot any civilian who makes a threatening gesture towards the unit.

"What if it's some guy giving me the finger—should I light him up, Sergeant?" McLeod grates. "Hell, this being New York, the whole city is now a free-fire zone."

"Shut up," Ruiz says absently, then tells them to deep six any personal effects, which will be stored in the hospital, and otherwise drop anything that is nonessential.

"And dump your Kevlar," he adds. "It's staying here, too. We'll be wearing the caps. Otherwise, bring as much ammo as you can carry. Let's go, ladies. We're on the move in ten minutes."

After Ruiz leaves them, Williams nudges McLeod with his elbow and jerks his head towards the NCOs huddled in an intense pow wow with the LT. "Look at them hashing their shit out over there. No more Kevlar, dawg? Something is definitely up."

As his fireteam's grenadier, Williams carries an M4 carbine fitted with an M203A1 grenade launcher under the barrel, which fires forty-millimeter grenades.

"Magilla didn't even react to my joke," says McLeod, completely stunned.

"You know all those people we lit up last night? I'm thinking there's a lot more of them than they're telling us."

"By all rights, I should be smoked with push-ups, nailed with extra fatigue or getting my ass chunked, as you so quaintly put it yesterday. But all he did was tell me to shut up. That just ain't right. My God, man. I think the Sergeant is scared."

"You're not listening, Ace," Williams says. "Let me break it down for you. There is some major shit going down here and we are walking into the middle of it and that's wacked. You feel me?"

"What I feel is terrified right now," McLeod tells him, nodding rapidly.

"And we thought the suck was back in Iraq where all you had to worry about was getting your nuts shot off in hundred and thirty degree heat. Gentlemen, welcome to the real suck."

The remainder of McLeod's and Williams' fire team, Corporal Hicks and Hawkeye, join them. Hawkeye begins gathering up their helmets while Hicks calls out to Corporal Wheeler, who leads the squad's second fireteam, and asks if there is any news about Boyd. Wheeler shakes his head, looking glum.

Wheeler already lost one man back in Iraq to the Lyssa virus, and then Boyd disappeared into thin air on his watch. Still shaking his head, he returns to his pre-combat inspection of Private Johnston, the sole surviving member of his fireteam, who everybody calls "The Newb" because he is only two months out of boot camp.

"What am I going to play drums on without my Kevlar?" says McLeod, but nobody gives him a reaction, making him feel even more agitated.

Ruiz jogs up and tells the squad that he got the OpOrder, and to gather around.

"All right, this is it. We'll be moving north on First Avenue in close column file on the west side sidewalk with scouts on our three o'clock." He turns to Hicks. "Ray, you're going to lead us there. I'd like you second in line. Who do you want on point?"

The soldiers blink and glance at each other. Even with the aggressive ROE, they expected to fall into a standard traveling formation with road guards to help block traffic. Instead, Ruiz is describing an attack formation, essentially a jungle file formation, for their one-mile foot march through the middle of New York City.

"Hawkeye," says Hicks, recovering quickly. "He's stashing our Kevlar. I'll tell him when he gets back, Sarge."

"Fine." Ruiz now turns to Wheeler. "Adam, the LT will be right behind you with Headquarters and Weapons Squad. Keep a tight hold on them."

"Roger that, Sergeant."

"After Weapons Squad, McGraw and First Squad will bring up the rear. That's the order of march for our column. We'll have Lewis' people moving parallel on our three o'clock for additional security and recon. They'll be marching down the middle of the Avenue, through the abandoned vehicles that are out there, so they'll be setting the tempo for the platoon's movement. Any questions?"

McLeod and the other boys understand the tactics. The LT chose column file as their traveling formation because the street is clogged with vehicles, and moving in single file provides easy communication and mobility. Adding a second column file is ideal for moving fast through dense foliage, hence its nickname "jungle file," and the LT probably believes it will be just as practical for quick movement through bumper-to-bumper vehicles and rubbish on the road. The second column complicates communication and movement but mitigates the main disadvantages of column file, which are greater vulnerability to a flank attack and inability to deliver much firepower against targets in front of the column.

The question on everybody's mind is about the big picture.

"We're treating a short march in Manhattan like a combat patrol," says Hicks. "Who exactly is the enemy and what is the threat level, Sarge?"

"Civil authority is breaking down," Ruiz says. "As we saw last night, the police here can't control the growing number of Mad Dogs. We're not cops. We don't have non-lethals. But we have to defend ourselves. We have been cleared to shoot anybody who attacks us even if they are unarmed. If you have time, call in the target. If you don't, take your shot. We are taking no chances with the Mad Dogs. Understood?"

"Hooah, Sergeant," says Hicks.

The other boys simply nod sullenly. They're not buying any of it, but they know better than to ask questions that have too fine a point.

"There's one more thing I want to tell you before we move out," Ruiz continues. "LT sent out a scouting party that got back just a little while ago. Word is we may see some horrible things while we're on the move. I will understand if what you see makes you sad, mad, whatever." His face darkens. "But if you break discipline and put the rest of the platoon in danger, I will put my boot so far up your ass I will be tying my laces in your mouth. Understood?"

"Yes, Sergeant," the boys answer.

"Like you mean it, ladies."

"Yes, Sergeant!" they shout.

"Any other questions?"

McLeod opens his mouth, but says nothing.

"All right then," Ruiz tells them. "Now fix bayonets."

Full battle rattle

The platoon steps off, two column files bristling with bayonets and strung out over sixty meters of ground. The boys are in full battle rattle, each carrying weapon and ammo, body armor, rucksack and two canteens full of New York City drinking water. It is a lot of weight but the boys feel light without their two-and-a-half-pound helmets. The air is muggy and the temperature is climbing in this late, last gasp of summer, making them sweat in their universal camouflage uniforms colored dark tan, light gray and brown in the desert/urban pattern. They move with weapons loaded, safeties off and cleared hot. Each soldier in the main column is spaced about two meters apart. Despite the low-grade racket caused by their clinking and banging gear, the platoon moves relatively quietly, shocked into silence by the scenes of devastation they'd been warned about by their squad leaders.

Behind them, the doctors and nurses who turned out to see them off begin to retreat back into the hospital, looking worried.

"Jesus," Williams says after several blocks, wagging his head. "This is mad, major-league, mother of all wacked."

"Are you rapping, Private?"

He glances behind to see McLeod, who grins and waves breezily over his weapon.

"Thought you were all nervous back there. This shit don't bother you?"

McLeod stares back wearing an innocent expression. "What are you talking about?"

Williams shakes his head in wonder.

The truth is that after nearly a year in Baghdad's most dangerous neighborhoods, seeing dead bodies and scorched property has become routine for PFC McLeod. The fact that the bodies are now American does not bother him. Instead, he feels annoyed. They offend him. McLeod has gotten through most of his young life using scorn and derision as a way to rationalize his failures, avoid traumatic stress reactions, and generally feel superior to everybody else. Scorn got him through Iraq, for example. He considered the Iraqis to be suicidal for continually taking on the world's most powerful military, and therefore one couldn't be blamed for helping by killing them.

And these New Yorkers, well, what we have here is a bunch of rich, successful people who got their comeuppance with a strong lesson in How the World Works. Specifically, that bad things happen to everybody regardless of who you are or what you've done, so it doesn't really matter who you are and what you do.

"When was the last time we were asked to fix bayonets?" Williams wants to know. "Boot camp?"

"What I don't get is if it's so bad out here that we can't walk a mile without a bullet in the chamber and bayonets fixed, then why didn't we just stay where we were?" McLeod wonders aloud. "It's like they're trying to get us killed."

"All I know is this place gives me the creeps," says Williams. "There must be hundreds of dead people on First Avenue all the way up to the East River Tunnel. And nobody's picking them up for burial. For some reason, that's the worst part of it."

From the back of the file, they can hear two guys from First Squad sing:

Study up on weaponry,
The M16, the M15,
Sammy knows the enemy,
Flim flam, big slam, tell the Major what you see.
Hut, hut, hut, hut!

The boys are starting to clown around to get their spirits up. Like McLeod, the other boys of Second Platoon have seen the worst and are already adapting to it, taking it in stride, getting their swagger back while they let their rage build up bit by little bit. Right about now, the new ROE does not sound so shocking to them. If Mad Dogs did this, then the soldiers are itching for some payback.

"Don't tell me Rollins is trying to rap back there," Williams adds, disgusted.

McLeod laughs. "Oh, man. It's even better than that. Him and Carrillo are actually singing that old Blondie song, 'Military Rap.' That's brilliant."

"Blondie who?"

"Come on, dude. Blondie. Blondie!"

"Like I said. Who?"

"Oh, man, this is really great," McLeod says with genuine feeling. "This mission has finally found its rock and roll soundtrack."

He suddenly notices that the singing cut off abruptly several moments ago.

"Private McLeod, shut yer dicktrap!" Sergeant Ruiz roars inches behind his ear, making him jump. "We are in a potential combat situation, and that means no singing and no chatting with the other girls! Williams, your muzzle's lazy: Don't point your weapon at Hawkeye's ass! He's on our side! Johnston, put that goddamn camera away: Stay alert and watch your sector, you moron! And Hawkeye, what the hell are you looking at up there? You're supposed to be leading this platoon."

"Sorry, Sergeant," Hawkeye responds.

"Right now you are the eyes of this platoon and you are looking at everything except the street. What's the problem, son?"

"Well, I never been to New York before, Sergeant," Hawkeye says shyly.

"What's that, Private?"

"Somebody told me the United Nations was around here somewheres."

"You were sightseeing," Ruiz says in disbelief.

"Yes, Sergeant. Like I said before, I am sorry about it."

"Get a good look before it's gone, Hawkeye," says McLeod.

The squad leader shakes his head, darkening with barely controlled rage. "Stay sharp and keep it zipped, ladies!" He turns around and sees Corporal Hicks trailing him, looking pale. "Corporal, I could use your help keeping this freakshow in line."

"Yes, Sergeant."

Ruiz lowers his voice. "You all right, Ray?"

"Yes, Sergeant," Hicks says. "I just saw. . .she looked like my. . . . Never mind, Sergeant. It doesn't matter." He looks dazed.

"Put it out of your mind, whatever it is," Ruiz growls. "We got a job to do."

"Roger that, Sarge," says Hicks.

Hawkeye suddenly turns and extends his flattened palm for all to see. Immediately, the column stops.

Security halt

The boys get behind the nearest cover and crouch, continuing to scan their sectors and provide three hundred sixty-degree security around the platoon. Within moments, Lewis' column on their right also scatters behind cover and stops.

Hawkeye makes a throat-cutting gesture, indicating danger ahead, and then taps his chest twice, asking for the squad leader to come forward.

Keeping low to the ground, Sergeant Ruiz scurries to join Hawkeye.

"What you got?"

"Not sure, exactly. But listen, Sergeant."

Ruiz closes his eyes. He can't hear anything. He wonders if maybe the platoon should do a listening halt, where they all get comfortable and settle into a complete silence. Finally, he says, "I don't hear—"

Hawkeye raises his hand, silencing him. Ruiz raises his fist for the platoon to see, telling them to freeze. Don't move an inch.

The screams become audible, carried on the shifting breeze on an east-west street ahead of them, barely penetrating the background hum of New York City.

"Some kind of trouble up there, seems to me," says Hawkeye. "Kind of sounds like a girl screaming for help."

"Like a lot of people screaming," Ruiz says. "Screaming bloody murder."

He keys his handset and softly relays what he has learned to the LT.

Bowman, about forty feet behind him, replies on the commo.

Is the sound coming from Thirty-Eighth or Thirty-Ninth Street, over?

"We think it's Thirty-Ninth Street, over," says Ruiz, glancing at Hawkeye, who nods.

War Dogs Two actual to all War Dogs Two squads: Fragmentation order follows, break. We will take an alternate route to the objective, break. Turn left here at Thirty-Eighth Street and proceed west, over.

"Turn on Thirty-Eighth. That's a solid copy, out."

Hawkeye looks down at his rifle wearing a sour expression. There are American civilians up ahead in trouble and the LT has ordered the platoon to march the other way.

Ruiz nudges him. "We're not police, Hawkeye," he says. "There's danger all around us here. LT's intent is to get the platoon to the objective on time and in one piece. It makes sense."

"I guess so, Sergeant," says Hawkeye. "I mean, it's not my place to say."

The Sergeant's eyebrows lift in surprise. He has never seen his boys so uncertain and sour about a mission. "You heard the LT. Go on, then. Lead us out of here, Private."

"Roger that, Sergeant."

Ruiz stands and moves his arm in a wide forward-wave, giving the signal to advance.

Hey, Army! Can you hear me?

The platoon hauls itself back onto its feet, grunting at the weight of rucksacks and armor and weapons and water, and trails after Hawkeye, making the turn onto Thirty-Eighth Street. Soon, they cross Tunnel Approach Street, where they weave their way through a pile-up of cars that crashed into each other during the night and became hopelessly ensnarled in a massive sculpture of chewed-up metal. Nearby, an ambulance is parked, its doors open and its lights still eerily flashing, a dead man lying on a gurney outside atop a glittering carpet of broken glass. His throat has been torn out.

They are moving into a residential neighborhood. As they approach the middle of the block, they hear the screams.

The cries appear to come from all around them, as if a crowd of howling ghosts were passing through them, making them shiver.

Then a man shouts down at them from an open fourth floor window, "Hey, Army!"

The soldiers of Third Squad look up at him.

The man is young, with swarthy skin, long black hair and heavily muscled arms.

"There are these two guys banging on my door trying to get in and I have to go out and pick up my insulin," he says. "Can you help me out here?"

Negative, Ruiz hears over his handset.

"Keep it moving," he tells his squad.

"The screaming is coming from these buildings," Williams says. "Hardcore, dawg."

"Hey, Army! Can you hear me down there?"

Williams glances up and sees people leaning out of other windows.

"Are you going to do something about these homicidal maniacs?" an old woman shouts down at them, immediately joined by a chorus of others.

"Isn't there anything we can do for these people, Sarge?" says Williams.

"Keep moving," Ruiz says.

The falling girl strikes the blue Toyota Camry on McLeod's right with a heart-stopping crash, her face plunging through the windshield in a spray of blood and hair. The car sags for a moment at the impact, setting off its grating car alarm.

"Christ!" McLeod shrieks, almost dropping his SAW.

Three of Lewis' boys open up on the fourth floor window, making the swarthy man flinch and duck back inside.

"Cease fire, cease fire!" Lewis is shouting. "What are you shooting at, dumbass?"

Kemper's voice grates over the radio: *War Dogs Two-Five to all War Dogs Two squads, cease fire, over.*

"Hold your fire," Ruiz tells his squad. "Keep your cool."

The squad is gathering around the corpse.

Keep it moving, out.

"Her freaking leg's twitching," McLeod says. "Oh, God."

"LT says, keep moving," Ruiz tells them, raising his voice to be heard over the car alarm. "There's nothing we can do here."

"LT's got no heart," Williams says, shaking his head. "That shit is ice cold."

"She's dead, Private," the Sergeant says. "And we're not. Let's go. Now."

Williams is starting to get a bad feeling about this mission, and his hunches are usually correct. He can feel the boys around him tense up, mad and powerless and itching to fire their weapons at something. He has a feeling that once they start shooting, they will all cross a threshold, and they may not like what they find on the other side.

"War Dogs Two-Three to War Dogs Two-Six. Coming up on Second Avenue now, over."

Proceed north on Second Avenue, over.

"Affirmative. Turn onto Second Avenue, out."

A moment later, Ruiz gets back on the commo.

"War Dogs Two-Six, this is War Dogs Two-Three. You better get up here, over."

I see them. On my way, out.

The intersection of Forty-Second Street and Second Avenue is dense with people fighting each other around a line of cop cars set up to block off access to Forty-Second. Several food delivery trucks are parked beyond, half unloaded.

There appears to be a pitched battle in progress.

Not here to reenact My Lai or Custer's Last Stand

The LT has called together the NCOs into a close huddle and tells them the situation on the ground has changed and as a result there is a new OpOrder for the unit. He speaks quickly, as the unit's presence has begun to attract the attention of desperate civilians in the area and the platoon needs to get back on the move fast. The people stand as close to the platoon and its umbrella of protective firepower as possible, wringing their hands and begging for help, while Third Squad holds them at bay.

"I can't contact Captain West," he says. "We appear to be on our own."

The non-coms glance at each other.

"Think we should take another route and go around?" says McGraw.

"Negative. We already tried that. We're now on Third Avenue and out of time. We pushed our luck as it is. I think this is like Iraq where the bad guys sleep from four to eight and then the bullets start flying. This city is waking up and it is like an ocean rising under our feet. We're just going to have to push through or we could be overrun before we reach our objective."

"Roger that, sir," the NCOs tell him.

They know as much as he does because he told them about Private Richard Boyd, the soldier who was bitten by a Mad Dog and within hours turned into a Mad Dog. The soldier who made him aware that the rules of the game had changed.

The infection is spreading at an exponential rate.

The Army gave him a big hint that this was happening with the bizarrely aggressive ROE. New York gave him a big hint with all the gunfire indicating flashpoints of Mad Dogs attacking Army and police units. And the Mad Dogs themselves gave a big hint when they began showing up everywhere in force.

But he knows they are spreading infection through their bites and spreading rapidly because PFC Richard Boyd went AWOL in an almost perfect state of health and several hours later turned up bitten and a Mad Dog.

Every hour, there are more infected and fewer of everybody else. At some point, it could be hours, tomorrow or the next day, the streets of New York will likely become too dangerous to walk even for a platoon of U.S. infantry armed to the teeth.

There isn't a military on the planet that has the force to meet this threat. Infection will keep spreading and spreading until there is simply nobody around to bite.

It's a simple numbers game.

"Stand back," Hawkeye says to the civilians.

"As you can see—" Bowman pauses as a civilian runs by, emptying a .38 at a pursuing Mad Dog and missing except for the last shot, which topples his assailant. The man continues on, stumbling and crying, unaware that he now has a dozen rifles trained on him. "We are facing a major open danger area ahead. The government is distributing food, and some type of riot appears to be in progress, which we are not going to try to suppress or we'll end up with another bloodbath on our hands. Understood? Speed is going to be our ally. We will cross the intersection in a platoon V formation, with each squad acting independently once we enter the open danger area. Any questions?"

"Satisfactory, sir," says Ruiz.

"Stand back, Ma'am," says Hawkeye.

"The rally point is the other side, if clear, or the Company HQ, if not. The squads getting across first will set up a defensive line until the platoon is reunited. Lewis, you will take the left. Ruiz, you will be going up the middle with HQ and Weapons Squad; I want good security for our gun team as they're going to be useless in this fight but I have a feeling we're going to need their services later. Okay? McGraw, you've got the right."

"Yes, sir," McGraw says.

"Stand back, I said!" Hawkeye barks at the crowd.

"One last thing, gentlemen," Bowman says. "We're not here to reenact My Lai or Custer's Last Stand. Regardless of what you see happening, our mission is to rejoin the Company with as few bullets and bodies as possible. That is our mission. Understood?"

"Hooah, sir," they say.

"Step off as soon—"

"What the hell are you doing?"

The civilians scatter as two men and a bald woman, drooling and gurgling, step forward and latch onto Hawkeye's limbs, pulling at them with their full strength. In an instant, he is shrieking and flailing.

Ruiz fires his shotgun, deafening all of them, knocking both of the men to the ground. The woman loses her balance and falls backward, then comes back snarling. Ruiz clubs her senseless with a single stroke of the butt of his weapon.

Lewis helps Hawkeye back onto his feet. The other boys look at the bleeding and dying civilians, and then Ruiz, with something like awe.

"Did they bite you, Private?" the LT asks Hawkeye.

"You saw what they were doing, sir," Hawkeye says, barely concealing his irritation while he rubs his left arm. "They tried to pull my arms off. Hurt like hell, too."

"I'm not making fun of you, Private. Did any of them bite you?"

"No, sir. Nobody did."

Bowman nods to Ruiz, then says, "All right, back to your squads. Let's move while we still have the freedom to do so."

"Hooah," they shout.

The soldiers deploy as fast as they can through the wreckage of the abandoned vehicles choking Second Avenue, then Bowman gives them the order to step off.

Speed is a type of security. If they can move fast enough, they can punch their way through with minimal loss of life and ammunition.

People come running past them, screaming for their lives, hugging or dropping their food parcels. Some begin clinging to the soldiers, who shrug them off and keep moving while their sergeants howl at them to *Go go go*, cursing a blue streak.

"Stay close to me, boys," Bowman tells Martin and Boomer.

Nearby, a man has jumped into one of the abandoned cars and is trying to close the door while a Mad Dog slowly forces it open. One of the soldiers drops the Mad Dog with a single shot. Bowman shoulders his carbine and unholsters his nine-millimeter sidearm. A woman flies by on rollerblades, shouting, "Heads up! Coming through!"

The platoon wades into chaos.

Exactly what you were trying to avoid

Third Squad moves fast among the cars and approaches the intersection, which is a scene of chaos. There are people everywhere, many of them infected. Mad Dogs are fighting uninfected people, uninfected people are fighting each other around the food trucks. Nearby, incredibly, two New York City police officers have wrestled a Mad Dog to the ground and are trying to cuff him, while five feet away a man is beating a woman to death in a frenzy with a broken hairdryer. One of the officers is bleeding from bites on his arm. The police cars' lights strobe red and blue, sparkling in the soldiers' eyes.

Mounted above the chaos, the intersection's traffic signal mundanely turns from red to green as it is programmed to do.

The air crackles with small arms fire and several people collapse to the ground. Second Squad has entered the intersection and is plowing ahead, shooting anything that looks hostile. First Squad is bogged down by civilians clinging to them for protection, their formation broken, while McGraw lays about him with the butt of his shotgun, trying to untangle his unit. The screaming is grating and endless, shredding their nerves.

"Get off me!" McLeod shouts, shoving his way through the civilians.

The infected appear to focus on whoever fired last, which is unnerving.

Hicks is crying as he bayonets a Mad Dog.

"Keep going!" he shouts.

"Don't make me shoot you!" McLeod is pleading, pushing against a woman's back with the butt of his SAW. She screams and drops a television set she's been carrying, which falls to the street with a crash.

People are running everywhere, but the soldiers are moving into the current, forming a dam, and then it's hand to hand.

Bowman fires his pistol into a snarling face, which disappears.

This is exactly what you were trying to avoid, he tells himself.

"Reform!" he cries, but there are too many civilians in the way, drawn to the soldiers' uniforms like metal to magnets. The civilians hold onto the soldiers' rucksacks, which are already heavy, and slow them to a crawl.

Williams fires a series of warning shots into the air, without effect.

A taxi and a delivery truck are lurching along with the flow of people in fits and starts, the drivers leaning on their horns. A woman climbs onto the roof of the cab and lies down, hugging her child close. Across the street, a man is defending his family with a baseball bat. Behind him, the plate glass front of a convenience store shatters and people begin looting. Its owner comes stumbling out, his head split open and pouring blood. The police cars' strobing lights bathe the scene in a surreal glow.

The stink is incredible, the dense sour-milk stench of the infected.

Then a wave of heat and thick, oily smoke descends upon them from a burning city bus down the street, choking them as it billows through the crowd until it suddenly lifts as fast as it had come.

"Go, go, go!"

Third Squad passes a group of people, drunk and staggering along through the melee, laughing and shouting, "Fuck it!" while working on popping the cork on a champagne bottle.

One of the revelers is shorn away and mauled to the asphalt.

The Lieutenant is panicking now, breathing hard, his vision shrinking to a box. He can't keep track of the blurred shapes around him anymore. The smoke falls upon them again like a wave, choking and blinding.

The last reveler throws the champagne bottle into the air, screaming, "I don't care!"

"Why aren't we moving?" Hicks is saying.

SPC Martin is wrestling with an uninfected man and teenage boy for possession of his machine gun. Next to him, the RTO is trading punches with a man twice his size. People are screaming and a civilian, his shirt off and leaking blood from his eyes and ears, begins shooting people randomly with a pistol.

Ruiz roars as a stray bullet takes off the top of the skull of a man who is running by, spraying him with blood and brains.

Two bullets rip into Sherman's radio pack, spinning him like a top.

The Newb grunts and falls to his knees.

"Sir, we can get through this," Kemper is shouting.

Bowman's field of view unfolds. His stress suddenly takes an entirely different and beneficial direction. Time dilates and he calmly, almost serenely, watches the horror unravel in slow motion, able to take in every detail.

His squad is still intact and they can get through this if they do whatever it takes. But if he chooses to live, life after today may not be worth living.

For some reason, at this instant, he remembers Winslow telling him, "Somebody has to survive, Lieutenant."

As Bowman did in the hospital, again, he makes his choice.

Loading a fresh clip, he quickly identifies the people bogging down his squad and shoots them one by one.

"Watch out, Mike," he says, and puts a round in a teenager's throat.

Slowly, the knot unravels and the squad is able to begin moving again.

The people he shot were not infected.

"Coming through, sir," Kemper says.

He racks a round in his shotgun and blasts the crowd in front of the squad.

A hole is instantly created as people moan and fall in a tangled heap of limbs.

"All right, move out," Bowman roars.

A block past the intersection, they stop, reload and set up a defensive line, panting. A woman is shrieking at them to go back and HELP THESE PEOPLE, HELP THEM.

"Sergeant, keep those civilians back or consider them hostile," the LT says.

But Ruiz isn't listening. "Where's Johnston?" he demands.

Two of the boys hurry over, huffing, carrying The Newb on a makeshift stretcher.

"He's dead," Corporal Wheeler tells him, sounding dazed. "Got hit by a stray bullet. It looked like friendly fire to me, Sergeant. One of our own guys shot him."

Ruiz spits on the ground, purple with rage.

"Second Squad, probably," the Sergeant says. "They were shooting everything that moved back there. Goddamnit. He was a good kid."

"Civilians, Sergeant," Bowman says quietly.

"I'm on it, sir," Ruiz tells him, glaring. "Wheeler, get his tags."

"Here comes McGraw and First Squad, LT," Kemper says.

First Squad is limping away from the intersection, firing behind them, dropping anybody who comes close. Two bloodied cops have joined them, toting shotguns.

"Where's Sergeant Lewis?"

"No sign of him," Kemper says.

"Try him on the commo."

"Friendlies coming in!" Lewis calls from behind them, running up with Second Squad.

"Friendlies on our six!" says Corporal Hicks, then calls out, "Reloading!"

"We made it through and set up a defensive line another block up the road," Lewis tells the LT. "Didn't know you wanted to rally here. Sorry, sir."

"It's all good, Sergeant."

Ruiz glowers at Lewis and says, "You and me are going to have some words later, motherfucker."

Lewis says, "Go to hell, Sergeant."

Second Squad begins covering First Squad's movement. The carbines pop and the bullets hum and snap through the air.

Bowman almost does not recognize Second Squad. In Iraq, they were boys who were much older than their years because of what they had done and seen. But now they are beyond even this scale. They are ancient now. It is in their eyes, he realizes. Looking ahead with thousand-yard stares, their eyes burn like cold stones as old as war itself.

The boys have become killing machines, like something out of myth.

He looks at Kemper, who also has the look. He guesses that he himself might have it.

There are two types of soldiers in the platoon now. Those who shot non-combatants, and those who did not. Those who shot uninfected people to save themselves and their comrades, and those who would have stayed in that intersection.

Those who will in the future, and those who won't.

Kemper nods to Bowman. He now understands the choice that the LT made back in the hospital. The choice to be damned, as long as it saved his men. A choice that was not expedient, but necessary.

"It was an emergency food relief operation," one of the cops is saying, his eyes gaping. "The food trucks drew a massive crowd of people, thousands. Then a couple of gangs of Lyssa victims came at us the other way, attacking and biting people." He's pleading with the soldiers around him. "There was nothing we could do!"

"You're all right now, buddy," one of the soldiers says to him.

Kemper whispers near the LT's ear, "Sir, if they're broken, we're it."

The other cop glares at Lewis' boys and says, "We're not staying with these murderers, Brian. We'll find another way back to the station."

Bowman checks his watch. The movement across the intersection—and intervening battle—lasted all of four minutes, and left them exhausted, bloodied and dispirited.

"You're on, uh, fire, Jake," he says, noticing smoke rising up from his RTO's radio pack.

"It's the radio, sir," says Sherman, sporting a black eye. "It's toast. But who knows, maybe I can fix it."

Bowman nods. If the radio is broken, the platoon is now cut off from the rest of the Army. They are officially off the reservation, at least until they rejoin their company.

"Sergeant Ruiz?" Corporal Hicks says. He is standing over Hawkeye, who sits on a curb, rocking back and forth. "He don't look so good, Sergeant."

Ruiz wipes blood from his face and crouches down to face the soldier.

Hawkeye shivers, sweating and pale, with his face buried in his hands. Getting the shakes is common after combat due to an excess of adrenaline.

The Sergeant put his hand on the boy's shoulder.

"You all right, son?"

Hawkeye removes his hands from his face. His N95 mask is gone. Ruiz sees a jagged hole where a Mad Dog bit and tore away a chunk of flesh from his cheek. The skin around the wound is swollen and inflamed.

"Sergeant," the boy says vacantly. "I don't feel so good, you know?"

"Just a scratch," says Ruiz, involuntarily jerking his hand away.

Hicks is calling for the medic.

They have little time to patch up their wounds and take stock of themselves. Bowman is issuing new orders. They are still shooting and using up ammunition, there are too many civilians in the area, and they are not secure. Time to move. Their objective is very close now. Within just a few blocks, they'll be back with Charlie Company in a defensive position behind some thirty-cals. Then they can rest.

Bowman will be happy to turn this mess over to the company CO and let him decide what to do.

The chain of command appears to have figured out the Mad Dog threat as well and is trying to consolidate its forces in New York. It's the smart thing to do, he believes: Hold what can be held and give up the rest. But the politicians are not going to want to give up anything. They are going to give the Army an impossible task. And officers do not always make smart decisions when surprised. It is going to be chaos.

In any case, it may be too late to consolidate in a city that is already beginning to swarm with infected.

Bowman, in fact, is now wondering how long, given a probable exponential spread of infection in the general population, Eighth Brigade will be able to remain effective as a fighting unit. He is aware that the ramifications go far beyond the Army and his tiny corner of it. He is just not ready to face them yet.

Right now, the end of the world is simply too big to even contemplate.

Chapter 5

I can't work like this!

Dr. Joe Hardy hustles into his office with Dr. Valeriya Petrova in hot pursuit, their labcoats flapping behind them.

"Here it is," he says, grabbing his putter from behind his desk. "Now we're in business." He turns around and begins to head back out the door, but his colleague blocks his way, staring at him coldly.

"Really, Doctor, this is no time for golf practice," Petrova says in her Russian accent.

"Watch me," he says, pushing past her.

"Are you drunk, Doctor?"

He laughs derisively. "No, hungry," he says, patting his enormous stomach. "Both make me irritable, so be warned."

She gives chase. "We need to discuss my findings."

"Findings!" He pauses a moment to face her. "Findings?"

"Yes. The implications are significant."

"Honestly, Valeriya, do you really think anybody gives a flying shit about your findings right now?"

"But they are significant, Doctor. Did you not agree?"

"Agree with what? Do you realize that we've got some serious problems that we are dealing with here?"

She looks surprised. "You did not get my email?"

Hardy laughs again and keeps walking, swinging his putter. Petrova stomps her right foot in frustration, her face flushed, and hurries to catch up with him, marching along at his side. What a strange woman, he thinks. Smoky, exotic looks and foreign accent that inspire lust. A masculine, abrupt manner that inspires loathing. Half the time, he doesn't know if he wants to buy her flowers or kill her.

Now Dr. Lucas steps out of his office, hastily repositions his glasses on his nose, and says, "Ah, Dr. Hardy, good to see you. Are you going to do something about the air conditioning or not? You may have, ah, noticed that it's freezing in here."

"He is right," Petrova says. "It is cold in this building."

Hardy sighs. "People, I'm the director, not the facility manager. Who, by the way, is MIA. There's nothing I can do."

"Well, I can't work like this, sir!" Lucas challenges him. "If you want me to keep at my research while we're going to be stuck living here for the near future, you could at least try to provide decent working conditions."

"Tape some garbage bags over the air vents," Hardy tells him, brushing past.

Dr. Saunders steps out of his lab, his wide balding head gleaming under the fluorescent lights, and shouts down the hallway, "Hey Joe! Any word from CDC or USAMRIID yet on our rescue before we freeze to death and starve?"

"No!" Hardy shouts over his shoulder, and keeps moving.

"Five minutes, Doctor," Petrova says. "That is all I ask. It is quite urgent."

They enter the employee break room. Hardy walks up to one of the vending machines and studies it for a few moments.

"Stand back, Dr. Petrova," he says.

"What?"

"Just move back two, maybe three steps."

"Why? You—here? Is this acceptable?"

"Yes, that's perfect, thank you."

He takes a deep breath just before swinging the putter as hard as he can at the machine. The club connects with the glass front and shatters it. The noise is startling. Glass shards spill onto the floor.

"Wow," he laughs. "Did you see that?"

"You could have warned me you would do this," Petrova tells him.

"Believe it or not, it scared me as much as it scared you."

Hardy looks down at himself, half expecting to see pieces of glass sticking out of his large, round body accompanied by his mother's voice yelling at him as a kid, *See, that's what you get for playing with things you don't understand, Joey.* Seeing himself unscathed, he pulls down his mask and reaches into the machine to plunder a package of peanut M&Ms, which he tears open with a hungry grunt.

"This was necessary?" his colleague asks him. "Please explain."

"Did you not hear me just say to that jackass Bill Saunders that CDC and USAMRIID are not returning my calls, meaning we are cut off from the outside world?"

Petrova nods. "I see," she says.

"Do you?" he says, munching rapidly. "There's a mob downstairs threatening to kill people if we don't hand over the magic medicine we don't have. We are under siege."

"Yes, I know all these things."

"Then, to top it all off, last night my daughter calls me to tell me there are some psychos attacking people in her building, and all the 911 lines are jammed." His shoulders sag. "Christ, between the siege and the power brownouts and all hell breaking loose outside, I don't know if it's even possible to finish what we started here."

"I understand things are hard," she says.

"Do you? So surely, then, you see why I don't care about your findings right now."

Petrova eyes him coldly. "Doctor. You know well that my husband and son have been trapped in London since all flights were grounded at the beginning of the Pandemic. My boy is three years old and I have not seen him or my husband in weeks. The cell phones are jammed and I have not spoken to them in seventy-two hours. I—" Her voice cracks for a moment as an expression of pain flickers across her face. "I think I understand how serious the situation is."

"I'd forgotten, Dr. Petrova," Hardy blusters, turning red. "I'm sorry."

"In fact," she says, collecting herself with a visible effort, "I believe I have a unique perspective on just how serious it really is based on my test results."

"All right, all right," he says. "I give. You've got your five minutes."

We are trying to cure the wrong disease

Petrova takes a deep breath and tells Hardy about what she found.

The Lyssavirus is transmitted like influenza, entering the body through the respiratory tract and attacking the lungs. The most common cause of death is a cytokine storm, a situation in which the body's immune system turns on itself. When the body encounters an invader, cytokines summon armies of immune cells to fight the infection. Normally, they stop, but sometimes, when a new virus is encountered, they can't. The resulting storm of immune cells lays waste to everything, damaging body tissues and organs, blocking airways and drowning the body in its own bloody snot. The malfunctioning immune system kills the body it was designed to protect.

In advanced cases, Lyssa enters the nervous system and attacks the brain, resulting in progressive viral encephalitis—steadily worsening inflammation of the brain—which kills its victim in less than a week. It specifically targets the limbic system, which governs a person's emotions, motivation and behavior. The result is artificial rage, popularly called Mad Dog Syndrome.

Laboratories across the country are trying to crack the disease and produce a vaccine—some competing, some collaborating—under direction from the Centers for Disease Control in Atlanta. Normally, Hardy and Petrova's laboratory facility, a Biosafety-Level Two lab located in the heart of Manhattan, would not even be working on a virus as dangerous as Lyssa, but it is already in the community, so there would be no real threat if it escaped the lab. And besides, the CDC and USAMRIID are desperate.

Hardy's team is actually getting close to their objective. If starvation and the mob and the brownouts and the cold don't finish them first.

"This I know," Hardy says. "Tell me what I don't know."

"My research has led me to the conclusion that the advanced dementia variant of the disease—what people call Mad Dog syndrome—is actually a separate disease."

In fact, she continues, the Mad Dog virus appears to have preceded the HK Lyssa virus. It is HK Lyssa's primitive ancestor. HK Lyssa is essentially a benign mutation of the Mad Dog virus that allowed it to survive by spreading more easily among humans.

"But in a few cases, HK Lyssa attacks the brain," she adds. "Once in the brain, the virus displays a remarkable trait: It reverts back to its primitive ancestor, the Mad Dog virus. HK Lyssa is therefore a—what is the term—Trojan Horse for Mad Dog. As you can see, we are wasting our time here trying to cure HK Lyssa."

"Hell, we've already isolated the bastard *in vitro* and we're working up a complete genetic characterization," says Hardy. "Don't be too hard on us. We have a ways to go, but we are getting close."

"What I am saying is we are trying to cure the wrong disease," she says.

"Bullshit," Hardy says flatly.

She stomps her right foot in frustration and says, "Oh!"

"What you're saying is fascinating, but academic. You said yourself that Mad Dog comes from Lyssa, so if we cure Lyssa, we cure Mad Dog."

"Doctor, listen to me carefully," Petrova tells him. "You know that Mad Dog and HK Lyssa come from the Lyssavirus family. Rabies is in that same family. While genetically very different, the symptoms are similar. The Mad Dog virus appears to be perfectly designed to transmit itself through bites and infected saliva. This is why the Mad Dog victim is so aggressive. He is compelled to seek out and infect others. This is an entirely new vector of disease transmission and, in my opinion, poses the greater threat."

Hardy grunts, interested now. "How does the virus operate?"

"When a Mad Dog bites an uninfected individual, the virus enters the body through the bite. It attacks the nerves and, undetected by the immune system, travels to the spinal cord. From there, it is mainlined to the brain. By the time the immune system detects the virus, it is too late. Very similar to rabies."

Hardy scratches his head in wonder. There were anecdotal reports of Mad Dogs transmitting illness through their saliva, but no real research in that area. The medical research community has been focused entirely on Hong Kong Lyssa as an airborne, flulike illness, and there were so few Mad Dogs. . . .

"What's the incubation period?" he asks her.

"It could be remarkably fast. My results suggest infection occurs within one hour and symptoms manifest several hours later."

"You mean weeks."

"No. I mean hours."

"But that can't be," he says, almost laughing. "It's impossible. Isn't it?"

"I have a hypothesis about the incubation cycle at this point," she tells him.

"But it's preposterous! If the disease is closely related to rabies and is a latent feature of HK Lyssa, then one would expect a period between exposure and becoming symptomatic to be more like its rabies cousin—anywhere from twenty to sixty days." He blinks. "Wait—what is your hypothesis?"

"I believe the disease may have been bioengineered and that is why it is so efficient."

Hardy breaks into a sweat. "Oh, Jesus. A terrorist weapon?"

"I do not know, obviously. But that is not important right now. What is important is given the aggressive mode of transmission and the lack of immunity in the population—even those who have caught Lyssa and recovered—the disease has a transmission factor that is likely equal to or greater than R2."

"Exponential spread. Of a disease that is transmitted through aggressive biting."

"It's almost impossible to confirm without field data," Petrova says.

"And then there's the incubation period of several hours."

"Yes. As I was saying to you, the implications of my findings are naturally quite significant."

"You can say that again," Hardy snorts.

"I would like to speak to some epidemiologists to discuss with them what they are learning in the field. Meanwhile, we will need to shift resources from curing the version of the disease transmitted by sneezes to the version transmitted by bites. Obviously."

Hardy rubs his hand over his stubbled face, staring over her shoulder in a daze. "I mean, you're kind of talking about the end of the world."

"You know my background. Ten years working with viruses like Ebola, Marburg, Lassa Fever. I am hardly an alarmist. I am only interested in facts. And the facts tell us that the Mad Dog strain is now taking over from its descendant because its victims are now spreading exponentially in the population. That is the disease we need to cure."

The blood suddenly drains from Hardy's face.

"Oh, God," he says, remembering. "Amy!"

Taking out his cell phone, he hurriedly punches a phone number.

"Yes! It's ringing," he says, pacing nervously. "Come on, come on. Pick up the phone." He suddenly feels an irrational rage at his daughter for making him worry. "I got her voicemail." His tone suddenly changes, becoming calm and smooth, a father's voice. "Hey honey, it's Dad. Just calling to make sure you're okay. Give me a shout when you get a minute, all right? I love you."

Outside the Institute, the country is falling apart because of the epidemic. Nearly twenty percent of the country's workforce is sick, consuming resources and producing nothing. And the numbers keep growing while supplies keep dwindling. Food and gas are being rationed, world trade has ground to a halt, the economy is crashing, and prices for everything from cigarettes to toilet paper are skyrocketing. Most states have declared martial law under the Emergency Powers Health Act.

On the radio, preachers are saying it's the Apocalypse.

But now this. Well, Hardy thinks, if Petrova is right, then it won't just feel like the end of the world. It really might be the end of the world. Infection will spread exponentially until everybody gets it except for those smart and supplied well enough to stay hidden for the next few weeks. Billions will die. The survivors, many driven mad by what they have seen, will live the rest of their days scavenging among the toxic ruins.

If she is right, the stakes in the race for a cure, already high, have just been raised to the ultimate level of a fight against possible extinction.

After hanging up, he glares at Petrova. "You're making me worry."

"I am simply the messenger," she says, staring wistfully at the phone in his hand. He can tell she is thinking about her family and wishes she had a little time so that she could try them again in London. He feels ashamed by this.

"Okay," he says. "Show me your test results. Let's hope you're wrong."

Then he freezes in his tracks and smacks himself in the forehead.

"Dr. Baird!" he shouts.

And rushes out of the room.

Puppets

Hardy jogs down the hall trailed by Petrova, his heart pounding in his chest. He just remembered that Dr. Gavin Baird entered the Institute last night shouting for help. On his way home, he got caught in a small riot of cops and looters outside a supermarket, and a child bit him on the hand, breaking the skin and drawing blood. Shaken, he returned to the Institute for antiseptic and a bandage minutes before the tall blonde and her mob showed up. Like the other scientists, he eventually gave up waiting and went back to work, disappearing into Laboratory West with Marsha Fuentes, one of the lab techs.

Hardy has not heard from either of them since.

Lucas leans out of his office, adjusting his glasses. "Do you know where the trash bags are kept?"

"Come with me!" Hardy roars.

"Should I come, too?" Saunders asks, then falls in with the rest. "Why aren't you wearing your mask, Dr. Hardy? Are you lifting the self-quarantine regime?"

Hardy pauses at the door of the lab, looking through the porthole but seeing nobody inside. "Has anybody seen Marsha since yesterday? Marsha Fuentes?"

The others glance at each other and shake their heads.

Hardy looks into Petrova's eyes wearing a sad expression. Then he opens the door and steps inside, holding the putter defensively.

Marsha Fuentes walks towards him from across the room, whimpering.

What is left of her, anyway.

She has been beaten black and blue. The left side of her face is purple and her eye is swollen shut. Her arm appears broken and, perversely, one of her breasts is completely exposed through a tear in her shirt and bra. She winces with each step.

"God, Marsha, are you all right?" he says, taking a step forward.

"She is one of them, Doctor," Petrova says.

He realizes that Petrova is right: The woman's throat is swollen, as if she swallowed crabapples that are now lodged in her throat. She's growling, making the buboes vibrate.

"Aw, Marsha," he says sadly.

"What's this all about?" Lucas says, sounding panicked.

"Christ, what is that smell?" Saunders says. "What was she working on in here?"

Baird went Mad Dog and beat the crap out of Fuentes. He also bit her. By the time she regained consciousness, she was already one of them.

Fuentes grins, leaking foam between clenched teeth.

"Maybe we should leave now," Saunders says, blinking.

"Where's Dr. Baird?" Hardy says. "We need to confirm that he's here and then we can get out and seal the room."

He turns to the right and sees the man several yards away, behind a desk.

"Jesus, Baird, you scared the crap out of me," Hardy says, forgetting for an instant what his colleague has become.

Baird is growling. His ponytail has worked loose and his long blond hair, clotted with blood, is splayed across his face and shoulders. He's a strong man, a weight lifter. His hands clench into fists.

Hardy can see his eyes through the veil of hair, burning like coals.

"Oh, shit," he says.

Baird launches across the desk, scattering papers and sending a PC crashing to the floor. He brushes aside the golf club that Hardy feebly raises to defend himself, seizes the back of the man's neck and sinks his teeth into his throat. Fuentes, her mouth foaming, latches onto Hardy's left arm and together, the infected scientists bear him to the floor screaming.

"Do something!" Lucas wails. "Somebody do something!"

Saunders shouts repeatedly, too terrified to make words.

Baird has ripped Hardy's throat out with his teeth. A fountain of bright red blood flies into the air. Hardy's scream becomes a gargle. His eyes are glassy with fear and understanding.

"Mom," he croaks.

Within moments, the lights in his eyes fade. His body relaxes.

The cell phone in the pocket of his lab coat spills onto the floor and begins ringing.

Petrova picks up the golf club and brings it down across Baird's back, making him flinch and yelp like a dog kicked in the ribs. She brings it down again, connecting with Fuentes' broken arm. She rolls on the floor, weeping with agony.

"Get out!" she says, wildly slashing at Baird again. "Lucas, Saunders, get out now!"

Despite the repeated blows, Baird is slowly rising to his feet, bleeding and snarling, while Fuentes is working her way back across the floor towards her on her knees, holding out her good hand in a splayed claw.

"Get out!"

Suddenly, she realizes that she is alone and that Baird is on his feet.

She backs up through the open door and hurls it shut.

A moment later, Baird's body slams against it and begins thrashing and clawing, leaving bloody prints on the porthole.

Inches away, on the other side, Petrova sits on the floor hugging her knees and crying, feeling the vibrations and frenzied pounding against her back.

Saunders and Lucas sit against the wall on either side of her, dazed and shaking from an excess of adrenaline.

Suddenly, Baird stops. The silence is startling.

Hardy's cell begins ringing again.

"He's dead," Lucas says, his teeth chattering. "He's dead, right?"

"They all are," Petrova says, wiping the tears from her face.

Gregory Baird and Marsha Fuentes died the moment the virus replicated enough to saturate their brains and subjugate their will to its own. The moment it began using their bodies as puppets for the sole purpose of violently passing itself on to new hosts.

She adds softly, "The Mad Dog strain is a parasite, and it has them now."

Petrova slowly gets to her feet, peers through the porthole, and gasps. Baird is grinning back at her, wheezing and dripping drool onto his bloodied tie and labcoat.

Viruses are the world's oldest form of life, primordial and ancient, and yet this mutant strain is something new, she realizes. It is a new force of nature, unleashed upon the world.

A new life form seeking its rightful place in the pecking order.

Baird and Fuentes are no longer making decisions on their own. They are rabid, acting solely based on the virus' simple program:

Attack, overpower and infect.

"Oh," she says, backing up. "Oh my."

"What is it?"

She turns, her eyes gleaming and wild, and screams: *"RUN!"*

Moments later, the door shatters off of its hinges with a crash and Baird spills into the hallway, howling with pain and rage.

Chapter 6

No sign of blue forces

Second Platoon, now a wedge made up of three rifle squads in diamond formation with HQ, Weapons Squad and the walking wounded in the center, reaches Samuel J. Tilden International Middle School ten minutes behind schedule. A growing crowd of civilians follows the platoon at a respectful distance, hoping for protection.

The school is a sprawling, three-story building consisting of a central trunk and two wings, accessible via a main entrance and numerous emergency exits. In the early days of the Lyssa epidemic, the City government closed all of the schools to prevent the rapid spread of infection among children, who were then taking the disease home to their parents. As the epidemic continued growing and began overwhelming the hospitals, the government tried to alleviate the pressure by opening Lyssa clinics at sites such as schools, the larger dance clubs and even the subway and train stations.

This school, turned into a Lyssa clinic, was where Quarantine placed the headquarters of Charlie Company, First Battalion, and its First Platoon. Yesterday, it was teeming with patients, medical volunteers and nearly forty soldiers, MPs, engineers and specialists, including at least one squad constantly manning a checkpoint behind a sandbag position constructed around the front doors.

Today, the entrance appears deserted. The street in front of the building is also empty of vehicles, restricted to official traffic only. Nobody comes out to welcome the boys of Second Platoon.

There are bodies everywhere lying on the street among fluttering papers and loose garbage, already starting to stink in the brisk air of this late September morning. The air is thick with flies.

They died from gunfire.

Second Squad is on point. Sergeant Lewis calls a halt. The LT hustles up, takes out his binoculars and scans the small, neat sandbag fort.

No soldiers are visible.

Bowman turns to Lewis and signals him to move.

The Sergeant whistles softly and Second Squad's fireteams rush across the open space to the sandbags, carbines held in the firing position.

Behind him, the civilians are getting nervous and asking why the platoon is stopped and they are not entering the refuge. Kemper explains that they must check out the area to make sure it is not dangerous. He tells them to stay out of the way for their own safety.

Second Squad disappears into the building. The scene is quiet except for the intermittent clatter of a machine gun somewhere far to the northeast.

"Every time we stay out of the way, we get slaughtered," one of the civilians complains.

Moments later, Lewis reappears at the sandbags and whistles, waving his hand in front of face to give the signal for all-clear.

"Now we can move," Kemper says to the civilian. "See how this works?"

"I thought how it worked is I pay taxes and you protect me," a woman in the crowd says, just loud enough for him to hear.

Kemper sighs, sorry that he tried.

The platoon moves forward, the civilians following closely.

"What the hell happened here?" Sherman wonders. The area in front of the school's doors is carpeted with bloody brass shell casings, the product of hundreds, possibly even thousands, of rounds being fired. The smell of cordite hangs in the air.

"Some kind of war," says Boomer.

"No sign of blue forces, sir," Sergeant Lewis reports to the LT.

The boys shuck their rucksacks in the hallway and take long pulls on their canteens. The civilians file past them, looking shell-shocked.

"Rest up," Bowman says. "We're on the move in five."

How a rifle platoon seizes control of a building

Sergeant Ruiz extends his arm over his head and gives a slight wave. Williams and Hicks get into position on each side of the door and give him a thumbs up.

Ruiz opens the door to the classroom and flicks the light switch. Inside, the rows of institutional fluorescent lights blink to life instantly.

He steps over the threshold, holding his carbine at shoulder level, ready to fire. Williams follows on his heels and turns left, while Hicks turns right. Behind them, Wheeler and McLeod pull security in the hallway, watching their backs.

The fireteam then loops around until they return to the doorway.

"Clear," Williams says.

"Clear," Hicks says.

"Clear," says Ruiz.

They have done this eight times already, and they are exhausted.

This is how a rifle platoon seizes control of a building, one room at a time. Once they entered the school, the LT placed his gun team and HQ, along with the wounded and civilians, near the primary doors, plugging the main entrance. This base became their foothold for action inside the building, while denying access to outsiders who might reinforce enemy forces.

This accomplished, the next step is to systematically clear the building. The three squads each entered a separate wing of the building, with the fireteams in each squad alternating as assault and support forces.

"All right, here's the stairwell leading up to the second floor," the Sergeant says, mopping sweat from his forehead. "Down there is the admin wing, which we got to clear before we can go up. McLeod, I am placing you here with your SAW."

"You're leaving me alone?" says McLeod.

Ruiz sighs loudly through his nose. "The rooms behind you have been cleared. We will be on your left, down that hallway. You lie here and point your weapon at the stairwell until we get back. Think you can manage that?"

"Since you put it like that—"

"Listen to me, dipshit."

"Okay, Sergeant."

"You got our backs. Do not screw up or nod off or rub one out or read a good book or whatever it is you do instead of soldiering. If you do, I will not assign you KP or smoke you with exercise. I will frag you. You will die. Okay? Do we understand each other?"

McLeod nods darkly. "Yes, Sergeant."

"All right, let's do this, ladies. Sooner we clear this building, the sooner we can kick up our feet."

"Roger that, Sarge," says Hicks.

"Take point, Private Williams."

"All right, Sergeant."

Williams turns the corner toward the admin offices and almost walks into the man standing there smiling down at him. A tall, skinny giant of a man, almost six foot five, wearing a neat suit and tie.

"Oh, sorry, sir," Williams says.

He glances up at the face and his bowels turn to water. The man's swollen, bruised throat bulges over the shirt collar, which is soaked with drool and mucus.

"Shoot him, Private!" roars Ruiz.

The man opens his mouth, making a bubbling, percolating sound deep in his throat, and reaches out with his long arms to embrace Williams.

The rifle pops and the man staggers backward, wincing in pain, his dress shirt now soaked red.

Williams blinks in surprise, then fires again as he was trained, putting the second bullet into the man's face, blowing off his jaw and ear. The man spins like a top and eventually falls to the ground with a meaty sound, his hair smoking.

The soldier laughs hysterically.

"Who shot him? Was that me?"

"Give me your weapon, Private."

Ruiz takes the M4 out of his hands, shoulders it and fires rapidly, *bang bang bang*, dropping three more figures at the end of the hallway.

"I'm going to make a soldier out of you yet, Private Williams," he says, handing him back his carbine and then retrieving his shotgun.

"Roger that, Sergeant," Williams says, blowing air out his cheeks. "Roger that."

A familiar voice from around the corner: "You guys all right?"

"Shut up and stay in position, Private McLeod," Ruiz yells back.

"Sergeant, look, it's a rifle," says Hicks, stepping forward and picking the weapon off the floor. "It's an M4." He wrestles with the bolt and snorts. "Jammed."

The Sergeant nods. He was afraid that at some point they were going to begin finding the shreds of First Platoon.

"And there's a blood trail. See it?"

The trail of blood droplets leads under a door to an administrative office. The fireteams quickly get into position, ready to take it down. Ruiz peers through the window set in the upper half of the door, which is similarly spotted and streaked with blood. The inside of the office is clean and brightly lit but otherwise appears empty.

He counts down with his fingers, *Three, two, one—*

The doorknob gives, but the door barely moves. Something's blocking it.

He pushes hard until the obstruction clears.

The soldiers step into the room, clear it, and then converge on its sole occupant.

The corpse lies tangled up in his own limbs. They recognize him as Charlie Company's RTO. He wears a crude tourniquet tied tightly around his leg, which has been mauled savagely below the knee. The top of his skull and brains are splattered up the scorched and splintered door, which he was blocking with his body.

Blocking, apparently, to keep the Mad Dogs out.

"This shit is cold," says Williams.

"He didn't want to become one of them," Ruiz says.

"Sergeant?" says Hicks, puzzled.

"Nothing," says Ruiz. "Just thinking out loud."

The man still clutches the pistol that he used to blow his brains out. As RTOs are not issued sidearms, the pistol is not his, although the soldiers recognize it as an Army-issue nine-millimeter.

The Sergeant crouches down and tears off one of the corpse's oval dog tags, then contacts the LT using his handheld.

"War Dogs Two-Six, this is War Dogs Two-Three, over."

War Dogs Two-Three, this is War Dogs Two actual standing by to copy, over.

"We have cleared most of the first floor of hostiles and have located a member of Charlie Company's headquarters staff in the admin area of the left wing, over."

What's his status, over?

"He's dead, over."

Any sign of War Dogs Six or other elements of his command, over?

"Negative. We have something positive to report, though. The man we found is the company RTO, and he has a working combat net radio. Over."

The boys glance at each other and grin. The man's death is horrible, the more so because this particular death, among so many, is closer to home for them as soldiers. But finding an intact SINCGAR is a stroke of luck. Communications can be as valuable as water and ammunition in the field. With a working field radio, the platoon can easily talk to Battalion. They can get things they need to live and continue functioning as a military unit in the field. Specifically, through direct communication with the chain of command, they can ask for news, orders, reinforcements, evacuation, rescue, air support, food, water, ammunition, equipment and medevac.

Outstanding, Sergeant, says the LT. *Can you send it back with a runner? Over.*

"Wilco, sir. Sending Private Williams now with the radio, over."
Solid copy, out.

"Collect these weapons and any ammo you can find," Ruiz tells the squad. "As for Doug Price here, we'll pick him up on the way back so he can be buried with respect."

A greater obligation

Lieutenant Bowman established his headquarters in the wide entry hallway of the school, surrounding a sprawling refugee camp of more than a hundred panicked civilians located directly adjacent to public lavatories and a water fountain.

At the end facing the main doors of the school, he placed his gun team, and at the other, facing the main stairs leading to the second floor of the trunk of the building, a SAW gunner detached from Second Squad.

This simple setup provides protection for the civilians while enabling them to access water and toilets, which he hopes will keep them calm, but not the soldiers' rucksacks, which are stacked near the front door under the watchful eyes of his gun team.

Sherman, holding an M4 carbine, scans the crowd for signs of trouble, shrugging at their requests for food, medicine, diapers, beer and cigarettes, plastic cups, blankets, rubbing alcohol, chocolate bars, more toilet paper and paper towels and soap, and a toilet plunger. He frequently glances at Hawkeye, lying groaning and sweating on a blanket under the care of Doc Waters, the platoon's combat medic.

Hawkeye is starting to stink.

"He's got Lyssa bad," the medic tells Sherman, dumbfounded. "He got bit by a Mad Dog and now he's turning into one. In hours. Something is definitely not right here."

"You think?" somebody mutters under his breath.

Bowman struck a deal with the civilians, allowing them to enter the platoon's defensive perimeter, and thereby become his problem, on two conditions. First, that they would not interfere with the operations of the men under his command. Second, that they would report any of them showing Lyssa symptoms, especially Mad Dog symptoms, so that they could be removed from the security zone and banished from the building.

So far, they have ignored the first promise and kept the second.

Beyond this, he is not sure what to do with them. He has orders to link up with First Platoon and Company HQ, and he will try to complete that mission for as long as he can. These civilians are only tying him down. And yet they are American citizens, and he has a greater obligation to protect them from harm.

His highest priority at this moment, however, is securing this building and giving his boys a well-deserved rest. They simply cannot keep up this pace. Already they are exhausted and using up their supplies at an alarming rate.

And the worst, he knows, is yet to come. Days of it. Even weeks of it. It may take a superhuman effort for his boys to stay alive just during the next twenty-four hours.

Doc Waters marches up to Bowman and says, "The men need to change their masks. They're getting caked with sweat and soot, and the men are forgetting to change them."

Bowman blinks in surprise. The platoon has bigger issues to deal with than Lyssa prevention. But of course the combat medic is right. Bowman nods and says he'll get on it.

"And sir," Doc Waters adds, "some of the men aren't wearing their masks at all anymore. This is majorly stupid, sir. We've had a rare morning, but the chance of infection is just as high now as it was yesterday." He glances at the civilians. "In fact, it's higher."

"All right, Doc," the LT says. "I'll see to it."

"Sir, we got incoming!" cries Bailey, the SAW gunner from Second Squad. He is lying on the floor, sighting down the barrel, which now rests on a bipod. "I got seven, no, eight hostiles on the main stairs."

The LT kneels next to Bailey and studies the Mad Dogs through his close-combat optic. They are Mad Dogs, seven of them sorry-looking specimens wearing paper gowns, and one wearing hospital scrubs. Three of them grin like clowns, their mouths and gowns stained red.

He wishes he could understand what motivates them. Don't they recognize their own friends and family? Why do they want to kill us? Why don't they attack each other?

The Mad Dogs pause and stand motionless, fists clenching and unclenching at their sides. They are still thirty meters away.

"What are you waiting for?" one of the civilians says. "Shoot them, for Chrissakes!"

Other civilians begin clamoring for them to open fire. A baby in the crowd starts screaming.

"Shall I light 'em up, sir?" says Bailey, gently placing his finger on the trigger.

"You know the ROE, Private Bailey," Bowman tells him. "We fire only if they threaten us. Right now they're not hostile."

The gunner glances up at him. "ROE, sir?"

"We're still operating under the rules of engagement issued by Quarantine last night."

"Well, they smell pretty threatening if you ask me, sir," Bailey says.

Bowman smiles despite himself.

Two of the Mad Dogs leap forward, snarling. The others quickly follow, sprinting with their characteristic loping gait.

They think like animals, Bowman thinks. They hunt in packs. Look at them go. They even run like animals. Why?

"You are cleared to engage," he says.

The SAW is a belt-fed light machine gun able to fire up to seven hundred fifty rounds per minute at an effective range of a thousand meters. It is a squad support weapon, typically used to set up a base of fire. It eats ammo fast and spits out a high volume of withering, murderous fire.

Bailey sights the first Mad Dog carefully and drops him with a single burst. He moves on to the next. Each time he shoots, the crowd emits a chorus of grating shrieks.

Bowman is starting to believe the civilians are actually trying as hard as they can to make his job irritating and complicated.

Then he tries to put himself in their shoes. As if several weeks of plague and chronic shortages weren't bad enough, their world is ending, they are refugees in their own land, and they are defenseless in a fratricidal war, hunted by a remorseless enemy that just hours ago was their son, their mother, their doctor, their priest, their oldest friend.

Now they're watching a SAW gunner cut some people in half.

Christ, he tells himself, the only reason you're still sane is you have a job to do. So try to cut these people a little slack, okay?

"Good shooting," he says.

"Sir? The Mad Dogs are a lot more aggressive than we were told, and there's a lot more of them than they told us there were."

"That's a very good observation, Private Bailey."

"I mean, is this, like, supposed to be the end of the world?"

"The Army has given me no such order," Bowman says.

The exchange reminds him of another important task he has yet to figure out how to do: Tell his people about the way the Mad Dog strain spreads, and what this means. Many of them, like Bailey, are already starting to put two and two together.

His handset chirps and Sergeant Lewis' voice deadpans, *War Dogs Two-Six, War Dogs Two-Six, this is War Dogs Two-Two, how copy, over?*

"War Dogs Two-Two, this is War Dogs Two actual, I copy, over."

War Dogs Two-Six, message follows, break. We have found an athletic facility in the main trunk, break. Hundreds, maybe a thousand, sick people on cots here, break. Some are in bad shape. Break. I see a lot of empty IV bags. Bedpans not being emptied. Meds aren't being passed out. Some of these people were apparently murdered in their beds. The survivors need aid. Over.

"Roger. I'll send Doc Waters down as soon as the building is cleared. Any sign of the CO or First Platoon, over?"

Negative. There's a lot of blood and brass. A lot of bodies who died of gunshot wounds. . . . No other sign of blue forces. Over.

"Any sign of medical staff, over?"

We see several body . . . parts that may be from the medical staff, over.

Bowman is starting to piece together what happened. First Platoon only had a squad manning the front entry. This unit was attacked from front and rear by Mad Dogs on the street and coming out of the gym. The rest of Captain West's command and First Platoon were attacked in isolated pockets, and probably destroyed. The medical staff was either slaughtered or infected and absorbed into the Mad Dog population.

"Friendly coming in!" a voice calls out from around the corner.

"Come on in, whoever you are," Bailey calls. "Mad Dogs can't talk, you know."

Bowman sees Private Williams come running up, carrying the SINC-GAR. Sherman rushes to greet him and immediately begins tinkering with it.

Negative contact, War Dogs Two-Six. How copy?

"That was a solid copy, over."

Correction: We have just found two riflemen from First Platoon. They're dead, over.

Bowman turns and glances over the civilians, some of whom stare back at him nervously. He can sense their distrust. It is almost palpable.

Somebody's got to survive.

"Have you discovered any provisions, such as food, blankets, medical supplies, over?"

Wait one. . . . Roger that, over.

"Continue with your mission, War Dogs Two-Two. Out." The LT calls to Williams. "Private, how many of the enemy have you seen?"

"Four, sir. All are, um, accounted for, sir."

"Go rejoin your unit, Private."

"Yes, sir."

There is no way only a few Mad Dogs overran a platoon of infantry and scattered them to the winds like this, Bowman thinks. There must be more of them, maybe hundreds. Where is the main force?

"Friendlies coming in!" a voice calls from the front doors.

"Come forward and be recognized!" Martin calls out, tensing behind his MG.

A soldier, blood splattered on his uniform and Kevlar, steps through the propped-open door and shows himself.

"Third Platoon here," the soldier says.

"Second Platoon here, boys," Boomer says. "Hey, looks like we beat you!"

"Hooah!" Martin yells, holding his fist in the air. "Yahoo!"

The doors open and the soldiers come staggering in. The boys of Second Platoon still in the area let up a ragged cheer. Even the civilians are grinning, hoping this means that law and order has returned to New York. But the cheers and grins fade quickly.

Some of the soldiers fall to their knees gasping, while others stare into space and walk like zombies. A few burst into tears, not even bothering to cover their faces. Several sit against the wall, light cigarettes with steel lighters, and hug their ribs.

"God, there's only fifteen, maybe twenty of them," Boomer hisses at Martin. "What the hell happened to the rest of their guys?"

An officer steps out in front of what is left of Third Platoon, wearing the insignia of a 2LT. Bowman instantly recognizes him as Lieutenant Stephen Knight.

Knight blinks into the fluorescent light of the hallway light fixtures. "Where's Captain West?"

Bowman weaves through the civilians until he is close enough to exchange a salute.

"Good to see you, Steve. It really is."

"Thank God you're here, Todd." His eyes widen in alarm. "Where are all your people?"

"Securing the building. Where's the rest of your guys?"

"I've got to report in," Knight tells him, shaking his head. "Can you take me to the CO?"

"He's not here, Steve."

Knight blinks rapidly, appearing dazed at the news. "But this is his headquarters," he says feebly. "His orders said for us to come here."

"We're still gathering intel on the situation here, but the Captain's command appears to have been overrun."

Another notch in the belt for the killah

In the school's east wing, Eckhardt, Mooney, Wyatt and Finnegan get in position to take down the school's chemistry lab, while Sergeant McGraw provides security in the hall with the other three boys of First Squad.

Eckhardt goes up the middle, while Mooney breaks right, Wyatt breaks left and Finnegan stays at the door in support.

Mooney immediately surmises that the room was used as a bivouac for elements of First Platoon. He sees cots, rucksacks, personal effects, helmets, gear and crates of ammo.

The beds are unmade. There are unfinished MREs on some of the chemistry tables.

Mad Dogs have been here. His nose burns from the sour stench lingering in the air.

Some kind of fight took place in this room. His boots crunch on broken glass, scatter the pages of letters from home. A light haze of smoke still hangs in the air. One of the cots is soaked through with drying blood, the blankets barely concealing a collection of body parts. Barely enough to be able to tell that whoever they belong to was human.

On the floor next to the cot, a neatly severed child's hand.

"Oh God," Mooney says quietly, swallowing hard.

He steps over a broken M4 and a handful of empty shell casings.

On the other side of the cot, three dead civilians lay in a heap on top of a soldier who died grimacing in pain. His scalp has been torn ripped off his skull and is sprouting from the mouth of one of the Mad Dogs, hair and all.

"No," Mooney says, then vomits neatly into the sink of one of the chemistry tables.

The other boys halt, waiting for him to finish. Nobody razzes him, not even Wyatt. Almost everybody has lost it at least once in the past ten hours.

Mooney rinses out his mouth and thinks for a moment. One squad, maybe two, were bivouacked here. Some got surprised while they were eating and were torn to pieces. Others got surprised in their sleep and were slaughtered in their beds. Most, however, seem to have vanished.

"It's okay," Mooney tells his comrades, feeling embarrassed. "I'm all right."

"Freeze," Eckhardt says.

The boys stop in place.

"I hear something," he adds. "Listen."

A wheezing sound among the cots and chemistry tables.

"I think there's somebody in here with us."

"One of those crazy people," Finnegan says, glowering with rage. "I'm going to kill him slow."

"Why would you say that?" says Mooney, spitting into the sink. "They're not people anymore. They're like animals. They don't even know what they're doing."

"Shut up, Mooney."

"He's a Mad Dog lover," says Wyatt, but nobody laughs.

"It might be one of our guys lying on the floor wounded," says Eckhardt. "Or a non-combatant. Think before you act, Finnegan. Now go get the Sergeant."

Finnegan signals to Sergeant McGraw that they have a possible contact, and the Sergeant enters the lab, toting his shotgun.

"All right now, let's clear this room," he says. "On your toes. Nice and slow."

The boys continue weaving their way through the cots and tables.

The wheezing stops, then starts again.

Mooney's heart is no longer in this. If McGraw were to suggest that they simply eat a bullet now and cop out on all this unreal horror, he would seriously consider it. He has not slept in more than twenty-six hours. During the last ten, he almost died after being chased by a horde of homicidal maniacs, hunted and shot down Mad Dogs during the cleanup at the hospital, reconnoitered the smoky horror show of First Avenue, marched a mile in full battle rattle, shot his way through a civilian riot, and cleared almost an entire floor of an abandoned middle school. He's bone tired and his morale, frankly, sucks.

Mostly, he is sick of the killing.

Soldiers get sloppy when they are this tired.

He feels a hand clutch his ankle. He staggers back, almost fainting.

An old man in hospital scrubs, dragging his gnarled legs behind him, leers up at him, sniggering and drooling. The hand reaches out and grips his ankle again. The bloody mouth opens in satisfaction: *Ah.*

Mooney screams and bayonets the man in the forehead, then promptly drops his rifle, falls on his ass and pisses himself.

The other boys gather around.

"Hardcore, Mooney," says Finnegan, excited. "Good on ya."

Wyatt says, "Another notch in the belt for the killah."

McGraw helps Mooney back onto his feet. "You okay, Private?"

"I think so, Sergeant."

"All right. Retrieve your weapon."

Wyatt laughs hysterically. Mooney glares at him. The noise returns. The boys instantly form a circle facing outward, establishing a defensive perimeter. Mooney pulls the bayonet out of the skull of the Mad Dog he killed, fighting back another urge to vomit and trying to ignore the unsettling sensation of wetness running down his pant leg.

McGraw signals at them to follow him across the room. Pausing at a secondary door leading into another hallway, he places his ear against it and listens.

Wheezing.

The sound electrifies them.

Mooney feels a hand on his ankle.

He looks down, his heart racing, but sees nothing there. He shakes his leg a little to free himself of the lingering feeling.

The sergeant makes a fist and punches the air several times in the direction of the door. *Prepare for action.* Mooney and the other boys raise their weapons, ready to fire.

McGraw opens the door.

The hall beyond is packed with Mad Dogs, many wearing paper gowns, others filthy and naked, waste running down their legs, shoving and drooling with their breath rattling in their chests. A wave of stink assails the soldiers, making them wince and their eyes fill with water. PFC Chen lowers his carbine and turns away, gagging.

The Mad Dogs begin growling.

Before either side makes a move, Mooney steps forward and kicks the door closed. Instantly, a score of hands begin clawing and banging on the door, which vibrates on its hinges.

"I didn't get to shoot my weapon!" Wyatt complains.

"That was quick thinking," McGraw says. "Private Mooney just saved our asses."

"What do you mean, Sergeant?"

"I think we just stumbled on an army of them," he explains. "The mother lode."

Payback time

The boys of First Squad exit the classroom out the other door and enter the hallway. McGraw points at his eyes with his index and middle fingers of his left hand, telling the security team to come forward. He holds his rifle over his head and points in the direction of the corner. He extends his flattened palm towards them.

The boys give him the thumbs up. They understand that the enemy has been sighted and is around the corner, and that they are to stay where they are.

The Sergeant quietly approaches the corner, peers around it, and instantly pulls his head back, holding up a finger to indicate that he guesses there are as many as a hundred hostiles occupying the hallway. He flashes several number signs and then bangs his fists together, telling them the enemy is about fifteen meters down the corridor.

Time to report this discovery to the LT.

He signals the squad to stay put in a defensive posture, and returns to the classroom. The Mad Dogs are still focused on the door, scraping at it with their nails. He gives the door the finger, and then keys his handset.

"War Dogs Two-Six, War Dogs Two-Six, this is War Dogs Two-One, how copy, over?"

War Dogs Two-One, this is War Dogs Two actual, standing by to copy, over.

"War Dogs Two, message follows, break. Be advised that we have identified a large group of Mad Dogs. Maybe two hundred of them, over."

Roger that, War Dogs Two-One. Outstanding. Do you have sufficient strength to engage and destroy enemy force, over?

McGraw grimaces and says, "Request alternative course of action, over."

Negative, over.

"I say again: Request alternative course of action. Over."

That's a no go. We have to secure this building. This has to be done or we will be forced to evac and find another building. And we'll have to clear that one, too. These are the facts we have to deal with. We literally do or die. Do you understand?

"Affirmative, sir."

Then complete your mission. Out.

He returns to the hallway. The boys look at him expectantly. Prepare for action, he signs to them, punching his first.

He tells First Squad's two SAW gunners that they will move forward, occupy the T intersection ahead, and set up a base of fire. The two grenadiers, Corporal Eckhardt and PFC Rollins, will shoot grenades into the enemy force from the flanks with their M203s, wreaking havoc while buying time for the SAW gunners to set up. The rest will provide support as well as security on their flanks.

The boys give the Sergeant a thumbs-up, their eyes gleaming with excitement.

They want to do this. They want action. For them, it's payback time.

McGraw raises his arm and does a single backstroke, telling First Squad to line up behind him in column file formation with the SAW gunners in the middle. He raises both arms and pushes his flattened palms toward each other until the boys tighten up their intervals to his satisfaction. The length of the column is now about the width of the hallway. Pumping his fist up and down, he tells them they will move at a slow run.

Finally, he does a wide forward "follow me" wave, telling them to move out.

His shooters jog into the open across the hallway, attracting the attention of the Mad Dogs, who snarl at them. A dozen immediately run towards the soldiers.

"Let 'em have it!" McGraw roars, unloading his shotgun at the closest infected and knocking them down with a single blast spraying more than twenty-five pellets of high-velocity buckshot. On his left, the boys hit the ground as Eckhardt and Rollins open up with their M203s, firing high-explosive forty-millimeter grenades over the heads of the Mad Dogs, tearing apart the infected crowded together about halfway down the hall.

Then the SAWs open up, tracers flying in blurred red sparks, knocking over Mad Dogs like bowling pins. They are far enough from the Mad Dogs that the weapons' beaten zones—the area of ground on which the cone of fire falls—covers the width of the hallway almost perfectly with minimal shifting fire. In other words, a turkey shoot. The guns spit out hundreds of empty shell casings, which ring against the floor and roll away. The devastation is so horrible, so complete and so disorienting that many of the Mad Dogs run straight into each other and into walls. But they do not stop. They do not appear to know fear, only an endless murderous rage that is now directed at First Squad's eight soldiers.

McGraw crouches behind one of the SAW gunners.

"You're aiming too high, " he says, watching the tracers. "Give them grazing fire, Ratliff."

More come spilling out of a side hallway. McGraw realizes he was wrong. There aren't two hundred Mad Dogs.

There are at least twice that.

A grenade becomes armed several moments early and explodes near the ceiling, bringing acoustic tile, fluorescent light fixtures, twisted metal tubing and water falling onto the heads of the onrushing horde. A severed arm flies spinning down the hallway and sails over Mooney's head, making him flinch.

"Did you see that?" Wyatt says.

"Out of HE, switching to buckshot!" Rollins calls out, coughing on dust and smoke.

"All right, Mooney, Wyatt, Finnegan, Chen, it's time to get in the game," McGraw says.

"About time," Wyatt yelps, and begins shooting with his carbine, a sustained series of metallic bangs. "Get some!"

"Rollins, you got any WP grenades?"

"I got three, Sergeant."

"Keep them handy in case we need to get out of here in a hurry and lay down some smoke to disorient the enemy."

"Not a problem, Sergeant."

"Take your time," McGraw tells his riflemen. "Choose your targets. Conserve your ammo. Make your shots count."

Mooney lines up his carbine's barrel using its iron sights, takes aim at the center of a woman's torso, and fires a short metallic burst on semi-auto, *pop pop*.

The carbine recoil hums against his shoulder, the spent shell casings fly into the air from its eject port, and then she is down. In close quarters marksmanship training, the Army taught him to fire two to the chest and one to the head to decisively neutralize an enemy. Here, however, he does not have to stop the enemy from shooting back, only stop them from advancing. No fancy shooting is needed; he only has to throw enough lead at each target to put them on the floor with the least amount of physical energy.

In fact, it is horribly easy for the squad to massacre all of these people. They are just flesh and bone.

"Reloading!" Eckhardt cries.

Mooney aims and fires again, and a man in BDUs just like his own drops onto the growing mound of corpses and body parts.

And again. And again.

The 5.56-mm rounds are high-velocity bullets that often plow straight through the body, tumbling in their trajectory and shredding organs and tissue as they pass through.

"Reloading!"

After a while, Mooney lets the training take over his body, giving his numb brain a rest and a chance to detach from the horror.

"How do you like me now?" Wyatt yells.

A pack of children dash towards the soldiers, snarling, hands reaching.

"Oh, Lord," Carrillo says, nearly blind with tears, and cuts them down with several bursts of his SAW.

"Reloading!" Mooney calls out.

The Mad Dogs never even get close.

Sergeant McGraw waves his hand in front of his face and yells, "Cease fire, cease fire!"

Mooney slumps against the row of metal lockers behind him and gulps air in quick gasps. The air is thick with cordite and an odor combining the rotten sour-milk stink of the infected with the sickly metallic smell of fresh blood.

The smoke hangs in the air like a shroud.

"That was starting to look a little dicey," says Ratliff, checking his SAW's ammo box. "I only got about ten rounds left on the belt."

Carrillo stares at the carnage while smoke rises up from his SAW, which started to overheat at the end.

"One of those kids looked just like my sister Jenny's boy," he rasps quietly, as if he is losing his voice. "But they're supposed to be in Florida. You don't think?"

"Naw," Ratliff says. He looks around for the Sergeant, sees that the man's back is turned, and pulls down his mask to light a cigarette. "Couldn't be."

"But it looked just like him," Carrillo says. "His name's Robbie."

"I can't believe this freaking carnage," Wyatt says. "It's ten times bigger than the hospital. It's mad sick, like a video game, yo."

Nearby, Chen quietly retches against the wall, moaning and mumbling to himself.

"It's not a game, you goddamn psycho," Eckhardt says, his face burning with shame. "You're not supposed to like it."

"We paid them back for what they did, that's all," Finnegan says grimly, kicking at the carpet of empty shell casings on the floor. "God knows the difference between a just kill and the kind you go to Hell for."

In Iraq, they had shot up cars, some filled with families, that disobeyed their orders to halt at a checkpoint. Men, women, children. An inevitable accident of war that filled many of the boys with regret and would stay with them for the rest of their lives. But this was intentional, against Americans, and on a colossal scale they never imagined possible.

And here was the Sergeant telling them they did a good job. That they secured the area and could rest soon. It's like getting a medal for My Lai. This is payback, and it tastes like ashes. They wanted this, they were hot to kill a million of those things after what they saw what happened to some of the boys of First Platoon, and now they are ashamed.

"They just kept coming," Ratliff says, shaking his head with something like admiration. "They wouldn't stop."

"They're not human anymore," Mooney says, his ears ringing and his headache returning with a vengeance.

"I'm starting to agree with you on that," says Eckhardt. "The way they looked at us. The way they moved. Definitely not human." He shivers. "It's like they were possessed by demons."

"Actually, they were possessed by a virus," Mooney tells him. "But you're not far off, Corporal."

"Did you see the ones wearing BDUs?" Ratliff says. "They were Army. Are we going to catch the bug and end up like that, too?"

McGraw is surveying the wreckage, stepping carefully among the mangled carpet of flesh, blood and human waste. An old woman, bleeding from a dozen wounds, crawls towards him on her hands and knees, hissing.

"I am truly sorry, Ma'am," he says, and shoots her in the head with his Beretta.

"Sergeant?" Finnegan says.

McGraw says, "If they can move, if they can bite, they're hostile. And we have to get through this hallway so we can clear the rest of this wing."

Mooney closes his eyes and wishes he were somewhere else. Instantly, his consciousness slides into black.

A bloody face lunges for his throat—

He jerks awake, adrenaline rushing through his body, and takes a deep breath.

"I am very sorry, sir," McGraw says. Another shot rings out.

Down the hall, a door opens and a voice calls to them:

"U.S. Army down here! Hold fire!"

"Same here," McGraw shouts back. "Howdy!"

"Is that Second Platoon?" the soldier says, stepping out of the room at the end of the hall, coughing on the smoke and stink. "Hooah, boys! First Platoon here!"

"We've been looking all over for you guys," McGraw says, grinning.

"We heard all hell breaking loose and stayed down. Oh Jesus, hell, what is this?"

The soldier is surveying the walls painted with blood and the piles of body parts and bodies, some of which are still moving, like a carpet of giant bloody worms.

His eyes roll back in his head and he faints. Other soldiers come out and gaze upon the slaughter in disbelief and shock, while a few run back where they'd come from to vomit in privacy.

Private Chen pauses behind Sergeant McGraw and swallows hard. He can't stop looking at the faces. The arms and legs, the guts and organs, the pools and streaks of blood, he can take that. But he can't take the faces. All those eyes looking back at him.

"We're all just meat, aren't we," he says.

"Maybe so," McGraw answers.

Chen can't take the hands, either. All those cold, open hands that feel nothing.

"I'm sorry, Sergeant."

The Sergeant turns, squinting. "What's that, Private?"

The feet. The hundreds of feet that will never walk again.

"That I can't come with you."

His voice has a shaky quality that makes everybody stop and look at him.

Chen laughs nervously as he puts the tip of his carbine into his mouth.

And promptly pulls the trigger.

Chapter 7

Can you help me?

Shivering in a ball under a desk in the Institute's Security Command Center, Petrova dreams that Dr. Baird has burst howling through the lab door.

She has dreamed this dream continuously since she fell asleep.

It is always the same.

She flees, and at first she is able to run faster than she ever has in a dream, faster even than she can in real life, but the fluorescent hallway is endless and its brightness rapidly dims as some ominous unseen presence eats the light. Suddenly, her strength begins failing and she can barely move despite mental pushes she gives herself in her sleep.

But this time the dream is different.

A phone rings shrilly, and she turns to see Dr. Baird at the end of the hall, grinning in triumph with bloody teeth and holding a clump of hairy, mangled flesh high over his head like a primitive trophy. Black fluid begins gushing from his eyes and grin.

Just meat, he says.

His face crumbles. Faster and faster, his head and arms dissolve as his body is converted into organic black fluid.

The liquid splashes against the floor and slithers forward like a million oily snakes, probing blindly, driven by an ancient program.

The liquid is pure virus seeking its new host.

She wants to scream, but she can't breathe.

The snakes coil and whisper in a million voices, *We are life.*

The phone rings again.

She turns and tries to run—

Baird bursts through a wall in front of her, broken cinderblocks flying in a cloud of dust, bellowing with rage and pain.

A phone is ringing.

I'm so cold, please don't make me get up—

Baird roars, shaking the building, making the light fixtures blink and fall out of the ceiling, but he is already fading.

Petrova's eyes flash open, her heart in her throat, her body clenched and gasping for air. Extricating herself carefully from under the desk, she quickly scans the operator desk and sees a phone with a red light flashing.

It rings—

She picks it up warily, still haunted by the dream and uncertain of everything.

"This is Dr. Valeriya Petrova," she says thickly, rubbing at a lancing pain in her neck. "Who is this?"

"Dr. Petrova?" a voice asks feebly.

"This is Dr. Petrova. Who is this?"

"Can you help me?"

Get the hell out of my lab

Lucas was taken first.

He ran several yards before he seemed to become winded and simply laid down and curled up into a ball. He barely struggled when Baird fell to his knees and sank his teeth into his arm.

After Petrova and Saunders turned the corner, Saunders slowed to a stop.

"We must go, Doctor," she said.

The scientist frowned as if trying to work out a complex math problem. "No," he said slowly. "We have to help Dr. Lucas."

"He has surely been bitten," she told him. "Which means he is already dead."

"You know, I don't even know his first name," Saunders laughed.

"You are ugly and I hate you," she hissed fiercely in a sudden fit of stress, surprised at herself for saying such things, especially since they were true. "Come with me. Now. Please, William."

"See what I mean?" His voice sounded weak and thin. "It's 'Bill.'

Nobody's called me William since I was ten."

He turned and jogged back around the corner to help Lucas, who was emitting a strange, high-pitched mewing sound, like a cat being slowly crushed.

"Please, William," she whispered.

She heard Saunders shouting. The shouts quickly turned into bloodcurdling screams.

"Oh," she said, and started running.

While she ran, she tried to remember how many people were trapped with her at the Institute. Hardy, Lucas, Saunders, Sims, Fuentes . . . Ten. There were ten people on this floor, and five of them were already either infected or dead.

She needed to warn the others, quickly, before Baird decided to go hunting.

And after that, what?

Find a safe place where they can hide and figure out what to do next.

She entered Laboratory East on unsteady legs and saw Dr. Sims and Sandy Cohen, a lab tech, working in gowns, masks, goggles and gloves. Sims was busy injecting reaction fluid into a strip of PCR tubes for a polymerase chain reaction test. Cohen was snapping digital pictures of Lyssa using the camera built into the lab's fluorescence microscope.

Petrova's eyes went straight to several glass Petri dishes on the desktop next to Sims. Each dish contained pure samples of Lyssa grown in cultured cells harvested from a dog's kidney.

At first, she was unable to speak, her mind numbed by the violence and adrenaline, somehow dumbfounded by the sight of her coworkers performing mundane tasks as if nothing had happened.

"Listen to me," she said shakily, then paused, suddenly out of breath.

Dr. Fred Sims, the oldest scientist on the staff at sixty-eight, turned and glared at the interruption. Giving Petrova the once-over, he quickly sized up her sweaty face, disheveled hair, spray of blood on her labcoat, and gleaming steel putter she still clutched in her hands.

"Dr. Petrova, you look unwell," he said, peering at her over the top of his spectacles. "Don't you think it's a bit early in the day for . . . whatever it is you're doing?"

"We are in serious danger."

"Now, if you please, get the hell out of my lab."

"Oh!" she said, blinking and stomping her right foot.

"I said, get out."

"Dr. Sims!"

"You. Are. Contaminating. My. Work."

"Frederick, listen to me," she said.

Sims' eyebrows arched with surprise. "Frederick, is it? Well. All right then, go on, tell me what's wrong, my child." He glanced over Petrova's shoulder. "And what in God's name happened to you, good sir?"

Petrova turned and watched Baird limp into the lab, his head twitching violently, smacking his lips, blood and foamy drool soaking his chin and T-shirt.

Cohen lurched to her feet and took several quick steps backwards. To Petrova, she seemed so helpless in her gown and mask and gloves, so cumbersome and slow.

"I don't understand," Sims said, his eyes widening with alarm. "This is very strange. What's this all about?"

Baird's bloodshot eyes focused on the golf club in Petrova's hands. He suddenly stopped, glowering, and growled deep in his throat, drool pouring out of his contorted mouth.

Cohen bumped into a chair behind her, knocking it over.

As if waiting for this cue, Baird lunged with a bestial snarl.

Cohen ran out of the Lab's other door, followed by Petrova.

Behind them, Sims emitted a single strangled cry.

The hallway was empty by the time Petrova reached it. Cohen had disappeared. She bolted down the hall as fast as she could on her heels, turned the corner, and ran directly into Stringer Jackson, making her nose sting and her eyes flood with tears. She had completely forgotten about him sitting in the Security Command Center, watching over them on the security screens.

She turned and pointed, stammering and blubbering, unable to express herself.

"I know," said Jackson. "I'm on it. Do you know how to get to the Security Center?"

Petrova nodded.

"Then go," he told her. "The door's unlocked. Go in and lock it. I'll be there soon."

She briefly wondered how Stringer Jackson, the retired, grizzled, middle-aged and overweight cop, was going to take on Baird in a hand to hand fight and win. But she did not care. She had done her part. It was up to the professionals to take care of things from here.

She did not see what happened next.

Within moments, she entered the Security Command Center and burrowed under the operator's desk, shaking with fear. The whirr and heat of the electronics almost instantly lulled her into a deep sleep.

Thank God he is not a Mad Dog

More like a mouse squeaking than a human voice.

Petrova grips the phone in her sweating hand. "Who is this, please?"

"I'm all alone and I need somebody to come and get me."

For some reason, she pictures her boy Alexander in her mind, speaking into a phone in a dark, bare room in London, all alone.

"Please, please tell me who is speaking," she says, panicking.

"Sandy. Sandy Cohen?"

"I know who you are, Sandy."

Petrova does not know her well. The woman is a lab tech like Marsha Fuentes, and has been working at the Institute for about six months. She always wear glasses with thick black frames, making her stand out in Petrova's memory.

"We just saw each other in the Lab."

"Obviously. Where are you?"

"I have to speak quietly or he'll come find me. What is happening here?"

"There are Mad Dogs in the building and they are turning other staff members into Mad Dogs by biting them," Petrova tells her.

"I'm not following you," says the feeble voice.

"Where are you, Sandy?"

"I'm in Dr. Saunders' office. I'm using his phone."

"Good. Please hold for a moment."

"Is this the security room? I was trying to call Stringer."

"Please be quiet for a moment, Sandy."

Petrova scans the images displayed by the digital projectors onto the large wall screens. One shows an empty hallway scarred by a long, dark smear on the floor, while the other shows an empty Laboratory East. She looks at the computer screen on the desk, which presents a series of icons used to control the security functions of the Center. The interface is fairly intuitive and within moments she is able to access images from all of

the Institute's cameras. She'd never known the place was so heavily mon-
itored, with cameras in all of its public spaces.

Things have changed a lot since she burrowed under the operator desk
and slept.

Baird is lying face down in one of the hallways at the end of a long dark
smear, twitching. Probably dying by inches because of his wounds. Who
knew how much damage his body had taken when she pummeled him
with the golf club, or when he burst through the door, or during whatever Jackson did to him after that.

On the other screen, showing the hallway outside Laboratory West,
Lucas and Fuentes are hunting together, sniffing at doors.

Petrova watches with interest.

They do not attack each other, only us, she tells herself. Is this the reason for the odor they produce? An olfactory cue that another person is
already infected, and therefore "safe"? How else would they recognize
each other?

They pass Saunders lying on the ground. Saunders twitches and slowly
gets to his feet. One of his ears has been gnawed off, but he doesn't seem
to mind.

Petrova pushes a button on her keyboard to bring up another image on
the screen.

The image shows the majestic main lobby downstairs, populated by a
mob of people, many of them waving at the security camera. A beautiful
blonde in their midst—whom Petrova recognizes from a TV series she
used to watch—is holding up a sign that says, *NOW! OR WE KILL THE OTHER
ONE.*

Despite her fascination with what is happening down there, it is not her
immediate concern. She forces herself to continue exploring the facility
on her screens.

Empty hallways.

An empty elevator lobby.

An empty auditorium.

An empty records room.

A corridor with a man's broken body propping open the door to the
east-side Men's Room. Petrova instantly recognizes him as Dr. Sims.

Her first thought: He is dead.

She cannot prevent her second thought, which fills her with shame:
Thank God. Thank God he is not a Mad Dog.

In the image produced on the other screen, Joe Hardy lies on his back in a large puddle of his own blood in Laboratory West. His eyes are open and his face is a mask of horror. Miraculously, he survived long enough to pick up his phone, which is now in his hand. She wonders if he ever answered it.

She suddenly cannot bare to look at him. She quickly brings up an image of another hallway. A pair of legs in men's trousers are protruding from one of the offices. Another person is hurt.

"Hello? This is Sandy. Are you still there, Dr. Petrova?"

"Just one more minute, Sandy."

"I was just thinking about Dr. Sims. He's dead, isn't he?"

"Please wait."

"We left him there and he died, right?"

"Sandy. Please. I am working on a way to get you out of there safely."

Petrova rapid-fires through the remaining images, all of them empty spaces, and performs a quick calculation in her mind: There are now five uninfected people at most, including Sandy Cohen and herself, cowering in their various hiding places, most likely in the offices.

Go back, a voice in her head tells her.

She cycles through the camera images in reverse order, searching randomly until she becomes frustrated. Whatever she was trying to tell herself, she's lost it now.

"What am I looking for?" she asks out loud, feeling irritated.

"Dr. Petrova? Is there somebody there with you?"

"No, Sandy. I am alone."

"Stringer isn't there?"

"I am speaking to my—"

The voice in her head suddenly shouts: *Stringer!*

Ignoring Cohen's questioning, she clicks to the image of Sims lying in the doorway to the Men's Room.

"Oh," she says quietly.

Behind Sims, in the mirror on the bathroom wall, she can see Jackson looking at himself, far enough from the camera so that the resolution is not very good, but close enough for her to see what he is doing.

He is poking very gingerly at his right eye. Or rather, his left eye, which only looks like his right eye in the mirror. Yes, he is poking at his eye.

Or rather, what is left of his eye.

Jackson, the retired, overweight, out-of-shape cop, beat Baird. But

Baird bit his face and ruined his left eye.

Jackson's clearly in shock. And almost certainly infected.

He has not yet turned, but it is only a matter of time.

Trust me

There are now four infected people in their section of the building, and two, possibly three uninfected survivors trapped inside with them.

"Sandy, listen to me," she says into the phone. "I am looking at the security camera feeds and they are showing me the corridor outside Dr. Saunders' office."

"Can you see if Dr. Baird is still around?"

"It is not Dr. Baird anymore, Sandy," Petrova says. "In any case, he is dead."

"Oh my God."

Petrova grips the phone, her hand and ear slick with sweat.

"Drs. Lucas and Saunders are now infected and have become Mad Dogs themselves," she says. "And Marsha Fuentes."

"There's three of them now?"

"I am afraid so. Actually, four. Stringer Jackson has been bitten. He has not yet become a Mad Dog, but I believe he will transform soon, which is why it is essential you try to get to me now, where it is safe."

"That's not supposed to happen. You can't become a Mad Dog if you get bitten. You only get it if the virus enters the brain. And no virus has an incubation period that short—"

Petrova sighs loudly. "I cannot get into the details, but what I am telling you is true."

"Well, I can't stay here forever with those things around, Dr. Petrova," Cohen says, her voice edged with hysteria. "You have to help me. You have to make them leave."

"I cannot do that, Sandy."

"Make them leave. Please. Please."

"Listen to me. I cannot make them leave, but I can see where they are by using the security cameras. That means I can tell you when it is generally safe to come to my location."

"You want me to leave here and go out there? Are you freaking nuts?"

"Right now, Dr. Lucas and Marsha Fuentes are in the auditorium and heading towards the elevator lobby," Petrova says, rapidly scanning the flipping images on the screens. She blinks, surprised at how fast the Mad Dogs move. "And Dr. Saunders, um, is now in Dr. Hardy's office."

"Saunders is too close!" Cohen hisses.

"If you go now, you can make it."

"What if there's another one of these Mad Dogs in one of the offices?"

Petrova admits the possibility to herself, but there is no other way to get Cohen to the safety of the Security Command Center without her eventually abandoning the relative security of her hiding place. There is no sure thing here. She has to take a chance or stay where she is, cut off from food and water and help.

"I know for a fact that there are no other Mad Dogs," she lies. "Trust me. Do you know the way to the Command Center?"

"But after I hang up, I won't know where they are."

"This is a good time for you to leave Dr. Sims' office and come here."

She can hear Cohen taking deep breaths, getting up her nerve.

"No!" she hisses. "I can't."

Petrova thinks for a moment, then says, "Do you have a cell phone? If you do, then we could stay on the line together, and I can walk you here safely."

"Yes, I have one. But all the lines are jammed, aren't they?"

"It is possible to get through. So try. Please." She reads Cohen the direct dial number of the phone in the Security Command Center. "Call now. Try a few times. If it doesn't work, then call me again using the interoffice line, which we know so far is reliable."

Before Cohen can respond, she hangs up.

The silence is startling.

Panicking, she flips through the images until she sees Baird lying on the floor. He is no longer twitching. He is dead. Really and truly dead. Thank God.

Aaa-aah-aaaahhhh

She bites her lip hard to prevent these little shrieks from sliding into uncontrollable hysteria. Wrapping her arms around her ribs, she rocks back and forth.

The phone rings, sending an electric wave of adrenaline through her body. She snatches up the phone, bathed in the glow of the screens.

"Yes?"

"I got through! I can't believe it."

"Keep your voice down," Petrova hisses.

"I'm on my cell."

"That is good. I will guide you, Sandy."

Petrova scans the images until she confirms the positions of the Mad Dogs and Jackson, who is still at the mirror, staring dumbly at himself and probing his ruined eye.

"This is a good time," she says. "You can go. But hurry."

"All right, I'm up," Cohen tells her.

Sandy Cohen appears on the left screen, dancing from foot to foot to restore her circulation. She is still wearing the white gown she had on in the lab, which flaps around her legs.

"Can you see me?" she asks.

"Go now. Keep going. Keep going. Keep going. Stop. Stop! Go into the office on your right. Now!"

Cohen disappears from the screen. Seconds later, Saunders appears, his hands balled into fists clasped against his chest and his head jerking like a bird's. He stops outside the office Cohen entered, appearing to sniff the air.

"Do not move even slightly, Sandy," Petrova whispers into the phone.

Saunders turns, runs down the hall and enters East Lab.

"Now. Go. Now."

The lab technician darts out into the hall on tip toes, looking both ways, holding the phone against her ear.

"Turn right at the end of the hall," Petrova tells her.

Cohen turns the corner and abruptly freezes in her tracks, putting her hand over her mouth.

Petrova curses herself. The horrors that she has already begun to digest are new to Cohen. She should have warned the woman about what she was going to see.

"That is Dr. Baird," she says. "He is dead. He is no threat to you."

"Oh my God," Cohen says.

"Be quiet," Petrova says. "Dr. Lucas and Fuentes are heading in your direction. You can make it, but you must go now."

She sees Cohen nod vigorously, dance around Baird's corpse, and begin walking rapidly towards the Security Center, looking over her shoulder every few steps to make sure nobody is coming up behind her.

Petrova says, "You are doing just fine. You are very close now."

"Almost there," Cohen huffs, already out of breath.

"You can do it," Petrova tells her.

The digital projector blinks out, the lights shut off and Petrova is plunged into darkness and silence so total she wonders if she's dead.

She sits in the dark, her heart pounding against her ribcage and her blood crashing in her ears.

The power has gone out.

The phone in her hand is dead.

She can hear Cohen shouting, "Hello? Hello?" out in the hall, the sound muffled and distant.

"Be quiet," Petrova hisses at the dark. "Be quiet or they will find you."

The woman is not far away. She's about thirty feet down the hall, in fact.

"The power's out, Dr. Petrova!" Cohen wails. "Help me!"

Petrova hears thuds against the wall.

"Oh, no," she says.

"Help me, please!"

Cohen is not being attacked. She is banging against the wall with her fists, which Petrova can hear in the Command Center.

That is how close she is. Closer even than Petrova initially thought.

"Come and get me! Please!"

And if she keeps this up, she is going to get herself killed or infected.

Petrova formulates a plan on the spot. She knows where the door is and believes she can find it in the dark easily. She will open it and guide Cohen to safety using her voice before the woman's screaming brings every Mad Dog in the place running.

Only she doesn't move. She is literally frozen with fear.

Cohen is still shouting for help.

Petrova begins to crawl back under the operator's desk, burrowing into the wires and the dust and the cobwebs and the residual heat of the electronics.

The last thing Petrova hears before she falls asleep is the horrible sound of a struggle that she takes into her dreams with her.

Chapter 8

We are the world's most powerful military
and we are being beaten on our own ground

Lieutenants Bowman and Knight, joined by their platoon sergeants Kemper and Jim Vaughan, stand on the roof of the Samuel J. Tilden International Middle School, which their units have cleared and secured, and listen to the gunfire in the city.

The school is only a couple of stories tall but even this high up, they have an almost antiseptic view of the city's Midtown district. The buildings block their view of the wholesale slaughter going on at the street level of the city. But they can hear it.

To Bowman, leaning against the parapet and gazing out into the smoky haze produced by scores of unchecked fires, it is as if New York itself were a giant body, its people healthy cells one by one being converted into virus that is beating the crap out of the body's immune system.

And to carry this analogy further, the immune system, well, that would be two brigades of infantry of the U.S. Army, about six thousand men and women in all—each a highly trained and heavily armed lean, green fighting machine.

We are the world's greatest military and we are being beaten on our own ground, he thinks. By the people we swore to protect, armed only with tooth and nail.

On the other side of the roof, Sergeant Lewis fires his M21 sniper rifle. He is up here fighting his own private war, shooting Mad Dogs down in the street behind the school.

"I still can't believe it," Knight says. "Is this really happening?"

"It's a numbers game, Steve," Bowman tells him. "You take five guys who develop Mad Dog symptoms. They each bite one other person and that one other person turns into a Mad Dog. Then that person bites somebody else. Every couple of hours."

Knight whistles. "Jesus, do the math!"

"Suppose just ten percent of the population of this city becomes a Mad Dog. Just one out of ten. And then suppose we had the men and the weapons and a safe position to shoot them down from."

Knight finishes for him. "There aren't enough bullets."

Bowman nods. "It's a numbers game. There's no way to stop this. It's only going to get worse. In a few hours, maybe a day, ten percent becomes twenty percent. A flood."

Across the street, a civilian in a private office has noticed them and is holding up a sign against his window that says: TRAPPED, HELP.

The officers move to another part of the roof, seething with shame.

They can only help those they can without risking the security of the unit. For a moment, Bowman thinks of Reinhold Niebuhr's Serenity Prayer, which his uncle Gabe, a recovering alcoholic in AA, taught him when he was ten years old: *God, grant me the serenity to accept the things I cannot change, courage to change the things I can, and wisdom to know the difference.*

"Who could pull the trigger that many times anyhow?" Knight wonders.

"Private Chen couldn't," Bowman murmurs. The soldier wouldn't be the last who would rather eat a bullet than fight this war, either.

Knight continues, "One of the reasons we got chewed up so bad all the way here is some of my boys just couldn't shoot Americans." He glances at his platoon sergeant, then looks away. "Have you, uh, shared your discovery with your platoon?"

"They're not dumb," Bowman says. "They know what's going on. It's just that nobody's said it out loud for them yet. They haven't had a minute to think about it."

"Yes," says Knight.

"I guess we'll have to tell them."

They flinch as the muffled boom of an explosion reaches their ears. A large cloud of smoke and dust billows out from behind a building between them and Times Square. Even yesterday, this would have been remarkable to them. Today, they take it in stride.

Knight laughs viciously. "We're going to tell them how their families, and everybody they know, are probably dying or being converted into those things out there."

"We're going to tell them to do their jobs, Steve."

Lewis fires his rifle, which discharges with a loud bang.

"It's getting personal, Todd. You better come up with something better than that if you want them to keep fighting for a country that's falling apart around them."

Bowman looks at Knight in surprise. "Why me?"

Knight smiles sadly. "You're the one who's in charge here, Todd."

"We're the same rank, but you've got seniority over me. You've got seniority over Greg Bishop of First Platoon, too. You're in command."

"On the way over here . . ." Knight looks at Sergeant First Class Vaughan, who stares back at him stonily, his expression inscrutable behind his N95 mask. "I was one of the people who couldn't shoot. I couldn't even give the order. I froze. It was Sergeant Vaughan here that got us out."

"Damn, Steve," Bowman says quietly.

He glances at Vaughan, but the NCO is a professional and while his face is flushed, making the diagonal scar across his face livid, his gray eyes give nothing away.

Knight says, "A lot of my boys are dead because I couldn't tell them to shoot."

Tears stream down the officer's face. Vaughan lowers his eyes. Knight looks away, gazing at the skyscrapers.

"Twenty-five percent casualties," he adds. "But you know what?" He hisses, fiercely, "If I could go back and do it all over again, I still wouldn't give that goddamn order."

Bowman says nothing. He had given the order to shoot. He personally not only shot Mad Dogs, he also shot down uninfected civilians who got in his way.

By any definition, he is a murderer and a war criminal. He knows it. His own platoon sergeant knows it. The two men were made from the same stuff; he saw Kemper do the same as him to get the platoon out of the riot and to safety.

And if they did not do what they did, if they were not war criminals, they might all be dead right now.

Nevertheless, he can't shake the feeling that he is damned.

The officers hear the piercing wail of a fire engine, punctuated by the bursts of its horn. It is a plucky sound amid the rattle of small arms fire and distant screams, reminding them that somewhere, out there, people are still fighting back against the rising tide of violence and anarchy.

The sound reminds them that it is not every man for himself out there. Not yet.

Similarly, the power continues to cut in and out, but somebody is still manning the controls at the power plant, and somebody is still delivering coal to burn to make electricity. In all the jobs that matter, from cop to soldier to paramedic to power plant operator, people are still doing their duty. Bowman finds strength in this idea.

Knight wipes the tears from his face and clears his throat.

"I wouldn't give the order," he says. "I guess that makes me a nice guy or something. But I have no right to lead Charlie." He sighs. "We should have stayed where we were. We were doing some good there."

"No," Bowman says. His eyes follow a pair of helicopters moving over the East River until they disappear behind a tall building. He takes it as a good sign that there are still birds in the air. "Captain West had the right idea trying to concentrate the Company. Warlord is spread out all over Manhattan and is vulnerable to being destroyed piecemeal. But it's too late. We got chewed up. We should have consolidated sooner."

"Maybe you're right," Knight says. "We shouldn't have been spread out in the first place, then. It's a mystery. I have a hard time believing that either the government or the Army didn't know about the infection rate among the Mad Dogs."

"Could be they were trying to avoid pushing an already panicked country into outright hysteria," Bowman says. "Could be that they honestly didn't know. Who knows? Right now, my situational awareness extends to what I can see with my own eyes."

"Well, if somebody higher up knew about this and didn't tell us, they may have just destroyed our brigade."

Bowman stares at him intensely and says, "Hell, Steve. Forget Quarantine. If somebody higher up knew and didn't tell us, they may have destroyed the U.S. Army."

Gaps in the chain of command

Sherman tries again to raise Warlord, the call sign for Battalion, and

Quarantine, which is Brigade's call sign, without success.

"Warlord, Warlord, this is War Dogs, do you copy, over?"

No answer from Battalion. The Battalion net is being overloaded with chaotic messages blending together into one long screech. From what the RTO can tell, War Hammer is screaming for reinforcements and ammunition, Warmonger reports the successful occupation of the old Seventh Regiment Armory Building, and War Pig says it has three men down and where's their goddamn medevac.

"Warlord, Warlord," Sherman says, then stops. It's useless.

Sherman switches to the Brigade net and tries to hail Quarantine.

Nobody answers. The only officer he can get a hold of, as they say in the ranks, is General Confusion. The voices on the Brigade net are less panicked than Charlie's sister companies, but equally confused. There are units missing, trying to consolidate, requesting orders, demanding resupply, on the move, taking casualties. There are gaps in the chain of command. Units are disappearing or moving without their commanders knowing it.

When Quarantine's XO finally makes an appearance on the net, it is apparently without his knowledge or consent, as he's shouting at somebody else in the room about a story that *The New York Times* is writing about the Army's sudden decision to lay waste to New York and almost every other major city in the country.

Somebody else, Sherman does not recognize the voice, says there is not going to be a *New York Times* tomorrow morning, and then the transmission cut out.

The civilian nets are even more ominous.

National Guard units defending City Hall have abandoned their positions and moved north, and protestors have occupied the building and are busy turning it into a fortress. The commander of the Guard unit was found dead at his post. The Mayor is missing. Right now, there is nobody running the government of New York City.

Meanwhile, operators are still calling first responder units, but units are not reporting back. The nets are going silent one by one, populated only by panicked operators asking over and over if anybody can hear them.

A cop gets on the net, says he has eyes on a group of vigilantes lynching five Lyssa victims from streetlight poles, and requests backup, but there is no help to give. Frustrated, the cop breaks protocol by asking the operator if there is a fucking plan.

Sherman senses that the government and the military are holding something back from the people who live here, but the people already know about it, and have begun to take matters into their own hands.

It is interesting, but ultimately not his concern.

He switches to Charlie Company's net and resumes his search for Fourth Platoon, which had been on Third Platoon's heels during the march to the school but suddenly disappeared and is now considered lost.

All of this makes for discouraging work for a radio/telephone operator, but a good RTO must have the patience of a saint, and Sherman is good at his job. He is not complaining. Even though he is not getting through to anybody, the traffic is more entertaining than he has ever heard it.

Things are bad, but like all crises, this too shall pass, he believes. He tells himself the government and the Army will fix it when those in charge finally get their heads out of their collective asses and do what needs doing. The United States survived the First and Second World Wars, Cold War, Spanish Flu Pandemic, Presidents Nixon through Obama, the Great Depression and the September Eleventh attacks. It can survive this lousy Lyssa Pandemic. Someday, he will tell his kids about how scary and exciting it all was, and he and his comrades will be called the Greatest Generation by their grandchildren.

He likes working alone so that he can take off his mask and smoke without any hassles. Lighting one up, he realizes that he is down to four packs now and after that, with all the supply problems he has been hearing about, there might not be any more cigarettes for a while. The thought fills him with panic. A lot of the boys smoke for fun, but he is an addict. He tries to put this unsettling train of thought out of his mind by throwing himself back into his work.

When he switches back to Brigade traffic, a strong, gravelly voice cuts through the babble:

This is Quarantine actual. Clear the net. Break.

The voice is calm, almost dry, but the effect is electrifying. Within moments, the chatter is reduced by more than half.

I say again: This is Quarantine actual. Clear the net. Break.

Sherman takes out his notepad and pencil, excited. He has only rarely heard Colonel Winters, the commander of the Brigade, get on the net in person.

All elements of Quarantine, this is Quarantine actual. Message follows, break.

You don't see that every day

McLeod paces just inside the doors to the school. About ten meters down the hallway, Martin and Boomer pass a cigarette back and forth, leaning on the sandbags of their MG emplacement. McLeod strolls over, cradling his SAW.

"*Salaam 'Alaykum*, boys," he says.

The gunners nod. McLeod watches in amusement as they turn away and pull down their masks to take a drag.

He adds: "You guys do realize that if one of you has Lyssa, the other now has it."

"Go to hell, McLeod," Boomer says.

"What do you mean?" Martin says.

"You're sharing a smoke," McLeod explains. Seeing their blank expressions, he shakes his head. "Never mind."

"This is not a good time to go around scaring people," Boomer warns him.

"What a crappy post," McLeod says darkly. "A freaking school. Look at this poster some kid made with a bunch of crummy markers: 'Welcome back' in a hundred languages. Christ, I'd rather be in goddamn Baghdad getting shot at."

"I'll bet you were one of the most popular guys in high school," Martin deadpans, making the AG snort with laughter. "Because you're such a comedian."

"Sleep deprivation makes me hilarious." McLeod yells at the ceiling, "I need sleep!"

"Why aren't you bunking with your squad, McLeod?" Martin says, winking at Boomer, who grins back.

"Magilla's got it in for me. Everybody else gets to sleep a few hours, while I'm stuck doing guard duty with—no offense—you guys."

Boomer bursts into laughter while Martin says, "You're lucky that's all you got."

"Are you kidding? What'd I ever do to anybody?"

"Have you ever tried seeing what would happen if you maybe shut your big mouth, McLeod?" Boomer says.

McLeod smiles and says nothing.

Boomer adds, "Looks like you're as popular in the Army as you were in high school, McLeod. Count yourself lucky you're not shoveling body parts into the basement furnace with the Hajjis—I mean, the civilians."

"Instead, you got guard duty," Martin says, gesturing toward the front doors of the school. "Hmm. Aren't you supposed to be like, you know, guarding?"

"Nobody's going to come here," McLeod tells him.

"It's a Lyssa hospital in the middle of a Lyssa plague," Martin says, taking off his cap and making a show of scratching his closely shorn head. "Hmm."

"Yeah, I wonder if anybody's coming," the AG says, cracking up now.

"Shush, I'm thinking," Martin says, still in character.

"Quiet for a sec," says McLeod. "Listen."

In the distance, they hear the roar of a diesel engine.

A large vehicle is approaching the school.

He adds, "Oh thank God, they're starting to pick up the trash again."

The MGR rolls his eyes and says, "Boomer, stay here, I'm going to go with McFly and check it out."

"Roger that."

"Lead the way, McDuff."

"You're a very funny guy," McLeod says. "It must run in the family. Just the other night, your mom—hey, that sounds military, doesn't it?"

The sound grows louder as they approach the doors and open them cautiously, peering out at the corpse-strewn street.

"Lookit, it's an LAV," Martin says, raising his fist. "Go, Marines! Get some!"

The armored personnel carrier, shaped like a large green boat on eight wheels, turns onto their street from several blocks away, its engine grinding.

"I want one of those," says McLeod.

"It's the LAV-R," Martin says. "See the boom crane on the back? It's got a winch so it can recover other LAVs that break down. The recovery model doesn't have much for defense, just the single M240 and some smoke grenades." He adds admiringly, "You should see the fighting version. It's got an M242 Bushmaster chain gun and two M240s. I saw one once. In action, too. It was freaking cool. The Iraqis call these babies the Great Destroyers."

"I hear she's single, tiger," McLeod says.

"They can go sixty miles an hour and drive underwater, man."

"Uh oh, they got company. Check it out."

The LAV-R has completed its turn and guns its engine to pick up speed. The vehicle is surrounded by a crowd of about twenty Mad Dogs running alongside it. A few somehow clawed their way on top and are beating on the armor with their fists.

The vehicle accelerates on the open street and the Mad Dogs begin to lag behind.

"I didn't even know the Marines were in Manhattan," Martin says. "We got no commo with them. Should we run out and try to tell them we're here?"

McLeod snorts. "Be my guest."

The LAV roars by on its eight wheels, Mad Dogs clambering over its metal body, followed by a swarm of infected, chomping at its heels.

Less than a minute later, the last Mad Dog runs by, a shredded red shirt flapping from his mouth. Then the street is quiet again except for the distant rattle of small arms fire.

"Well," says McLeod. "You don't see that every day."

Every kill is a broken chain of infection

The naked obese woman chases the teenaged boy down the street, arms outstretched and breasts rolling. They pass two charred corpses that lay smoking on the sidewalk outside a burned-out convenience store. His sneakers crunch on broken glass.

With a loud bang, the woman drops to the ground, writhing and moaning.

The boy stops, grips his knees, and totters, panting, almost too tired to stand on his own. His entire body, clad in a bunny hugger and jeans, is flushed and drenched in sweat. After making sure the woman is no longer a threat, he lifts his face to scan the nearby buildings, searching for his savior.

In doing so, he reveals an inflamed and swollen bite mark on his cheek, smeared with blood and drool.

His roaming eyes find a tiny silhouette on the roof of the building across the street. His mouth spreads into a big, toothy grin. He raises his hand to wave hello.

The top of his head explodes.

On the roof of the building, a puff of smoke rises.

Sergeant Grant Lewis peers into his ranging telescopic sight, scanning the ground for additional targets. He sits on a stool he found in an art classroom, resting the rifle on a bipod on the parapet next to an unfinished MRE.

The street below opens up to him in detail.

Bowman collected the NCOs back at the hospital and explained what his scouts found: Private Boyd had gotten bitten during the night and then turned into a Mad Dog by morning, like something out of a zombie movie. It explained everything. For Lewis, it all fit—the huge number of Mad Dogs running wild attacking people, the change in mission, the new ROE. Hawkeye catching the Mad Dog strain from a bite on his face confirmed it. The rate of transmission for this disease is incredible.

And if we don't do something about it, he tells himself, we are going to be wiped out.

As a result, Lewis has come up with his own ROE: If you are a Mad Dog, or if you are bitten and are going to become a Mad Dog, I am cleared hot to kick your ass.

The M21 is a semi-automatic adaptation of the M14 bolt action sniper rifle. The advantage of the M21 is the shooter gets a quick second shot, which is ideal for target-rich environments. A cam built into the scope mount adjusts the sight to compensate for the bullet's trajectory. The magazine he is using holds twenty 7.62-mm bullets.

There are no targets in view. The street is empty of life. The air smells like smoke. But they are out there, close, circling. He can hear their growling and their sad, plaintive cries carried on each fresh breeze.

The longer he stays up here, the longer he can delay having to listen to Sergeant Ruiz chew his ass about alleged fratricide. Nobody wanted to kill The Newb. Nobody wanted The Newb to die. Friendly fire is a common thing in combat. Things were very confused trying to cross that intersection. Accidents happen all the time in war.

He can also avoid Sergeant McGraw, who has been moping under his own personal storm cloud, wondering how he missed the fact that PFC William Chen was cracking from the stress right under his nose. Wondering if he could have prevented the poor kid from blowing the back of his head off, which of course he couldn't. Every soldier has a different way of reacting to stress. Every soldier has a different breaking point. If they themselves do not know what it is, how are you supposed to know?

Lewis shakes his head in wonder. The way his fellow NCOs have chosen so far to react to this crisis is making him lose a little respect for the rank of sergeant.

He leans back in his chair, stretches, and takes a swig from his canteen. He hates the taste of New York City municipal water, but like all guys with experience in the field, he is used to making do. He has food and water, which is all that counts. A grunt can burn up to four, five, six thousand calories a day on a high-stress mission like this one. You either lose weight or you eat every chance you get and replace the calories.

Across the street, two guys in suits and ties are smoking cigarettes on the roof. One of them is leaning over the parapet to take a look at Lewis' kill. The other sees Lewis looking back at him and sheepishly holds up his index and middle finger to make a V. He is either communicating "victory" or "peace," Lewis isn't sure.

To a real soldier, Lewis believes, it is the same thing.

The pause in targets gives him time to reflect on Charlie's predicament.

Bowman is going to try to consolidate Charlie with Battalion and Battalion is going to try to hook up with Brigade, Lewis guesses. It's a big effing mistake. It is exactly the kind of smartass strategy some soulless egghead would dream up. He can picture the egghead now, showing the Brass a big color-coded map of the USA and telling them the parts they can hold with armor and the parts they are going to have to give up for a while. He will rattle off casualty estimates and label civilian casualties under his plan as "acceptable."

And the Brass will grunt and nod. A lot of these guys served in the Cold War and believed America could fight and survive a nuclear exchange with the Soviets. This many million will die, this many million will survive. They have heard this type of language before and they speak it fluently. As long as we come out on top, right? Of course, it is not their families dying—oh no, not these rear-echelon motherfuckers.

And then the environmental nuts will come along and say how this is going to be good and very cleansing for the planet. Global population will be rewound to before the birth of Christ, and the planet will bounce back and flourish and Man will live in harmony with nature from thence forth. We are the real virus here, multiplying and consuming until we kill the host that sustains us. We must end this world to save it, right? Of course, this is all freaking fine in theory until it is your family that is doing the dying.

No, the smart thing to do, Lewis believes, is for everybody to stay where they are, make the Air Force earn its pay for a change by keeping everybody supplied, and then punch out patrols to go deep into neighborhoods and shoot down every Mad Dog they see. Every kill is a broken chain of infection, slightly improving humanity's odds.

Meanwhile, hand out guns. Give everybody and his mother an old surplus rifle and sixty rounds, a flyer explaining how to use it, and a license to kill for a month.

But Lewis knows the Army and the Army is not going to do that. He believes the Army's going to react to the first punch in the nose the Mad Dogs gave it by retracting all its limbs inside its shell. Instead of putting the Mad Dogs down while they are still dispersed, the Army is going to let them build an army that will wipe the human race off the face of the earth and give it back to the birds and the bees.

Movement down in the street. Lewis peers into his telescopic sight and sees a woman and child running, holding hands. They are so beautiful that he daydreams for a moment about his wife Sara and their boy Tucker, far enough away from him that they might as well be on the Moon. The woman is a young mom, in her mid twenties, with long straight blond hair and a slim, athletic body clad in a tight T-shirt and jeans, while the daughter is virtually a smaller version of her mother, maybe seven years old.

I'll protect you, he thinks. On this one street, you will be safe. Go in peace.

He blinks, looks again.

The mother has been bitten in the arm. The wound has been hastily bandaged and a length of unraveled gauze, stained almost black with dried blood, flaps behind her.

She is already dead. All he has to do now is stop her from taking who knows how many poor saps with her to the grave.

He takes aim and prepares for the shot, but freezes on the trigger pull. If he kills the mother, the girl won't have a protector. She won't last five minutes on these streets.

But the mother has been bitten. If he does not kill her, she will later go Mad Dog and then kill or infect her daughter.

He can't decide what to do. The Bible story about King Solomon enters his mind. Two women are fighting over a child and Solomon's answer is to take a sword and cut the child in two. When one of the women says please don't do this but instead give the child to the other, Solomon knew instantly that she was the real mother and gave her the child.

The smart move, the safest bet, is to kill both of them.

A thought pops into his head: *We must end this world to save it.*

His view of the mother and daughter is now blocked by the corner of the building.

Picking up the rifle and cursing a blue streak at himself for losing his concentration, he runs to the other side of the roof and quickly repositions his weapon on its bipod. He finds the pair after a cursory scan of the street, aims the barrel of his rifle at the back of the woman's head, and exhales.

It's all freaking fine in theory until it's your family that's doing the dying.

He releases the trigger. He can't do it.

Lewis spits over the parapet in disgust.

Across the street, a man in an office is waving at him and holding a sign that says: TRAPPED, HELP.

Lewis spits again.

"Welcome to the club, buddy," he says.

The more I see her, the more I think it's unfair that she's scared of me, and this makes me pissed off, and then I think about it some more, and then I decide—

Sergeant Ruiz peeks into the classroom through the window set in the door and sees Third Squad sprawled asleep on top of their fartsacks where they'd been billeted, surrounded by leftovers from rapidly devoured MREs. One of them cries out in his sleep, making the others stop snoring long enough to frown and twitch for a few moments.

Again he thinks about his young wife and infant son in Jacksonville, Florida. Should he try to call her now?

What if she doesn't answer the phone?

Would he go over the hill and try to get home to his family, like Richard Boyd?

Maybe, but look where that got Boyd. The LT said half his face got bitten off and he'd been transformed into a Mad Dog.

He hears footsteps, turns and sees 2LT Greg Bishop approaching from the end of the hallway, gesturing angrily at his trailing NCOs. Probably complaining again about Bowman's order to McGraw to shoot down all those civilians. Said it was inhuman, even with the ROE. Said Bowman doesn't deserve to take command of what's left of Charlie Company. Said even some Nazis during WWII refused to follow orders and participate in wholesale slaughter.

Ruiz shakes his head in disgust and resumes his own walk to the gym, where a thousand people lie moaning and dying on cots arranged in nice, neat rows. Healthy civilians are moving among them changing sheets and bedpans and IV bags, supervised by three hapless, red-faced corpsmen and a handful of nurses from the day shift who made it to work. Others are disposing of corpses and disinfecting the area with mops and rags. The LT told them: We have food, water, blankets. We can protect you, feed you and shelter you. But if you stay, you work. And you work hard.

It is unpleasant labor, and there is plenty of shirking, but many of the civilians are happy to have something to do to take their minds off their problems. The ones who are working are the toughest, the ones you can count on. The others just can't take what's happening to them and their world. They quickly wandered off and nobody has seen them since. Many of these people have lost everything, and it was torn away bloodily in front of their very eyes. They are in shock, and many of them will never snap out of it.

It was a good idea, in any case, to give the civilians something to do. The LT is smart for an officer, Ruiz thinks. If Bowman commanded the way Bishop says he should, First Platoon would still be trapped in that classroom, under siege and starving by inches, and Second Platoon would have been scattered to the winds on Forty-Second Street.

Ruiz likes to make things simple. Here is how he sees it:

Bowman is working hard and doing what it takes to keep his boys alive.

Bishop is a douche and is complaining instead of working.

And Knight, well, word is some of his own guys want to frag his ass. Word is that when the Mad Dogs came out of the woodwork and started ripping his boys to shreds, he refused to fire, and instead told them to run for it.

Ruiz shakes his head. The reality on the ground has changed, and if we do not change with it, we will die. Those who cannot accept reality, as it is, should not command. Bishop, for example, believes Bowman should have called in units equipped with riot control gear and captured the Mad Dogs nonviolently.

The man is either insane or in denial about their predicament.

That leaves Bowman as the ideal man for the job as the guy least likely to get them all killed within the next twenty-four to forty-eight hours.

Ruiz sees a few civilians patrolling the gym, toting M4 carbines. He exchanges a nod with one of them, a middle-aged marine with experience in Panama and the first Gulf War. Another one of Bowman's innovations—arming those civilian volunteers having prior military experience with Charlie Company's spare carbines. They are now Bowman's police force, used to make sure none of the Lyssa patients goes Mad Dog and makes trouble, while giving the rest of the civilians somebody to complain to besides the soldiers.

Bowman said he is not interested in a humanitarian mission. He is trying to keep Charlie Company combat effective. He is looking at this place as hostile territory and the Mad Dogs as enemy combatants, the way he was told to do by the Brass. The guys in the rear with the gear are not right very often, but on this, they are absolutely goddamn correct.

Ruiz walks down a row of Lyssa victims lying in their cots, looking into each face. Most are in bad shape, as the Mad Dogs showed a preference for spreading infection to those lying in their beds who were closest to recovery. But a few smile back at him.

There is hope in this place. It makes him feel good. They are doing some good here. The LT said there's plenty of supplies, including ammunition, and a lot of sick people to protect and help recover.

He also said not to get too comfortable.

If Charlie Company moves, Ruiz wonders, should I try to leave?

How would I get home?

Does it matter? If what Bowman said about Boyd is true, then the Mad Dogs are going to try to wipe this planet clean of human life. Maybe one out of twenty is now a Mad Dog, and they are already bringing the country to its knees.

The rate of infection is unbelievable.

It is a horrible thought, but our only hope of stalling the Apocalypse, he thinks, is that the Mad Dogs kill a lot more people than they infect, reducing the rate of infection. If the infection rate is arithmetical instead of exponential, they might have a chance at stopping them through brute extermination. The way the Iraqis were doing it just before Charlie was sent home. (It is strange to think that the countries most likely to pull through this are failed states with brutal societies and lots of guns and ammo.)

In any case, if America is doomed, why should he stay? Why not at least try to get to Janisa and Emmanuel? In a contest between his family and his platoon, there would be no contest. If his love for his wife is passionate, his love for his son is primordial. He would, in fact, saw off his own arm for his kid. He would systematically kill all of his comrades. His true duty in a crisis like this, at the end of the world, lies with his family.

The only problem is he is here and they are there, and he would die before he could reach them.

A young woman hurries by, her dark eyes wide with alarm. Doc Waters, exhausted and in a fine rage now, shouts after her to bring back as much amantadine—a generic antiviral drug—as she can carry.

Even with the mask, Ruiz can tell that the girl is pretty, just like his Janisa. The idea that his wife and son are in danger fills him with grief.

He will try to call her. But first he has to check on one of his boys.

Hawkeye has been tied down to his cot with restraining belts, sweating and reeking, the bandage on his cheek stained a rusty brown, his throat beginning to swell into a mass of golf ball-sized buboes. He tries to smile upon seeing Ruiz, but the smile quickly morphs into a grimace, his skin the sickly gray color characteristic of infection.

"How are you, Hawkeye?"

"Been better, Sergeant," he rasps, his voice underscored with a vibration that occasionally culminates in a growl when he exhales. "You come to help me?"

"I brought an extra pillow for you, like you asked."

"I can't swallow. I'm goddamn thirsty all the time but I can't stand even looking at water. Just seeing an IV bag pisses me off. I'm pissed off all the time."

"It's unfair, Hawkeye."

"No," Hawkeye hisses. "It's the germs. They're making me pissed off. They're putting thoughts into my head. You see that pretty girl who just walked by? The one with the big black eyes you could fall into?"

"She just walked by here," Ruiz says. "Sure, I saw her."

"Of course you did—she's beautiful," Hawkeye chuckles, then grimaces again. "She's kind of scared of me. Every time she walks by, she looks at me real scared. And I think, don't be scared, miss, I'm Cameron Ross, I'm a good guy, I'd never hurt you. And the more I see her, the more I think it's unfair that she's scared of me, and this makes me pissed off, and then I think about it some more, and then I decide *I want to chew up her face so she can't see me anymore.*"

Ruiz takes a step back without thinking, gazing down in horror at the soldier.

"Everything makes me so damn pissed off, Sergeant. Every minute that goes by I can feel myself getting more pissed off. I don't want to die hating everybody and everything." He glances down at his hand, and Ruiz sees that he is holding a photo of his girlfriend. "I want to die while I still love them. I'm dying either way, Sergeant. That's a fact. I'm not scared. I just don't want to die hating my girl, or my own mother. Do you get it now, *or do I have to drill it into your fucking skull?*"

Ruiz nods and says softly, "I get it, Hawkeye."

Hawkeye growls deep in his throat, then closes his eyes and sighs. "Thank you, Sergeant."

Ruiz takes the pillow he brought, places it over the boy's smile, and presses down.

"Bye, Hawkeye," he says, tears streaming down his face.

The boy struggles for about a minute, then lies still.

When Ruiz is done, he notices the room is strangely silent except for the general moan of the Lyssa victims lying in their beds. He looks up and sees almost everyone staring back at him. Several of the civilians slowly nod in understanding, while others cover their faces to hide their tears.

He is not the first person to have to do this for a friend.

Feeling tired in his bones, Ruiz begins walking in the direction of the west wing, where he hopes to find an empty classroom where he can call his wife. Immediately, the people around him resume working as if nothing happened.

Corporal Alvarez approaches and salutes. He says the Lieutenant wants the entire company to muster. LT has talked to Quarantine, he says.

Quarantine has new orders for Charlie Company.

It's us or them, gentlemen

Gentlemen, the Lyssa virus is much more of a problem than we have been led to believe. The Pandemic has taken many lives and caused severe shortages and panic. But now the game has changed and our mission has expanded. The Army is no longer simply concerned with protecting infrastructure. We are fighting for the survival of the United States. I know that sounds dramatic, but there's really no other way to put it.

Right now, outside these walls, there is no local government. No food distribution. No medicine. There are almost no firefighters putting out fires. Only a handful of police offers are still doing their duty. Many of the hospitals have been abandoned, like this one. It's fast becoming the law of the jungle out there.

There is a reason for this.

Warlord has suffered major losses as well. Captain West and his head-quarters staff are MIA and presumed dead. Colonel Armstrong is dead, and so is the Battalion XO, Major Reynolds. Captain Lyons of Alpha is taking over Battalion.

Gentlemen, be quiet. There's more.

As you know, I have been placed in command of Charlie. I have received new orders directly from Brigade. All units in our AO have been ordered to consolidate into the next highest level at an easily defensible location. This means Alpha, Bravo, Charlie and Delta Companies are going to concentrate and reconstitute Warlord. Quarantine wants Battalion squared away until he needs us.

These orders make sense. They are also simple as far as we're concerned because our current position is the rendezvous point. Everybody is coming to us. All we have to do is wait. A citywide curfew is going into effect at seventeen hundred hours. By eighteen hundred, the Battalion should be reconstituted under Captain Lyons.

Now it's time to tell you the real problem that is behind all this. What I have to say may shock you, but at this point probably will not surprise you.

At first, we were told that Mad Dog syndrome is common only in the most severe cases of Lyssa, where the virus attacks the brain. Turns out this is wrong. Turns out the Mad Dogs apparently carry an entirely different strain of the virus in their saliva. When they bite people, those people become Mad Dogs.

In fact, once bitten, they can become a Mad Dog within hours.

Gentlemen, be quiet.

Gentlemen—

Thank you, Sergeant.

The number of Mad Dogs is increasing at a rate that we cannot understand. We have seen with our own eyes that they are dramatically growing in numbers and that they attack and seek to infect, without fear or mercy, any non-infected person that they see. The level of threat is increasing by the minute and will increase until the Mad Dogs are either all dead or they exhaust the supply of people they can infect.

Now you know why we have no choice but to concentrate Battalion or cease to be in the game helping America get through this crisis. Gentlemen, I am not kidding when I say that we are fighting for the survival of our country. Possibly the human race.

The situation is unprecedented.

All right, listen up.

Things have changed, and we need to adapt.

First, there will be no more talk of "baby killers." If you think the Mad Dogs are still people, your sentimentality is going to get you and the man next to you killed. Mad Dogs are not people anymore. They are puppets controlled by the Mad Dog virus. The virus tells them to attack and infect, and they do it. These people probably have no knowledge of who they are, what they are, or what they're doing.

And if they do know, but have no choice, then God help them. Either way, if you kill a Mad Dog, it is a mercy killing. It's that simple.

Mad Dogs do not carry weapons and they look like you and me, but do not let appearances fool you. These things are the deadliest foe that America has ever faced and the most dangerous enemy you will ever meet in combat.

There will be a lot more killing. We are in a hostile country, surrounded by a hostile army, close to being cut off from resupply and medevac, and the enemy is hunting us in a war of extermination, fighting us using tactics against which we never trained.

This is an enemy that does not take prisoners. That does not negotiate. That requires no supply, knows no fear, and attacks relentlessly. The virus does not fight for land or money or politics or religion. It fights to survive by infecting, or killing, all of us.

I am telling you this so you can get your head on straight. If you want to stay alive, you're going to have to get some fight in your gut and see this situation for what it is.

A war with unlimited spectrum. Total war.

It's us or them, gentlemen. These are the facts on the ground.

Right now, you are probably getting very worried about your loved ones. I have family in Texas, some in Louisiana, who I think about every day. But I can't get to them. I'd never make it. If I walked out that door, I'd be dead, or a Mad Dog, within twenty-four hours.

If you want to help your family, then do your job.

Somebody has to survive this.

Civilian law enforcement is being wiped out. That leaves us. We're all that's left between a rising tide of Mad Dogs and annihilation. So your family's only hope, our country's only hope, is that the Army stays together long enough to make a difference. From now on, once a unit is destroyed, it cannot be replaced. It's gone.

One of you asked me if this is the end of the world. My answer was not a very good one. I thought of a new answer, and I like it better.

Whether the world is going to end or not is literally up to us.

As for me, gentlemen, I say it's not.

Chapter 9

They do not deserve to take it all from us

The sun is shining and the streets are jammed with people enjoying the end of summer. In Central Park, hundreds lie on blankets in Sheep Meadow, sleeping or reading. Several boys with their shirts off throw an orange Frisbee back and forth, while a dog playfully barks and scampers between them. Christopher sits on a bench bouncing Alexander on his knee. They both smile eagerly as she approaches them barefoot and laughing. Alexander demands ice cream. Valeriya Petrova suggests a ride on the Merry-Go-Round instead and he shouts for joy before realizing he's been fooled, suddenly declaring his interest in both ice cream and a ride.

What flavor, Alex? Christopher asks.

Alexander looks up at his father and cries exultantly: Vanilla!

Her eyes flicker to Christopher, deliciously aware that he is unaware of being watched, and knows they are getting older every day and that some day they will die and there will be nothing and they will never be together like this again. Instead of making her sad, the thought fills her with a strange elation that she is alive and not dead, that she still has time, that they all have time, before even just this single perfect day ends. And her son has even longer and all the world lies before him.

Tonight she will make love to her husband and whisper thank you in his ear as she does at times when she feels like this, when she cannot contain the beauty of her life and the joy her family brings her.

Harsh white light shatters the darkness.

The building groans to life as its systems reboot.

Petrova lies under the desk, shivering with her eyes clenched shut.

You must get up, she tells herself. You must not give up. You must survive for them.

No, stay and dream a little while longer. Maybe the dream is true. Maybe, outside, the world has returned to normal. *People in the park, laughing and playing. Lying on the warm grass, reading a paperback—*

No—

Outside, she knows, the world is dying.

Everybody she has ever known, everybody she has ever loved, everything she cherished as part of life, is being destroyed.

She knows that she is probably going to die here without ever seeing the sun again. Without ever seeing her son again.

So far away.

Mankind will not cross the Atlantic again for perhaps hundreds of years. London may as well be on another planet. Within a generation, even the word "London" may cease to be generally remembered in North America. Knowledge that there are other continents at all may slowly be forgotten as future generations struggle to survive.

All this because a tiny little biological machine simply wants to live.

If the virus could think and speak, it would say it has a right to try to multiply, to fight for dominance, to survive. Survival, in fact, is the virus' sole purpose. It is designed to survive. That is what makes it so strong. It was virtually the first form of life on the planet, and it will be the last.

But it is not better than us, she thinks. Stronger, maybe. But not better.

Can a virus make its human puppets paint a sunset, for example, that reflects the soul of the real thing? Possessing mind but not thought, does it understand the concept of science, progress, the betterment of the species? Has it ever looked up with its borrowed eyes at the stars and wonder if there are other planets that can support life, perhaps life it can talk to? Can it understand charity or love or empathy or mercy? Has a Mad Dog, roaming the streets feverishly searching for a new host, ever felt anything in its extremely short life span beyond a toxic level of pain and rage?

They do not deserve to take it all from us. They are just machines. Living software. They will kill everyone and destroy everything, only to die off themselves and disappear as fast as they came, leaving despair and ruin behind. And this security equipment and all the other human machines will simply lie here rotting for years under layers of dust, perhaps to be picked up generations later by uncomprehending descendants.

It is unfair—

A sudden burst of anger gives her just enough strength to move her hand.

With great effort, she reaches across the carpet. Her body follows, as slow as a snail, but as determined. Fear weighs down on her with its own special gravity, and she wonders if she will make it. But soon she is standing, looking into the security screens, where she sees Sandy Cohen lying broken on the floor outside.

Dead.

We are just meat to them, she thinks. They consume us and throw away the wrapper.

Even the air feels heavy in her lungs.

If you do not want to die here, get busy doing something else, she tells herself.

Her eyes flicker to a pack of cigarettes on the desk. Jackson was a smoker. Petrova quit four years ago, before she got pregnant with Alexander. Has not touched one since.

Just one, she decides. To help me think.

Petrova ignites the tip of the cigarette and inhales deeply, feeling guilty about it in part, strangely, because she is doing it in a public place. In more ways than one, ingrained habits die hard. She coughs. She inhales again and does not cough. Like riding a bike. Within moments, the head rush assails her brain.

So much for quitting, she thinks. It was agony to quit, and she is throwing it all away for three quarters of a pack of Marlboro Lights. And not even menthol, which she prefers. On the other hand, between the epidemic and the Mad Dogs, she doubts she is going to see an abundance of cigarettes anywhere anytime soon. Perhaps forever.

She suddenly realizes that she does not have much time. The power might go out again, and if it stays off, she will have no way to survive.

She begins to take stock of her surroundings. Most of the desk drawers are stuffed with paper records, logs, office supplies and old manuals. The bottom desk drawer contains a half-full quart bottle of whiskey, an almost full carton of cigarettes, a condom, a heavily dog-eared copy of *Juggs*, a package of salted peanuts, and a clipboard holding some sort of training schedule. She removes the peanuts and devours them greedily.

Lovely, she thinks. The only things I have lots of are cigarettes and pornography.

One of the storage bins holds flashlights, which she removes, tests and sets aside.

But no guns or other weapons. Petrova knows that the security staff carries at least a billy club and a TASER, but Jackson either has these items on him, lost them during the fight with Baird, or discarded them afterwards. That just leaves her golf club, next to which she places a small steel fire extinguisher and a box cutter tool.

Petrova finds the bathroom adjacent to this main room and uses it, smoking a second cigarette on the toilet with the door open and the light off. For a few moments, the smoking dampens her hunger.

She snaps her fingers, stands up and flushes. Pausing at the sink, trying not to look at herself in the mirror, she hurriedly washes her face and hands, and dries them with paper towels. Then she goes back to the operator station.

The security system, she realized, must include a way to prevent the migration of airborne microbes and toxins in the event of an emergency.

After several minutes, Petrova shuts off the HVAC system with a primitive cry of triumph. Instantly, the air-conditioning stops breathing ice over her skin. Soon, the air will get stale, but at least she won't be freezing anymore.

This small act of control gives her a sense of optimism and fuels her courage.

"I am very sorry, Sandy," she says to the screen, then flips the image.

To get out of here, she must either escape or be rescued.

Don't look behind you

Marsha Fuentes lies twitching and wincing on the floor in one of the aisles in the auditorium. Lucas is in the elevator lobby, blinking and sniffing the air. Saunders is in Laboratory West, pacing back and forth. Stringer Jackson is still standing at the mirror, rocking back and forth, his ruined eye weeping mucus. Drool dribbles from his lips.

He has turned.

Down in the lobby, the beautiful blonde appears to be arguing with some of the men in her mob. She holds a pistol in her hand, which she taps against her leg as she talks. The people down there have figured out that when the Institute went into lockdown, not only was the lab sealed, so was the entire building. They are upset about it.

Behind the woman, Petrova can see a group of people lying on the floor in the corner. Lyssa victims. Some of the mob are sick and getting sicker. But none of them appear to be going Mad Dog. At least, not yet. She reminds herself that with standard airborne Lyssa, the odds are very low.

The woman is now waving the pistol over her head and pointing at the sick people. The men walk away sheepishly.

Reluctantly, Petrova tears her eyes from the screen. If she is going to be rescued, she has to act fast. She gathers up the fire extinguisher, which she intends to use as a missile, and her golf club. The box cutter she puts in her pocket as a weapon of last resort. She takes a deep breath in front of the door, hesitating.

It is either this, or get back under the desk.

She takes off her shoes to make less noise while she walks, opens the door and gingerly steps outside.

The hallway is empty, except for the bodies, and dead silent. She hurries past Sandy Cohen, who lies like a marionette with her strings cut, her limbs at odd angles and her grinning head facing the wrong way. Further down, she scurries past Baird's body, lying on its side like a downed bull. Footsteps echo down distant hallways.

Turning the corner, she creeps up to the bathroom where Sims still lies on the floor, his stiff body propping open the door. Stringer Jackson is inside.

Now for the hard part.

She darts by the open door, willing herself not to be noticed.

Immediately, Jackson begins snarling.

"Oh damn," she says, breaking into a run.

Behind her, the door is flung open, slamming against the wall with a loud bang, and Jackson spills out of the bathroom snorting and growling, stumbling over Sims' body.

Petrova looks over her shoulder, slowing down, and sees Jackson recover and begin loping towards her, his eye leaking yellowish-green sludge, bellowing a nasal *ka ka ka* sound through slavering jaws.

As a scientist, she knows all sorts of facts about the human body. For example, she knows that human jaws, clamping down to bite, can exert more than four thousand pounds per square inch.

Moments later, she comes to a sliding halt in front of her office. Slipping in, she slams the door, locks it and puts her weight against it, praying for it to hold.

But Jackson does not try to break the door down. Instead, he begins growling and pacing. She can hear him sniff at the air, sensing that she is there. She is trapped again, and this time, she has no access to the security system.

Petrova puts down the golf club and fire extinguisher and sits at her desk. The act is so familiar to her that for a moment, she feels like everything is back to normal. Her PC's screensaver displays a screen-sized image of her, Christopher and Alexander looking up at the camera, grinning. Christopher took the photo himself, holding the camera at arm's length over their heads. Alexander, held in Petrova's arms, is reaching up towards the lens. The photo was snapped with a digital camera near the end of a perfect day in Central Park. The image holds her, transfixed, for several moments.

Jackson shoulders the door during his pacing, startling her.

Time to get to work. She picks up the phone, which blares a loud rat-tat-tat signal. Same with the handset to her fax. A wave of sweat breaks out on her forehead and armpits. Her first dead end.

She opens her hard drive and tests her connection to the email server, which appears to be working, giving her a connection to the outside world.

Smiling now, she opens the secure FTP site the CDC set up for them to share their work. It is also operational. She grabs everything she can find related to her discoveries, doing a broad data sweep, and dumps it all onto the server.

While it is uploading, she writes an email to her contacts at the CDC and USAMRIID, cc'ing as many people in the virology community that she can think of, summarizing her findings and stating that she has a pure sample of the Mad Dog strain. She tells them that she and her colleagues are close to producing a formula for a vaccine but a mob has entered the building's lobby, locking them in, and they require rescue. Then she clicks SEND.

It is a simple plan, but she believes it will work. By now, the world outside must know that the Mad Dog strain is the real threat. The Centers for Disease Control will want a pure sample. She has a sample, as long as the power does not fail for good and spoil it. In particular, they will want a vaccine, which is why she lied and said they were close to producing one.

So now all she has to do is wait for the government to come and rescue her. A simple plan.

Unless her contacts are all dead.

Unless there is no CDC or USAMRIID anymore.

Unless somebody else has already done the research she is offering.

Her stomach growls. Petrova opens a drawer in her desk and pulls out her purse. Rooting around inside, she produces a box of orange-flavored Tic Tacs, pours what is left into her palm, and rapidly devours them. She does the same with a pack of gum, gnawing the flavor out of it and then swallowing it whole.

There are no emails from Christopher in her in-box.

She tries the *Guardian* website, but there are no stories. The website is up and running, but no stories have been posted since yesterday. What could this mean?

Other news sites carry stories of riots, some with video showing Mad Dogs chasing down screaming people, dragging them to the ground and mauling them. The stories are few in number and poorly written. Other sites, such as YouTube, have either crashed or been shut down. The social networking sites are flooded with frantic pleas for help.

She cannot give up hope that her family is alive, but after several minutes, she stops her search for hard news as she is getting nowhere and only wasting time at this point. She wants to return to the Security Command Center as soon as possible, as that is where she left the flashlights. She can live without food, even water, for days, but the idea of being trapped here without light is horrifying.

If things are as bad outside as she thinks they are, the power will eventually go out.

She just has to somehow incapacitate or get past Jackson. And, if it is not too much trouble, stop by the employee lounge long enough to pick up some food out of the machine that Hardy broke open, so she does not starve to death.

She listens for a moment. Jackson has stopped pacing. The corridor is quiet.

Petrova slowly rises from her chair and tip-toes to the door. Still nothing. She gets down on the floor and tries to look under the door. Slowly rising to her feet, she gingerly places her ear against the wood to listen.

From inches away, she can hear a sudden loud, guttural snarling.

"Oh," she whispers, backing away.

She wishes that she had planned further than sending email to CDC and

USAMRIID.

But she has an idea.

You are stronger than us, she thinks, but we are smarter than you.

Going back to her computer, she brings up a letter and sets it to print a hundred copies. Within moments, the printer begins churning out pieces of paper.

For several moments, she stares at this mundane routine with something like longing, then tip-toes back to the door, holding the fire extinguisher and golf club. Putting the club down, almost without thinking, she abruptly jerks open the door and steps aside.

Jackson roars into the room, races to the desk and knocks the printer onto the floor, where it lands with a loud crash.

Petrova stands there stupidly for several moments, unable to believe her plan worked. She jumps outside and slams the door before Jackson throws himself at it, pounding and clawing and kicking and yelping in a mindless fury.

She backs away from the door, panting.

Dr. Lucas is standing almost next to her, blinking without his glasses, sniffing the air.

He begins to growl.

Petrova left the golf club inside the office. She aims the fire extinguisher and sprays him with a jet of white foam pressurized with nitrogen, hoping to blind him.

The scientist coughs and sputters for a moment, pawing at his stinging eyes and yelping, then goes berserk, waving his arms wildly around his head and biting at his hands and forearms, flinging foam in all directions. Petrova can only watch in amazement as his teeth rip cloth and tear away pieces of flesh, soaking his face and arms with blood.

More than four thousand pounds per square inch.

Backing up step by step, she finally turns and runs, leaving Lucas to howl and tear at his clothes and flesh in his blind rage. By the time she returns to the Security Commander Center, she is shaking so hard that she can barely open the door.

On the screen, the beautiful blonde is holding up a sign that says, YOU MADE ME DO THIS. Next to her, several worried-looking men are forcing the other National Guardsman, his arms still tied behind his back, to his knees.

Petrova watches, transfixed by this new drama.

Throwing the sign down, the blonde marches to one of the Lyssa victims lying on the floor, a young girl, and rubs her hand all over the girl's face until her hand is slick with mucus. She holds the hand high over her head, showing it to the camera.

"Oh," says Petrova. "No, no, no. Please do not do that."

As she marches back, her mouth moving soundlessly, the soldier's eyes go wide and he begins to struggle struggling wildly against his captors, who can barely hold him.

The blonde smears the snot over his face and lips, then begins scribbling on the piece of poster board, which she holds high for Petrova to see: ONLY YOU CAN SAVE HIM.

"We do not have a vaccine, you stupid bitch!" Petrova screams, throwing the fire extinguisher against the wall. "Stop killing people!"

The rage boils up inside her, comes pouring out. She races to the security system's graphical interface and begins studying it.

"You want to come inside," she mutters in disgust, her accent thickening. "This is what you want. We shall see."

She clicks an icon on her screen, which turns from red to green.

On the screen, the crowd of people appear startled, then burst into cheers, laughing and hugging and pointing at something that is happening off screen. The blonde looks down at the soldier, who stares at the floor. Alone among the cheering mob, they are weeping.

The people are pointing at the elevator lobby. They have won against the stubborn scientists who have been hoarding a vaccine.

The elevators are coming down.

Chapter 10

You know, my dad. . . .

Mooney sits on the floor next to his sleeping bag in the classroom that First Squad has claimed as a sleeping area, airing his feet and cleaning his carbine. After a lot of firing, a good cleaning is necessary. He wants his weapon functional—not ready for parade—so he is field stripping and cleaning it fast. Around him, some of the other boys are doing the same, getting ready for action. The room stinks of sweaty socks and cleaning solvent.

Wyatt swaggers in carrying a plastic garbage bag with his left hand. Behind him, Mooney sees one of the boys from Second Squad mopping the floor out in the hallway, whistling while he works. Everybody is dying, the world is ending, but the Army likes things clean, Mooney tells himself. It will be a nice, neat, orderly Armageddon. The last man alive, please turn out the lights.

"Booty," says Wyatt, spilling the bag's contents onto the floor in front of Mooney—a small mountain of half-melted candy bars, cartons of juice, warm cans of soda, and pancaked Twinkies, cupcakes and donuts.

The boys whistle, eyeing the loot enviously.

"What do you think, Mooney?" Wyatt says, offering one of his lopsided grins that make his large brown Army glasses—the type the boys call BCGs, or birth control glasses, since there's no way in hell of getting laid while wearing them—appear crooked on his face.

Mooney studies his comrade for a few moments while he swabs his gun barrel with a cleaning rod and patch. He is starting to feel like he has adopted Private Joel Wyatt, although he is not sure why, since he basically can barely stand the screwball soldier at this point. Or maybe Wyatt has adopted him, and he is not strong enough to resist: Joel Wyatt can be like a force of nature. In any case, when you feel like you are going to die soon, you tend to start feeling pretty forgiving about things. All the irritating stuff stops being real and no longer matters. Just ask Billy Chen about how much he sweated the small stuff before he ate a bullet.

"Where'd you get all that, Joel?" says Ratliff.

"I jacked the rich kids' lockers," Wyatt says, beaming, sifting through the candy with his hands. He adds hastily, "It's not like they're coming back."

Ratliff starts to laugh, but it fades quickly.

"You keep touching other people's stuff and you're going to get sick, Joel," Mooney says, then reconsiders. "OK. Screw it. Give me that Mars bar."

"What's the magic word?"

"Now," Mooney says, glowering.

Wyatt grins again, his cheeks bulging with chocolate, and hands him the candy bar.

Mooney takes a bite and chews slowly. An instant later, he is wolfing the rest of it down, gnawing rapidly until his jaw muscles protest from the sudden overload. Now here is something to live for. Nothing ever tasted so good in his life. He reaches and grabs a carton of apple juice, spears it with the straw, and sucks it down in several long gulps. The sugar rings his brain like a bell.

"That's my stuff!" Wyatt whines as Ratliff comes over and grabs a pack of cupcakes.

"There's plenty for everybody," Mooney says.

"That's what your mom. . . ." Finnegan says, his voice trailing off. Nobody laughs. Instead, the boys stare off into some point in space and the atmosphere begins to fill with despair, like a fast-acting poison. Mooncy can't stand it anymore.

"Everybody come and get a candy bar," he says. "Joel's buying."

The boys swipe at his pile, almost picking it clean. "Thanks, Joel!" they tell him.

"Yeah, thanks a lot," Wyatt tells Mooney.

"We have appointed you our new morale officer," Mooney says.

"Why? Didn't everybody find the LT's speech uplifting? 'Good day, uh, gentlemen, I'm the LT. Blah, blah, blah, uh, the world's ending, and you're still in the Army.'"

The boys laugh, chewing on their candy.

"You didn't happen to find any beer in the lockers, did you, Joel?" says Finnegan.

"Or a couple of joints, maybe?" Carrillo wants to know, laughing.

"How about valium?" says Ratliff.

"Southern Comfort?"

"Codeine?"

"Heroin?"

They sound like they are horsing around, but Mooney can tell they are dead serious. They have recently learned that the road of duty now leads face first into a brick wall, presenting a choice that Billy Chen refused to continue making and that they are still trying to avoid. They are not sure what they now owe, and to whom. They do not want anything to do with Lieutenant Bowman's total war, but they see no way out of the Army and no way home and besides, home may not even be there anymore.

A few hours of escape would be welcome.

"I had a teacher who kept a quart of whiskey in his drawer," Finnegan says. "We'd sneak in during lunch period and take a few sips, and replace it with water."

"I can't believe a year and half ago I was graduating from high school," says Carrillo, eyeing the student desks stacked against the far wall. "Man, I've seen a lot of shit."

"Eighteen going on forty-five," Ratliff says, and Mooney smiles, nodding.

"Man, I would kill for an ice cold bottle of Bud," Finnegan says.

"Screw Bud," says Ratliff. "Heineken's the best."

"I only drink the good stuff," Carrillo boasts. "Guinness on tap."

"Carrillo likes to eat his beers."

"The domestics are just yellow water, you guys. You're drinking carbonated urine."

"I like Bud."

"What about Corona?"

"Hey, man, what's the difference between a half and half and a black and tan? I could never figure that out."

Rollins finishes his Hershey's chocolate bar, sighs and stares at the wrapper wistfully. "I just thought of something," he says. "If things are as bad as LT says, I wonder if they're making more of these chocolate bars or if this is all there is for a while."

"Or movies," says Finnegan. "Live concerts. Football games. *Hustler.*"

"PlayStation," says Wyatt. "*Sports Illustrated*'s swimsuit issue."

"Hot chicks, dope, rock and roll, and beer," says Ratliff.

"My old man won't like that," Corporal Eckhardt says across the room, scrubbing his carbine's firing pin and bolt assembly with a toothbrush and solvent to get rid of carbon residue. "He can really put it away. He can down two six-packs a night, pass out and then wake up the next day and go to work."

"Sounds like a swell guy," says Wyatt, snorting.

"My old man's a psycho. If anybody can survive this thing, he will."

"My dad's an accountant," says Finnegan. "He hates violence. He almost had a heart attack when I joined the Army and he found out they were sending me to Iraq."

"My dad's got a basement full of guns," says Carrillo. "He loves his AK47 more than he loves my mom. He's a real jerk. Jerks like him always make it."

"Kind of shows you what kind of world is going to pop out the other side of this giant asshole," Mooney says.

"Yeah, all the pussies will be dead," says Eckhardt.

"And all the psychos will be running the place," Mooney says. "Think about it."

The soldiers fall silent, trying not to think about it.

"My girl," Ratliff says fiercely but quietly, almost to himself. "She's tough. She'll be okay. Her dad owns a gun. I taught her how to shoot. She's going to make it."

Finnegan looks out the window, squinting into the sunlight. Suddenly, he starts laughing uncontrollably. Everybody looks at him.

"You know, my dad," he says, then stops abruptly, his laughter trailing off and his face slowly going blank.

Moments later, an air raid siren interrupts their gloom, slowly winding up somewhere in midtown Manhattan. A siren across the river begins wailing in response, then another from somewhere farther away, tinny and distant. The grating sound builds until it is almost deafening.

Mooney looks out the window. The quality of the sunlight tells him it is late afternoon. Seventeen hundred hours, to be exact.

The citywide curfew is now in effect.

The boys slowly rise to their feet. Their plan is to rustle up some supper for themselves. After that, they have a funeral to attend.

In two hours, the American sun will set, and it will be oh-dark.

One man, at the right place at the right time, making a difference

Three police officers, clad in head-to-toe black BDUs, body armor and bulky clear-visor helmets, tread slowly down the street, newspapers scuttling around their boots and clinging to their legs. One of the cops leans on a comrade for support, while the third, a tall woman with a long braid protruding from under her helmet, brings up the rear, dragging her clear ballistic shield. They are all exhausted, but it is her turn to fight. They were going east at one time, but got turned around and are now heading west, towards the sounds of gunfire.

Gunfire means people. Security.

Night is falling. Around them, the streetlights flare to life in the dusk.

As if awaiting this signal, two Mad Dogs bolt out of a nearby apartment building, past construction scaffolding with posters plastered all over it advertising an aging pop singer's farewell tour, and race towards the riot control police, yelping.

The woman assumes a fighting stance, raising her truncheon and shield, while her comrades sink to their knees on the asphalt behind her, panting.

She waits for the Mad Dogs to approach, taking deep breaths, then quickly sidesteps the first, a middle-aged man in hospital scrubs, who runs by and comes to a skidding halt. Moments later, the other, a large man in coveralls, comes flying at her, snarling. She body checks him with her shield, stunning him, then brings her truncheon down on his skull, killing him instantly. An instant later, she pivots and backhands the first man with her shield, making him spin until he trips over his own feet.

The woman staggers back, almost finished by the effort, her shoulders sagging under the weight of her armor and weapons, while the man scrabbles his way back onto his feet and begins pacing in front of her like a nervous cat, howling.

They were working riot control near Grand Central Station, barring thousands of people from attempting to board the trains that stopped running days ago, the station having since been converted into a Lyssa clinic. Then hundreds of Mad Dogs appeared and began tearing into the frantic crowd and biting everybody in sight.

The riot control unit advanced, trying to separate the Mad Dogs from the uninfected, and found themselves trapped between the two.

Only tear gas saved them.

The cops fired CS grenades, which burst in huge clouds of brilliant white gas. Mad Dogs and uninfected people alike ran blindly through the clouds, tears and mucus streaming from their eyes and noses, clawing at their clothes and burning skin. Dozens of people bent over and began choking and vomiting. The Mad Dogs suffered the most. Tear gas reacts with moisture on the skin and in the eyes, and Mad Dogs are soaked with sweat and saliva. Tear gas also burns the nose and throat, and the infected already find it enormously painful to swallow because the Mad Dog strain paralyzes the nerves in the throat to force production of saliva.

The unit was broken, the cops scattered and trying to return to their station. For this group, it has been a running fight lasting nearly a mile along a circuitous path. There were five of them in the beginning. But one was chased into a plate glass window, and the other died heroically in front of a Staples store to buy time for this friends to escape.

The man in scrubs, growling, leaps through the air—

And falls to the ground with a loud bang.

A puff of smoke rises from a nearby rooftop.

Sergeant Lewis, sitting on a stool on the school's roof nursing a wad of Red Man dip in his cheek, sees another Mad Dog come running at the cops from the apartment building. He sizes up the man, aims center-mass at his body using his scope, and drops him with a shot between the shoulder blades.

The cops duck for a moment, glance at each other, and then begin looking around for the shooter.

This I like, he thinks, taking a quick moment to spit. Clear-cut ethics. One man, at the right place at the right time, making a difference.

Now all we need to do is put every man with a uniform, a gun and some training in the right place to wait for the right time. Break the chain of infection everywhere and roll this plague back into Pandora's Box or wherever it came from.

Small arms fire begins cascading to the south, and he glances in that direction, wondering what kind of trouble Alpha and Bravo Companies have gotten themselves into. They should have shown up an hour ago. They stepped off late and they are meeting resistance along the way. Now they are losing the light.

He turns back just in time to see another Mad Dog, an obese woman in a jogging suit, running towards the woman cop, who braces herself and raises her truncheon to strike.

Damn.

He fires and misses.

Damn!

The M21 is a semi-automatic weapon, however, which means he gets another shot. He fires again. The woman flops to the ground, convulsing and pouring blood from a smoking hole in her back.

This is my street, he thinks, spitting tobacco juice. I give you free passage. You will be safe as long as you travel here under my protection. Next time, don't bring a billy club to Armageddon.

He glances up at the sky. Just enough daylight to make good on this promise. Feeling magnanimous, he waves, hoping they see him.

They are not looking up at the buildings, however.

They are trying to run.

Peering into his scope, he sees one of the cops, crawling on hands and knees, while the other man staggers away, lurching on tired legs, following the woman cop who sprints ahead of them with all of her remaining strength.

"God," he whispers in awe.

Beyond the three cops, a moving wall of Mad Dogs is advancing down the street, hair matted and disheveled, dressed in rags, filthy and trailing their own waste.

Thousands of them.

The horde tramples and grinds down the first cop like road kill without breaking its stride. The second stumbles and falls to his knees. Almost instantly, the mob plows into him with the force of a car, tosses him into the air like a doll, and quarters him neatly, spraying a cloud of blood into the air.

The woman cop stops in the middle of the street and turns around, bracing her shield and holding her truncheon over her head, her braid spilling down her back.

Lewis' rifle bangs: A Mad Dog drops. Bangs again, and another falls. He is trying to make a hole for the woman, but he knows it is useless. He sees the faces of the infected as he kills them. Their faces have no expression, only moving when their mouths contort into snarls and yelps, while their eyes remain fixed with an alien stare.

He fires again and again, draining the magazine.

Save one bullet for her, he tells himself.

No, she can make it.

No, she's already dead.

His rifle clicks empty.

The cop swings her truncheon once before disappearing into the throng, which swallows her whole, instantly, as if she never existed.

"God damn you bastards!" Lewis roars in a sudden blind rage, standing and shaking his fist. "I'll kill every one of you!"

His radio crackles in his ear.

Who are you shouting at, Sergeant?

He turns and sees the officers and senior NCOs clustered on the other side of the roof, staring at him.

Lewis wipes his eyes and keys his handset.

"You'd better come see this, LT," he says. "You'd better come right now."

Job security

McLeod flips the girl onto her stomach so he does not have to look at her face, particularly her eyes, which are wide open and glassy and staring. He bends down, grabs her ankles using latex gloves, and begins pulling her across the street, followed by a dense cloud of flies. Her dress hikes up, exposing her bare legs, and her face drags along the ground, leaving a thick smear of coagulated blood from the bullet hole in her throat.

"Oh, God," he says, repulsed, trying not to look, humming loudly to shut out the sound of her face rasping against the asphalt.

"Hold up, Private," a voice says behind him.

"Roger that," McLeod says, flinging the girl's legs down and staggering away from the corpse.

"Here. Take this." It's Doc Waters, holding out a Q-Tip.

"What's this for?"

"It's Vicks vapor rub. Rub some under your nose and it'll cut out the stink."

McLeod smiles, waving flies away from his face. "Thanks, Doctor. You're the best."

"Not in your nose, Private. Under it. There you go. Technically, you should not even be putting it under your nose. But it should help against the smell of the dead."

"I don't care what it does to me, as long as it works." McLeod begins sniffing dramatically. "How about that. It does work."

"You know, you really shouldn't stack corpses like that. You should have used body bags. If you need to move them again, you'll have to use a shovel."

"Not enough bags, I guess. Shovelers, we got lots of."

"I see." Doc Waters gestures at the three other soldiers dragging corpses into the fly-covered pile near the front of the building. "So you're not the only one in the shitter, Private. Who are these guys?"

McLeod grins. "They're the misfits from First Platoon who started fighting after the LT's speech telling us how everybody we know is dying back home."

Doc Waters eyes him. "When was the last time you got some shuteye?"

"What is this wondrous thing you call 'shuteye'?"

The combat medic sighs. "Sergeant Ruiz doesn't have the authority to give you an Article 15 punishment. I'll put in a word with him about how hard he's riding you."

"Why? Look at me, Doctor. I'm working outside. Exercise, sunlight, fresh air."

The truth is he has not been this tired since Basic. He remembers sleeping on his feet all the way to some range in the middle of nowhere, stuffed into a cattle car with the rest of his training company. That was nothing compared to this. One thing he can thank the Army for: a deep appreciation for the simple things in life that are absent during combat, like a hot shower, air-conditioning, greasy burgers and fries, time for yourself, driving a car going nowhere in particular, privacy, a girlfriend. And decent sleep.

They flinch at the high-pitched crack of carbines down the street. First Platoon boys providing security for the cleanup detail, dropping Mad Dogs at the perimeter.

"And my own bodyguards," McLeod adds, then turns and shouts, "Keep 'em coming! Get some!" He grins. "They keep killing Mad Dogs over there, and me and my new friends keep stacking them nice and neat over here so we can burn them later for public health. Do you know what I call that, Doctor? Do you?"

"No, what do you call that, Private?" Doc Waters asks, his patience suddenly exhausted.

"Job security!"

The medic chuckles despite himself, shaking his head.

A soldier calls from the front doors of the school. "We got more people coming in, Doc. You want to check them out?"

"You're a piece of work, Private," Doc Waters tells McLeod, and returns to the front doors of the school, where four civilians are being held at gunpoint.

"I try my best, Doctor," McLeod mutters, bending over and grabbing the girl's ankles. "I try my best."

First Platoon's Sergeant Hooper tells the detail to stop work for the day and come get some chow.

"Roger that," says McLeod, dropping the corpse's legs again, stripping off his gloves and walking over to the curb, where the boys from First Platoon are already washing their hands and tearing the plastic wrapping off their MREs.

The MRE provides twelve hundred calories and contains a main entrée, side dish, plastic spoon, bread or crackers and spread, sports drink or dairy shake or some other beverage, seasonings, pack of gum, candy such as Tootsie Rolls or a pastry, flameless ration heater, matches, napkins and moist toilette.

Tonight, McLeod has scored chicken and dumplings. Excellent, he tells himself. He pockets the moist toilette. He's been saving them up and intends to take a quick whore's bath after his work here is over.

"What'd you get?" one of the other soldiers says.

"Beef brisket," another answers him.

"I'll trade you chili and macaroni."

"All right."

"My mom used to make this incredible chili. She'd get the beef from Costco—"

"How can I eat this shit while I'm listening to you talk about your mom's home cooking?"

"Who has Tabasco sauce?"

"Who's got C4? Let's make a fire and heat this shit up and eat it right."

"No fires, boys," Sergeant Hooper says, standing nearby with his thumbs hooked in his load-carrying vest. "Chow down that supper fast."

Small arms fire erupts to the south.

"Stop making more work for us!" one of the grunts calls out. "We're taking five over here."

"That's not our guys," McLeod says. "It's farther south. It's Alpha. Or Bravo."

"Listen to General Patton here."

McLeod says, "The curfew is on. The new ROE says anybody they see walking the street after curfew is hostile and they are cleared hot."

"Finally taking the gloves off," one of the grunts says, nodding. "Second Platoon's LT is full of crap. We take the gloves off and put these mutants down, we'll have this city cleaned up in no time." He glares and his face turns red. "There ain't no world ending. My mom and sister are doing just fine."

"Okay, peace, brother," says one of his comrades. "I don't feel like fighting with you about it again."

"Next time, I won't try to break it up," says the third. "You dicks got me in trouble."

"And what about you, McLeod?" the first grunt says in a menacing tone. "Is the world ending? What do you think?"

"Oh, I think whatever you think," McLeod says cheerfully.

The soldier blinks, then says, "Well, okay, then."

McLeod goes back to eating, tuning out the soldiers and listening to the sound of gunfire all around the city as Warlord's companies slowly grind their way through the wreckage to consolidate. It is a disturbing sound. It is the sound of a lot of people dying.

Is the world ending? You betcha, he thinks.

He remembers feeling a perverse thrill at the LT's speech. The end of the world. Yes, sir! No more taxes, credit card debt, dance clubs, snooty cheerleaders, asshole jocks, careers, bank accounts, retirement worries, gym class, bad TV shows, plastic surgery, stupid politicians, megachurches or the constant feeling that you are in a hole and can't get out. No more stupid rules that hem you in from every side.

Life is about to get a whole lot simpler. Just the law of the gun, and McLeod is hanging out with the people who have the best guns. As if to lend weight to this thought, the shooting to the south suddenly intensifies.

With each death out there, the world's memory is getting shorter. A man could become reborn in this struggle and rename himself. No more living in the shadow of his great politician dad and his class clown past. During every screw-up in high school, McLeod would stand before his dad with a defiant smile, but the bastard never so much as blinked at him, too sanctimonious to lose his temper or even scold him his wayward son. Over time, the screw-ups got bigger, bolder, to get a reaction, any reaction. His upper-crust mother finally broke down, but he never won against dear old Dad of Steel. When he got caught shoplifting for the second time, his dad was through cleaning up his messes quietly behind the scenes, and McLeod was given a choice of jail or the Army.

When you screw up in the Army, you get a big reaction. Guaranteed.

McLeod smiles to himself as he realizes that Dad will probably survive after all. All the bigshot politicians are probably being squirreled away to secret bunkers. Even though his dad's side is out of power right now, all the oligarchs stick together. First thing they'll do when they get out is nuke the Chinese and hand over everything that's left to the rich people. Can't come out the other side of Armageddon and make a fresh start for humanity without bringing all our old problems with us, right-right?

He'd been looking forward to college, though. He loves to read and used to fantasize about spending hours cracking open volumes in the college library, growing smarter by the minute with the knowledge of the ages in his hands. He wanted to sit on the floor with a bunch of intellectuals who would appreciate his true genius. He wanted to study philosophy and try to figure out if there is any point to all of the misery he has already seen in his young life.

But there won't be any more of that for a long time, he thinks. By the time the human race gets through this nightmare, in a few generations we'll be lucky to be able to read a book.

"We should elect a new leader, like Bishop," one of the grunts is saying. "Then we could do our own thing."

"Know what I'd do? I'd go out and get some pussy. I'm freaking horny as hell and if we're all going to die, why aren't we going out and getting us some chicks? Especially since most of them seem to be dying."

"You know what happens when civilians walk up to the door and Doc Waters takes them away? He makes them strip so he can check them for bites."

"Even that chick that came in about an hour ago?"

"Oh, definitely."

"Man, she was definitely hot."

"You can't elect your own leaders in the Army," McLeod says. "If we stop following orders, there will be no more Army. We might as well all go off on our own and start looting and raping now until we're killed a few hours later."

"Yeah, that's what we're just saying, yo."

McLeod grins. "What could you possibly steal that has any value any-more? Food, water, ammo, a safe place to sleep—these are the only things worth anything anymore. And we got them right here."

"Oh, is there some pussy in my MRE that I missed?"

One of the other grunts chimes in, "What do you care what we do, McLeod? They sure as shit didn't put you on this detail because you're some super soldier."

McLeod smiles to himself.

Then he stands up suddenly, spilling his unfinished chicken and dumplings onto the asphalt, his heart racing.

That sound—

Their security detail comes running past, heading into the school.

Like a flood—

He sees them coming.

"Into the school and down on the ground, boys!" Hooper roars.

They bolt inside, shut the doors, and throw themselves onto the floor. Hooper crouches by one of the doors, peering out of the window cut into its top half, through which the day's final threads of sunshine are now streaming. His eyes grow wide and he jerks his head back, his chest ris-ing and falling rapidly. His face has turned chalk white.

The first Mad Dogs run past the school. Hooper raises his fist to tell the boys to freeze, but they are scarcely even breathing. McLeod cannot see the army rushing by outside, but he sees the shadows dancing across the walls and ceiling, and he can hear them loud and clear, the tramp of their feet on the asphalt. He lays his ear to the ground and listens to the thun-der. Tries to picture their pounding feet: boots, tennis shoes, broken high heels, sneakers, bare feet. The ground vibrates under his ear.

The seconds crawl by while the flood of humanity continues to flow past them. How many people is this? he wonders. A thousand? Five thou-sand? Ten?

It's like a stampede of animals, he tells himself, which brings a sudden flash of insight. Animals stampede because something scares them. Are the Mad Dogs as scared of us as we are of them? Is that why they are so hostile—are they simply defending themselves?

McLeod slowly becomes aware that the Mad Dogs are growling. At first, it is like a river of individual sounds babbling in competition, but after a few moments, he begins to sense an underlying pattern. A rhythm emerges, repetitive and forceful. It is not a sound of fear. It is a sound of purpose and violence, like a religious chant or a tribal war song. The sound moves down the street like a massive locomotive and underneath it McLeod hears a constant ominous buzz that vibrates deep in his chest and makes his head ache.

Maddy is going to war.

Moaning, McLeod bites down on his sleeve and clenches his eyes shut.

The stampede gradually fades into the distance until silence returns.

"Jesus God," one of the boys finally says. "I think I crapped my pants."

The others crack grins, whistle, blow air out of their cheeks.

Sergeant Hooper opens one of the doors just enough to take a fast look around outside.

"Where are they going, Sergeant?" McLeod asks him shakily.

"Wait," says Hooper, holding up his hand.

The boys fall silent, watching the NCO.

McLeod suddenly knows where the Mad Dogs are going.

To the south, the constant crackle of small arms fire is escalating.

Final protective fire

Bowman and Knight lean against the roof's parapet and squint at the looming skyscrapers, now glittering with lights against a darkening sky. Behind the officers, Kemper and Vaughan chew on their cigars near one of the rooftop HVAC units, murmuring in a communal cloud of smoke. Sherman sits by the combat net radio, monitoring the nets, while Lewis scans the street with his sniper rifle and a fresh mag.

"The shooting's stopped," says Bowman.

"See anything?" Knight asks him, peering through his binoculars.

Bowman shakes his head.

The gunfire, steadily rising in volume over the past few minutes, stopped abruptly several moments ago. The vacuum was instantly filled with the clanging of a store alarm somewhere in their neighborhood, the buzz of distant helicopters and the dull roar of thousands of air conditioners, even though the evening is cool.

Bowman warned War Hammer Six by radio about the army of Mad Dogs headed his way. Captain Lyons thanked him for the intel and abruptly signed off. Alpha's commander had few options as to what he could actually do with the information. He could either advance or retreat, and retreat at this point would mean surrender.

Lyons is a good officer, and would think things through. Bowman tried to imagine what was going through his mind. He could slow Alpha's pace to give Bravo a chance to catch up and consolidate their firepower. But it is hard enough just to move one company through streets choked with cars and rubbish; two companies would be an unwieldy force of about a hundred and sixty men. And how much more firepower could he really bring to bear by combining their forces in firing zones that consisted of streets and doorways?

No, the LT tells himself. The Captain will not anchor Alpha's fate to Bravo's by waiting around in a hostile area, especially with Bravo having so much ground to cover, but instead go the other way, force marching his command to take advantage of the failing light before night fell. So he will place his boys in a formation favorable to mobile defense and move hard and fast. But how fast can he push a company of eighty men on these streets, fighting for every block?

Not very, apparently. Alpha stepped off over an hour and a half ago and is still at least a mile south of the rendezvous point.

At least he has the curfew in his favor, Bowman thinks. Right now, everybody on the street is hostile and Alpha, Bravo and Delta are cleared hot against anything that moves.

Knight glances up the sky. "He's lost the light," he says.

Bowman grunts, glancing at his RTO.

Sherman says, "War Hammer is reporting heavy casualties. . . . Some dead, most bitten. . . . Quarantine is turning down his request for a mede-vac. . . ."

Bowman and Knight glance at each other. When Charlie's sister companies finally show up, they are going to have to quarantine or otherwise do something with soldiers who were bitten. But this will be Lyons' decision to make, not Bowman's.

Bowman tries to picture what is happening at Alpha's position. Lyons' boys are tired and probably running low on ammo after killing who knows how many Mad Dogs. Some of the soldiers are dead and have to be carried, while a larger number have been bitten and surely know they will become Mad Dogs themselves within a few hours.

Will these soldiers continue fighting for Lyons even though they know their bites are death sentences? Will some of them turn their weapons on themselves? Or will they simply wander off?

What would you do if you had a rifle in your hands in a lawless city and only had a few hours to live?

"War Hammer is telling Warmonger to pick up the pace," Sherman says.

Bowman nods.

Small arms fire erupts in the west, quickly turns into a steady volume of fire. It is Delta Company, attempting to push its way through fresh resistance.

Lieutenant Bishop comes up from behind.

"What have you got?" he says, taking out his binoculars.

"See for yourself," Bowman says without turning around. He is annoyed with the officer and is going to have to get him squared away. It is bad enough having Stephen Knight around. The man is clearly broken after what happened to his platoon. But Bishop is mouthing off to the NCOs like a politician, always saying what they should be doing instead of simply accepting command decisions and making the best of them.

Loud gunfire explodes to the south, close to their position. The shooting has a terrible urgency to it this time, making Bowman's heart pound. A series of flashes like lightning illuminate the outlines of nearby buildings, followed by ear-splitting booms.

He blinks and remembers visiting his uncle's ranch on July Fourth when he was a kid. At night, stuffed on hot dogs and birch beer, he and his cousins retreated into the pastures, alive with fireflies and the singing of the dog day cicadas, and watched the fireworks light up the sky and explode with terrifying bangs.

Knock it off, he tells himself. He has done well armoring his mind against the destruction of the past as well as the terrifying idea of future extinction. His only weakness is the escape offered by pleasant memories of home. These memories helped get him through Iraq but here, they will only slow him down and make him weak when he needs to stay sharp and focused. There is a time and place for pain. . . .

The Way of the Warrior and all that. The macho stuff the lifers talk about. It is a philosophy that tells you to embrace pain so that it makes you stronger. Well, that certainly applies here and now. He wants his feelings cauterized. In his case, there is nothing macho about it. He simply believes that a lot of his men will die if he does not stay strong, uncaring, unfeeling.

The shooting suddenly cascades into a deafening, crackling roar punctuated by flashes, pops and booms he can feel deep in his chest.

"That's FPF," Knight murmurs.

Final protective fire. A defensive tactic. When it is put into play, the unit fires every weapon it has to stop the enemy from advancing and save itself from being overrun. It is the option of last resort. The meaning is obvious: Alpha is in trouble.

Bowman is amazed at the number of Mad Dogs. In the past five hours, they must have doubled in population. The easy explanation is they overran the hospitals and infected thousands of people in their beds, along with a full night and day of infecting anybody who ventured outside their homes. There must be tens of thousands at this point, possibly even hundreds of thousands, running towards the sounds of the gunfire from all over the city. The average rifleman carries more than two hundred rounds. If every bullet for each of their weapons found its mark, a single company could theoretically kill twenty thousand of the enemy.

Would even that be enough?

He reminds himself that First Squad alone, burning through almost all of its ammo, killed hundreds of Mad Dogs in less than fifteen minutes. Alpha can win this fight.

Kemper, Vaughan and Sherman join the officers at the parapet, their eyes gleaming.

Eleventh Cavalry air units are buzzing over the battle, weaving around the skyscrapers. An Apache helicopter suddenly buzzes low and fires a pair of Hellfire missiles at the street.

Kemper flinches and says, "Christ, that's close."

A second helicopter drops a TOW missile, guides it to its target, then veers off like an angry hornet. Fireballs expand and rise above distant buildings. Heat and light.

Kemper adds, "Unless. . . ." But says nothing more.

Bowman nods. Unless the friendly units are serving a dual purpose on the march. Either they make it to the rendezvous and consolidate and therefore become an effective player in this game, or serve as bait to lure the enemy into a killing zone for the Cavalry. General Kirkland, leader of the Sixth ID, may have issued a standing order to his air units to destroy concentrations of Mad Dogs regardless of whether there are friendly units near the target.

This does not piss him off. Bowman understands its logic. Kirkland is desperate and flailing and fighting to win to save a dying country, staking everything on this one night. Bowman realizes that he would do the same thing in the General's shoes. It is basic utilitarianism: The needs of the many outweigh the needs of the few. Military decisions in war are often based on such ethics.

Confirming Kemper's suspicion, Sherman looks up from the radio and says, "They're not calling in those air attacks. They've got men down."

"Sir, I. . . ." Vaughan says, struggling for words.

"We need to get out there right now," Lewis says, finishing for him.

"We will follow our orders and stay in position," Bowman says, looking through his binoculars.

"Sir," Lewis pleads. "Let me take out Second Squad."

Bowman glares at him. "That's a no go, Sergeant. Are we clear?"

"Crystal," Lewis says tersely.

Bowman sounds confident, but is actually feeling anything but. In fact, he is itching to get Charlie into the game. Could this be a decisive battle? he wonders. Is Lewis right that we should spread out and shoot down every Mad Dog as early as possible before it becomes too late? Should I lead my men out there to support Alpha or Delta, and perhaps put an end to this once and for all?

Or is it already too late—for Alpha, for Delta, for all of us?

It all depends on the infection rate, Bowman knows. Manhattan has more than one and a half million people living on it. If one percent of them are now infected, that would be about sixteen thousand people. If five percent, it would be eighty thousand.

If ten percent, it would be a hundred and sixty thousand.

"Warmonger is reporting a large body of Mad Dogs from the west," Sherman says.

Even when given clear orders, Bowman believes a field commander must act on his own initiative as facts change on the ground. On the other hand, a commander must recognize that he does not have perfect situational awareness and should never make emotional decisions. The fact is, nobody really knows what is happening. Everybody is guessing. And bucking orders to support Alpha or Delta, the two companies closest to Charlie's position, would be a major risk to his own boys.

On the other hand, American soldiers are in trouble out there and need help.

The only way to find out would be to literally "do or die."

As if reading his thoughts, Bishop says, "We'd never get there in time, Todd. There's nothing we can do."

"War Pig is calling in a danger-close fire mission," Sherman says.

"We have arty support?" Knight says, incredulous.

Bowman shakes his head. Quarantine said nothing about artillery support. Artillery is a sledgehammer, too unwieldy for this situation. Even after everything he has seen, it would be almost too fantastic to contemplate—American artillery, planted miles way, firing HE rounds for effect into the middle of New York City.

In any case, the request itself is a bad sign. That's Captain Reese, a good officer and a cool hand in a firefight, leading Delta. A danger-close fire mission is when an arty strike is called in within six hundred meters of your position. Practically on top of your own head. It's another sign of desperation. Like Alpha, Delta is in trouble.

"What the hell?" Bishop shouts.

The skyscrapers are suddenly going dark in groups, as if a series of giant light switches controlling the glittering skyline of New York City were being flipped off one by one. The streetlights shut off. All of the lights shut off.

Kemper says simply, "Blackout. . . ."

The world is plunged into darkness.

The gunfire suddenly slackens, becomes haphazard.

The men gasp. The boys out there were caught flatfooted by the dark. Would they have time to put on night vision goggles or produce battlefield illumination? If they could get their NVGs on, they would have the advantage and might even turn the tables.

They see the flashes in the west and south where the companies are making their stand. The gunfire in the west sputters and slows.

Then it stops.

The men gasp again. Either Reese fought his way out, or he and his boys are dead. Surely, he got through and is back on the march. It is hard for these men to conceive of an entire company being destroyed.

In the south, a single flare rockets up into the sky and deploys a small parachute, producing a fiery, eerie glow as it begins its lazy descent to the earth.

Immediately, the gunfire intensifies, but then it too sputters, stops, flares up, dies.

The helicopters buzz in closer, firing missiles, raking the streets with devastating strafing fire. Then one by one they detach from the engage-ment and fly away.

The city is silent except for the ringing in their ears.

"Is that it?" Lewis asks. Tears of rage are streaming down his face. "The power goes out and Battalion gets overrun? Just because of some bad goddamn luck?"

Nobody answers him. Everybody knows there was a lot more to it than that. They know it was doubtful whether they could have fought their way through anyway. They realize now that they are facing an enemy that is stronger than they are.

And they are alone.

Bowman says quietly, "Jake, I want you to raise War Hammer for me."

"All companies stopped broadcasting," says the RTO. "The net is clear."

"Try, Jake."

"Yes, sir."

Above, the sky opens up in a brilliant display of stars not seen in this part of the world since the Blackout of 2003. The tiny blinking light of a satellite lazily crosses the sky.

"No response, sir," Sherman says in the dark.

The men stand in the dark in a stunned silence.

"Jake," the LT says carefully, "I want you to raise Warmonger and War Pig and ask for a sitrep."

Sherman blinks in the gloom. "Sir?"

"Now, Jake."

"Yes, sir."

The darkness bears down on them, forcing their thoughts inward. After several moments, the RTO says, "No response, sir."

Bowman nods, feeling lightheaded.

In one night, the world just got a whole lot smaller. Much smaller, and infinitely more dangerous.

While there is life there is hope

First Squad marches down the hallway, the beams of their flashlights playing on the shiny floor, a display case filled with trophies, dull rows of lockers and acoustical ceiling tiles. Mooney, Carrillo, Rollins and Finnegan carry Private Chen in a black body bag.

After the power went out and the emergency generator restored the lights in the gym, they heard the news via Joe Radio—the rumor mill—that the other companies had been destroyed.

Mooney believed it. His comrades didn't.

His BDUs are stiff, dirty and stained. His uniform would probably stand up on its own if he took it off. Probably run after a bone if he yelled fetch. He is exhausted from endless work, his left eye won't stop twitching from stress, and his nerves take a flying leap every time somebody clears his throat. But the news about the slaughter of Warlord while trying to walk several miles across Manhattan has electrified him.

All of his worries have suddenly evaporated. He does not care about Laura or how he wishes he could spend a few hours listening to his favorite records. He does not care about Wyatt constantly bugging him. Deep down, he does not even care if this is the end of the world.

All he cares about, at this very minute, is whether he is going to survive and for how long.

This war, this total war as LT put it, has gotten very personal and Mooney simply can't really think of its ramifications beyond that. He does not want to die. Nothing else matters.

After the news circulated about Warlord, the NCOs went up to the roof to find LT while the civilians either stood around in stunned silence or started bawling.

It was the perfect time to slip out for the funeral.

They were ordered to burn Chen's body with the civilian dead, but the boys had another idea. If things were as bad as LT said they were, most of the empty classrooms would be staying empty for a long, long time.

Tonight, PFC Chen would be entombed in his very own mausoleum.

Multiple footsteps approach from behind. Mooney's heart leaps into his throat, his left eye trembling.

Ratliff wheels, raising his rifle, and challenges: "Mets."

"Go to hell, Ratliff," a voice answers from the darkness.

Ghostly forms emerge from the gloom. It's Third Squad, wearing bright green glow sticks hooked onto the front of their load-bearing vests.

"You're supposed to say, 'Yankees,'" Ratliff says, suddenly out of breath.

"Oh, Mad Dogs can talk? Can you get that light out of my face?"

Corporal Eckhardt lowers his rifle and says, "Next time, say 'Yankees' and you won't get shot, Private. What you got there?"

Corporal Hicks says, "We heard what you were doing for Billy Chen."

"Whatever you heard, you heard wrong," Eckhardt says defiantly.

"It's not like that. We'd like to do the same for two of ours." Hicks gestures behind him. "This is The Newb. The other is Hawkeye. We don't want them burned up in a pile. We want them to cross over to the other side whole, with honors."

Eckhardt glances at the other boys of First Squad. Mooney nods. There is plenty of room where Chen is going.

"Where's the class clown?" he says, obviously referring to McLeod.

"Sarge gave him sack time," says Hicks.

"All right," Eckhardt says. "We scoped out the last classroom on the left and got everything set up there. We found an American flag. You got something to cover up your guys?"

"We'll make do," Hicks tells him. "You lead. We'll follow you."

Together, they bring the bodies into the classroom. All of the desks have been pushed against the walls, which are adorned with posters of animals, a human skeleton with all of his bones labeled, and a skinless man with all of his muscles labeled.

Earlier in the day, one of the boys wrote on the chalkboard:

HERE LIES PFC WILLIAM CHEN. HE WAS A GOOD SOLDIER AND LOYAL FRIEND. HE WILL BE MISSED. MAY HIS DEATH BE A LESSON TO US THAT WHILE THERE IS LIFE THERE IS HOPE.

RIP

Mooney and the other boys pause for a moment to read the message. They grunt, impressed. They set down the body bag and unzip it.

The boys stagger back, gagging.

"Like rotten cheese and eggs," says Finnegan, retching.

"Is he alive?" says Rollins. "He's moving!"

"Quiet, he's trying to say something. . . ."

"Jesus," Mooney says, swallowing hard to force back his bile. "Some flies got on him before we zipped him up and laid eggs in him. His face is moving because *it's filled with maggots.*"

"Damn," says Rollins, paling.

"Zip him up, Mooney, goddamnit," Eckhardt orders.

Mooney closes the bag.

"Still stinks in here," says Corporal Wheeler.

"Not as bad, though," Eckhardt points out.

"Smells like one of my farts after I get the MRE with chili and beans," says Wyatt.

"Joel, shut up," Mooney says, feeling light headed at the mention of food. "Just stop talking."

The boys push several of the student desks together and lay the bodies on top of them.

"Check this out," says Williams. "Somebody carved into this desk, *'SCREW MR. SCHERMERHORN.'* That's all right."

Nobody laughs. Eckhardt drapes the American flag over the three body bags.

The carvings on the desks give Mooney the creeps. The memory of the normal world haunts this school in a very real way. It is too easy to close one's eyes and picture thirty bored teenagers trying to stay awake so they can figure out what their biology teacher is telling them.

Standing here in this classroom makes him feel like he is in a museum.

Eckhardt and Hicks eulogize the boys who were killed while everybody else says their own farewells by placing their right hands over their hearts, a gesture of respect they learned from the Iraqis. Eckhardt says he didn't know Billy Chen well, apparently nobody did, but Chen was Army and that made him family. Hicks describes Hawkeye's uncanny marksmanship, which very likely would have destined him to become a sniper if he wanted to make the Army a career. Tells how Hawkeye always got stuck on point and never complained about that or anything else. Wheeler and Williams make them laugh by describing jokes McLeod would play on The Newb while he was asleep—tying his shoelaces together, dunking his hand in warm water—the usual barracks pranks. Eckhardt says each of these men died for their country.

The boys glance at each other, uncomfortable. What does that mean anymore? They know what dying means, they've seen enough of it, and it is not hard to imagine themselves rotting inside those body bags instead of their friends, infested with maggots. But what country? Most of them are in a state of flat denial but even they know America is going through a crisis from which it will emerge looking entirely different. What comes out the other side, in fact, may no longer be recognizable anymore as "America."

An awkward silence descends upon the funeral. Nobody knows what to say.

"What if it's true?" Ratliff says hesitantly, obviously afraid he will be ridiculed for saying something this honest.

"How can it be true?" Wyatt says. "A bunch of unarmed Hajjis can't just wipe out a battalion."

"Why would they be making that shit up for, dawg?" Williams says. "To boost your morale? You all know it's true but you just don't want to face it."

Nobody answers him.

"Well, if it's true, then what are we supposed to do with one lousy company?"

"Keep our heads down, if we're smart," Williams tells him.

"You got that right," some of the other boys murmur, nodding.

The other boys chime in.

"Give this thing a chance to blow over."

"Wait. We're going to be okay, aren't we? Right?"

"They're not going to airlift us out?"

"Don't count on it. Where would they land the birds—outside in the street?"

"We got good people leading us," Hicks says. "We should be okay."

"Captain Lyons was good," Rollins says. "And now Alpha's gone."

"And Reese. And Moreno. They were good, too."

"They were following orders. Kirkland and Winters told them to march and they marched."

"Exactly my point. What if they call up LT and tell him to march?"

"If I was LT, I wouldn't even answer the phone."

"I know the LT," Eckhardt says. "He'll follow his orders."

"If the Army is in this bad shape, why should he risk his neck?" Williams says.

"Why should any of us?" says Ratliff.

The boys fall into another awkward silence.

Finally, Mooney says, "You guys are going to laugh, but I'm sticking with the LT because I want to see kids go to school here again."

Nobody laughs. The boys watch him curiously.

He says: "It's like this. . . . Billy Chen died fighting for his country. Seems to me that country is disappearing around us. If it keeps going, we might end up being all that's left of it. We walk away from our jobs, then America is gone. That's how I feel about it. So I'm going to do my job and keep America alive long enough so it can get back on its feet and be normal again some day. That's my mission."

The boys shift restlessly, murmuring and nodding. Mooney has planted a seed in their minds stronger than patriotism. He is giving them a condition for victory in this war without heroes, without winners. He is reminding them of home at peace.

They are picturing picnics and pickup trucks, girlfriends and first dates, street hockey and drive-in movies, granddads playing checkers in the park, long drives on summer nights, a favorite song on the radio, arguments about politics, getting up early for church on Sunday, holding jobs and cashing paychecks. Even the petty worries and needs that no longer seem important—like bills to pay and credit cards and what everybody else is wearing and the latest street slang—all of it strikes the boys deep in the soul, making them nostalgic for the mundane world that is ending.

There is a difference between going to Iraq to fight for your country and being in the situation they are in now, literally fighting for your country's survival. If they can keep even a shred of the old America alive, they feel like they will win.

Mooney wants to stay alive, and there is safety in numbers. But it is not enough to stay alive. A man must also have something for which he wants to live as well.

Chapter 11

I want to tell my story first so you won't forget me

The only thing that kept us alive so long was the small firing zones. The Maddies had to bunch up and for a while there, we were shooting fish in a barrel. They came at us in twos and threes out of doorways, around corners, out of cars—they even came flying out of windows. We had maybe sixty men when we stepped off. We were armed to the teeth and cleared hot to shoot anything that moved. No identifying targets. Just shoot and scoot. We also had a good leader. Captain Reese was a damn good officer and I would have followed him anywhere, even after he cracked. It took us a while to get used to the fact the enemy wasn't shooting back at us. After that, we went to town.

After ten blocks of being in a meat grinder and shooting at a sustained rate of fire, though, we started to get tired. It was like being under harassing fire except it was bodies they were throwing at us, not bullets. The abandoned vehicles all over the street forced us to take it slow and screwed up our firing lanes, making us waste ammo. There were cars and trucks and glass everywhere from one abandoned traffic jam after another, and the shadows from the light poles were murder. We saw over and over again where somebody with a big truck or SUV panicked and tried to ram his way out, pushing vehicles into pileups. Some of the cars were on fire and pumping out this thick, oily smoke. Civilians were screaming from windows and throwing shit at us to get our attention.

By the time we'd gone twenty blocks, we were down to forty, fifty men. A few guys got killed, but most of our losses were from guys who just melted away into doorways of apartment buildings. You'd turn around, and suddenly they'd be gone. Some walked away because they'd got bit and they knew this was a death sentence. Others probably just thought it was suicide to keep pushing and they'd had enough. I don't think they're cowards. I really don't. This war is bigger than all of us, almost too big to even understand. People break easy when they try to get their head around something this big. A war where winning feels like losing, and losing, well, it means you're dead.

Anyhow, the Mad Dogs showed up in force from two directions. There were thousands of them out there in the dark, coming fast, all of them growling with each breath so that they sounded like a train. If you ever saw the movie *Zulu* with Michael Caine, it was like that—thousands and thousands of people running in waves against aimed rifle fire. No, better, I remember I once saw a crowd of a couple thousand kids stampede at a heavy metal concert. Now imagine all those people are running at you and they want to tear you to pieces with their bare hands and teeth. I saw them coming and I pissed down my leg. There's no shame in that. It happens to a lot of guys, right? Never happened to me in Iraq, even when the bullets went buzzing right by my ear like wasps. Funny if you think about it. I had to come home to learn true fear.

It's down there? God, this place looks like an insane asylum. Freaking stinks, too. Listen. Just let me tell the rest of my story before you put me in, please. I didn't fight my way here all night just to get pushed into one of these rooms and forgotten about. I came because I wanted to feel something, anything, like home again, just one more time. And I want to tell my story first so you won't forget me.

Thank you. I mean it.

So there we were, already low on ammo and with a horde of maniacs coming at us out of the darkness, and we tore them a new asshole. We unloaded everything we had on them. No more shoot and scoot. We were a mobile defense, and it was time to defend. We propped the MGs and SAWs on the hoods of cars and rained lead. They were ripped to shreds. Bodies were cut in half. Heads popped off of bodies and flew into the air. It was incredible, like being in some warped virtual reality game. You're going to think I'm one sick puppy, but it felt good. It felt like survival. I didn't see them as people anymore, but as a group, as a whole, like this one big monster. The more they died, the more I lived, you know? I wanted them to keep coming. I wanted them all to die.

And I still honestly thought we'd make it. At that time, despite our fatigue, our ammo situation and our losses, getting overrun was the last thing on my mind. But then rifles started jamming. One of the MGs overheated. I fired mag after mag at a rapid rate of fire until I had almost nothing left, and still they kept coming. Waves of them. Overhead, the helicopters were circling, watching us, and then when things got dicey they strafed the Mad Dogs with the chain guns and, oh Lord, entire sections of the horde just exploded and disintegrated.

Things went to hell in a hurry after that.

An Apache came in low, blinding us with his light, and started dropping rockets and now vehicles were being flipped and tossed into the air, like: *Wham! Wham! Wham!* Hot metal was flying everywhere, ringing off the vehicles and clattering off the walls and ripping through the bodies of the guys in my squad. In an instant the Apache screamed overhead and was gone, I was squinting through the afterglow in my eyes and shooting, and then I noticed that my entire squad had literally disappeared. It was just me and my Sergeant, who was bleeding from his ears and stone deaf and staring in a daze. It wasn't Maddy that killed my squad; it was blue on blue fire. It was right about then that Captain Reese got a little confused because he started screaming into the radio calling for an arty strike almost on top of us to keep the Hajjis from overrunning our position. He completely freaking lost it.

That's when I knew I was a dead man. A river of blood was literally flowing around my ankles like something out of the Bible. Moments later, the power went out and everything went black. And that's when the real horror began.

We had no time to put on NVGs or shoot a flare. We were firing randomly in the dark on full auto, backing up until we formed a square around Captain Reese with bayonets fixed. The muzzle flashes showed glimpses of the Mad Dogs tearing Second Platoon apart, so close you wanted to puke from the stench. They were screaming in the dark. It was hand to hand and the guys were dying fast. And what was I doing? Shit, my heart was pounding like a drum and I was pissing down my leg. I could barely move, I was shaking so bad.

First Sergeant Callahan tried to pull the Captain away to the safety of a nearby building, but the man stood his ground, shooting his pistol while somebody popped smoke in a crazy try at concealing him. The Maddies swarmed around him and ripped him apart by the handful. I only barely survived after being picked up and thrown into the air by the mob—it was like getting hit by a baseball bat everywhere on my body at once—and crawled under a truck. All around me, the horde just kept coming, running past, rattling the vehicles and making the ground shake like a herd of elephants.

Maddy died by the thousand but he wiped us out and barely broke his stride doing it. And after all that, I lived to hike it back almost the entire way here before some goddamn kid pops out the back of a minivan and gives me this on my hand. But I'll tell you, it's just as well, because I'm so tired. In fact, I don't think I've ever been this tired.

Is this my new home?

Any, um, other last requests?

PFC Mooney opens the door to the classroom and waits. He and Wyatt have heard the same stories told repeatedly by shell-shocked survivors trickling in since last night. Mooney does not know what to say to the soldier. What is there to say? What does one say to a man whose friends were violently torn apart right in front of him and is now doomed to die from a poison busily replicating itself in his brain?

"I don't get a roommate or nothing?" the soldier wants to know.

"Everybody else who got bit is already starting to turn," Mooney explains. "You could be the last one. They might attack you. We don't know."

"It would have been nice to talk to somebody else from Delta and cross over together."

"Sorry, man."

"It's okay. I guess it doesn't matter. You're gonna die some day whether you get that last smoke in or not. I'm just glad the war's over for me."

"We left a few books in there that we got from the library. Classics. Help you pass the time. I don't know, maybe you'll like them. We also put the word out in case any of the survivors want to stop by and talk with you through the door. You still got a little time."

The soldier nods. "Right. Okay. Thanks."

Mooney notices that the soldier's left eye is twitching.

"Any, um, other last requests?" says Wyatt.

"No, I'm good," the soldier says, walks into the classroom, and approaches the window, looking out into the sunshine. He breathes deep and says, "I'm telling you, it sure is—"

Mooney has already begun to close the door. Wyatt passes him a handful of nails, which he hammers into the edge of the wood door to secure it to its frame.

The survivors trickled in all night and the next day, telling their horror stories. Half of them were bitten but had nowhere else to go. The LT did not want to kill them or turn them out so he came up with the idea of converting part of the school's west wing into an asylum.

Wyatt raises the plundered surface of a desk and Mooney begins hammering until it covers the bottom half of the door and its frame. Once the door is completely covered, Mooney nails one of the soldier's dog tags into the wood—name, rank, serial number, blood type and religious preference—while Wyatt scrawls the boy's name with a pen knife.

Mooney waits patiently until Wyatt is done carving. He can hear the Mad Dogs in the other classrooms pacing and growling. They were soldiers once, these lost boys. This is where they turned, and this is where they will eventually die and be entombed.

Wyatt picks up his carbine and says, "Let's get out of this freaking zoo."

"You say that again and I will take you out, Joel."

Wyatt smiles but says nothing.

Mooney pauses to touch the name Wyatt carved into the wood, struggling through his exhaustion to commit the boy and his paltry details to memory.

PFC James F. Lynch has blood type A and is a Christian, no denomination.

The real problem isn't people leaving the Army. . . . The real problem is the Army leaving us

Sergeant Pete McGraw glides his thumb over the rabbit's foot in his pocket, his personal talisman given to him by his wife before his first tour in Iraq and her death in a car accident on an icy bridge in Maryland months later. The smooth fur of the rabbit's foot comforts him. After everything he has seen and been through in three tours of duty in Iraq and now this bag of dicks, he firmly believes luck and Margaret's spirit watching over him are the only things standing between him and oblivion. In his other pocket, he fingers a bent bottle cap he kept on a whim from the first beer he ever had with his girlfriend Tricia, a slim blonde beauty with braided hair down to her waist who shares his passion for hard drinking and motorcycles, among other things. He wears a medal engraved with an image of St. Michael, patron saint of soldiers and cops, on a chain around his neck, next to his dog tags and a 7.62-mm bullet. The bullet, the type of round used in AK47 assault weapons, is the bullet that was going to kill him back in Iraq, and as long as he wore it, it couldn't fulfill its purpose.

From here on out, he is going to need all the luck he can get, seeing how the world is ending.

He falls in with the other NCOs cramming into the school principal's offices, an open workspace and lobby with several adjoining private offices that Bowman established as his headquarters. The men nod to each other as they enter, smelling like sweat, gun oil and stale cigarette smoke. A sergeant that McGraw knows from First Platoon catches his eye and gives him a courteous nod, and McGraw wonders at how quickly things change. Just two days ago, the other NCOs were looking at him and his squad like they had blood on their hands and swastikas tattooed on their foreheads. Now they regard his boys with something like respect. His boys popped their cherry in this war early. But if he is getting respect, the NCOs from the other companies who survived the massacres are looked upon with something like awe. They went to hell and back and survived.

The non-coms gather around 2LT Bowman, who stands with his hands on his hips next to a large tourist map of Manhattan, complete with call-outs of businesses such as Barnes & Noble and Burger King, thumb-tacked to the wall. The RTO pushes his way through the bodies, races into one of the private offices, and slams the door. Knight and Bishop come out of one of the other offices and hustle to Bowman's side. Kemper is shading Staten Island and Battery Park red with a Magic Marker. Bowman is already greeting them in a quiet voice, and McGraw can't hear him.

The sergeants blink in the fluorescent light and sip their lukewarm coffee, bags under their eyes and carbines slung over their shoulders, murmuring to each other. Sergeant Lewis is sharing some of his chaw. As Bowman finishes his welcome, they settle down to listen. McGraw does a rough headcount; there are so many NCOs in their unit now that the crowd spills out into the hall. Some he recognizes from the other platoons of Charlie Company, others are survivors from the massacre of Alpha,

Bravo and Delta. These are the best men the Army has, McGraw thinks. The lifers. They are the bedrock of the Army, these modern-day Centurions. It takes years to make one of these men, and once they are gone, they cannot be replaced.

All of them now report to a young second lieutenant who happens to be the most senior officer alive in the entire battalion. McGraw watches him and thinks: We're lucky the man's competent. It could be much worse. They could have Knight, who is only nominally still in command of Third Platoon, or Bishop, the type of officer who risks lives to advance his career. McGraw has been hearing rumors that Bishop has been telling some of the NCOs that he wanted to lead a party out to try to help the other companies during the massacre. The sooner LT gets him squared away, the better.

"Jake has been combing the nets to come up with a list of assets and threats," Bowman says. "Mike has been marking them on this map. If we're going to survive, gentlemen, we need information."

The NCOs periodically stand on tip toe to improve their view, squinting at the map. McGraw sees a series of colored circles, squares, long smears and triangles littering the length of Manhattan and the river coasts of the boroughs and neighboring states. It is pathetic. In just a few days, the Army has lost control of most of New York City and its population of more than eight million. The color-coded geometric shapes float on the map like islands in an ocean.

We really do have our backs up against the wall, he realizes.

Bowman traces his finger across the map and stabs a red square at Battery Park.

"This here is actually what's left of a mechanized infantry brigade of marines sent to reinforce Warlord before Command decided against it," he says. "They've got two platoons at Fort Clinton and the rest are stationed in Staten Island, which used to be Twenty-Seventh Brigade's responsibility. After the government here collapsed, Colonel Dixon declared martial law and cleared Staten Island of Mad Dogs."

Some of the sergeants grin and nudge each other.

"They, uh, do like to take the initiative, so I hear, sir," Kemper says, making the men laugh.

"Yeah, well, Manhattan's got a hell of a lot more people than Staten Island," Hooper says, reminding them that they work for a rival branch of the military and not to give the jarheads too much credit for anything.

"I could get some work done around here if I had some LAVs, too," another sergeant says.

"Hooah," somebody mutters.

"Give me some Bradleys and about thirty bulldozers, and I'll unfuck this island double quick," somebody shouts from the back, and the NCOs cheer.

"The Marines have got their own problems," Bowman says loudly, regaining control. "The only reason the Marines are on Staten Island to begin with is it was being used as a staging point to reinforce us here in Manhattan. The boats dropped off two platoons in Battery Park, then the Brass called off the game and the units ended up stranded. Now they're effectively cut off from their main force and they are not being resupplied."

The NCOs stop smiling. If military units in the area stop being supplied, then eventually they will start looting to survive, and once an army crosses that line, they cease being an army and become a rabble—part of the problem, not the solution.

Bowman adds, "Meanwhile, Dixon's low on food, ammo and fuel, he has a man down out of every four, and he's now governor and de facto chief of police of an island with nearly five hundred thousand people on it. That's a half a million people getting hungrier, sicker and more pissed off by the minute."

The sergeants bury their faces in their coffee mugs, chastened. Bowman returns to the map, pointing at police stations where at least a few cops are trying to hold it together, Financial District and municipal buildings occupied by ragtag National Guard units and the Brigade's civilian affairs unit, a bridge still held by military police and engineers, and Twenty-Six Federal Plaza, where a handful of FBI agents, immigration officials, Federal judges and their families are apparently holed up. Manhattan is riddled with islands and pockets of friendly units, but nobody is strong enough to link up with anybody else or project their power. The marines at Battery Park might as well be on the Moon. The only real estate any of these units truly controls is right under their feet.

McGraw believes there could be up to fifty, even a hundred thousand Mad Dogs in Manhattan alone. The population grew fast because the problem started mostly in the hospitals and there were thousands upon thousands of people there, lying helpless and easily infected, like tightly packed kindling awaiting a spark. The good news is the Mad Dog population does not appear to be growing as fast as it was. The hospitals have been emptied and most people are staying home, denying the virus a plentiful source of new bodies. In any case, the Mad Dogs now appear to be concentrated into sizable mobs that often end up killing anybody they come into contact with instead of infecting them. Soon, the number of Mad Dogs on the streets is going to start declining as they suffer a massive die-off. The war might end soon if everybody just stays hidden and waits.

Somebody asks about the three yellow boxes in Brooklyn and Queens.

"I was getting to them," Bowman answers. "As far as I can tell, they're deserters. Nothing bigger than a platoon at this point, but it's another thing that Twenty-Fifth Brigade has to worry about that's out there."

The sergeants glance at each other. The country must really be on the brink of collapse if the Army is starting to fall apart.

But the real problem isn't people leaving the Army, the LT tells them.

He adds quickly: "The real problem, it seems, is the Army leaving us."

His finger traces along Brooklyn's western coast, a long green smear.

"This is Second Battalion, Twenty-Fifth Brigade, commanded by Colonel Guzman. He's in a good position."

Another green smear along the north coast of Queens.

"This is two companies of First Battalion, Twenty-Fifth Brigade, commanded by Colonel Powers. He took a real beating last night and is barely holding it together."

He points at a red X in the South Bronx.

"This is the last known position of the other two companies of First Battalion, Twenty-Fifth Brigade, commanded by Captain Marsh. We have lost all contact with his command. It is believed to have been destroyed."

The NCOs murmur and step from foot to foot, suddenly restless and angry.

Bowman taps his finger on a blue square in midtown.

"This is us here. First Battalion, Eighth Brigade."

He points to a blue rectangle in Jersey City, to the west.

"This is Second Battalion, commanded by Colonel Rose," he says. "We're what's left of the Crazy Eights."

"Wait, where's Quarantine?" one of the NCOs calls out.

Bowman shakes his head. "We have lost contact with Quarantine. Colonel Winters and his command are MIA. We are now trying to. . . ." He gives up talking as the non-coms begin murmuring loudly among themselves.

Their headquarters, and all its logistics and signal units—even the brigade band—has disappeared without a trace somewhere across the Hudson River in Jersey City.

"Listen up!" Kemper roars, quieting them instantly.

"The Twenty-Fifth is being loaded onto transports to be taken down the coast to Virginia," Bowman tells them. "Immunity is withdrawing from the region. As far as I can tell, the new strategy is to consolidate in the more rural areas of the country, where the Mad Dog population is smaller and more dispersed, particularly the bread basket—"

"What about us, LT?" McGraw says. "What are we doing here?"

Bowman shakes his head.

"That's just the thing. I honestly don't know. Eighth Brigade has not been issued evac orders for the time being, and Division isn't telling us why."

"What about Los Angeles? Is it being abandoned? I got people there, sir."

"This is a goddamn disgrace!"

Several of the other sergeants start shouting at once.

"I already told you everything I know," Bowman yells over them.

Sherman is pushing his way through the crowd. He reaches Kemper and hands him a piece of paper.

The LT adds: "So we're going to hunker down here for a while and reorganize our unit. We're also going to start training for a new mission."

Kemper reads the note and glances sharply at the RTO, his face reddening.

Bowman continues, "We're going to try to salvage the equipment H&S Company left when they got overrun. They had weapons, food, water, medicine in storage. An ammo dump. If we don't get it, the locals will pick it clean. We need those supplies to remain combat effective."

"How are we supposed to get to H&S?" says Ruiz. "They were over a mile away from here when they were overrun."

Bowman smiles and says, "We're going to innovate."

Kemper approaches and says something into the LT's ear. By the time he finishes, Bowman is visibly angry, leaving the sergeants wondering.

"Put it on the map," says the LT.

The Platoon Sergeant draws a yellow border around Second Battalion in Jersey City. Bowman turns to the NCOs.

"Uh, Jake has just heard from Division that we are to avoid any contact with Second Battalion over in Jersey City," he says. "Colonel Rose and his XO, Major Boyle, are reported dead. Captain Warner is in command, and he is refusing to obey orders."

"Look on my works, ye mighty, and despair!"

McLeod finishes mopping the hallway in the Asylum—what the boys call the wing where they put the soldiers turned Mad Dog—and walks slowly down the virtually empty hall, reading the names carved into the boards nailed over the doors. The visitors are all long gone, as the inmates have all turned Mad Dog.

He passes by one that reads, *JAMES LYNCH.*

Behind the boarded up door, he can hear Maddy pacing in his boots, growling.

"If you had a longer life span, I'd join you," McLeod says. "Seeing as your side seems to be winning this thing, and all."

James Lynch snarls and throws his shoulder against the door, making McLeod take a step backward, almost spilling his bucket. Down the hall, Private Becker from Third Platoon, posted on sentry duty, watches and shakes his head.

McLeod grins and waves, then checks his watch. Lunch time. He decides to take his MRE onto the roof to watch Sergeant Lewis bang away at Maddy with his rifle.

He arrives to find the roof empty except for a smiling Private Williams, leading one of the female civilians by the hand. They disappear behind one of the HVAC units.

McLeod walks to the parapet, sets down his SAW, and looks out over the city.

New York.

What a view. Even dying of this horrible cancer, it's beautiful.

"Look on my works, ye mighty, and despair!" he says into the chilly air, quoting a poem he read once in English class, in what seems to him now to have been another life. *"Allah akhbar."*

It has never been so quiet. There are no cars moving, no shrill sirens, no babble of voices. Smoke drifts over the looming skyline as fires rage unchecked. Garbage and sewage are tossed out of windows into streets choked with corpses.

Mercifully, the wind blows south, carrying the stench out over the ocean.

A single helicopter buzzes in the distance. McLeod recognizes it as an observation helicopter. Division's air support is wasting no more fuel or ordnance on New York City. The sky belongs to the birds now, feasting on the dead.

He rips his MRE open and looks down at the street.

It is deserted. Nothing for Sergeant Lewis to bang away at except drifting garbage and a pack of feral dogs, even if he were here. Soon, even the dogs are gone.

Like looking at the frozen peaks of mountains, once the majesty wears off, New York's skyline could not be more depressing for human survival. There is no money, only a barter economy with little to barter. Few people here have the skills they will need to survive for the next few months. There is no electricity, no plumbing, no sewage, no health system, and little hope for the future. And oh yeah, if you step outside for the next few weeks, you will probably be killed. Long term, your prospects are even worse.

Across the street, somebody taped a sign on the window of a private office, facing outward, that says, TRAPPED, HELP. The office appears to be empty.

"Mind if I join you?"

McLeod turns and sees a middle-aged man wearing a neat suit, cardigan sweater and tie, fiddling with a transistor radio.

"Sure." He nods at the radio. "What are you getting?"

"Nothing local, obviously," the man says cheerfully. "But I am receiving an AM news station out of Pittsburgh. The government has a cure for Mad Dog disease, they say. It's only a matter of time now before they fix this and we can get things back to normal."

McLeod checks out his lunch. Pork rib. With clam chowder as a side. He rips open a packet of barbecue sauce and slathers it onto the ribs.

"You think so?" he says.

"Sure," the man says.

"So what did you do before?"

"I am a professor at Columbia University."

"I was going to go to college."

"You still can, my boy. You got your whole life ahead of you." He sets the radio down on the parapet and takes out a pipe. "Mind if I smoke?"

"Help yourself, Professor," McLeod says, his cheek bulging with food.

"You can call me Dr. Potter."

"Okay, Dr. Potter."

"I'm joking, young man. You can call me Dave."

McLeod shrugs. "Okay, Dave."

They listen to the radio together. A reporter recaps a statement that the Secretary of Health and Human Services made earlier in the day.

Blah, blah, blah, McLeod thinks.

"Do they do any local reporting, Dave?" he asks.

The question appears to startle Potter, who finishes lighting his pipe before answering. The puffs of smoke smell like cherries.

"No," he says. "They always report from the FEMA bunker at Mount Weather down in Virginia. Which is natural, since that's where the government is these days. CNN and MSNBC and CBS, they're all there. They are still operational. That's a good sign."

McLeod chews slower, suddenly depressed, until he can barely swallow.

The truth is the networks are not really there anymore. They are just repeating whatever the government tells them. The media, like all the other institutions Americans recognize, are being whittled down to facades. It is so obvious that even a guy like McLeod can figure it out, but so horrible that even a college professor will not acknowledge it.

"I have a feeling," McLeod says, "I'm never going to get to go to college."

Which means he is going to have to learn how to be a soldier after all, he realizes. He doubts there will be many other career choices for him in the near future. Soldier may not be the best profession, but it sure as hell beats "scavenger" and "serf."

He flinches as two fighter planes scream directly overhead, briefly washing the roof in flickering shadows. USAF F16 Flying Falcons. Twenty-seven thousand pounds of thrust pushing up to fifteen hundred miles per hour.

"Look at those suckers go," McLeod says.

The planes soar through the sky in unison until they disappear over the buildings to the southwest, appearing to slow as they bank over the East River.

"I should have joined the Air Force," he adds. "Last I heard, Maddy can't fly."

Moments later, they begin their return, zooming back towards the northwest. Four black dots emerge from their torsos, drop rapidly away, and fall hurtling through the air towards the earth in a forward trajectory.

"Holy shit," says McLeod.

Each of those dots is an unguided two-thousand-pound bomb.

"Hum? Is something wrong?" Potter says, toking on his pipe.

The dots drop out of sight. A moment later, a distant flash, followed by grating thunder. A column of black smoke rises over the cityscape of southern Manhattan.

Potter shouts over the echo, "What in God's name was that?"

"I think the Air Force just blew a big hole in the Williamsburg Bridge, Dave," McLeod says, shaking his head in wonder as another pair of F16s roars past, heading south. "It looks an awful lot to me like they're sealing off Manhattan."

The last man standing

Four days ago, First Battalion numbered more than six hundred fifty combat effectives. It now has a combat-ready strength of less than two hundred. All of the officers are dead or missing except for 2LT Todd Bowman and the other two surviving lieutenants from the four original companies of Charlie Company.

Bowman reports these numbers after Immunity, the call sign for Major General Kirkland's divisional command, contacts War Dogs Two by radio during a sweep of units still operating in the region.

Holding the SINCGAR handset to his ear, Bowman stands ramrod straight at attention, even though he is alone in the Principal's personal office except for Jake Sherman, who sits nearby chewing on a thumbnail. Junior officers often do this during those rare occasions when a Major General gives them a call.

Kirkland congratulates Bowman on keeping his command intact, appoints him commander of the Brigade and, in recognition of his accomplishments in the field, promotes him on the spot to the rank of Captain.

The old ways apparently die hard. After everything he has seen, this unusual field promotion surprises Bowman more than anything that has happened yet.

Kirkland says he has a mission for him.

After the call is terminated, Captain Bowman turns to Sherman and says, "The wonders never cease."

"Congratulations on your promotion, sir," the RTO says, beaming.

"Thank you, Jake. Even if it is for being the last man standing."

A simple misunderstanding

Bowman leaves the office and sees the NCOs waiting for his return, nursing their coffee mugs and murmuring among themselves in the open office area.

"All right," he says, returning to the map. "That was Immunity. I have new orders direct from General Kirkland. We have been given a mission."

The NCOs settle down, watching him with expressions that are suddenly wary and suspicious. It suddenly strikes him in a flash of insight that Second Battalion was probably offered the mission first. Lieutenant Colonel Rose accepted it. Then his men, seeing such a mission as suicide for themselves, rebelled and shot him.

Ironically, Rose probably would have ordered First Battalion to take on the mission and kept his battalion out of it, since the mission objective is in Manhattan. But before the Colonel could delegate the mission to Bowman's people, his men killed him.

A simple misunderstanding.

After that, Major General Kirkland turned to one 2LT Bowman and appointed him commander of the Brigade.

There's a lesson here. He would have to tread carefully.

"Our mission involves a research facility located on the west side." He stabs the map with his index finger. "Right about here. Can everybody see? We're going to this facility to secure a group of scientists and help them evacuate the city."

"Uh, LT, sir?" asks one of the sergeants from Third Platoon. "With all respect, that sounds like suicide, don't it?"

"We're going to make it to that facility with no casualties if I can help it," Bowman says, looking the man in the eye. "We're going at night, which will help. By the way, it's Captain, not LT. I was promoted and placed in command of the Battalion."

Actually, he was placed in command of the Brigade, but the whole thing—a 2LT being promoted to head a brigade—sounds too ridiculous even to him.

"Congratulations on your promotion, sir," another sergeant from Third

Platoon says. "But going out at night is definitely suicide. We saw that the other night. The massacre happened after the blackout."

"Actually, the blackout probably saved what was left of the companies from being completely wiped out," Bowman answers. "And the survivors made it all the way here, mostly unharmed, using their NVGs. We're going to do the same for this mission."

Some of the NCOs nod at this.

"We can't silence our weapons, though," another sergeant says. "You shoot off a few rounds in this town, and every Mad Dog in the place comes swarming at you from everywhere at the gallop."

"We won't be firing our weapons," Bowman says.

"Sir?"

"We'll be making our way with the bayonet."

The NCOs guffaw and whistle in respect. The plan has balls. They just might make it.

Bishop raises his hand. "Sir? I have a question. Why are we risking our necks at all? The Army is abandoning us here. Technically, we're on our own."

Bowman frowns. "We're not being abandoned. We're going to be—"

"All I'm saying is we're safe here and we should consider whether the risk is worth our lives."

Bowman shakes his head. He does not want to argue with Bishop in front of the NCOs. But they have a right to know what's at stake.

"I'll tell you why this mission is important," says the Captain. "This team of research scientists has found a cure to the Mad Dog disease. And there's a helicopter ride out of here for us when the mission is completed. We're going with the scientists."

"With all respect, sir, that's bullshit," Bishop says. "I'm not buying it."

The NCOs gasp at the breach of discipline between officers in front of enlisted men, then begin murmuring—some against Bishop, some for him.

"He's right!" one of the sergeants from Bravo says.

"I'm not going out there again," a sergeant from Delta mutters.

"Even if we get out of here, they're just going to use us like cannon fodder in some other city. You know?"

"Embrace the suck, gentlemen."

"Shut up and listen to the CO!"

"I say call a vote!"

"I'm only asking a fair question, Todd," Bishop says. "We've been lied to too many times already, and it's gotten too many good men killed."

Kemper roars, silencing them all, "You will address him as 'Captain' or 'sir,' Lieutenant! And you will not argue with the Captain or question his orders in front of enlisted personnel. That means shut the hell up right now!"

Bowman glowers at both of them, barely containing his rage. "Both of you get out of here. Get out of my sight. Now. I'll deal with you later."

"Yes, sir," Kemper says. "Sorry for my outburst, sir."

As he passes Bowman, he winks.

Bowman is almost too stunned to understand, but then he gets it. Kemper knew that Bowman did not need a champion to defend him, that what he needed was for his people to respect his authority and obey his orders. Kemper showed the NCOs that he obeys Bowman, while also silencing Bishop by immediately ending the public debate.

"We are not a boys club," the Captain tells the sergeants. "We do not vote. You are either in the Army and you follow orders in a chain of command that goes all the way up to the President of the United States, or you are a deserter and scum. Understand?"

"Yes, sir," the NCOs answer.

"Now listen up. This is important. If we weren't going out on this mission, we'd still be going out to retrieve supplies from H&S, or sit here and starve. The NVGs are either going to get us there or we are returning here. After we complete the mission, the Army will lift us somewhere else that's safer than being in the middle of the most densely populated city in the goddamn country. Not to mention a deathtrap, since the Air Force has started blowing the bridges in a crazy attempt to prevent the Mad Dogs here from migrating. Damn, in just a month or two, what you see outside the window today might be considered the good old days of peace and plenty. I think, given the facts on the ground, this mission is our best and only real option for long-term survival. Hooah?"

"Hooah," the NCOs answer, some louder than others. Some not at all.

"We step off at zero four," says Bowman. "Be ready, gentlemen. That is all."

One of you is a traitor

The boys of First Squad, Second Platoon immediately start grumbling as they wake up in the darkness. By the time they get out of their sleeping bags, shivering in the night air that has grown increasingly colder over the past few days—this being the first week of October—they have progressed from bitching to full-fledged whining.

A lot of soldiers are gung ho for the cool stuff that happens here and there in the service, and constantly gripe and moan about everything else that happens in between. But this is real dissent. They were just getting comfortable here and starting to feel like they might be able to wait this thing out and come out the other end alive. They have food, water, electricity, heat, security in this place. A few of the platoon's Casanovas even found the time, amidst the endless hard work, to strike up relationships with women in the building.

Mooney was the only one not surprised when Sergeant McGraw told them last night that they were bugging out. He had already sensed the change in the air. He saw the signs and portents and understood that nobody was going to make it out of this thing without intense suffering. The TV stations going off the air one by one. Paper money only having value as kindling. The complete breakdown of distribution systems for food, medicine and clothing. The rumors of Army units simply taking their guns and walking off the job.

It all happened so fast.

Soon, he believes, people will be burning library books to keep warm in between hunting each other for food and using the Hudson as a toilet and washing machine.

"You didn't really think the Army was going to leave us alone, did you?" says Carrillo. "We're one of the only units in the area that's still obeying orders."

"We're one of the only units still alive," Ratliff says.

"They at least had to try to get us killed," Rollins says, but nobody laughs.

"Quit your bitching and gear up, boys," McGraw says, stomping into the room. His sleeves are uncharacteristically rolled up, revealing his hairy Popeye forearms with a skull tattooed on one and crossed rifles on the other. "I want you out in the hallway, against the far wall in single file, ready to move, in fifteen. Drop your fartsack, Ratliff. Your poncho, too. We're going light. Bring lots of ammo and otherwise only what you need. We're leaving everything else for the Hajjis."

The boys burst into laughter. They've taken to calling the Mad Dogs

"Maddy" and the civilians "Hajjis" over the past few days, and hearing one of the NCOs do the same—especially their own blunt, burly Sergeant McGraw—is hilarious to them.

Many of these boys will leave their warm sleeping bags and risk their necks tonight purely out of devotion to their NCOs. They respect the non-coms. Wherever they go, the boys will follow.

"Anybody got any more glow sticks?" Rollins says. "I can't hardly see shit in here."

"Use your NVGs," Mooney says. "It'll be good practice."

McGraw turns at the sound of Mooney's voice, points at him, and says, "You." He points at Wyatt. "And you."

"I didn't do it," Wyatt says.

"Get your shit on, meatballs," McGraw tells them. "You're coming with me."

"Yes, Sergeant," Mooney says darkly. The other boys are already tearing into MREs for breakfast. His stomach growls.

They are on the move after a few minutes. The boys of the other squads are already spilling out of the other classrooms in the wing and filling up the hallway. Most squat against the student lockers in grim silence, their carbines between their knees. Some race out of line to use the john before the company steps off. Somebody from First Platoon cranks up "Welcome to the Jungle" by Guns 'N Roses on a CD player to get their juices flowing and wake up the Hajjis.

At the end of the hallway, McGraw tells them to wait, his eyes on the Platoon Sergeant, who is arguing with several civilians.

Somebody calls out for fresh batteries for his NVGs. The boys here are finishing up their last smokes, dropping the butts and grinding them out with their boots. Then two soldiers from First Platoon's Weapons Squad show up carrying a crate of ammo between them, and start passing it out.

Top up, they say. Put a mag in every spare pocket. Bring as much as you can carry.

Mooney steps closer to the Platoon Sergeant and listens in on his argument.

"You will be okay here if you keep your heads down and don't attract attention," Kemper is saying. "There's plenty of food. We had crews filling up every bottle and bucket in the place with tap water. You've got extra gas we siphoned from the refrigerated trucks, so you've got a good supply of fuel for the generator."

"Your duty is to help these people, Sergeant," one of the civilians says.

"My duty is to follow my orders."

"You work for us, goddamnit."

"I work for the U.S. Army, Ma'am."

Kemper walks away, nods to McGraw, and continues down the hall, which suddenly grows increasingly loud and chaotic as the NCOs begin ordering and dressing their squads for the movement. Adding to the confusion is the fact that the CO made some last-minute changes to the order of march, promoting some of the sergeants to the rank of LT, combining squads, and otherwise rebuilding a new overstrength company on the fly from the wreckage of a battalion. Some of the boys are shouting out names, panicked; entire squads appear to be missing.

Mooney turns around and sees Martin and Boomer tagging along with their .30-cal M240. Martin gives him a thumbs up. Mooney frowns. He never knows if Martin is being nice or an asshole. In Iraq, giving somebody a thumbs up is the same as giving them the finger.

"You know what's going on?" he whispers.

Martin shakes his head, grinning.

"No talking," McGraw says.

They turn the corner and enter an empty hallway. Soon, the sounds of what's left of First Battalion recede into the gloom.

Kemper switches on the SureFire flashlight attached to his carbine.

"Turn that thing off," a voice says in the dark. "I'm right here."

"Yes, sir," Kemper says.

Captain Bowman steps out of an empty, dusty-smelling classroom, a glow stick dangling from his load-bearing vest. The monochromatic light stick, like the NVG phosphor screen, is purposefully colored green since the eye can distinguish between more shades of green than other phosphor colors. He's the only one of them who has a light source.

Kemper says to the MGR and AG, "I want you to set up the thirty-cal here, pointing that way. We're going to the end of this hallway. If you hear shooting, you keep your cool and hold your fire. If I say shoot, you start shooting anybody with a flash light or a glow stick. But only if I tell you to shoot. Is that clear, Specialist?"

"Hooah, Sergeant," Martin says.

"Good man."

The Captain gives Mooney and Wyatt the once-over. Mooney stands at attention and says, "Sir, Private Mooney reports!"

Wyatt echoes the ritual.

Bowman smiles at them. "Always you two. At ease, men."

"What are we doing here, Sarge?" says Boomer.

"It's personal," Kemper answers.

Martin and Boomer finish setting up the M240. The group moves down the hall.

Ahead, in the darkness, Mooney hears murmuring voices, occasionally punctuated by a strident yell. His stomach begins a series of flying leaps. He suddenly feels certain that something bad is happening. And that something very, very bad is going to happen.

The Captain is talking into his handheld.

"I've got a couple of the men with me, but I'll be coming around the corner to talk to you alone," he says into his handset. "All right?"

Mooney gave up his own radio after his recon mission, so he doesn't hear the response. But the Captain keeps moving, so it must be all right.

"Here I come now," Bowman says, raising his hands in a gesture of surrender. "Hold your fire. Don't shoot. We're just going to have a conversation."

The Captain turns the corner and disappears.

Kemper follows closely until he reaches the corner, then squats down, listening. McGraw whispers to Mooney and Wyatt to prepare for action on his command.

Mooney drops to one knee, feeling the comforting cushion of his kneepad, sweating in his BDUs. His heart pounds against his ribs and his blood is crashing in his ears. The moment Captain Bowman disappeared around the corner, the tension began mounting until it has now become almost impossible to breathe.

"Todd, sorry we have to meet like this," a voice says.

Lieutenant Bishop, Wyatt whispers.

"Same here," Bowman answers.

"Well, we're not going, as you can see. We're going to stay here and rebuild."

"I understand."

"We don't want anything to do with your war. We're not in the Army anymore. And we're not going to die to keep the memory of a dead country alive."

"I understand. But I still need to talk to the men."

"Go right ahead. There's nothing you can say to change their minds, though. They already survived one massacre. They're not going to walk into another."

"Men!" Bowman says.

The Captain's voice echoes through the hallways until it becomes a ghostly murmur.

"Men!" he repeats. "You can stay here. We're not going to force you to come with us. What's done is done. It's all right."

"That's nice of you," Bishop warily. "What do you want in return?"

"One of you is a traitor against the United States, and must be punished."

"And who—what are you doing?"

A pistol bangs loudly, echoing sharply in their ears with an almost physical impact, making them flinch.

Another *bang*. A wave of cordite in the air, tingling the nose.

Mooney can sense McGraw tensing ahead of them. He can smell the man's nervous sweat as he prepares to rush forward and provide cover fire for the Captain. But nothing happens. The seconds tick by. The deserters do not shoot.

The ringing in Mooney's ears slowly fades.

"What's done is done," Bowman says. He calls out into the gloom, "If we are forced to return, you will be accepted back into the Battalion with no questions asked. If we don't come back, take good care of the civilians. I am intending to tell the General that you volunteered to stay behind. There will be no dishonor for you, as long as you stay true to yourself and the people in your charge. While they remain alive and well, you are still in the United States Army."

After a few moments of silence, Bowman adds, "Well. God be with you men."

"Thank you, sir," the boys whisper in the dark.

Moments later, Captain Bowman returns, his glow stick almost glaring in Mooney's eyes. The light is trembling, and it takes Mooney a moment to realize it is the Captain who is shaking. The man just shot down a fellow officer while a dozen, two dozen—it could have been scores—of deserters aimed a variety of automatic weapons at him.

"We can't use them if they're broken," Bowman says. "We have truly become a volunteer army tonight." He looks dazed and exhausted. "Bishop was a traitor, though. That I did to fulfill my duty to the Army. Things may be falling apart, but we still are the U.S. Army."

Kemper and McGraw nod somberly. There is no need to explain.

Bowman sees Mooney and Wyatt, takes a deep breath, and smiles. "Thanks for the backup, men."

"You're welcome, sir," Mooney rasps, his mouth dry.

"Now let's see if we can get the hell off this island tonight."

Thrust and hold, move.
Withdraw and hold, move.
Attack position, move

The boys file out of the school's front doors two by two, a long tan line that snakes through the dark, bristling with bayonets. The first squad in the column fans out to form a wedge, making the formation look like an arrow. The NCOs walk alongside the column, keeping a tight grip on their squads. While they will be moving in company strength, each squad will be acting independently, since there is no talking and no talking means no communication up and down the chain of command.

They all know where to go, how to get there, and what the rules of engagement are. No shooting unless it is a matter of life and death. Safeties on. They will push through with the bayonet. Speed, surprise and night vision will be their allies on this mission.

Near the front of the column, Mooney marches along in his NVGs, a pair of goggles that look into an amplified electronic image of the outside world on a green phosphor screen. This allows the soldiers to see even in starlight, which is all that is available tonight, by amplifying ambient light thirty thousand times and then creating an image rendered in green. The soldiers can see Maddy, but Maddy can't see them back.

Maddy can, however, hear them making an awful racket. The column rattles along, boots crunching glass and kicking cans and bottles, coughing on waves of stink circulating through the otherwise silent city. But despite the noise, the Mad Dogs do not attack. They appear to be dormant.

Mooney hears a scuffle on his left, followed by a hideous *thunk* sound and a sharp yelp. He turns just in time to see his sergeant pull his shovel out of a woman's head and shove her corpse to the asphalt. McGraw signals to them: Don't stop, keep moving.

The Sergeant whispers in the dark, "Sorry, Ma'am."

Mooney cannot stop himself from wondering who she was before she crossed over and became one of them. An important movie producer? A magazine editor? A meter maid? A substitute teacher? Did she have a husband or was she single? Did she have kids? Was she planning a vacation in Mexico over the winter?

Was she a terrorist who was going to blow up New York?

Was she a scientist about to discover the cure for cancer?

We'll never know.

Many of the infected are walking barefoot across broken glass, leaving trails of blood behind them. Others have gaping flesh wounds that are leaking pus from scores of infections, not just from the germs transmitted by bites, but because New York has become an open sewer over the past several days. Their stench is horrific, slowly winning its war against the vapor rub the soldiers have slathered under their noses. These people are scarcely human anymore.

But Mooney does not hate them. He just can't see them as monsters. Several days ago, they were regular people. It is hard to hate slaves. They have no choice.

Ahead, he sees more infected. There are clusters of them standing listless in the dark, apparently sleeping on their feet, their shoulders rising and falling as they pant with rapid, shallow breaths. Others sob and cry out as if from deep sadness.

The stench grows in strength, making his stomach waver at the edge of a convulsion. He tells himself not to cough, not to make a sound.

He passes a Mad Dog who has sensed their presence and is trying to find them blindly, his eyes blinking in the dark. The man suddenly moves into the blind spot of Mooney's peripheral vision. NVGs offer the advantage of night vision even in near total darkness, but have three big disadvantages that are unnerving and even dangerous.

Soldiers used to 20/20 eyesight during the day must quickly adapt to a reduction in visual acuity to 20/25 to 20/40 at best. In other words, the NVGs produce a fuzzy image. While the fact there is no moon tonight is probably saving their lives, it is also giving their NVGs very little ambient illumination to work with.

While the NVG visor is binocular, the actual lens is monocular, robbing its wearer of depth perception. The boys stumble along, adapting the way they walk so they can maintain balance. Some occasionally flinch when they see Maddies wandering around, because they are not sure how far away they are.

Meanwhile, soldiers used to having a greater than one hundred eighty-degree field of view must adapt to forty-degree tunnel vision. The soldiers must wag their heads constantly to see if Maddy is coming up on their sides, where they are virtually blind.

Mooney hears the Mad Dog sniffing the air and growling on his left. He wags his head in time to see his squad leader bash in the man's skull with his shovel.

McGraw does not apologize.

Mooney's mind races: Investment banker? Famous actor? Father of three?

He is trying not to think about his turn on the front line stabbing these people in the dark and pushing them to the ground. He has shot lots of people over the past few days, and even bayoneted the sniveling thing on the floor in the science classroom back at the school. But he did that without thinking. Shooting somebody is one thing. Intentionally putting a knife into a person's body is another. Most soldiers hate the weapon.

Second Squad steps out of line and squats, exhausted by the fighting, waiting for the rest of the column to pass so that they rejoin it as its last section. It is now First Squad's turn to be on point.

Mooney takes a deep breath, constantly moving and analyzing the objects swimming in a dozen shades of green in his limited view.

Ahead, floating in the gloom, the pale bodies of Mad Dogs sleep in their strange huddles and wander among the ruins of an abandoned traffic jam, stumbling over torn luggage and dead bodies.

The air is suddenly pierced by wailing, one of the infected crying out in sadness and pain.

The column is not supposed to deviate from a straight line until the first turn four blocks ahead. If Maddy blocks the column, bayonet him, push him to the side, and keep moving. Those are his orders. If he disobeys, he might get everybody killed.

The Mad Dog directly in front of him appears to be vibrating on his green phosphor screen, his large body undefined and fuzzy and his long matted beard writhing like a sizzling nest of worms. His left eye is swollen shut and leaking black fluid from an infection. His mouth yawns open. He appears to be grinning.

Mooney falls into a boxer's stance, left foot forward, body erect, knees slightly bent, balancing on the balls of his feet.

He was trained for bayonet fighting. There are four attack movements that he learned back in Basic: Thrust, butt stroke, slash and smash. There are friendlies on his left and right, so he is limited to the thrust. The basic idea is to put the blade into any vulnerable part of your opponent's body.

The biggest problem is picking the spot. It is during this moment of thought that the revulsion sets in. Many soldiers simply aim center-mass at the enemy's torso. Either they do not have time to think, or they don't want to.

Mooney pulls the stock of his M4 close to his right hip, extends his left arm, and lunges forward on his left foot with all his might, spearing the Mad Dog between the ribs and pushing him. The man shrieks, stumbling backward and almost taking the rifle with him. Mooney pulls hard and retrieves the blade, which slides out of the man's body reluctantly with an awful sucking sound.

Maddy stumbles to the left, trips over a fallen motorcycle, and doesn't get up.

Another Mad Dog steps out of the gloom, an old woman dressed in the rags of a hospital gown, blood splashed on her face and chest. Her toothless mouth gapes at him, gurgling a stream of bubbling drool rich with virus.

Thrust and hold, move. Withdraw and hold, move. Resume attack position, move. Take a step forward.

Next to him, Finnegan curses quietly as his carbine is wrenched out of his grasp. He chases after it and retrieves it, stumbling and gasping.

After ten minutes of this, slowly carving their way through two blocks, Corporal Eckhardt taps his shoulder and takes his place at the front of the column.

Mooney falls back in line, feeling an overwhelming compulsion to tear off his NVGs and let the world go black. The tendons in his aching arms seem to have hardened into steel and a sharp pain lances through his left wrist. Bayonet fighting is punishing work. He is dying for a drink of water.

Sergeant McGraw steps out front and holds up his hand. The boys drop to one knee with a general clatter, panting. The Mad Dogs ahead have a gleaming green halo around them, against which they wander as dark silhouettes. Apparently there is a fire ahead producing a lot of light and threatening to expose them.

Mooney wags his head to have a quick look around, and also try to clear his head of the claustrophobic sensation that he is trapped inside a horrible dream.

The infected are everywhere.

We will carry this action with the bayonet

After the column grinds to a security halt, Bowman lifts his NVGs and is instantly plunged into darkness. He raises his carbine and peers into the red-dot close-combat optic, which provides night vision and also magnification.

He quickly surmises that the front half of the column has become embedded in a large force of Mad Dogs. Not one of the main bodies of thousands, but a force of several hundred at least, moaning and wheezing in the darkness. They stand in clusters, panting in sleep, or wander around aimlessly, pressing close against the column, sniffing the air and growling, lashing out when they walk blindly into the bayonets. And at the rear of the crowd, some type of fire, probably a car fire, is burning in the middle of the street.

His unit is in trouble. Maddy is blocking the street in large numbers and is now virtually surrounding one-fourth of the company like a herd of blind predators. If the column tries to push through at the point of the bayonet, they will become increasingly visible as they get closer to the fire. Then they could have a real battle on their hands, and on unequal terms.

The Captain flips his NVGs back over his eyes. Above the street, he suddenly notices, many of the windows are glowing green with candlelight. All around them in this seemingly dead city, people are still trying to survive.

You're leaving all of them to die, he tells himself.

He forces this crushingly depressing thought out of his head with a grunt.

Keying his handset, he murmurs, "All Warlord units, this is Warlord actual. Hold position until further notice, over."

Jogging down the line, he finds Sergeant Lewis at the back of the column, and sends him to the far left, then sends the next squad to the far right, repeating this until he has created a line of troops spanning the street.

After deploying his troops, he finds an abandoned car, gets in, and gently closes the door.

"All Warlord units, this is Warlord actual," he whispers. "If I have taken you out of line, I name you Team A. The rest of you still in line are Team

B. On my mark, Team A will charge and push Maddy back. Once we make contact, Team B will join the attack. We will carry this action with the bayonet. There will be no shooting.

"The research facility is just over eight blocks from here. A little over half a mile. After we begin our assault, we will keep moving as fast as possible. This will be the mission's release point. After we begin, you will be responsible for getting your unit to the objective on your own.

"Step off on my mark. Good luck and Godspeed. Wait, out."

Getting out of the car, he gets into position next to Sergeant Lewis, who turns and acknowledges his presence with a nod.

"Step off in five, four, three, two, one, go," says the Captain.

Team A begins jogging forward in a bristling line. The line quickly becomes ragged as some of the boys stumble over garbage and corpses, others lag from exhaustion, and some painfully run into fire hydrants, street signs and even cars after misjudging how far away they are. Bowman can hear his breath come in short, sharp gasps.

The first Mad Dog appears. Bowman spears him, the force of the momentum of his thrust almost shocking the carbine out of his grasp. He retrieves the blade with a colossal effort and shoulders the man out of the way, knocking the wind out of both of them. The man goes down.

Another takes his place, snarling.

Ahead, the crowd continually thickens until a virtual wall of bodies appears ahead of them in the green gloom. Some of the boys, unable to help themselves, shout high-pitched war cries to amp up their courage as they rush forward into battle.

The line crashes home. Maddy reels from the shock, dozens dropping to the ground writhing with bayonet wounds. The survivors attack the soldiers, then Team B stands and begins its own assault in a line punching through the middle of the throng.

If this were any normal enemy with a healthy fear for their own lives, they would be fleeing as fast as they could run in the dark. But this is no normal enemy. It is an enemy incapable of fear or reason. To Lyssa, the human body is disposable, just a meat puppet with a five-day expiration date. Even the individual virons in each body have no real interest in self preservation, only in the overarching survival of their genetic code. The individual viron is just as much a slave to its ancient program as its infected victims are.

A flurry of small arms fire punches holes in Maddy's ranks.

Nobody gave the order to shoot. It happened suddenly at five different places at once. There are too many Mad Dogs for them to kill in hand to hand fighting. The soldiers' line has been broken in several places as some squads were able to push forward while other squads were stopped cold. With a broken line, the Mad Dogs' superior numbers began to tell as they began to surround and overwhelm the soldiers.

One exhausted soldier panicked when a wounded Mad Dog on the ground sunk her teeth into his boot. He shot her in the head, blowing off several toes in the bargain.

Moments later, everyone is firing.

Above them, civilians are leaning out their windows, shouting themselves hoarse.

What's done is done, Bowman tells himself. He thumbs off the safety on his carbine and begins shooting Mad Dogs at a nearly cyclic rate of fire, a round every few seconds, draining mags and reloading without breaking stride. The crackle of small arms fire turns into a roar as the entire company lights up the Mad Dogs. Muzzle flashes burst along the line, almost beautiful to watch on their NVGs. Tracers stream through the air. A grenade explodes, a massive green fireball erupting into sparks and fiery blobs. The air begins to fill with luminous, pale green smoke clouds.

The civilians are cheering.

"All Warlord units, this is Warlord actual," he says into his handset. "Keep moving. Keep moving."

The use of live ordnance proved decisive. The company shot its way through the mob with very few casualties.

Eight blocks to go. About three quarters of a mile.

All around them, the city has begun to stir with the tramp of thousands of feet as the Mad Dogs awaken from their haunted dreams of the time before the plague.

If the soldiers move fast, and there are no other mobs between here and the research facility, they can do this.

"Go, go, go!" Bowman cries.

They make it.

Chapter 12

We're the U.S. Army

Sergeant Lewis leads the first grab team up the stairs while the rest of the company pulls security down in the Institute's lobby, waiting their turn. It is pitch black in the stairwell, robbing them of vision as NVGs are useless without some ambient light to amplify, so they turned on the SureFire flashlights mounted on their carbines, fitted with red lenses. The resulting beams appear a brilliant green on their NVGs, but are barely visible to Maddy's naked eye.

The squad pauses on the stairs.

"It's good and locked, Sarge," says Corporal Jaworski, trying the door that Lewis believes leads to the labs.

"Who's got the C4?"

"Here, Sarge."

"Give it to me, Reed."

Lewis takes the block of C4, sticks it onto the door and begins setting the charge while the squad retreats to a safe place down the stairs.

"Fire in the hole!" he shouts.

The boys crouch and put their heads down, cupping their ears.

The detonation roars down the stairwell with a sharp boom that they can feel from the base of their skulls to the tips of their toes. The explosion blew out the lock and buckled the door, which now rocks precariously on one hinge in a pall of tangy smoke.

"Move!"

The squad hauls itself to its feet, raises their carbines, and enters the hallway in a tightly packed diamond formation, scanning for targets.

Lewis knows Maddy has been here. Between the Vicks and the smoke, he cannot smell them, but he saw the corpses laid out in the corner in the lobby, apparently dead from disease and carpeted with flies, and the National Guardsman with a hole in his head. There is evidence of strife everywhere in this place.

He also saw, outside the doors of the research facility, the Special Forces team lying scattered on the street like road kill. Their story was easy to figure out. Immunity must have airdropped them in an initial attempt to evac the scientists. A single helicopter depositing them on the roof of a nearby building. The attempt obviously failed.

Now it is our turn, he tells himself.

His shooters move as one down the corridor, their flashlights exploring the gloom, until they reach the elevator lobby.

The corpses lay on top of each other, locked in a death grapple. Two wear labcoats, marking them as scientists, while the other eight are in street clothes. A few have the marks of Mad Dog infection. The stench of death is powerful here. Several blood trails lead away from the area to closed doors.

"What the hell happened here," says Parsons, whistling.

"Lot of dead Hajjis, a couple dead Maddies," says Jaworski, holding his hand over his mouth to keep from gagging. "Gunshot wounds, strangulation. This poor guy got his throat torn out."

"This shit is ice cold, yo," says Turner.

"Turner, talking like that only makes you sound more white," says Perez.

"Hey, this chick looks exactly like that chick on TV," says Bailey. "You know?"

The boys gather around.

"Yeah, that show with the robots. What's that show?"

Nobody can remember the actress' name or the show's.

"Looks just like her, though," Jaworski says. "I know exactly who you mean."

"Contact!"

The boys fill the corridor, searching for targets. The green flashlight beams swing wildly and abruptly converge on the center torso of a Mad Dog loping at them from the far end of the corridor, her labcoat flapping around her legs and her arms outstretched in the dark, trying to find them using her sense of hearing alone.

"Put her down, Reed," Lewis says, patting the top of the soldier's head.

"Roger that, Sarge," the soldier says.

He releases the safety on his weapon, aims using its iron sights, blows air out his cheeks and applies gentle pressure to the trigger. His M4 discharges with a mechanical cracking sound. The burst blows the woman's shoulder off. She stumbles drunkenly for several steps, then falls to the floor twitching in a widening pool of blood.

"Good," the squad leader tells him. "Now go count your coup."

They are under a standing order from Bowman to make sure anybody who is down is actually dead, but without wasting precious ammunition. That means finishing the job with the rifle butt or bayonet. The NCOs started referring to it as counting coup to try to make it more palatable to the boys so they would actually do it. Lewis is incredibly proud of his troops for the strength they are displaying.

Reed gets up, jogs to the woman, and stabs her in the neck with his bayonet.

"She's down," he calls, then suddenly holds up his fist.

The squad freezes in place, listening.

Reed waves at them to move up.

"You got something?" says Lewis.

"I heard a sound in a room down there on the left, Sarge."

"Let's check it out," he says.

Lewis is not hopeful, however. The mission appears to be a bust. The scientists are either dead or infected along with these other civilians who came here for God knows what reason. He is hoping this still means the Army will extract them, but he has a feeling they won't. No scientists, no evac. If they find no survivors, they will be stuck in Manhattan.

"I heard something in there, Sarge," Reed says, pointing at a door bearing a discrete sign that says, SECURITY.

It is locked.

"If there is somebody inside this room, open the door," Lewis says.

He hears a muffled groan, but nothing more. The door does not open.

While he prepares some C4, the boys take a knee and pull security around him, listening to the sound of small arms fire erupting in another part of the facility. It is the second grab team, putting down another stray Mad Dog.

Lewis shouts at the door: "If you are inside and can hear me, we are going to blow the lock. Get as far back as you can and get on the floor!"

"And if your name is Maddy, stand right next to it," Bailey says, making the boys laugh.

The squad retreats to a safe distance.

"Fire in the hole!"

The door blows and the squad pours into the smoking hole, carbines at the ready, sweeping the room.

"Clear!" the boys sound off one by one.

"Sarge, I got a survivor!" Perez calls out. "In the bathroom back here!"

"Holy shit," Parsons drawls.

The woman lies shivering on the floor curled up under a pile of labcoats, some of them torn and darkly stained, clutching a flashlight that has stopped working, its batteries drained and dead. She lies surrounded by empty bags of snack food and candy wrappers and an odd collection of beakers, test tubes and planters, some filled with water. She apparently has been saving the toilet as a final backup water supply and using a trash can as a toilet instead, surrounded by rags torn from a labcoat for toilet paper.

Lewis is flooded with admiration. This woman somehow managed to stay alive for several days in virtual total darkness and with little food or water, while the Mad Dogs hunted her in the dark by sense of hearing and smell.

This is one tough broad, he thinks.

Her eyes searching blindly in the dark, she starts shouting.

"What's she saying?" Perez asks.

"I think she's talking in Russian," Jaworski says.

"Right—but what's she saying?"

"How the hell do I know what she's saying? My people are Polish, not Russian, and I only speak American."

Lewis drops down and squats on his haunches.

"Ma'am, it's all right," he says several times until she begins to calm down. "I am Sergeant Grant Lewis with the U.S. Army, and we're going to get you out of here."

The woman licks her lips and says dryly, "Army?"

He cracks a glow stick, which gleams bright against the dark, and holds it out to her. She seizes it with both hands and stares at its light intensely, tears streaming down her face.

"That's right, Ma'am," he says, flipping up his NVGs and grinning in the green glow. "We're the U.S. Army."

I survived

Feeling warm and safe in a pair of sneakers and oversized BDUs, Valeriya Petrova wolfs down the MRE that the soldiers handed her, washing it down with long pulls on a canteen. She blinks in the bright Command Center, its lighting the result of a few easy repairs of the emergency generator in the downstairs electrical room.

Petrova marvels at the dull, institutional colors in the Command Center, washed in fluorescent light. After days of darkness, even the dull is starkly beautiful.

She survived. Later, she will wonder why she alone survived among all of the people trapped in the building, both the research team and the mob; she will certainly feel survivor's guilt. But not now. Right now, she is exultant just to exist.

The medic calling himself Doc Waters stands nearby, studying her closely with his arms crossed, making her nervous. Does he expect her to drop dead? She has lost weight and she is undernourished, but she is not starving. She was able to stay hydrated even after the power failed. She can't run just yet, but she can walk just fine.

The truth is she has never felt more alive.

In any case, the time of running is over. She is with the military now. She is safe. The boys around her—they strike her as incredibly young, these beefy kids—keep talking about helicopters coming to get them. Soon, she will be airlifted to a secure place where she can isolate a new sample of the Mad Dog strain and finish her work on a vaccine.

The door opens and a young man appears. The soldiers straighten their posture and stare at him in respectful silence for a few moments as he enters the room, marking him as an officer, a leader.

He sits across from her and smiles.

"I'm Captain Bowman," he says.

"And I am Dr. Valeriya Petrova."

"I hope you find your new clothes acceptable, Dr. Petrova."

"After wearing the same clothing for the past several days, I am finding this uniform perfectly comfortable, Captain Bowman."

Neither insist on familiarity, on being called by their first names. The truth is she needs him to be Captain Bowman, her savior, and he apparently needs her to be Dr. Petrova, the scientist who can stop the plague.

"Doc tells me you're feeling well," he continues. "That you're fit to travel."

"Yes."

"Good," he nods. "Can you tell me what happened here, Dr. Petrova?"

How can she explain the nightmare? The madness, the murders, the infection, the blood. The weak and slowly dying mob intentionally infecting the Guardsman and coming up in the elevators only to be savaged and infected by a berserk Dr. Lucas and Dr. Saunders. The endless darkness with little hope for survival, staying sane only by imagining herself in Central Park, on a blanket in Sheep Meadow, reading a book while nearby her husband and child laughed and played.

The screaming in the corridors as they all died one by one.

The slowly dimming hope that rescue would come.

The darkness that began to seep into and shroud even her memories.

"I survived," she says, shivering.

He nods again. He understands.

"We survived, too," he tells her. "Just yesterday, I was a second lieutenant."

Now it is her turn to nod. She is not familiar with the military, but she gets the idea. The Army chain of command in the area has sustained significant losses.

"So the world outside. . . . It is bad?"

"Dr. Petrova, it's so bad, there may not be a world soon."

"I do not suppose you have any news of . . . Europe."

"Sorry. My situation awareness was once limited to New York, and is now limited pretty much to this building. I only know ground that my men can hold by force."

She swallows hard to choke back a sob. The Army is not in command of the city. They are refugees, like her, seeking flight. And if that is true, the same must be true in all of the big cities. Washington. New York. Los Angeles. Chicago. London.

He adds, "Dr. Petrova, my superiors have instructed me to secure both you and whatever projects you were working on." His eyes look hopeful. "A cure, I understand?"

Petrova's eyes flicker to the other soldiers in the room.

"Clear the room," Bowman says, his eyes never leaving her face.

The boys file out reluctantly, leaving her alone with the Captain, Doc Waters and the man who is apparently Bowman's second in command,

Sergeant Kemper. This man frightens her for some reason. While the soldiers are mostly boys, quick to grin even in their desperate circumstances, the sergeants strike her as very hard men.

"The Mad Dog disease is a separate disease," she says, then pauses.

"I'm listening," he tells her.

"Lyssa, as you know, is bad enough, but it is a Trojan Horse for the Mad Dog strain, which revealed itself by presenting a new vector for transmission—saliva. Biting."

The Captain exchanges a glance with Kemper.

"That matches our understanding of the situation," he tells her. "Go on, Doctor."

"I isolated the Mad Dog strain and produced a pure sample, but it was ruined when the power went out and we lost refrigeration in the labs. I already forwarded my work electronically to CDC and USAMRIID before the power went out for the last time. But I need to get back into a proper lab with a proper staff to produce another pure sample and finish my work on a vaccine."

Bowman does not appear to be satisfied with the answer. He stares at her intensely and says, "You seem to be saying there is no cure, only a vaccine, and that it will be a long time before we have such a vaccine in any quantity."

"That is correct, Captain."

Petrova lowers her eyes. She knows they rescued her at enormous risk to themselves, and her answer is not very satisfying to them. In part, they are here because she told a white lie to push CDC and USAMRIID to rescue her. But the scientific process is not like a military process, with quick, definitive results. One cannot shoot and kill a virus with a rifle. Science is a slow, laborious, collaborative effort. A pure sample must be grown in a cell culture. Then it must be tested for susceptibility against antiviral drugs. Then it can be distilled to produce a vaccine through a painful trial and error process. Make it too weak, and the host gains no immunity. Make it too strong, and you kill the host.

Her discovery is a major breakthrough, and it is the best shot they have at defeating the virus. Not immediately, but over time.

But the Captain was obviously hoping for immediate results. The world is ending right now. Soon, there may not be an America to defend anymore, if what he told her about the outside world is true.

"I am sorry if you were looking for more definitive results," she says.

"Even if I had a vaccine in my hands right now, it would still take months to manufacture in significant quantities, assuming the biomedical factories are still working."

"My men risked their lives coming here," he tells her. "Obviously, we can't tell them that you have a cure and that they can be vaccinated before we get picked up. But if you want to promote a slight fiction that it will take less than months, I wouldn't correct you."

"I see. . . ."

"I hope you do, Doctor. We'll be moving out within a half hour, as soon as our birds get in the air. We may have to fight every step of the way to reach them. If the men feel like they are fighting for an important cause, it might help instead of hurt."

She is nodding now.

"We understand each other, Captain. I will help you any way I can."

They wanted to make a better world

Captain Bowman stares at the beautiful scientist sitting across from him and realizes that he and his men might end up dying for her today. They are risking their necks simply because she has the best theory on how to cure the disease. They will fight in the next few hours, and they might die without seeing the sun again, to get this woman back into a working laboratory so she can produce a vaccine. A vaccine that will not be ready until the Mad Dogs have virtually overrun America and destroyed everything he loves about it.

All this effort for a cure that will come too late.

It is the classic Army bull, but he should have known better. He should have known she would not deliver instant salvation. A quick fix to a global disaster like this would be highly unlikely, if not impossible. Life is so much more complex than he'd like it to be. Many soldiers complain about this, but he is mentally flexible and accepts the complexity of life as a law of nature.

In short, it figures. But he wanted to believe.

The fact is, if he were General Kirkland, he would make the same call. This woman is the only scientist who spotted the real threat. She may be the best shot America has at producing a vaccine. She is a primary asset in a war that must be won, plain and simple. Even if there is not enough time to make a difference, America must try to find a cure. Where bullets and bayonets failed, medical science might still, one day, prevail. If she dies and nobody else steps up to cure Lyssa, the virus will have won the war against mankind even as it slowly burns itself out, perhaps permanently, perhaps to rise again.

Dr. Petrova is also our ticket out of here, he tells himself. At this moment, she is more valuable than we are. Without her, we might be left behind. The situation is unstable, chaotic. The Army is apparently in a shambles during its retreat from the cities, shedding units and equipment in the confusion and constant attrition. He had to bargain with Immunity, in fact, just to get them to live up to their promise of airlifting all of them out. Immunity had taken a line that they would extract the scientist from a nearby roof, and then they would see what they could do about rounding up a few CH-47s to evacuate Bowman's troops. Perhaps in a few days, assuming the Mad Dogs would all be dead then. For Bowman, there were too many what-ifs, assumptions and empty promises. He knows Immunity is heading south and within a few days, it will be far away and may not even exist. No Chinooks, no scientist, he told them. He will catch hell for that later, he knows. Possibly lose his command. They might even put him against a wall and shoot him. But his men will survive, if only to fight again, and perhaps even die, another day.

"I have to ask one thing, Dr. Petrova," he says.

"Yes," she says.

"Two things, actually." He stumbles a bit. "Yes, two things."

She eyes him curiously.

"Of course."

"My first question is: How did this happen?"

"I developed a hypothesis. But a scientific hypothesis, you see, is only—"

"I understand, Doctor. What's your theory?"

"My apologies. My theory is based on several observations. The virus is too perfect. Lyssa somehow snaps back to its Mad Dog ancestor once it enters the brain. The incubation period defies belief. It must have been bioengineered."

Behind Bowman, Doc Waters gasps.

Kemper says, "A terrorist weapon?"

"Why produce a terrorist weapon that will kill so many people on all sides?" Doc Waters says.

"Maybe the terrorists think they'll survive it and come out ahead,"

Kemper says. "Maybe they think it will level the playing field."

"It sounds too good, though. It must have had government sponsorship."

Petrova says, "Actually, you are both incorrect."

She hesitates, apparently afraid of offending them.

"In my opinion," she adds.

"Go on, Doctor," Bowman says. "You're the expert here."

"Viruses are highly proficient at penetrating human cells and inserting DNA," the virologist tells them. "It is what they do. Because of this, viruses normally thought of as deadly have begun to be used as Trojan Horse delivery systems for genetic material or drugs that can cure other diseases. Before this happened, gene therapy was an exciting area of biomedicine with tremendous potential."

For example, she adds, a modified and benign form of HIV, the same virus responsible for AIDS, has been studied as a delivery system for diseases such as hemophilia and Alzheimer's. Herpes may be proficient for targeting and destroying cancer cells. Even Ebola, one of the world's deadliest diseases, has been studied as a delivery vehicle for a benevolent retrovirus that can repair cells and help combat diseases such as cystic fibrosis.

"I believe researchers in Asia were working with a modified rabies virus as a new gene therapy asset, and something went wrong, obviously," Petrova concludes.

"You can say that again," Kemper says.

"The rogue experimental virus entered the community but quickly mutated into what we call Hong Kong Lyssa—a respiratory disease similar to avian influenza. Perhaps it was accidentally mixed into the experimental vaccine formula. Such mistakes have happened before at biomedical facilities."

"How could they even tamper with nature like this?" Doc Waters demands, his face reddening. "They basically destroyed civilization."

"Please," Petrova says, her nose wrinkling with distaste. "You have medical training, Mr. Waters. Certainly, you can appreciate that the release and spread of the disease is an odd occurrence, a one in a million circumstance, a very small risk for incredible gain for humanity. The world took far greater risks harnessing atomic energy. This was not the product of some sinister plan. The intent was to strip the virus of those attributes that made it deadly and insert benevolent genetic material into the hollow protein shell. The virus is not supposed to replicate or attack cells. It is a very careful process. I cannot imagine what went wrong, although something certainly did go wrong."

"You can say that again," Kemper says.

"I can tell you gentlemen one thing positively about the people who did this. The only thing I know for certain about them and what they did. They were trying to cure diseases that claimed millions of lives. They wanted to make a better world."

"So did Hitler," Doc Water mutters.

"Oh," Petrova says, obviously offended.

"It's a hell of a thing," Bowman says, preparing to rise. "As far as theories go, I can't think of a better one." He does not hold her responsible for what happened. Instead, he admires her strength and intellect. The fact of her survival over the past several days marks her as a remarkably resilient and resourceful woman. "Thank you, Doctor."

"You said you had two questions for me, Captain."

"I did, as a matter of fact," Bowman says, grinning. You'll probably find the question a little strange, possibly even improper. Aw, hell, I guess I'll just ask flat out. If we survive this, can I take you to dinner, Dr. Petrova?"

Petrova smiles and displays the gold wedding band on her left hand.

"Captain Bowman, that is a flattering invitation," she answers, "but as you will observe, I am a happily married woman."

Bowman smiles and nods.

"That also figures," he says dryly.

Time to kick my ass?

McLeod finds Sergeant Ruiz alone in the elevator lobby, leaning against the wall with his hands deep in the pockets of his BDUs, seemingly lost in thought. The CO has authorized the company to take off the N95 masks until the march, and it is strange to see Ruiz's face again. Most of the soldiers took advantage of the fact they had to wear masks 24/7 and grew scraggly beards, but not Ruiz; he is clean shaven. A gung ho mo fo, as they say in the ranks.

McLeod says: "You, uh, wanted to see me privately, Sergeant Ruiz?"

The NCO steps away from the wall, the muscles of his bulldog torso straining against his uniform, his eyes intense and staring. As he approaches, McLeod flinches, but holds his ground. This is it, he thinks. The hour of reckoning.

Magilla is finally going to kick my ass.

Ruiz continues until he stands directly in front of McLeod, looking him up and down while the soldier stands at attention.

"Private McLeod, you are one sorry sack of shit," he says.

"Yes, Sergeant," McLeod answers, meaning it.

"A big greasy shit stain on my otherwise spotless record of training the world's finest combat infantry."

"Yes, Sergeant."

"I got one question for you."

Do you want to get punched in the face or stomach?

"The question is: Are you ready to man up, son?"

"Sergeant?"

"McLeod, this unit has been in constant danger for the past four days. Our battalion has lost about two-thirds of its strength during that time. A good number of our casualties were sustained by mobs of people who tore our guys apart with their bare hands. While all this was going on, have you fired your weapon even once?"

"Um," says McLeod.

"Speak up, son."

"No, Sergeant," he says clearly.

"It's not a test," Ruiz tells him. "At ease."

Just tell me when you're going to do it. Don't sucker punch me. That's all I ask.

"I said relax, Private. Relax and listen good. I'm trying to teach you something."

"Yes, Sergeant," McLeod says, swallowing hard.

"Do you know what time it is, son?"

Time to kick my ass?

He answers, "It's about oh-five-forty-five, Sergeant."

"That is affirmative. Outstanding, Private. Do you know when the sun rises? I'll tell you when. Today, the sun will rise around zero-six-twenty. Do you know what that means?"

McLeod chews his lip, sweating.

The Sergeant says, "Don't hurt yourself, Private. It's not a trick question. I'll tell you what it means. It means that even if Immunity were to put birds in the air right now and we left this facility right now to meet them up in Central Park, we still wouldn't have enough time under darkness to conceal our movements. That means we will be taking some, most or all of this trip in daylight exposed to Maddy. What would you do if you were in command?"

"Me? I guess I'd ask the General to wait until tomorrow night."

"Outstanding, Private! But the General just told you it's now or never, do or die. Division is pulling stakes and trucking south. In twenty-four hours, all their birds are going to be far gone, committed to other missions. There'll be empty sky around here as far as the eye can see. So it looks like we have no choice. We're moving out, and we'll be walking in Maddy's shadow." Ruiz puts on a sad face. "How does that make you feel, Private?"

"Feel, Sergeant?" McLeod clears his throat. "Well, honestly, it makes me—"

"Do not answer that question, Private."

"Yes, Sergeant."

"Get your shit together, son!"

"Yes, Sergeant."

"What's holding you back from kicking Maddy's ass? Are you scared?"

I just want

"Yes, Sergeant. I'm scared."

Ruiz shakes his head, circling McLeod like a shark studying its prey.

"You got to man up, son. Fear is your bitch. Do you understand?"

to go to school

"Yes, Sergeant."

"When Maddy hits you, you got to hit him back tenfold. Hooah?"

and read books

"Hooah, Sergeant."

"If you survive the next one or two hours, you can survive anything. You are really and truly the baddest motherfucker in the world. Really and truly the best. Am I right?"

and be left alone.

"Yes, Sergeant."

"Remember son, pain is temporary, but honor is forever. This is about how you see yourself in your old age. What you tell your grandkids about what you were doing during the plague. So are you a warrior? Or are you chickenshit?"

McLeod relaxes his stance and looks his squad leader in the eyes.

Time to be honest with this guy for once.

"Sergeant," he says, "I never was a warrior and I doubt I'll ever be one. You know it and I know it. But I'll do right by you. You've always done right by me. You may not think I think that, but I do. So I'll do right by you. I'll kick ass today for the squad."

Ruiz blinks.

"All right, then," he says finally. "Just be aggressive with that SAW."

"Hooah, Sergeant," McLeod says, coming to attention and saluting.

The NCO shakes his head, regarding McLeod with his intense stare. "You really are a piece of work, Private. Anybody ever tell you that?"

McLeod grins and tells him, "Every day, Sergeant."

"Be aggressive on this march, McLeod," Ruiz says darkly. "I'll be watching. Now get your shit-eating grin out of my sight before I kick your ass all over this building."

Brave or stupid, take your pick

First Squad sprawls on the floor in full battle rattle, wolfing down MREs and catching last-minute smokes but otherwise ready to move. Mooney and Wyatt share the last pack of cupcakes from the rich kids' lockers. Ratliff is hunched over a boot, finishing his repair of a broken lace. Carrillo pulls the plates out of his body armor, as the boys have been ordered to ditch the extra weight so they can move as fast as possible. Finnegan reloads the last bullets he just cleaned into a magazine, which will improve the odds that his carbine will not jam. Like Sergeant McGraw, who was spotted earlier playing pocket pool with his lucky talismans, the boys have their superstitions: Finnegan kisses the magazine before loading it into his carbine. Rollins runs off to find the chaplain after being told the man is leading a group of soldiers in prayer in another room.

Mooney sits against a wall, his carbine between his knees and his mouth blissfully full of stale cupcake, and listens to the sounds of the boys sharing stories and seeking each other out in fellowship. He is intensely aware of everything around him and his own place among them. Like the other soldiers, he has an innate knowledge that every passing minute is bringing them closer to a confrontation with Maddy in daylight. In just a half an hour, he might be dead, his body torn to shreds by a homicidal mob. Life is particularly precious to the doomed. Every moment that passes, he experiences like a snapshot. And he is filled with intense fraternal love for all of the other soldiers because they might die, too.

The thing is, if they will die, at least they won't die alone. In the end, after all, that is all a soldier truly owns in combat—the possible comfort of dying among friends. That is why soldiers consider other soldiers their family. They look the tiger in the eye together, at the edge of oblivion.

It is sad to think, though, that for those who do die today, war will be the only thing they have every truly experienced.

"So this Hajji's up on the roof firing an RPG—remember that guy?" Carrillo says, almost shouting as he reminisces. "Every time Second Squad shot at him, he ducked down, then popped up to fire again, only he wasn't even firing at us."

"Oh right, he kept shooting at that yellow station wagon parked near that factory," Finnegan chimes in. "And we were like, 'What's he shooting at? Does he need glasses or is he just an idiot?'"

"They had Second Squad boxed up nice and neat in a kill zone and that dude could have done some serious damage to those guys, but he kept firing at the vehicle," Ratliff says, laughing.

"That's right, it was a VCIED!" Carrillo says, his eyes gleaming and slightly vacant, reliving the moment. "That car was wired up like a big brick of C4 but didn't go off. So he tried to make it blow by hitting it with a grenade."

"Only he couldn't shoot for shit," Wyatt points out.

"Some of them could," Mooney says, instantly regretting it. The laughter dies down into a smattering of chuckles. Now they are starting to think about the rest of that horrible day fighting in the alleys, streets, courtyards, houses. By the end of that day, they were exchanging point blank fire with insurgents in the middle of people's living rooms. They cannot remember whether the insurgents were Sunni or Shi'a, jihadist or nationalist. But they do remember how Torres died in the house to house fighting, how Simmons lost both his legs.

"Yeah," Carrillo says softly, trying to hold onto the moment.

"Hey, what about that night, when the Tank Team showed up, and that crazy Hajji took on an M1 Abrams with an AK?" Finnegan says.

The boys howl with laughter, rekindling their mirth with fresh memories. Mooney grins. The AK47 rounds bounced harmlessly off the tank's composite armor, already scorched and scratched by numerous RPG hits and heavy machine gun fire. At first, the tankers could not believe what they were seeing, then decided if it's a duel the insurgent wanted, they would oblige. The tank ground to a halt in a cloud of dust, its turret swiveling, and lowered its rifled tank gun. Moments later, it fired a round that lit up the street like daytime for a moment, vaporizing the Iraqi instantly.

"Like a fly swatter squashing a gnat," Finnegan adds.

"Brave or stupid, take your pick," Corporal Eckhardt chimes in.

Again, the levity does not last. This time, the image of the lone Iraqi pointlessly shooting at a sixty-ton armored monster bearing down on him—its steel-clad treads squealing and its big gun lining up to belch instant death in the form of a 105-mm HE round—does not strike them as quite so darkly comical today.

The prospect of going up against Maddy again this morning, in fact, is suddenly making them identify with that plucky but seemingly suicidal insurgent.

Brave or stupid, take your pick.

And yet they too would try.

Not quite saving the world, but I'll take it

Kemper knocks on the door with the nameplate that says *JOSEPH HARDY, RESEARCH DIRECTOR*, and enters to find the CO sitting on the edge of the desk, studying his wrinkled map of Manhattan that he has thumbtacked to the wall.

Kemper places his hand over his heart and says, *"Salaam 'Alaykum, sir."*

Bowman usually answers, "Hooah" to this greeting when it's given by a fellow veteran of Operation Iraqi Freedom—specifically, Operation Together Forward III, in which all soldiers learned Iraqi customs as a strategy to win hears and minds—but today he says earnestly, *"Wa 'Alaykum As-Salaam,* Mike."

And unto you be peace.

Kemper's eyes flicker to the map.

"The plan is solid, sir," he says. "The men know what to do."

"I have endless faith in the men," Bowman answers. "But almost none in plans."

Kemper laughs, lighting one of his foul-smelling cigars.

Bowman continues: "A million things could go wrong and get us all killed. It's going to be a hard day, Mike. The ultimate test."

"Yes, sir."

"This will be the last military operation before America gives up on New York. Once we're gone, the city will be ceded to the virus."

"If Maddy lets us leave, sir."

"And if Immunity sends us those birds." Bowman checks his watch. "It's already too late. We're going to be making part of this march in broad daylight."

"I don't suppose you can get the General to postpone the extraction for a day."

"I'm afraid that's a big November Golf, Mike."

"You don't want to go now, while it's dark, and wait for the birds at the Park?"

"What if they don't show? We'd be stuck out in the open. This is a good position we've got here. We've got electricity. We may end up having to stick around."

"Speaking of which, there is another alternative, sir, that I didn't want to bring up in front of the other men for obvious reasons."

"Stay here?"

"Do what everybody else is doing. Take care of number one."

Kemper realizes that only in a crisis as bad as this are they able to even talk this openly about desertion.

"And then what?"

Kemper shrugs. "Maybe try to get back to the high school and sit this thing out until Maddy finally drops dead. Try to get the people here fed and organized somehow after it's over. They're going to need a government. Perhaps this is where our duty lies?"

"Yeah. You've seen how good we are at nation building."

Kemper exhales a cloud of smoke and laughs again.

Bowman shakes his head.

"Seriously, Mike. I don't know about you, but I'd like to stay in this war as long as I can. We raised our right hand to uphold the Constitution against all enemies, and if ever America needed us to fight an enemy, it's now. In any case, we've got to get the scientist out. Who knows, maybe she really can cure this thing. The world can't have a vaccine right now, but it might need one later. It's not quite saving the world, but I'll take it."

The Platoon Sergeant nods. "I figured on you feeling that way, Captain."

"That's the mission."

"It's a bag of dicks, that's for certain."

"Hooah, Mike."

"Anyhow, you asked to see me. What do you need?"

"Right. It's like this, Mike: I need an officer to command Second Platoon."

"What about Lieutenant Knight?"

"I've made him my XO."

"Ah. Smart."

"Mike, I'm offering you a promotion to the rank of first lieutenant."

"Right. Ah, sorry, sir, but I'm going to have to say thanks but no thanks to that promotion. If you're really feeling magnanimous, sir, you can promote me to Sergeant Major. But even First Sergeant would be a nice step up in pay grade."

The CO grins. "Afraid all your friends would ditch you, Mike?"

"If I became an officer, sir, whose incompetence would I bitch about all day?"

Bowman laughs out loud and says, "So be it. The battalion will be reconstituting as an overstrength company, and it's going to need a First Sergeant, so you're it."

He extends his hand to Kemper, who shakes it warmly.

"Congratulations," he adds. "It's a well deserved promotion. Although I don't know about that rise in pay. Money's becoming worthless. For all I know, they're going to start paying us in MREs."

"Thank you, sir."

"Same to you, Mike. Thanks for everything. . . . I wanted to let you know, whatever happens, that I appreciate everything you've taught me."

"You're paying me back for it. You're starting to teach me a thing or two."

"Well," Bowman says, embarrassed.

"Do you mind if I take that map, sir?"

"Help yourself."

Kemper takes it down from the wall, folds it carefully, and puts it in a pocket of his BDUs.

"Souvenir, sir," he says.

I must be in good hands with soldiers who have a name like that

The elevator takes Petrova and a squad of gawking soldiers down to the lobby, where the rest of the company has assembled and is ready to leave the building. When they are not staring at her—the famous scientist they believe holds the secret to curing the plague—she likes to watch them work. These kids seem to know what they are doing. They move like clockwork and are well led by their NCOs, the professional warriors.

The company begins to file out of the building in sections. First, two platoons exit in a paired column, one soldier swinging left and one swinging right to provide a defensive perimeter on the street so that the rest of the company can safely exit. Then Captain Bowman, trailed by his machine gunners, whom he calls the Alamo Squad, leads the rest of the company outside.

Petrova blinks in the dim light, marveling at the sky, which she has not seen for days.

The air is chilly and the sky is gray and cloudy.

The helicopters took too long to get in the air. Dawn has come and the column will be moving in daylight. The gray sky is already filled with screaming birds, feeding on the dead.

She cannot believe the carnage. The cars smashed against each other at odd angles on a road of garbage and broken glass. The blood splashed across the ground and pooled in the potholes. She steps over random torn luggage, battered children's books, a pattern of cracked CDs. People's entire lives spilled onto the ground. Without its owners, it is just garbage.

The air smells like smoke.

My God, Petrova tells herself, it is not even a city anymore, but a wasteland. She was picturing a city in a crisis, not already fallen.

This was her home, and she is leaving it forever.

At last, the CO gives the order to move out. The company gets onto its feet, weapons and gear clanking, and begins its march north at a brisk pace. She feels safe being surrounded by so much legendary American firepower, and yet feels completely vulnerable in the open like this.

The Mad Dogs are out there in their armies, hunting the uninfected. Petrova can sense them. Their growling gently touches her ears as whispers on the breeze. Their marching vibrates under her feet, a deep rumble in the distance. If the Mad Dogs brought the greatest city in the world to ruin like this in days, what does this puny group of boys hope to do with their rifles and bombs and machine guns? They would shoot an ocean, hoping to kill it.

She passes the burned wreck of a Chevy Malibu. The charred, blackened skeletons of the driver and his family are still inside. The driver's grinning jaws hang open, as if laughing silently at the fools passing him by. The horror of it slaps her in the face.

She presses her hands over her mouth and swallows hard, painfully aware that the soldiers around her are watching to see how she will react. They are not being malicious. They are visibly anxious. If she starts screaming, she could put their lives in danger.

But Petrova does not scream; she steels herself and keeps walking, passing one horror after another. Overhead, the black birds cackle, as if laughing at them all.

She turns to the soldier marching next to her, a tall, slim twenty-year-old with intelligent eyes, apparently part of a handpicked detail assigned to guard her.

"What is your name?" she says as quietly as possible.

"PFC Jon Mooney, Ma'am," he answers earnestly, if mechanically.

She tentatively holds out her hand.

He stares at it, then takes it with his own gloved hand, gripping it firmly.

"I've got you, Dr. Petrova."

"Thank you, Jon."

The boy's face lights up at hearing his first name.

"I'm Joel," the soldier on her other side says. "Do you want a Kit Kat bar, lady?"

Petrova smiles and shakes her head politely. She is too nervous to eat and besides, she lived on junk food out of the vending machine for days and is now thoroughly sick of it. They've gone several blocks without incident but they have so far to go, and the sky continues to lighten as the sun rises above the horizon.

Above, people are waking up to the noise the column is making as it weaves its way through a street choked with cars, and begin shouting down at them from windows. Some ask for help killing a Mad Dog loose in a stairwell, public corridor or even in a neighboring room. Some ask for food and water and medicine. Everyone ask for news, any news.

Are you here to help us?

Who sent you?

Is it over?

Petrova looks down at her feet, her face burning at the thought the

Army is not fighting its way into New York to save its people, but sneaking its way out to save just her alone, abandoning everybody here to a likely future of disease, starvation and death.

This city was her home. These people are the New Yorkers she shared its sidewalks, subways, restaurants, museums, parks, taxis, cafes and treasures with.

"What is your unit?" she asks Mooney, hoping to distract herself. She instinctively trusts this seemingly sensitive young man. His eyes have not died like most of the other boys'. Their eyes have seen too much killing and they've been turned partly into what they hate, killing machines capable of thoughtless, wholesale slaughter. Those creatures roaming the streets are, in a sense, the living dead, but some of these soldiers are the dead living. Jon Mooney is one of those who are still alive. He is still human. She can tell by looking at his eyes, where the soul shows itself.

"First Squad, Second Platoon, Charlie Company, First Battalion, Eighth Brigade, Seventy-Fifth Regiment, Sixth Infantry Division. They call our brigade the Crazy Eights, Ma'am. Technically, we're all that's left of it."

"The Crazy Eights," she says.

"That's right."

"I must be in good hands with soldiers who have a name like that."

Mooney grins and says, "We're the best at what we do. You're safe with us."

"So what is my special name?"

"Ma'am?"

"President Kennedy was known as Lancer. I must have a special name."

"Actually, you do. You're, uh, 'Doctor Killjoy.'"

"Oh," she says.

"The names aren't very important, Ma'am. They're almost pulled out of a hat."

"It is okay," she says. "But it is not as good as 'Crazy Eights.'"

The soldier laughs, while the people in the windows above continue shouting.

Can I come with you?

Are you here to stay?

Do you guys need any help?

The noise has already attracted a stream of Mad Dogs, who are quickly bayoneted. Then the first shots ring out. The gunshots reverberate in the street, echo down the canyons formed by the buildings. These sounds in turn flush more Mad Dogs out of their hiding places. Snarling and snapping their jaws, they come running at the column from alleys and side streets and out of buildings, only to be speared or shot on sight.

Petrova suddenly feels her body clench with fear. She squeezes Mooney's hand fiercely, her arm trembling. The soldier holds on and does not complain. He is looking up at the buildings, frowning at the sudden change in atmosphere. He hears it, too.

A bizarre rumbling sound, like a million cardboard boxes being punched in the distance.

The civilians in the windows are crying out to them in panicked voices, pointing south. The NCOs at the rear of the column shout into their radios.

Letting go of Mooney's hand, Petrova climbs onto the hood and then scrambles up onto the roof of a Ford Ranger pickup truck, ignoring his protests.

Panting, she turns and looks south.

A moving wall of people races towards them, raising a colossal cloud of dust that drifts high in the air, wafting against the sides of skyscrapers.

Deep in the flood of Mad Dogs, cars and trucks appear to slide as they are jostled by the crowd, like they're floating on water.

A million Bairds, all rushing headlong towards her in a compact, twitching mass, driven by a single mind.

She screams.

If you can't run . . .

Captain Bowman stands on the roof of a blood-spattered yellow taxi, carbine slung over his shoulder, looking through binoculars and whistling at the horde of Maddies bearing down on his command from less than two thousand meters away. Around him, the company streams past, preparing to shed squads every block to form lines facing south.

He is faced by an overwhelming force, and has few options. He can't run, at least not very far, because Maddy runs faster. He can't hide because the helicopters will be recalled if the company doesn't show up at the scheduled time, and they will be trapped here; besides, there is no guarantee Maddy will not follow them into the buildings.

If you can't run, and you can't hide, you have to fight.

The strategy is settled. The rest is tactics.

Maddy has numbers and speed, but Maddy can't shoot a gun. He is only dangerous if he can get his hands on you. So if you want to live, keep your distance.

Bowman's plan calls for deployment in depth, with the lines collapsing like a bag after contact with the enemy. Each squad will dump ordnance on the tightly packed Maddies and, once the enemy gets too close, hoof it to the rear, passing the enemy off to the next line.

As long as they do not run out of bullets or make any mistakes, they should be able to keep themselves safe.

He doubts it will work, actually, but he feels he has no other choice.

By deploying his troops in depth, basically spreading them out, he might wear down and destroy this very large body of Mad Dogs while leapfrogging all the way to Central Park. The problem is their formation will stretch out over a half mile, leaving the flanks vulnerable to other large bodies of the infected that he believes may be converging on his people. If this happens, his force will be cut into two or more pieces, and any units unlucky enough to be cut off will be destroyed. And the mission will certainly fail.

A thick trail of black smoke billowing from a burning dumpster begins flowing across the avenue, chased by a sudden change in wind and blocking his view. He puts his binoculars away and spares a moment to glance up at the sky, wishing he had air support. Even a single recon helicopter would be helpful.

Warlord Six, this is Warlord Seven, over.

Warlord Seven is the senior enlisted man in the battalion, Kemper.

Bowman keys his handset and says, "Go ahead, Mike, over."

Be advised that Warlord Five is leading a detachment east, over.

"Say again, over."

Warlord Five is leading a detachment east on Thirty-Eighth Street, over.

"Wait, out," he says, fighting a mixture of rage and panic.

Warlord Five is the XO.

The company is moving north, and Knight is leading some of the boys east.

The man is committing some incredible blunder, completely misinterpreting his orders, and dangerously close to getting them all killed.

Bowman realizes he has seconds to fix this.

He keys his handset again.

"Warlord Five, this is Warlord Six, how copy?"

Warlord Six, this is Warlord Five, go ahead, sir.

"Steve, what are you doing? Get those people back in formation before we have a disaster on our hands."

Negative, says his XO.

Wrong answer

Lieutenant Stephen Knight, holding a pair of binoculars and watching the turn where he led Alpha, Bravo and Delta away from the main column, grunts with satisfaction as threads of brilliant white smoke begin to drift into the intersection.

His plan is simple: He is going to hit Maddy as he enters the intersection, then leapfrog east rapidly while the rest of the column continues north.

Bowman screamed at him for several moments over the radio but quickly realized they were wasting time they did not have, and decided to adopt Knight's plan on the spot.

Good old Todd. He has a flexible mind.

Knight is convinced his plan will succeed. Charlie's rear guard popped smoke to conceal the company's retreat and hauled ass north. Meanwhile, his own force will draw Maddy off of Charlie and keep them busy for a while.

Maddy is not going to make a fool out of me again, he tells himself, grinning.

Vaughan comes jogging up after issuing orders deploying the rest of their force in depth, stacking them facing west, with a strong rear guard. Around them, two squads of soldiers, their first line, have found comfortable firing positions and are waiting for the order to shoot, locked and loaded.

Knight puts his binoculars away and winks at the man who had been his platoon sergeant and is now a first lieutenant, commanding what is left of Alpha.

"I just got off the com with the CO," Vaughan says. "I ought to shoot you in the goddamn head. You just killed us all."

The soldiers closest to them, hunched over their weapons, raise their heads and blink, wondering what is going on.

"This is the only way to accomplish our mission," Knight says.

"My boys died because you froze," Vaughan roars, unholstering his nine-millimeter and chambering a round. His face is flushed, making the ugly diagonal scar appear livid on his face. "Now they have to die so you can redeem yourself!"

"What the hell?" one of the soldiers says.

"Oh man, I knew this mission was messed up," another mutters.

"This is the right thing to do," Knight says calmly.

"I outrank you now, Steve. You had no right to do this to me!"

He raises the pistol, takes a step forward and aims it at Knight's forehead.

"I don't care if you shoot me, Jim. What's done is done."

"You had no right to do this to these boys!"

One of the soldiers calls out: "Contact!"

Without taking his eyes off the pistol in Vaughan's hand, Knight takes a deep breath and screams with all his might: *"FIRE!"*

The line erupts with a storm of gunshot, turning the first wave of Mad Dogs into flying fragments of meat and bone.

Vaughan lowers his pistol, shaking his head sourly.

More Mad Dogs turn the corner and race towards their line until stopped cold by another volley.

"They're taking the bait," Knight says triumphantly. "See that, Jim?" He raises his carbine, sizes up a Mad Dog in his scope, and fires his first rounds. "I knew it'd work!"

If the entire game is going to be lost, there is nothing to be lost by sacrificing a pawn, he tells himself. Because with the game lost, the pawns die anyway.

The tracers stream down the street, every fourth bullet a red streak created by a trail of burning phosphorous. A thirty-cal machine gun opens up, lacerating flesh and snapping bones. A forty-millimeter grenade falls from the sky, bounces off the roof of a car and explodes in mid-air, decapitating a dozen Mad Dogs at once.

And still they come, pouring around the corner, stumbling over the dead, their feet splashing in a lake of blood and writhing bodies and body parts.

"Reloading," somebody calls out.

"Bring it!"

"Get some!"

One of the soldiers raises an AT4, a lightweight recoilless antitank rocket launcher good for area fire up to five hundred meters, and disengages its two safeties before cocking the mechanical firing pin. Estimating the range, he adjusts the tube-shaped weapon's plastic sights and takes aim.

"Fire in the hole!" he screams.

He pulls the trigger and fires, producing a mushrooming, fiery back blast from the rear of the tube. The finned missile ejects and closes the distance between the soldiers and the Mad Dogs in a half-second, skimming the top of the crowd before disappearing into the building beyond. A moment later, it detonates with a blinding flash, rocking the building, which belches its flaming guts onto the street.

A wave of smoke and dust descend upon the Mad Dogs, shrouding them from view.

Knight is laughing, draining a magazine at a cyclic rate of fire, shooting randomly into the dark veil.

They must all die to wipe out his sin and pay his debt to the dead.

"Fall back!" Vaughan is shouting, waving his handgun. "Back of the line!"

As the boys stream toward the rear, the former sergeant grips Knight's arm and shouts into his ear, "LT! Do you have a plan for getting us back to the main column?"

"Of course!" Knight grins, his eyes gleaming with their own pale light. "It's simple. We kill them all!"

"Wrong answer, sir," Vaughan says.

The handgun discharges in his other hand, putting a bullet through Knight's calf. Knight screams and collapses, clawing at his leg.

Moments later, it's raining body parts

McLeod runs across the open intersection, firing his SAW from the hip, hitting almost nothing and screaming his head off. The other boys of Third Squad run alongside, their faces red and sweaty, huffing as they lay down their own wild suppressing fire. The bullets shatter windows, punch holes and blow out tires in vehicles, rattle off walls, snap through the bodies of the Mad Dogs.

Everybody is doing more running than shooting right now. The column is still retreating north after Knight's defection, and it is turning into a rout. The XO's ploy helped them escape the first horde of Maddies, but thousands more are pouring into the area from the east and west, and the column is being flanked on every street.

As the rear guard, Third Squad's only hope is to outrun Maddy before the column is broken and they are cut off.

Behind them, a soldier from Third Platoon pauses to lift a Javelin launcher to his shoulder, his aim wobbly as he gasps for air.

"Fire in the hole!"

The missile instantly strikes an SUV standing like an island in the middle of a flowing river of infected, crumpling its door like aluminum foil just before it detonates with a boom the soldiers can feel in their feet. The fireball sends half of the vehicle ripping through the crowd like a giant bowling ball before crashing through a nearby plate glass storefront, while the other half flies spinning into the air.

The soldier leans back and howls in triumph, then shouts after his fleeing comrades, "Don't tell me you guys didn't see that!"

He is instantly tackled to the ground by a mob of the infected coming up behind him. He shrugs them off, struggling to flee, and topples under the weight of an endless stream of Maddies. Behind them, a score of infected stagger by, on fire from head to tie and flailing blindly, screaming in agony. A moment later, the soldier is permanently obscured from view by a wave of black, oily smoke. A living flood of Maddies pours out of the smoke racing headlong after the column. They are scarcely recognizable as human anymore, filthy, hair greasy and matted, covered in bruises and open sores, gaunt and dressed in bloody rags.

They are the living dead.

"Contact left!"

Ruiz is ahead of the squad, swinging his arm like a baseball coach on third base waving his runners home for the big win, screaming, "Go, go, go!"

The boys stop firing and pour their last energy into a flat out run to get across the next intersection before they are cut off and slaughtered.

They pass Ruiz, who yells "Frag out!" and throws a grenade down the street at their pursuers. Moments later, it's raining body parts.

Then they're running across the next intersection as a column of Maddies bears down on them fifty meters away from the west.

"Captain says we're clear up ahead," Ruiz shouts when they're halfway up the next block. "We're walking to the next intersection."

"Roger that!" the boys shout back, panting.

"Now give me fire while we take five, and make it hot!"

The boys yell exultantly, pouring a storm of hot metal into the approaching Mad Dogs, who disappear in a cloud of red mist. The fire immediately eases as the soldiers marvel at their incredible firepower.

"Keep firing!" Ruiz roars at them. He's obviously tired of withdrawing under pressure, and wants to make some breathing room.

A grenade explodes near the burned-out wreck of a car in the middle of the street, flipping it. McLeod steadies his SAW against the hood of a Toyota Corolla and begins firing in controlled bursts. He will not switch to cyclic fire unless he has to do so to stay alive; he does not want to risk overheating his weapon. Once it jams, it is out of action and that's it, he will be out of the game.

He notices an inviting door leading into an apartment building. A few minutes running up the stairs until he gets to the roof, and he can wait this whole thing out.

But he does not move.

Every time I fire my weapon, he tells himself, I consent to this freakshow.

He spares a glance at Sergeant Ruiz, then fires a burst that cuts a skinny woman in half. He is not going anywhere as long as that son of a bitch is still alive. He promised Magilla that he would do his part, and he intends to keep the promise, unsure why it is so important that he do so.

He is vaguely aware there is also a moral dilemma involved. The only way he can successfully escape into one of the buildings is if the rest of his squad—including Williams, who has put up with his crap longer than most would—stays in the street fighting while needing every gun, especially his SAW, on line.

"Hey, they're popping smoke behind us," somebody says.

At the next intersection, their comrades in Second Platoon, the column's advance guard, disappear behind a wall of smoke heading north, while the remains of First and Third Platoons are moving east. It is Lieutenant Knight's crazy plan all over again.

"Prepare to withdraw on my command!" Ruiz calls out.

Fire slackens as the boys get set to break off contact and haul ass.

Time to retrograde.

I'm not afraid

Knight slowly pulls himself onto his feet, grimacing with pain at the bleeding hole in his torn and bruised calf muscle, and sees the first Mad

Dogs racing toward him from only twenty meters away.

"Vaughan!" he screams. "Vaughan, help me!"

Leaning back against a car, he reaches for his carbine, but it is gone. All he has is his nine-millimeter. Gritting his teeth against the pain, he quickly unholsters it and squeezes off several shots into the approaching horde, dropping bodies onto the street.

The Mad Dogs bear down on him, their slavering jaws champing.

Knight laughs suddenly, his eyes shining, feeling lightheaded and weak from the loss of blood.

"I'm not afraid of you," he says, and empties the rest of the clip into their snarling faces.

The infected do not know what fear is.

They rip him into pieces, ignoring his screams, and fight over what is left. They gnaw and bite even at the morsels, trying to infect his dead flesh with living virus.

The rest rush by in their thousands, pressing onward into the crashing rifles of Alpha's lines.

One last card to play

Bowman watches his new rear guard pop smoke, concealing their retreat as First and Third Platoons head east, hoping to draw Maddy off the main column, now reduced to a pathetic twenty-five troops. Nearby, Kemper is yelling at everybody to clear the net, which has become congested with incomprehensible, screaming voices.

In less than fifteen minutes, his command has been scattered to the wind and is now entangled in a decisive engagement against a superior enemy, facing defeat in detail.

"Vaughan's holding," Kemper tells the CO. "He says they're starting to swing north soon and move towards the extraction point."

"Roger that," Bowman says, trying to feel hopeful.

A Mad Dog runs out of a nearby building, loping with his hands splayed into claws, spittle flying as he snarls. Without thinking, the Captain shoulders his carbine and cuts him down with two rounds.

Killing Maddy has become routine, almost instinctive now, without remorse or regret.

His company is at the edge of the abyss now.

Knight, acting on his own initiative, split their force in the face of the enemy and the bastard was right. Bowman realizes that if they stuck to his original plan, the column would have been hit in the flank in several places while engaged and destroyed piecemeal. He saw no other alternative at the time. Knight was willing to sacrifice himself and the men as pawns in a game; Bowman was not. No wonder the crazy bastard kept his ideas to himself until the last possible moment.

A mark of a good commander is to roll with the punches in the field. Not only did he decide on the spot to run with Knight's plan, he decided to implement it again when faced with an unwinnable fight against another collection of mobs converging on them. Almost all of First and Third Platoons volunteered to act as a diversionary force and hopefully Ruiz, part of the rear guard, will have the sense to join up with them instead of leading Maddy through the smoky veil that right now is their only real protection.

They are doing a good deed, but there is no need for anybody to sacrifice his life for a cause. Once things get too hot, they can simply melt away into the nearest buildings until danger passes, and gradually find their way back to the school.

Their decision was heroic, but also practical. They could all stay together and die valiantly, or break off and stay alive but give up the possibility of extraction.

"Contact left!" Corporal Alvarez calls back from the advance guard.

"Orders, sir?" Kemper says.

Bowman asks about the size of the force, and Alvarez tells him.

Christ, how many of these monsters are there?

Roll with the punches.

Another mark of a good commander: Keep one's options open.

The problem is they are almost out of options. Bowman has one last card to play, and decides to play it.

It is his turn to go east.

Contact

Ruiz is no fool. He understands why the Captain popped smoke, and turns the corner to follow First and Third Platoons—already setting up to hit Maddy as he enters the intersection—instead of running through the smoke to rejoin the rest of Second Platoon. The other soldiers cheer as they turn the corner, happy for the extra firepower and to have a pro like

Ruiz around. His combat skills are practically a legend in Charlie Company. The man has warrior spirit in his heart and ice water in his veins.

"Who's in charge here?" Ruiz asks Sergeant Floyd, a former corporal whom Bowman promoted to take over the remnants of Third Platoon.

Floyd looks Ruiz up and down, his face pale and his eyes bulging.

"You are, Sergeant," he says.

"All right. You're too bunched up. I want these men here to spread out—"

"Contact!"

Ruiz screams: *"FIRE!"*

The soldiers whoop as the line erupts with a volley. Instantly, the first ranks of the Mad Dogs collapse, their bodies torn and gushing blood, instantly replaced by fresh ranks. They're all making the turn. For a second time, Maddy has taken the bait, sparing the main column.

"Where do you want my SAW, Sergeant?" McLeod shouts over the din.

"Pick your own ground, Dorothy," Ruiz growls, racking a round into the firing chamber of his shotgun. "We'll be on the move in less than a minute."

McLeod deploys his bipod on the hood of a yellow cab, lines up his sights center mass on one of the leading Maddies, and fires his first burst. The gun bucks against his shoulder, making his teeth vibrate. He continues firing, empty shell casings and links popping out of the weapon's eject port and clattering onto the hood of the car. The tracer rounds strobe, flashing and guiding his aim into torsos and faces and limbs and skulls. The stream of hot metal pulverizes everything it comes into contact with.

"Frag out!"

He notices that the Mad Dogs are close and getting closer. Floyd made a mistake: He set up too close to the intersection without giving his first lines any breathing room.

"Reloading!"

Ruiz has already seen the same problem, and is ordering the first line to withdraw. The fire slackens as the boys come off the line.

"Contact!"

"Where?"

"The mothers are behind us!" somebody screams.

At the next intersection, First Platoon has been split in half by a massive horde of Mad Dogs converging from the north and south.

In just moments, most of Ruiz's command has become cut off and surrounded.

"Shit," he says.

"Our father, who art in heaven," McLeod says. He is suddenly unable to remember the rest of the prayer, his mind blank.

"Contact!"

"Man down!"

The Mad Dogs are ripping the boys apart in the intersection and pouring into the side streets, driving everything before them.

"FIRE!" Ruiz roars at anyone in earshot, then turns and blasts his shotgun into the infected coming the other way. "FIRE YOUR WEAPONS!"

Contact.

Some of the soldiers panic and flee to nearby doors, trying to escape into the buildings lining the street. Most of the doors are metal and locked, while others are fronted with glass and easily broken with rifle butts. The soldiers cry out in fear and rage as they open the doors but find their way inside blocked by furniture stacked into crude barricades by people living in the building to keep out the infected.

There is no escape from this.

At what moment did Custer, seeing all those warriors running up the hill with murder in their eyes, realize that he was toast? McLeod wonders. What did he do about it? Did he just sit down on the grass and wait to be tomahawked, taking his last precious moments to reflect on his short life, maybe sneak in one last combat jack?

Or did he keep shooting, wasting those moments but doing it anyway just so he could prolong his life by several more seconds?

Hell, when I die, he tells himself, I want to be doing something fun, not firing a gun.

He wills himself to stop shooting, but his fingers do not obey him.

I guess that solves that mystery, he tells himself. The instinct of self preservation trumps all. Quantity is better than quality. Now is probably a good time for cyclic fire, then.

He fires the SAW in rock and roll mode, spraying death almost blindly into the crowd.

Look at me, he thinks, I'm goddamn Rambo.

"That's the stuff, Private!" Ruiz roars, firing his shotgun and chambering another round, ejecting a smoking empty shell. "Hit him back tenfold!"

"I'm trying!" McLeod answers him.

"Reloading!" somebody calls out.

"I hate this goddamn Army," Williams says, struggling to clear a jam in his carbine. An instant later, the Mad Dogs swarm over him, turning his scream into a sickening wet gargle as two pairs of jaws sink into his throat and rip it open.

"Our father who art in heaven!" McLeod rasps, tears streaming down his stubble, mowing down the Mad Dogs still biting frantically at his dead friend's face, tearing away pieces of flesh and spitting them out.

Nearby, Corporal Hicks falls on his ass, one of his arms mangled and bleeding and the other holding his carbine, still shooting while the rest of the soldiers struggle to form a defensive square and fix bayonets.

A grenade flies into a second-story window and instantly detonates with a flash, ejecting glittering hot glass and flaming debris down onto the street, followed by a drifting veil of smoke and dust.

McLeod staggers and bumps into Ruiz, who is slowly retreating while rapid-firing his M4 Super 90 shotgun. The air is thick with smoke and the stench of infection. As the smoke descends upon the street, he catches glimpses of Hicks and Wheeler being torn into shreds. They reach the defensive square only to find it already gone. Back to back, McLeod and Ruiz create a three-hundred-sixty-degree zone of death for the Maddies.

The SAW grows hot in his hands, and suddenly clicks empty.

"Final protective fire," Ruiz says, then stumbles away, dropping his smoking shotgun. He is clutching his neck, blood running through his fingers.

"Sergeant?" McLeod says, unable to believe his eyes.

Ruiz is indestructible. He can't die.

He was not bitten; a stray bullet caught him.

"Emmanuel!" the man gasps, falling to his knees.

"Man down!" McLeod screams automatically, knowing it is useless to call for help.

He rushes forward to pull the Sergeant to safety but is suddenly shoved to the ground in the swirling melee of soldiers and infected. A Mad Dog trips over him, knocking the wind out of his lungs. Gasping for air, he sees Ruiz on his hands and knees, struggling to stand up, surrounded by Maddies hanging onto him and biting every inch of his body.

"Sergeant!" he calls out.

A knee cracks against the back of his head. The world goes black except for a few colorful sparking stars. By the time his vision clears, Ruiz has already been transformed into road kill, a headless and armless torso crushed and studded with fragments of glass.

"You motherfuckers," he says, crying with helpless rage. "You didn't have to do that to him. You didn't have to do that."

A grenade explodes nearby, sending charred and broken bodies collapsing around McLeod and soaking him in blood and smoking scraps of flesh. Another cloud of smoke and dust flows across the crowd. The high-pitched screams of the dying penetrate the loud ringing in his ears. Sobbing hysterically, he crawls between the running legs through the filth and glass until he is able to pull himself into the yellow cab and curl up shaking in a fetal ball in the backseat. The car rocks and jolts like a boat in the storm as the infected pour around him, finishing the slaughter of the doomed boys of Third Platoon.

Outside, the screams reach a crescendo.

Our father, who art in heaven

The crackle of small arms fire begins to die out. A Mad Dog runs into the side of the cab, smashing its face against the window and cobwebbing the glass. The foul-smelling corpse in the driver's seat sways with the impact, its head rolling and grinning.

Our father who art in heaven

Our father who art in heaven

A final flurry of gunshots, then nothing but the tramp of thousands of feet and a primal, almost triumphant growl from thousands of mouths.

Our father

I had no choice

There were once ten of them. Now there are four heading north through a wasteland, dirty and tired and bloody, while infected mobs pound the garbage-strewn alleys and side streets in a never-ending hunt for fresh meat.

They are the last of the main column after Bowman took the rest of the platoon east to divert the Mad Dogs: McGraw, Mooney, Wyatt and the scientist, Dr. Petrova.

They march in single file close to the buildings, staying in the shadows. With each step, the gunfire and shouting recedes further behind them until they can see the greenery of Central Park beckoning to them and promising sanctuary.

More than once, they have had to hide to avoid bands of Maddies, all heading south towards the shooting.

A metal garbage can rolls into view from behind the next corner, trailing garbage, and comes to a halt in the gutter. Slimy rats pour out of it, scrambling for cover.

Petrova groans with revulsion, her nails digging into Mooney's arm. She has faced every horror without faltering but his arm, the usual target of her channeled hysteria, is now covered with scratches and bruises.

Mooney accepts the abuse without complaint. He likes the attractive scientist, but that is only part of it. The pain keeps him from screaming in fear and revulsion and grief himself.

McGraw has called a security halt. Chewing on his handlebar mustache, his eyes wide behind his tinted sunglasses, he signals that he wants Mooney and Wyatt front and center.

Mooney gestures at Petrova, but the Sergeant does not care. There is nobody else. The last time they ran into a mob of infected, Carrillo, Finnegan, Ratliff, Rollins, Eckhardt and Sherman were cut off, climbed into the bed of a pickup truck and made a stand.

And now they are dead. They know this because they had to come back for the radio and found their bodies scattered like mangled, discarded puppets.

Wyatt offers Mooney one of his gimpy grins, making his big glasses crooked, and then winks. Mooney nods, wearing an expression of hopeful sadness. They've brought each other luck so far. They can't die now.

McGraw punches the air, pointing.

Prepare for action.

Mooney and Wyatt creep up to the corner, weapons held ready to shoot. Other than two charred, burned-out police cars at an abandoned checkpoint, the street appears empty. Perhaps the garbage can just fell over. It happens.

He is about to signal that the area is clear. Then he sees movement.

It is a dog. A pack of them. Filthy, feral dogs, feasting on a child.

"Hey!" he says.

Wyatt hisses at him to shut up, but he cannot stand the sight of that boy being eaten.

"Git!"

One of the dogs slouches closer, its lips peeled back and its ears flat, snarling in defense of its meat.

Mooney looks down at his bayonet. He is not allowed to shoot unless it is a matter of life and death; otherwise, it is the bayonet. But he does not want to get into a knife fight with a pack of feral dogs carrying God knows what diseases.

He picks up a beer bottle off the ground and throws it at the dogs, who scatter with snarls and yelps, licking their bloody chops.

"Dude, check it out," Wyatt says. "Hajjis on our three."

Four teenage boys stand across the street, wearing dirty hoodies and looking at them.

Wyatt adds, "You think they're infected?"

Mooney shakes his head, unsure. He raises his hand and waves.

The boys exchange a glance. One waves back.

"I don't think so, Joel."

The boys start walking towards them, glancing both ways, out of habit, before crossing the street.

They are holding baseball bats, but of course they would be armed. It would be madness to go outside without some type of protection. But Mooney is not in the mood to take chances anymore.

"That's close enough," his says, raising his carbine.

The boys stop in the middle of the street, their eyes vacant, and exchange a long, meaningful glance. They turn back to the soldiers. One of them grins.

As he grins, saliva leaks down his chin. He is infected, but has not turned yet.

They suddenly sprint forward, swinging their bats.

"Stop or I swear to God I'll shoot you dead," Mooney says.

One of the boys runs clumsily into Wyatt's bayonet, spearing himself, while another hits him in the arm with a bat, hard enough to make him drop his carbine. They close to grapple. Moody swings his own carbine to slash at the other two boys with his bayonet, but they dodge out of reach and pause, their mouths open and laughing soundlessly.

One breaks left and the other right—

McGraw's shotgun discharges with a deafening bang, killing one of them instantly. The two survivors flee, leaving one dead and the other trying to pull his bleeding body across the street, keening in his death throes.

"Finish him quick, Mooney," McGraw says. "Count your coup."

"Roger that, Sergeant."

If the blast did not bring Maddy running, the kid's grating death wail will. It is best to finish him quick. Mooney takes a deep breath, raises his carbine with the bayonet pointing down, and brings it down into the boy's back.

The knife pierces the boy's body clean through, impacting the street below with a jolt that resonates up Mooney's arms and neck. For several moments, the boy writhes under the bayonet like a fly pinned to a wall. Then he falls still, bleeding out onto the asphalt.

"Dead now, Sergeant," Mooney says.

"Then let's go," the Sergeant says.

Mooney pulls his bayonet free and stands over the corpse, exhausted. He notices Petrova staring at him, wide-eyed with horror.

"I had no choice," he says weakly.

"Your eyes," she whispers.

Mooney blinks. What does she see?

"Are you wounded, Private?" McGraw asks Wyatt.

Wyatt, standing aside with his hands jammed in his armpits, wags his head, looking pale and tired.

"I'm good, Sarge," he says. Wincing, he bends to pick up his carbine.

"What's wrong with my eyes?" Mooney demands.

But Petrova is not paying attention to him. She is looking up at the pale gray sky.

He follows her gaze and senses the change in atmosphere. Then he hears the sound coming from the southeast: the thunder of rotors. It rapidly grows in volume until three CH-47 helicopters roar over nearby rooftops at more than a hundred fifty miles per hour, red lights blinking on their bellies.

"Get on the horn with those Chinooks and tell them we're coming," McGraw shouts at Mooney, who has been carrying the SINCGAR since Jake Sherman died. "Tell them to hover at the rendezvous point until we reestablish radio contact!"

Mooney begins chanting into the radio, trying to contact the pilots.

Roger, War Dogs Two-One. We copy.

"I've made contact," he tells the others.

The group lets out a ragged cheer. Only Wyatt looks sour, staring after the disappearing helicopters glumly and muttering something to himself.

"You see that, Joel?" he adds. "We might just make it."

Seeing those massive birds cross the sky was one of the most beautiful things that Mooney has ever seen.

He feels like he will be home again soon, wherever that may be.

The opposite direction

McLeod opens his eyes and slowly extricates himself from the cab's backseat, his face sticky with drying blood and his ears ringing at a deafening volume.

He stands and takes a deep breath.

The sky spins, filled with the distant echo of gunfire.

He falls to his knees, vomiting messily onto the bloody ground.

Somebody hands him a canteen and he drinks greedily, spits.

"How," he says, and groans at the pain in his head.

The street has been turned into a nightmare landscape made up of hills of dead people and body parts and lakes of blood. Here and there, a wounded Maddy writhes on the ground, eyes and mouth gaping like a fish out of water. Civilians from nearby buildings silently pick at the dead, scavenging. The women mourn the soldiers, weeping as they search the bodies for food, blood splashed up to their elbows. The men pick up the carbines and look wistfully toward the sounds of shooting to the north. Everybody is pale with wide, panicked eyes; several people have paused in their work to vomit against a nearby wall.

McLeod shrugs off the hands trying to help him up and staggers to the place where he last saw Ruiz. His feet squish in boots filled with warm blood. He can't find the man's remains but knows he is there, buried in the scattered human wreckage.

"Sergeant?" he says, and breaks down coughing, his throat hoarse and sore.

Wait, he tells himself. The world does not know how to mind its own business. There are people out there who are going to try to stop you. You must be ready to fight.

He bends to pick up a carbine and pistol, load his pockets with ammo, and scavenge a few MREs and a canteen.

"Did I do right?" he says.

He bends over and coughs, spitting repeatedly.

"Did I do right by you then, Sergeant?"

The civilians gather around him as he starts moving in the opposite direction of the sounds of gunfire. They step out of his way and touch him lightly as he passes. Behind him, a woman sobs quietly.

He pauses long enough to touch his heart and say quietly to himself, "*Shookran*, Sergeant," then continues on his way.

He will break into a music shop and play every instrument. He will set up house in the New York Public Library and read every one of its books. Life is short, and this is the greatest city in the world, filled with treasures.

From now on, he vows, nobody will ever tell him what to do again.

You made it this far for a reason

Mooney's heart pounds as the double-prop Chinooks land in Sheep Meadow, the thirty-foot-long propeller blades savagely chopping the chilly air during their descent and sending waves of swirling dust and slivers of grass roaring across the field.

Each of these twelve-ton machines is nearly one hundred feet long and can transport more than fifty soldiers. Today, they will take on only four new passengers.

Next to him, Dr. Petrova is crying.

"We played here," she says, feebly gesturing at the field. "All of us."

He can barely hear her. The noise is incredible.

"That was my spot, under that tree," the scientist adds.

The loading ramps at the rear of the helicopters' fuselages drop, unloading Special Forces fireteams that fan out and establish security. Several start shooting at distant targets, dropping the first Maddies attracted to the heavy thumping of the rotors.

One of the soldiers stands and waves.

"That's our cue," McGraw shouts. "Let's go!"

The wind blast is strong, tugging at their uniforms and making them cough on the waves of dust. Mooney takes Petrova's hand to steady her as they half run, half limp to safety.

"We're almost there," he tells her, unable to believe they are going to make it.

The woman is pale and weak, murmuring to herself.

But this was his home, she says.

"Whose home?" he asks. "Keep moving, Ma'am!"

We ate ice cream last summer.

The soldiers rush forward to take her arms and help her onto the helicopter. Mooney starts to follow, but notices that McGraw and Wyatt are hanging back at the ramp.

"I'm not going with you boys," the Sergeant says.

"What?"

"I'm staying behind!"

Mooney looks at him helplessly. Is the man insane, hoping to get killed, or simply freakishly loyal, willing to take the incredible risk of fighting his way back to the Captain? Does he expect Mooney to stay with him, too?

It's not fair, he thinks.

McGraw says: "I'm quitting the Army!"

Wyatt laughs into the howling wind.

The Sergeant explains, "This was my last mission. I'm done. I'm going to keep my head down until it blows over, and then try to get home to my girl. Good luck to you boys. I wanted you to know I'm proud of you."

"Thank you, Sergeant," Mooney says with a lump in his throat.

"Good luck, Sarge," Wyatt says.

"Luck I got plenty of," McGraw says, winking. He salutes quickly and then he is gone, jogging lightly past the Special Forces teams as if the world were just beginning, not ending.

"I'm staying, too, Mooney," Wyatt tells him.

"You quitting?"

"Naw," Wyatt says. He pauses for a quick farmer's blow and then adds sourly, "One of those wanking wanktards back there bit me in the armpit. The infected one got me."

"Christ, Joel," Mooney says, too stunned to understand what he is hearing.

"Hurts like hell. I can actually feel the little mothers in my brain. Guess I'll go somewheres and eat the rest of my chocolate bars. Maybe go swim in the pond back there. Maybe rob a bank. Who knows; a lot can happen in a few hours before I turn into a zombie."

Mooney's voice cracks. "But what the hell am I supposed to do without you?"

Wyatt offers up his gimpy smile. "You'll manage okay on your own, boss. But I'll have to find a new sidekick."

One of the Special Forces soldiers appears at the top of the ramp and says, "Coming or going, make a choice. We got company."

"I'll see you around, Joel," Mooney says, holding out his hand.

Wyatt ignores the gesture, backing away awkwardly in the raging wind, smiling and offering a comical salute with his middle finger.

"Contact!"

Several soldiers rush down the ramp and begin firing at a horde of Mad Dogs breaking from the trees and streaming into the back of one of the other Chinooks parked across the lawn, overrunning its guards in hand to hand fighting. The distant bodies flop onto the grass, while others disappear inside the massive helicopter, which suddenly lurches into the air.

One of the soldiers grabs Mooney and shoves him roughly inside, where he lands on the floor shouting in panic. He scrambles into the seat next to Petrova, who screams at the sound of the gunfire, covering her face in her hands.

"No more killing," she pleads.

An NCO runs down the aisle towards the pilots, roaring a command to get the bird into the air right now.

"You're going to be okay, Dr. Petrova," Mooney says. "You made it this far for a reason. You had all those chances to die and you didn't. You can't die now."

The helicopter suddenly lifts hard, rising at a speed of twenty-five feet per second. Gravity sucks at his stomach and toes.

A Special Forces medic works his way down the aisle until he reaches Petrova and begins shouting questions at her: Has she been bitten? Is she otherwise injured? Does she have any other medical conditions affecting her well being? Does she want water?

Turning away, Mooney hops frequencies on the combat net radio, searching for Charlie's net. The air whistles through the cabin, making it difficult to hear. Then his ears pop and the voices come through clear as a bell.

That's our ride up

We can't

Man down!

Can the birds give us cover?

If anybody's got an MG, we need

He finds the sounds of their voices, even describing a losing fight, strangely comforting. They are still alive down there, and as long as they are still alive, there is hope.

We got contact

Could use fire support on the left

Establish a base of fire
Then break off with the other assault team
Clear the net, morons!

Mooney notices that the Special Forces guys are staring intently out the windows of one side of the helicopter, swearing. Turning in his seat, he sees the Chinook that was infested with Maddies flying erratically in the sky, its tail swinging back and forth, the loading ramp still open and spilling bodies that fall hundreds of feet to the ground below.

"Come on, come on," one of the soldiers says. "Keep control."

Mooney knows how they feel. Their friends are dying in the other helicopter, and there is nothing they can do about it.

The distressed helicopter roars west, veering towards the majestic, castlelike towers of the San Remo Towers building with the others pursuing at a safe distance. The men suck in their breath, expecting to see it crash and dissolve in a fireball inside one of the towers, but it pulls back, lurching and trying to stabilize. It is still too close, however: The props suddenly break against the side of the building and the violent stresses rip the Chinook in half with a burst of fire and smoke. The two pieces flop over and fall like stones to the earth, where they crash into pieces.

But while Mooney cannot tear his eyes away, he is only partly continuing to pay attention to this drama.

On the radio, the voices are screaming.

A fool's errand

Second Platoon pauses to fire a ragged volley against the pursuing Mad Dogs, then starts running again, leaving a trail of brass and links and Maddy corpses.

Bowman lingers for a few moments, providing cover fire. He knows he is going to have to give his exhausted boys a rest soon. The platoon is starting to shed stragglers and everybody's aim is getting wild. Maddy, meanwhile, does not seem to get tired. Plenty of the infected suddenly stop and keel over, their hearts bursting in their chests from the severe exertion, but the rest keep coming. They are the strongest and the fittest and there are always more to replace the fallen, it seems.

The same could be said of us, he tells himself, only when one of us falls, there are no replacements. There is nobody else. These men are the best but they are also the last.

He lobs a grenade into the endless horde and starts running again, flinching at the explosion that he hopes will buy them seconds.

The objective was to reach the rendezvous location at Sheep Meadow, but then Private Mooney radioed to tell him that the birds were back in the air with Dr. Valeriya Petrova safely aboard.

Their mission is now over. It was complex, extremely dangerous and partially successful. Now they have a new mission, simple but even more challenging: Stay alive.

Six blocks ahead, Vaughan's force was stopped cold at Columbus Circle, a wide traffic area at the southwest edge of Central Park, and set up a defensive position at its center, around the statue of Christopher Columbus. He is barely holding and is screaming for reinforcements. Bowman is taking Second Platoon there. Everybody else is dead. There is nobody else. Between him and Vaughan, the unit has maybe seventy shooters left.

Vaughan picked the spot for his stand well. As a junction for Broadway Central Park West, Fifty-Ninth Street and Eighth Avenue, Columbus Circle was kept clear of civilian traffic and there are no vehicles around, offering beautiful open firing lanes with good kill zones. They have too few guns and are virtually surrounded; both units now need to rejoin to concentrate their firepower.

After that, it is either them or Maddy in a classic showdown.

The only other option is to disperse his command: Everybody break into the nearest building, find a safe place to hide, and pray Maddy does not come in looking for you. But then what? Only the NCOs have communications. Everybody would be spread out and stranded in different buildings, possibly already filled with Maddies, with little food and water. Out of the frying pan and into the fire, as they say. Their only ultimate hope for surviving is to somehow get everybody into a safe place or defeat Maddy here. Now.

Ahead, the boys are slowing their pace.

Trouble ahead, Lewis says over the radio.

Bowman doubles his effort, sprinting to the head of the column, where Lewis and Kemper are observing another large body of Maddies blocking the road ahead.

A grisly parade of Mad Dogs, loping along in a ragged column, tall and short, skinny and fat, naked and clothed, bald and hairy, black and white and yellow, are pouring out of a street ahead and turning to move north along Eighth Avenue towards the sounds of Vaughan's guns. It's strange, but they look almost cheerful.

Second Platoon's situation, meanwhile, is dire. There is a huge enemy force directly in their path and another right behind them, and Bowman has seconds to make a decision.

One final rule of command: A good leader must do whatever it takes.

"Who's holding M203s?"

The boys come forward while Martin and Boomer deploy the M240 machine gun against their pursuers to buy some time. The air fills with the thirty-cal's staccato bark.

He tells them: "Load up with Willy Pete."

The boys do what they're told, loading their grenade launchers with WP grenades. White phosphorous burns fast and produces an instant cloud of smoke, making good smoke grenades. But it also ferociously consumes anything combustible and the only way to stop it burning is to smother it.

As a result, it is one of the most controversial potential anti-personnel weapons available, but ideal for the Captain's purpose. The grenades will kill and maim many of the Mad Dogs directly and produce so much smoke that the platoon will have a chance of blasting its way through while the enemy is confused and partially blinded.

"Satisfactory, sir," Kemper says, nodding, then issues his own orders.

The boys break apart, some going forward and some back to the rear.

They shoot.

The grenades arc high into the air and land in the midst of the Maddy column moving into its right turn onto Eighth Avenue. The WP rounds burst, burning fiercely amid the tightly packed Mad Dogs, setting many of them on fire and turning them into screeching human torches while blinding others with instant banks of smoke.

"Go, go, go!" Kemper roars.

"We get through these Maddies, and we've reached the Circle!" Bowman promises.

"Hooah!" the boys shout, rushing forward in a line bristling with bayonets, firing as they move, dropping Mad Dogs by the dozen.

"We're coming in, Vaughan!" Bowman shouts into his mike.

Roger that, out.

Blasting their way past the intersection, they sprint the last block, gasping for air, finally catching sight of Vaughan's boys formed up in a square formation ahead.

"HOOAH!" Vaughan's boys cheer, some of them breaking off firing to stand and make a hole, raising their caps and weapons as Second Platoon joins forces with them.

"Boy, are we glad to see you guys," Bailey yells, coming to a stop and coughing a massive wad of phlegm onto the ground. "Now where do you need my SAW?"

Bowman approaches Lieutenant Vaughan, who stands scowling at the battle with his cheek bulging with Copenhagen dip. The men salute, then shake hands warmly.

"Vaughan, this is your show. Where do you want us?"

The LT shrugs. "We're pretty much surrounded, so pick your own ground, sir."

Bowman nods and raises an eyebrow. "Mike?"

"We'll take the east and get in this game if you can hold the other sides," Kemper says. "The men are tired of running and they're itching to kick Maddy's ass."

"Roger that, First Sergeant," Vaughan says, and then they part ways to give their orders and place their squads.

Bowman deeply admires the LT. Getting his unit out of the grave Knight dug for them was nothing short of incredible. The other newly promoted lieutenants immediately named him their leader to create a unified command. Leapfrogging east, he found a building they could pass through. As each squad fell back from the front in the collapsing bag, they entered the building, cut through, and came out the other side, rallying in an empty street a block away from danger. Even the last squad got out without casualties. That was before almost every street in the area became jammed with snarling Mad Dogs.

Only Knight died, giving his life for his men. Or at least that is how Vaughan put it. All sorts of things happen in the field. You take a bunch of boys armed to the teeth and put them in an extreme situation where they are desperate to stay alive, and all sorts of things happen, Bowman knows. He knows all too well.

The soldiers deploy quickly, the formation shifting and growing larger as Second Platoon takes over the eastern edge of the square, with the MG rocking at the northeast corner and two of the SAWs at the other. The Mad Dogs continue pressing in, coming in waves. The square lights up with muzzle flashes, coughing clouds of smoke into the air.

"Reloading!"

"Frag out!"

Several soldiers scramble out of the way of the back blast of an AT4.

"Fire in the hole!"

Lewis is pacing behind his squad, observing their fire, offering suggestions to his boys. Kemper stands nearby, shouting, "Don't waste your ammo! One bullet per Maddy, in the chest! Put him down and move on! Make every bullet count!"

This is it, Bowman tells himself. The Alamo. The final battle.

We can do this.

"Reloading!"

The Mad Dogs come out of the smoke drifts, their legs splashing through an apocalyptic sea of blood and writhing limbs, their eyes burning with hatred and their mouths contorted with pain and rage.

An endless tide of gray faces.

The boys pour fire into their unprotected bodies without mercy, knowing they are fighting a war of extermination.

Empty shell casings fly into the air and clatter to the concrete, rolling away to form piles around the feet of the formation. Tracers stream through the clouds of smoke. Grenades explode in fireballs and plumes of smoke, flinging torn and broken bodies to the ground. An anti-tank missile bursts in a blinding flash, sweeping the southeastern quadrant of the Circle clear of life for several seconds, leaving a thick smoky haze.

The final battle.

We can do this. . . .

This is Bowman's mantra—his prayer.

It only takes minutes, however, for the battle to turn against them.

One by one, the boys lower their weapons and cry, "I'm out!"

The fire begins to slacken. Anti-tank rocket launchers are discarded after they fire their last missiles. Grenades begin to run out. Magazines are passed from hand to hand. Some of the boys curse and struggle with jammed weapons. Others stand stoically, carbine held in the ready position for bayonet fighting, waiting for the end. Many turn to their Captain with pale faces, looking for an answer, any answer, other than death. They are afraid to die.

"It's like Steve said once," Bowman says. "There just aren't enough bullets."

He leans his empty carbine against the base of the statue and blows air out of his cheeks.

"This is going to hurt a lot," he mutters, shivering a little despite himself. He unholsters his two nine-millimeters, holding one in each fist, and waits for the end.

He finds himself fixating on tiny details: Broken windows in one of the buildings across the street. Pale faces looking down. The trembling leaves of the skinny trees planted around the statue. The inviting green of the Park across the street to the northeast, where the massive Maine monument stands, honoring the VALIANT SEAMEN WHO PERISHED IN THE MAINE BY FATE UNWARNED, IN DEATH UNAFRAID. Time dilates: The minutes appear to stretch into hours.

The Mad Dogs continue to die like flies but they are closer now, pushing through the haze, waiting patiently for their moment.

Bowman calls out: "Lieutenant Vaughan!"

"Sir?"

"See that building directly to the west of our position. The Time Warner Center?"

"Yes, sir."

"That's the rally point. Perhaps some of us can make it through. Pass the word."

"Yes, sir."

Kemper and Lewis join him, and he tells them the plan. The building looks so close. It's right across the street.

"I can get my boys there," Lewis says, his eyes blazing. "I know I can."

"Then see to your men, Sergeant."

Kemper lights one of his foul-smelling cigars and sighs.

"My last one," he says.

Bowman watches the wall of Mad Dogs steadily inching towards their perimeter as the fire continues to slacken, and waits for Vaughan to tell him the boys are ready to charge. He leans back against the cool stone of the statue, taking a deep breath, willing his racing heart to slow down.

It is a fool's errand, he knows. They can charge, and maybe somebody will survive, but not all of them, and maybe not even some of them.

The Captain damned himself to save his men days ago and then sacrificed their lives for this mission. The mission is everything, and yet even a mission as noble as this one, saving a scientist who might save the world, doesn't seem worth the price. When these boys are gone, there will be none like them ever again.

So they will charge and finish it.

A fool's errand, yes. But if even one man survives, it will be worth it.

He says, "What did I do wrong, Mike?"

"This still ain't about you, sir," Kemper says.

Bowman grins. Then he laughs out loud.

He says, "You can't win 'em all, Mike."

"It's a bag of dicks, sir."

"The men are ready to move," Vaughan says.

Bowman tells him to give the order and lead the boys across.

As for him, he has decided that he will stick around for a while. He doesn't want to run anymore. Suppose he did and somehow survived. To where? To do what then? To survive how? For what tomorrow?

Better to die fighting, on your feet, like a man, for a country you love, before it disappears forever.

Kemper says, "Sir, I'm proud—"

Who will inherit the earth?

Petrova looks out the window and briefly says farewell to her home and all of the parts of her that she is leaving behind.

After hovering near the base of the San Remo Towers searching for survivors, the Chinooks climb the air and head southwest, suddenly offering a bird's view of Columbus Circle.

"Oh," she says, sucking in her breath and touching her chest, feeling her heart pound against her ribs.

It is here that Captain Bowman's dying company, a single ragged square barely visible through drifting currents of gun smoke, has chosen to make its last stand.

She sobs, seeing what they cannot—endless legions of infected pouring into the Circle and choking the streets beyond, their march raising clouds of dust over the city.

Hopeless.

The square suddenly moves, breaking towards the Time Warner Center, crossing a short distance before slowly dissolving in waves of smoke and infected. Some of the soldiers break off and run in all directions, flailing as they are caught and torn to pieces. Moments later, it is impossible to tell the soldiers and infected apart.

A last flurry of muzzle flashes in the haze. A plume of smoke rising from a burst grenade. A blinding flash, fire and dust. Then nothing.

The infected fill the Circle, wandering aimlessly, as if the soldiers never existed. In fact, the Mad Dogs have probably already forgotten about them.

Petrova cries for the boys, hot tears flooding her cheeks.

The Crazy Eights, people called them.

I will remember you, she vows to herself. And I will repay you.

"Oh God," Mooney sobs in sudden anguish, looking like a broken old man at the age of twenty. In a single morning, all of his friends have died and he has probably never felt more alone. Seeing him like this, Petrova remembers lying curled in a ball under the desk in the security room of the Institute, wishing she were somebody else, somebody without so much fear and pain. Now it is her turn to offer comfort. She takes his hand in hers, and they share tears over the death of his comrades.

As the helicopter continues to lift into the cold gray sky, she sees more and more of the dark crowds circulating through the city's arteries. New York belongs to them now, the insane, the mad, the infected. They will die like flies over the coming days and make the city a graveyard, leaving a nightmare of disease and starvation for the survivors. Civilization will recede as the virus does, leaving the survivors forever afraid of its return. Their descendants will virtually worship the virus and its power.

She wipes her face and turns in her seat, still holding Mooney's hand but emotionally turning inward, trying to stay strong so she can continue fighting this war. She is suddenly painfully aware that the Special Forces, buckled into their seats, are casting fierce, hopeful glances at her, wondering if she, and what she represents, was worth the lives of their friends.

What she can promise them, just as she is now promising the lost boys of Eighth Brigade in her heart, is that she will kill this virus. There will be other viruses, other plagues, but the Mad Dog strain will never again return to threaten extinction. When she is done with the virus, humanity will be able to return to its rightful place on the earth.

She will also honor the soldiers with her memory. Integrity, courage, loyalty—these and the other Army values seemed cute, even corny, to her several weeks ago, but will be in all too short supply in America's future, she knows. Such men from the past will not easily be replaced by the next savage generation shaped by the plague.

Petrova believes with her whole heart that humanity will survive this apocalypse. But with men like Captain Todd Bowman dead and gone, who will inherit the earth?

LaVergne, TN USA
03 April 2010
178102LV00001B/195/P